SILVERWOOD

The first thing that struck me was the odour. The entrance hall smelled faintly of ammonia, as though its black and white marble tiles had been mopped with one of those disinfectant solutions used in school gymnasiums. Always, in my memory, the unmistakable fragrance of freesia had permeated Silverwood. It, too, had come to be associated in my mind with wealth. To me, freesia smelled of money. I suppose the scent was simply a favourite perfume of Ada Prudhomme.

She was still there. Her portrait hung where it had always been. She'd been beautiful. She had an expression of pleasant indifference, as though her mind were elsewhere. Her lips were faintly pursed, and those remarkable blue eyes had a trace of mockery about them, as if, perhaps, the artist were telling her a tedious anecdote while she was thinking about her honeymoon.

SILVERWOOD

Joanna Barnes

A STAR BOOK
published by
the Paperback Division of
W. H. ALLEN & Co. PLC

A Star Book
Published in 1986
by the Paperback Division of
W. H. Allen & Co. PLC
44 Hill Street, London W1X 8LB

First published in the United States of America
by Linden Press/Simon & Schuster, Inc. 1985

Copyright © Joanna Barnes 1985

Printed and bound in Great Britain by
Anchor Brendon Ltd, Tiptree, Essex

ISBN 0 352 31696 9

For J.L.W.

1964

PART ONE

Elodie Swann

I have reached the age where I sometimes glimpse the dead for
one clear, bright moment before their features are eclipsed by
those of the strangers who have taken their place. I have seen my
own brother a short distance away, across a street, and crossing,
failed to find him anywhere. Just yesterday, leaving Sunday
services, I recognized a young doctor who had once treated me
for influenza. Without thinking, I called out to him, only to
remember that he had died near Anzio in the Second World
War.

It is not surprising, then, that I often catch sight of Ada.
Sometimes she is striding smoothly ahead of me in a crowd, her
stature still striking and her head held high in that taut, thrusting
attitude that I associate with a thoroughbred racehorse lunging
towards victory. I have seen her seated beyond the shiny windows
of a passing automobile, visible only in imperious profile like the
face on a coin. Once I felt, with utter certainty, that it was she,
until I realized that the car was a battered, rusty relic of a Ford,
not Ada's style at all.

I don't know what goes on at Silverwood these days. I've not
been there since the day of Ada's funeral and that was long ago.
The trees, those silvery-barked eucalyptus, growing in such
profusion, make the house invisible from the road, so there is no
way of knowing if her twins are there or some new owners or
perhaps only the ghost of poor Farkas, trespassing in the deserted
gardens.

Most of the land around Silverwood has been sold for development. The new streets are smooth, black macadam not yet
hummocked from earth tremors or the subterranean thrust of
roots. They are planted with spindly jacaranda saplings too slight

to provide shade. Along these stark sunlit streets are row after row of tract houses painted, astonishingly to my mind, in the dainty pastels of a baby's nursery.

That phrase, 'from the road,' gives away my years, but in fact I do remember when Sunset Boulevard was only a bleak, monotonous stretch of dirt leading through some dusty fields of barley and beans to the sea. That was before the Beverly Hills Hotel, before Pickfair or Silverwood, before the electric railway surrendered to the Studebaker and the wide screen yielded to the television tube. There was nothing on the land above Sunset Boulevard where Silverwood now stands hidden among the tall trees. Coyote and deer, rabbits, raccoons and rattlers populated the bushy hills above the flatlands. In Hollywood where we lived fashionably close to Monsieur DeLongpré's gardens there was a city ordinance prohibiting the herding of more than two thousand sheep at a time through the public streets.

But I am straying from my subject. Lately, I regret to say, that happens too often, as my companion, Mrs Evans, is fond of informing me. She is also prone to telling me not to dwell in the past. When you're eighty years old, as I am, the future is hardly a subject for contemplation, and the present seems less vibrant than life used to be. But Mrs Evans has a point. I was thinking of Silverwood and of Ada.

We were both considered beauties, Ada and I, each in our own time. She was an imposing figure by any standards. She was nearly six feet tall, with piercing blue eyes and pale blond hair. She had high cheekbones, a slim, prominent nose that stopped just short of detracting from her other features and a mouth which barely escaped the vulgarity of looking voluptuous. Unlike many big women, she held herself unabashedly erect. Her hair was always knotted high on her head, in defiance of her height and the influence of fashion. Despite her stately bearing, there was an appealing aura of slight dishevelment about her. Inevitably, a halo of golden strands would have sprung loose from her topknot, giving her the look of a disconcerted Valkyrie swooping into battle. This imperfection often saved her from appearing a rather forbidding figure.

When we first met, I assumed Ada was my age. It never

12

occurred to me that she might be a good deal younger than I. For some reason, I always assume that tall people, being bigger, are older.

I can remember my amazement at hearing that Victor Prudhomme was going to marry Ada, of all people. A long time later, I asked him how he had decided to settle down with her. He answered, 'When one makes the decision to marry, an appropriate mate will appear on the scene. It's like any enterprise, really. When the timing is right, the details fall into place.' Victor was not a sentimentalist. I wondered how much or how little he knew about his bride. Certainly, the information I possessed about her might have given pause to the most ardent groom. Victor breezed into that marriage without giving it a second thought, or so it appeared at the time.

Nobody, needless to say, could have been more different from Victor Prudhomme than Sam Farkas. He might as well have been a Hottentot for the element of incongruity that he presented in Ada's company.

Farkas had a son, a slight, shy boy with skin the colour of milky toffee and eyes like bittersweet chocolate drops. David, I believe his name was. Poor child, he never seemed at ease at Silverwood. Probably his father's presence there was as much a puzzle to him as to anyone.

How peculiar memory is. Most of the time I am hard put to recall what I did the day before yesterday, yet when I think of Silverwood or of Ada, I am like a cat catching its paw on a ball of twine; the more it tries to pull away, the more the thing unravels. I sit in a shambles of strands and shreds, not really successful at weaving my recollections into anything useful or even decorative.

A year or more ago, Ada's granddaughter came to see me. That would be Andrew's oldest child, Daphne. She looked to be in her twenties, with dark hair, a heart-shaped face and Ada's remarkable blue eyes. She had a sweet, solemn demeanour, not unlike her mother's. 'Miss Swann,' she inquired, 'would you mind if I asked you some questions about my family?' I didn't mind her asking questions and told her so. 'But you must take into account that I am of the old school,' I added, 'and we're not

13

in the habit of telling all. We don't prevaricate, you understand, but we don't spill everything, either.'

She was constructing something she called an 'oral history of the Prudhommes.' When I told her that under no circumstances would I commit my elderly ramblings to some clever Japanese tape recorder, she backed off politely and asked only that I clarify or supplement the facts she'd already gathered. I'm sorry I didn't match her curiosity tit for tat with my own inquiry about the status of Silverwood. It accidentally slipped my mind. Certain other things, things about Ada, slipped my mind, too. But this was deliberate. For as long as she lived, Ada and I had an unspoken pact of sorts. For good and proper reasons, neither of us said much about the other. Even though Ada was gone now, I saw no profit in betraying her confidence.

I wonder what sort of shape Daphne's endeavour finally assumed. Did hindsight and the cumulative memories of various friends and relatives lend form and meaning to a hundred scattered glimpses of the past? For her sake, I hope it did, though I doubt it. Ada had a way of editing the truth, not to say tailoring it, that precluded anyone's forming finite conclusions about her for which she might be called to account. No matter that she's long gone: Ada was strong, mark my words. I dare say she contrived to make certain her 'history,' as Daphne would call it, was remembered as imprecisely as she'd like it to be.

And who can blame her? One's vanity rebels at the thought of being totted up with mathematical finality like a flimsy string of numerals solidified into an immutable sum. I, for one, envy Ada her lacunae and her talent for the oblique. Seen from here at the far end of life, nuance becomes more rewarding than mere fact.

David Farkas

Late in the spring of 1962, I returned to California to stay, although I hadn't planned it that way. In retrospect, I couldn't have come back to the States at a better time. The Kennedys were in the White House, and the whole nation seemed buoyed by that spirited, stylish young family given to serving God and country and evidently enjoying every minute. Their gusto was contagious. Optimism rode on the wind that spring. You inhaled it. It was almost difficult to believe that I had ever felt differently about my country.

I'd been in my twenties when I'd quit our cottage in Santa Monica and consigned the contents to the auctioneer, the Goodwill and, in the case of a few mementoes, my Aunt Ruth on Long Island. The only things of my father's that I took with me when I left were his books and photographs.

In the intervening twelve years, I'd returned to America occasionally to sell bonds for Israel by giving talks before various Jewish philanthropies and Zionist groups. I was a fair success on that circuit, and every Hadassah mother, it seemed, had a daughter who'd always wanted to meet an architect. I suppose it was inevitable that I should ultimately be sent to Los Angeles, since there were at least as many Jews there as in Tel Aviv where I was living.

I'd forgotten the dank gloom of spring in southern California. Had I been looking forward to my homecoming, it might have dampened my enthusiasm, along with the slick streets and dripping greenery. But long ago I'd stopped thinking of the place as my home, probably out of a tenacious loyalty to my father, to whom finally it had been so inhospitable. In fact, the sombre chill of the weather at once brought back to me the emotional climate of my last year there. It had been a time of outrage, frustration, grief and, at the end, only the sort of disgusted fatigue left to someone who has retched himself dry.

Not only had I not given a damn about returning, but I had become used to being air-expressed to my lecture dates like a machine which, when activated, spoke for the allotted time and was then forwarded to its next destination. Sometimes I found myself looking in the phone book next to my hotel bed in order to remind myself what city I was in.

This time, however, I was to be billeted with the son and daughter-in-law of my host, Rabbi Hillel Pressman. I liked Mike and Sonia Pressman from the moment they met me at the airport. He was an illustrator for Disney, and she was a librarian at UCLA. They lived in the Los Feliz area in one of those twenties-style Lloyd Wright houses that look like landlocked ocean liners. They were (and are, I should say, because we have since become close friends) a pair in whom enthusiasm for life effervesced with an energy that swept along friends and acquaintances as well as near-strangers like myself. By the time we arrived at the HMS Pressman, as Mike's father liked to call the place, they were talking about giving me some sort of party before my departure on Friday, and I was in a mood to accept the offer.

It was an easygoing affair. Mike played jazz piano with a group that included a neurosurgeon on sax, a couple of copywriters from an ad agency on cornet and drums and a bass player who looked as if he belonged with the Harlem Globetrotters but who taught physics at Loyola. They were wailing out a funky, lickerish version of 'Trouble in Mind,' when the blond next to me tapped on my knee.

'I've been watching you. You don't remember me, do you?'

'I'm afraid not.' I raised my glass to her. 'My loss.'

'We went to Beverly Hills High together. My name was Miriam Rappaport. It's Freeman now. That's my husband on the saxophone.'

'Yes?' It took me a moment. 'Didn't you have an older sister? The Rappaport I remember had a slight overbite and brown hair.'

'That's me. Or was.'

'I think I just stuck my foot in my mouth.'

'No, you didn't. David, I just wanted to say – ' The music swelled to a brassy blue crescendo. She waited until the melody had died down. 'I just wanted to say that I was sorry about what happened to your father.'

'Me too.'

'He was one of those rare adults who never talked down to us kids. I always liked him.'

'So did I.'

'Nowadays, most people are pretty embarrassed about the whole business.'

'Fellas, fellas!' Mike rose from the piano. 'Let's take a breather, yes?' He pushed the bench aside with his knee and went to the bar.

I was relieved when Miriam's husband beckoned her away to meet someone. Until now, I had almost managed to convince myself that I was a stranger in a strange city, feeling singular and solitary, enjoying my detachment.

'David.' Mike sat on the arm of my chair. 'Did Sonia mention going to see ACTS before I take you to the airport tomorrow?'

'I don't believe so. What sort of acts?'

'A-C-T-S, the American Cinema and Television Society. It's housed in a grand old heap of stone, one of those mansions that'll never be duplicated, at least in our lifetime. You really ought to take a look at it as long as you're here. It's not open to the public, but we're members. I have an errand to do there in the morning, and Sonia suggested you might like to mosey around the building for a half hour or so while I'm about my business.'

'Suits me, but I can always take a cab to the airport, if it's more convenient.'

'Not at all. You'll get a kick out of ACTS. It's a landmark of sorts.'

My antennae should have quivered at that point, but maybe I'd had too much wine. Perhaps I just didn't want to recall any local landmarks, architectural or otherwise. Since I'd earned my degree at SC, I should have realized that anything deserving of Mike's description had to be something I'd seen.

Mike was driving, and I was gazing out of the car window,

17

surprised at how little of the landscape seemed familiar. We were passing through what I judged to be a fairly new subdivision, acres of terraced homesites in varying states of construction. Here and there realtors' signs were stuck in the ground, advertising a newly completed house or a vacant lot for sale. Scrawny saplings, supported by stakes, stood at intervals along the pavements, looking like those bony, near-naked survivors of the camps, ashamed, of all things, of their appearance. The houses were bastard versions of various styles, from Hawaiian modern and California ranch to English Tudor and French Provincial, all sporting the obligatory two-car garage. About the only thing they had in common was an overlarding of wrought iron grillwork at the entrances and the fact that the exteriors were the colour of Easter eggs. Until then, I had never entertained the possibility of a half-timbered Tudor painted robin's-egg blue.

'Amazing,' I said.

'*Dreck*.'

'I meant to say how strange it seems not to have my bearings. I should know where I am and I don't. I used to live somewhere near here.'

At the end of a cul-de-sac, Mike paused before a pair of concrete gateposts and hit the horn lightly. A uniformed guard appeared from a kiosk a short distance beyond, shading his eyes against the sun. Mike pointed to a red decal on his windshield, and we were waved up a curving driveway carved out of a handsomely landscaped hill. 'Do you still have family here?' he asked.

'No.'

'Did you live in Beverly Hills for long?'

'Quite a while.'

We followed a series of arrows marked 'Parking Area' to a wide plateau divided by islands of oleander with spaces striped and numbered for well over a hundred cars. Mike parked and locked his station wagon. He motioned towards a couple of tall Italian cypress trees at the edge of the parking lot. 'The steps are over there. Follow me.'

'What exactly is the purpose of ACTS?'

'The society preserves film and tape so that historians, sociologists and just plain movie and TV buffs can have access to them for study. We have educational workshops for promising writers, directors and editors. For the best ones, we provide internships at the studios. Then there are the occasional lectures on subjects like production design and special effects. We have an annual fund-raiser here, one of those wingdings with two bands and a big tent and the full complement of stars, but mostly ACTS relies on grants from private enterprise with the emphasis on the entertainment industry.'

'Good God.' My voice came out sounding oddly hoarse. I could feel the hot pressure of tears behind my eyes.

Mike halted on the steps that led from the parking terrace down to the gardens and, beyond, to the house. 'Is anything wrong?'

I shook my head.

'David? You look like somebody just kicked you in the *kishkas*.'

I wiped my eyes on the sleeve of my denim jacket. 'It was unexpected, that's all. I know this place. The people who lived here were our neighbours.' They were more than that, really, but at that moment, I couldn't have explained to him the connection between us and the Prudhommes.

From where we stood, it was evident that the ragged gardens had been receiving only desultory care. The grass was patchy, and Mr Yamada's precise geometric boxwood maze looked like something that had melted.

'You go ahead,' I told Mike. 'I'll catch up with you inside.' What I didn't say was that I needed some time to collect myself before I walked through those wide doors again.

'Are you sure?'

'I want to look around the grounds.'

'I'll be in the reference library. It's the large room at the far left end of the main hall.'

That would have been the dining room. It had a vast fireplace framed in black marble with a tracery of fine white veins that, as a child, I used to imagine were violent slashes of lightning against a night sky. There were two glittering chandeliers overhead. Their light sparkled on the immense crystal and silver epergne that stood in the centre of the long mahogany table in which, if I leaned past my white linen placemat, I could see my face. There were twelve chairs around the table and- to either side of the fireplace, a pair of antique sideboards painted with scenes of waterfowl. On the far wall hung a massive gilt-framed mirror that reflected the windows at the opposite end of the room. Looking into it, I imagined a lunatic Lewis Carroll world that ran amuck just out of sight beyond the symmetrical topiary trees outside the windowpanes. The existence of this secret bedlam kept me amused when adult conversation turned to matters that bored or confused me.

I was amazed at how intact my memories of Silverwood had remained over the years. Maybe I had thought they could only be unearthed like ancient artefacts from an archaeological dig, covered with soil and dust, perhaps so fragmented that they couldn't be glued together at all.

But here was the old croquet lawn. There had once been a gazebo between it and the bowling green beyond, where I had spied my father, his head in his hands, sobbing, one day not long before he went away from here for good. I hadn't the nerve to go to him, I remember, and turned away to walk home. I've never resolved whether I acted out of cowardice or embarrassment or whether I was respecting his privacy.

I walked down the cypress allée towards the swimming pool and found it empty, with cracks running through its turquoise tiles. The windows of the pool house were dirty, but I could see that the floor was strewn with dead leaves, a few broken pieces of lawn furniture and some rusty gardening tools.

Descending one flight of the semicircular pair of stairs to the lower terrace, I passed above the scowling gargoyle that used to drool continuously into a little pool from his niche in the stone wall. His mouth was dry now, and the pool was overgrown with the orange nasturtiums that had once neatly bordered it. Farther along, I found the old lily pond. The lotus were gone, and the water was so dark with algae that it was impossible to see whether it still contained any fish. As the path neared the house, I came upon the beautiful round triple-tiered fountain that I had once thought the most elegant object I had ever seen. I sat down on one of the curved white marble benches beside it and gazed at the weeds that sprouted from the three basins.

As nearly as I could figure, the parking lot had replaced the old stables and riding ring. There had been a caretaker's cottage, a barn and several garages, some large greenhouses, a potting shed and an immense household garden in which were grown not only the expected vegetables and herbs but things like artichoke, asparagus and several exotic kinds of melon as well as lavender to line the dresser drawers. I recalled a grape arbour, too, and a strawberry patch. These, plus the orchards, the pasture and the hilly fields beyond, where Tony, Drew and I had raced our horses on one of the rare occasions when they allowed me to encroach upon their twinship; all else, in other words, save the deteriorating landscape adjacent to the house had apparently been sold off for a housing development. Why, I wondered, had neither twin wanted to live at Silverwood?

It never occurred to me, I now realize, to entertain any curiosity about *my* old house which lay over the brow of the hill to my right, near the foot of what had once been the main driveway to Silverwood. Such was the pull of this place that I was more interested in why the Prudhomme twins had abandoned it than I was in my own past.

Here, near the house, the grounds hadn't been allowed to go to seed as they had elsewhere. The broad circle of gravel in the auto court was evenly raked, and if the pool in the centre no longer held its twin dolphins spouting crossed arcs of water, at least someone had thought to plant it with some sturdy, proletarian geraniums. As I approached the door, I glanced down the tree-lined drive, remembering the first time I had walked up it, chilly, scared and holding on to my father for dear life. Now I stooped to pick up some fallen eucalyptus leaves and crushed them in my hand, inhaling the pungent fragrance that I knew so well. These towering trees, with their silver-grey trunks, had given the house its name.

The Prudhommes, with the aid of a sizable fortune, had aimed to create a family seat that looked as if it had existed for decades, if not centuries. Only as an architecture student had I learned from some photos of famous English houses that the place was a

21

knockoff of a Tudor manor named Langehurst Hall which was located someplace in Derbyshire. They'd done a hell of a job, I thought, looking up at those limestone walls traced with trumpet vine. The turrets and arches, the oriels and ornamental stonework were nothing if not aristocratic. The soft crunch of the gravel underfoot reminded me that I had once thought that the sound of automobile tyres on this driveway epitomized Old Money.

I paused in the shade of the porte cochère to read the brass plaque that had been affixed to one side of the entrance. 'The American Cinema and Television Society,' it said, and underneath, 'Members and Guests Only.' Above the wrought-iron and plate-glass doors, chiselled in stone, was a cartouche in the centre of which had been cut a single large 'P.' I pushed down on the iron handle, and the right-hand door swung inward.

The first thing that struck me was the odour. The entrance hall smelled faintly of ammonia, as though its black and white marble tiles had been mopped with one of those disinfectant solutions used in school gymnasiums. Always, in my memory, the unmistakable fragrance of freesia had permeated Silverwood. It, too, had come to be associated in my mind with wealth. To me, freesia smelled of money. I suppose the scent was simply a favourite perfume of Ada Prudhomme.

At the thought of her, I looked quickly to my right.

She was still there. Her portrait hung where it had always been, on the wall halfway up the stairs to the second floor. To my left, above the opposite staircase, there had been a portrait of the same dimensions, a picture of the twins at about ten years of age, but it was gone now. I stood there in the entryway at the top of the wide steps leading down to the main hall and studied her face at length. She'd been beautiful, to be sure, although I judged the young woman in the painting to be twenty at the outside, and I'd not met her until she was forty or so. The figure in the frame was seated in an ivory-upholstered gilt armchair, wearing a gown of what appeared to be pleated salmon-coloured silk, rather like a Grecian robe. She was looking slightly downward and to her left, her gaze falling towards the doorway behind me. She had an expression of pleasant indifference, as though her mind were elsewhere. Her lips were faintly pursed, and those remarkable blue eyes had a trace of mockery about them, as if, perhaps, the artist were telling her a tedious anecdote while she was thinking about her honeymoon. The portrait, I knew, had been painted while she and Victor Prudhomme were abroad on their wedding trip in 1913.

Its most striking feature was, of course, Ada's fabulous emerald suite. At the base of her throat lay a necklace of matching graduated gems, surrounded and connected by diamonds. The pair at the centre looked to be a good five carats apiece of brilliant green, which meant that the total had to be in the neighbourhood of fifty carats of emeralds for the necklace alone. The bracelet was of the same style, though its stones were all the same size. The drop earrings each contained two emeralds, the bottom one somewhat larger than the one at her earlobe. I guess it would be a compliment to say that Ada held her own, despite the scintillating competition of her jewels.

Ada (though certainly I never dared call her anything but 'Mrs Prudhomme') was an *eppes*, a personage, in my eyes. She intimidated me, although I don't think she meant to. Ada didn't so much enter a room as overtake it, like a vessel under full sail. She would sweep into the solarium or the music room, breasting tides of conversation or melody, immediately commanding attention without a word or gesture. Looking back, I suppose there was a time I hated her, though not for long. I was under the impression that she had invaded the intimacy that had existed between my father and me since my mother died. It had seemed, for a while, that she'd swooped down upon us like a great pirate ship, cut loose my mooring line and left me adrift on my own.

I heard the click of footsteps coming towards me up the marble steps. A lean, blond fellow about my age gave me a grin, pushed his shaggy forelock back with splayed fingers and, looking from Ada to me, said, 'What's your guess? Is she someone's idea of camp or did she will a fortune to ACTS?'

'Neither. This was her home.' I was taken aback by the tone of my voice. I sounded defensive, proprietary. Before I could apologize, he'd made his exit.

I walked down to the main hall, gazing up at the coffered ceilings, my hand on the smooth wood of the banister. My fingers came to rest on the newel post which was topped by a carved pineapple. Tony and Drew, I remembered, used to toss their jackets here and leave them for the butler or a maid to put away.

I guess I had once been young enough and sufficiently exposed to the opulence of movie sets to take this place in stride. Now, having spent some years designing *kibbutzim* of cinder block, its magnificence dazzled me all over again.

Ahead of me was the triple-arched entrance to the solarium. I ducked my head inside only for a moment, as there seemed to be a lecture in progress. A perspiring gent with a white-rimmed tonsure and tobacco-yellowed moustache was expounding the different means of creating 'cinematic suspense' to an audience of a couple of dozen, seated on metal folding chairs. I wondered what my father would have made of that word, 'cinematic.' 'So? All the world's a *mavin*,' he'd likely have said with a shrug.

My father, though he often called me 'Dovid,' rarely spoke Yiddish except in private. I cannot imagine him having used it in Ada Prudhomme's presence, but a word or two must have slipped out over the years they knew each other. I've no doubt that when thes lapses occurred, she (who, by the way, pronounced her name 'Ah-dah') merely smiled that abstracted smile of forbearance which appeared on her face in reaction to any social blunder and remained fixed there until the embarrassment had blown over.

To my left, the door that had once led to the music room lay open, revealing an unattended office containing two metal desks, some vinyl-covered chairs and a wall of filing cabinets above which, on the linen-fold panelling, were hung three rows of old photographs in black dime-store frames. I went in for a look, stopping to stub out a cigarette left smouldering in a tin ashtray on the carved mantel where, in bas-relief, a pair of snarling manticores were separated by a festoon of laurel.

Some of the pictures were yellowed photos of Silverwood in the old days. Others looked like studio publicity stills, probably donated to ACTS. They had been hung randomly, without regard for chronology. Here was Deanna Durbin singing to an audience of GIs, a configuration of Busby Berkeley dancers, the late Victor Prudhomme astride one of his polo ponies. Charlton Heston in the remake of *Ben Hur* and a group of helmeted aviators gathered beside a biplane, among them Mary Pickford and Charlie Chaplin. It took me a minute before I realized that the young face in the centre of the top, far-right picture was my own.

Perhaps it had been a Thanksgiving dinner party. There was no sign of Christmas or birthday decorations. We were gathered on the lawn outside the drawing room, with the reflecting pool in the background. I appeared to be in my late teens, gangly and wearing a rather sheepish grin. Next to me, slightly shorter than I, was my father, holding his pipe in his hand and squinting amiably into the sunlight. Ada stood beside him, poised, erect, self-confident. 'She is a fine actress,' my father had once said. He'd nodded, thoughtfully, affirming this opinion, and repeated it. 'Ada's a fine actress.' This struck me as funny because I doubted that she'd think it a compliment. It had taken me years to glean even a notion of what he meant. Even then, I had to admit, the more I learned about Ada Prudhomme, the more she seemed to retreat into a mist of ambiguities, always out of reach.

To her other side in the photograph was Tony, his arm clasped about the waist of his wife, Nita. I'd once thought Nita Paris the sexiest pinup I'd ever seen, with her sultry dark eyes, masses of unruly black hair and full pouty mouth.

Dosie, Drew's wife, stood on my right, holding her youngest child in her arms. That dated the photo late in 1945, the year Tony and Nita married and the baby was born. I remembered that Dosie had died bizarrely not long afterward. How typical of her that WASP nickname, Dosie, was. Her full name was Dorothea, although I never heard her called that. Her father, the formidable Hale Hunt Outerbridge, industrialist, philanthropist and run-of-the-mill anti-Semite was posed beside her with his wife, Dorcas. Dorcas, as ever, appeared impeccably turned out in a dark suit with a peplum, a bowed, checked blouse adorned with two strands of her mothball-sized real pearls and a handbag and shoes that matched. She was, by conventional standards, an attractive woman, though not quite a beautiful one. Her blond hair was curled under at the shoulders, pageboy style. Not a strand, needless to say, had strayed out of place. She was leaning slightly on the arm of her husband. Her smile, I thought, looked forced.

In front of the grownups were Dosie's and Drew's older children. Dexter must have been all of four, a towhead, wrinkling his nose at the camera. Daphne was a couple of years his senior, a delightful child, in my memory. She was an artless, inquisitive little girl, always perceiving the subtleties of adults. Where, in that tribe of marmoreal ancestors, had she picked up her sensitivity? She stood there, evidently taking the photography very seriously, her hands at her sides, as delicate and graceful as a butterfly that had paused motionless for a moment on the broad lawn.

Looking at those familiar faces brought back to me the first time I had entered this house. To be sure, I'd furtively explored the grounds a few times. I'd been curious, like any small boy, as to what grandeur lay hidden behind the stone wall separating our property from the Prudhommes'. Once, I recall, I had been apprehended by the head gardener, Mr Yamada, who'd shouted at me in Japanese and chased me away, brandishing a murderous rake.

The night I met Ada Prudhomme we had a violent windstorm, the kind that wrenches boughs from trees, sends shingles skating off roofs and turns the flying debris into dangerous projectiles. My father and I were in our living room, listening to the steady shriek of the wind and the sounds of unidentifiable objects colliding, scraping and splintering in the dark outside. The lights went off. 'Thank God Tilly isn't here,' said my father, lighting the pair of candles on the mantelpiece. 'She'd be having conniption fits.' Our housekeeper had gone to Fresno for a nephew's wedding. 'Wait a minute.' Dad abruptly snuffed out the candles. 'We should go up and check on Mrs Prudhomme.'

'Mrs Prudhomme? What for?'

'She's alone, Dovid. She has no husband to look out for her.'

'She's not alone. She probably has lots of servants.' I was eight years old at the time, and I didn't like the idea of venturing from the cosy security of the living room.

'It's not the same. Someday, God forbid, you may know the loss of a partner. Come on, Dovid, fetch your jacket. What kind of neighbours would we be not to look in on her on a night like this?'

The moon was eerily bright, despite the air being full of dust and dry leaves. I could feel the grit against my teeth and in my eyes as I passed through the open gates and trudged up the gravel drive, holding fast to my father's hand.

A few flickering lights played in the dim recesses of the vast overshadowing house. As we drew near the black cave of the porte cochère, I asked, 'Can't we go back? They've lit candles.'

'It's a scary night, Dovid, I agree. But that's no excuse for not doing the decent thing.' He raised the giant knocker and brought it down on the ironwork of the front door. I jumped as though the sound were a gunshot.

A shape materialized from the darkness within and set a candle aside.

The door opened slightly, and a man's voice spoke. 'Who is there, please?'

'Sam Farkas, from down the hill. My boy, David, and I came up to make sure Mrs Prudhomme was all right.'

He turned from the door and addressed another form in the hallway below. 'It's Mr Farkas, ma'am, with his son.'

The door opened. My father gave me a gentle push and followed me inside. The butler handed his candle to Ada Prudhomme as she came up the marble steps towards us.

I had seen Mrs Prudhomme passing through the gates in her automobile, but I hadn't realized how tall she was. Her dress rustled like crisp dollar bills as she moved, and with her came a fragrance so exquisite that, apprehensive though I was, I wanted nothing more just then than to be close to her. It was more delicious than orange blossoms or jasmine or roses. I could not imagine anything smelling so sweet.

'Mr Farkas.' She held out her hand to my father who, instead of shaking it, took it in both of his.

'When the electricity went off, I thought to pay a call to see that you weren't having any trouble up here. This is my son, David.'

'Hello, David.'

'How do you do, ma'am.'

'We've a frightful mess in the morning room,' she told my

27

father. 'A tree limb smashed the window. There's glass everywhere.'

'Is there anything we can do?'

'Thank you just the same. Safford will see to it.'

Suddenly there was an earsplitting crash, followed by the chinkling of broken glass. I started, my heart pounding. Wind gusted through the hall.

'Heavens,' she cried, 'again! It's the solarium!'

I could hear the butler's footsteps racing along the hall. Mrs Prudhomme turned and dashed down the marble steps, my father and I close behind.

I followed her across the darkened hallway with no inkling that our lives and the life at Silverwood had just merged.

Nanny Beale

From the beginning, I never got along with Mrs Henderson. Now I'd say that's a good thing, too. Had I not been on the lookout for another position, Mrs Biddeford wouldn't have heard of me and written. And I wouldn't have gone to Wellesley on my day off to meet her. She was interviewing me, she said, on behalf of her sister-in-law who was having a difficult time expecting. I didn't meet Mrs Prudhomme that day. She wasn't feeling fit. It was Mrs Biddeford, Mr Prudhomme's sister, who hired me. I never met Mrs Prudhomme 'til several weeks later, after the boys were born, after the nurse who'd tended them those first weeks had gone on another case. I'd not expected there'd be two of them, which isn't to say the prospect frightened me. We'd been eight in my family. Dan was the eldest, then Catherine. They both chose the Church. I was next, then Mary, Maureen, Patrick, Angelica and Sean. The last three were born when I was already in my teens. My mother, rest her, used to say the angels had sent me to help her. Strange, isn't it, that someone like myself should love children so much and never want her own. The truth is, even if they're your flesh and blood, children are vagabonds. The very day they come into your life, they're heading out of it.

Some, bless them, keep a warm spot in their hearts for the places and people of their youth and never entirely forsake them. Daphne – she'd be Mrs Prudhomme's eldest grandchild – is that kind. The poor lamb lost her mother at an early age, and I expect that's why she's reluctant to lose touch with the remaining traces of her childhood, including myself. I wasn't a bit surprised when Daphne wrote to me, asking me to set down my memories of Silverwood so that she might have them as a keepsake. 'Begin at the beginning, Nanny dear,' she wrote. I did exactly that, starting with how Mrs Biddeford had interviewed me on behalf of her sister-in-law, Mrs Prudhomme, who was then expectant.

As I told Daphne, the twins, Anthony and Andrew, came into my life (or, more properly, I came into theirs) in Holy Week of 1917. I didn't burden young Daphne with details. I kept my account to the point. Still, I recall clear as can be how I'd packed my things, gone early to church and sat waiting in the little sitting room off the Hendersons' kitchen for Mrs Biddeford's chauffeur to fetch me. I didn't like that, instead of calling me 'Miss Beale,' he called me 'Winifred' right off, as if I were a parlour maid or a laundress. He was high and mighty, that one, saying, 'Winifred, if you'll follow me out to the Hudson, please.' The Hudson, indeed! If he thought he could impress me with Mrs Biddeford's Hudson, he'd another think coming. I wasn't a green girl just off the boat. I'd come to Boston a full three years before, when I was twenty. Besides, Mr Henderson had a Lagonda of the exact sort owned by Russian royalty. I was beginning to think I might have made a mistake, when Mrs Henderson came out to say good-bye to me, all charm and breakfast honey glistening on her lips, a honey-bear hiding teeth and claws behind that sweet, sweet smile. I was as glad to go as I dare say she was to be rid of me. We hadn't ever hit it off, mostly because she wouldn't let me do my job. She was forever interfering, slipping in at night to give the youngest an extra bottle because he'd sounded fretful or telling me it was too windy to take the children outside or wanting to play with them just when it was bath time.

Mrs Prudhomme, praise the Lord, was of another stripe. She left me to my business from the first. The nurse had gone that morning, leaving a spick-and-span nursery to her crédit and two pages of notes about the twins' feeding. They were bottle babies. Mrs Prudhomme prided herself on being a modern parent, though in my private opinion nothing compares with mother's milk. The twins – I can remember this as though it were this Wednesday past – were in a single bassinet. Two tiny cubs, their faces screwed up, mewling, their small arms waving. I picked up the one nearest to me.

'That is André,' Mrs Prudhomme said. She lifted the other baby from his bedclothes. 'This is Antoine. His face is slightly less full than André's. It's not as difficult to tell them apart as you might think.'

André began to wail. 'He's hungry,' I told her. 'I'll feed them both as soon as I've washed up.'

She laid Antoine back on the mattress. 'I'll leave you to get acquainted with them.'

Mrs Prudhomme wasn't the type to interfere. I think she was a bit overwhelmed by the twins, afraid that they were too much for her to handle. It always seemed to me that she felt more at ease with them after they began to walk and talk. She wasn't a woman to hover over her children like some of them do. In Mrs Prudhomme's life, her husband came first; then came the children. That suited me nicely, thank you.

As it happened, I held Mr Prudhomme's babies in my arms before himself even set eyes upon them. He and his wife had been visiting from California when Mrs Prudhomme had experienced some discomfort with her pregnancy. Mr Prudhomme became worried and insisted that she remain with his sister, Mrs Biddeford, while he returned to the West Coast to conduct his business.

When he arrived from California to take us back there, I had the twins dressed in little white embroidered dresses that Mrs Biddeford had given them. The two ladies had gone to the station to meet Mr Prudhomme, and the first I knew of them was the sound of his voice in the front hall downstairs. It overwhelmed the women's like a great low roll of thunder drowning out the sparrows in the trees. It was deep and robust, the sort of voice that could reach clear to the last pew of a cathedral and touch the sinner sitting in the shadows there. You hear such voices among the Irish and the Welsh, but not often among Americans. I felt at home with the man before I ever met him.

They were coming up the stairs now. I dabbed a bit of drool from Antoine's mouth and brushed the soft dark down back from André's forehead.

Mr Prudhomme paused in the doorway and nodded to me. He was tall and lean and dark-complected, with a strong, angular face that might have seemed harsh, save for a ready smile and the glitter of good humour in his eyes. His gaze came to rest on the bassinet. Almost casually, he approached it. That was the way he moved, nonchalant and graceful as a big cat. He was the most elegant gentleman I've ever seen, yet without a trace of self-consciousness in his manner.

He inspected the babies with considerable care, starting with their tiny feet, as though, if he weren't satisfied, he might order them both wrapped up, marked 'return to sender' and dispatched by the afternoon post. Neither Mrs Biddeford nor Mrs Prud-homme said a word. When he finally looked into those little faces and recognized the spit of himself there, you could see him give up his heart on the spot. He cleared his throat. 'They're smaller than I'd thought.'

Mrs Prudhomme laughed nervously. 'But they're perfect, Victor, in every way. They'll grow quickly; won't they, Nanny?'

'Indeed they will, ma'am.'

Mr Prudhomme turned and looked me up and down. 'Nanny Beale, is it?'

'Yes, sir. Wouldn't you like to hold them?'

He backed off a step from the bassinet. 'One at a time perhaps. It won't upset them?'

'Nonsense,' answered Mrs Biddeford, handing him a diaper.

'What's this for?'

'Protection.' She smoothed it across the shoulder of his suit.

'If you'd give me your attention, sir. Be sure to brace the little head with your hand. Like this.' I put the baby into his arms.

The child looked up at him, blinking sleepily. He stared down at his infant son in silence for a moment. 'Which one is this?'

'That's Antoine, sir.'

'It's *who*?'

I glanced hastily back to the bassinet. 'Antoine. André is here.'

'*For God's sweet sake, Ada!*'

Mrs Prudhomme's cheeks grew flushed. She appeared about to cry.

Mrs Biddeford whisked the child from his arms and handed him his other son. 'They look just like you, Victor, in your baby pictures. The very image.'

He glanced at the boy, then at me. 'Alphonse, did you say?'

'No, sir. André.'

'Just as bad, if you ask me.'

'I had thought – ' Mrs Prudhomme began.

'Spare me your ersatz elegance, Ada.'

'Victor, you said whatever I wanted – '

'I didn't mean you could hang a pair of ludicrous names on the poor little bastards.'

'Victor! In God's name!' She seized the baby from him and held it close.

'I'm sorry.' He turned to me. 'Forgive my wording, if you will, Nanny.'

Mrs Prudhomme put the child in its bassinet. 'Under no circumstances do I want to hear that kind of language – '

'Or?' Mr Prudhomme laid a hand on her arm and put his face close to hers.

'Everyone has limits, Victor.'

Mrs Biddeford cleared her throat. 'Ada thought, Victor, that since there was a tradition of French names in our family, you'd want to maintain it. Haven't you always been proud of our French ancestry?'

'They'll be ragged to bits, saddled with a pair of pretentious pantywaist names like that. Good grief, Ada – '

'Perhaps we could carry on this discussion downstairs, Victor.'

So the babies became Andrew and Anthony, and as soon as they could walk Mr Prudhomme took to calling them Drew and Tony, which I suspect he thought more manly still.

Rumour has it that Mr Prudhomme was a hard man when it came to business, but we at home never saw that side of him. Actually, he was an easier sort of presence than Mrs Prudhomme. He didn't mind having a laugh with you. He was more relaxed with the staff than his wife was, though I can't think why. We showed them each the same respect.

By the time we'd been a day or two on the train back to California, Mr Prudhomme would pop into the drawing room next to theirs, where the babies and I were travelling. He'd hold the boys and stroke them and banter with me just as though we were old acquaintances. It was kind of him to put me at ease like that. To tell the truth, I'd not realized how very big America was until it began to roll by me unceasingly for days and nights, a continuous flow of strange place-names, curious vegetation and vast, barren tracts that might as well have been at the far side of the moon. I was sorely missing my own green country and feeling a bit sorry for myself, but I could always depend on Mr Prudhomme to cheer me up. The babies' mother looked in on us now and again, pausing to see that they were comfortable and not fretting. She wasn't one to pick them up, though, and fondle them, though she loved those boys fiercely all her life and saw to it that they had nothing but the best. I think, now that I look back on it, that Mrs Prudhomme felt she had little in common with infants. Then too, it was my impression that she'd had those children only to please her husband. When Mr Prudhomme was happy, his wife was happy. Pleasing the Mister came first in her life, and I guess if he'd wanted ten children, she'd have given them to him.

Mind you, that's only what I sensed, but as my own darling mother used to say, I was born with the gift of extra sight. Messages come to me without any kind of explanation.

That was why, when I saw the house, I was afraid. In those days, before Silverwood, they had a home in Hollywood, and the first time I ever laid eyes on that place, I knew it had a spell on it. I can't say I had a vision exactly, since I saw nothing save that big dark green house crouched on a rise above the road, looking like some huge moss-covered monster come from a damp cave to claim his territory. That house meant us no good. It was a broody place, full of shadows, with porches all 'round so the sun never penetrated the gloom. It was full of noises – creaks and groanings and rustlings. There was a giant Negress named Verna in the kitchen (I had never before been in a home that employed the coloured) who said that the rustlings were the traffic of rats. There were rats in the palm trees, she said, and late at night they crawled about the porches and the roof, looking to get inside.

At certain times of the year in California, there are violent windstorms, the air dry and hot as the devil's own breath. Around that house, the wind shrieked like a band of banshees circling the place. Doors slammed, and the windows shuddered so hard you waited for them to splinter. From the chimneys came a sound like the first moanings of the dead rising from the grave on Judgement Day. I spent a lot of my time there on my knees, I can tell you, praying to the dear Lord for deliverance.

I don't think Mrs Prudhomme liked the house much, either. It had been her husband's before they married, and it was never intended as a family kind of place. There wasn't even a proper playroom for the twins. We were crowded there, the children, their parents, myself, the cook, Verna, and her husband, James, who served as houseman. Yet I was lonesome, wanting the company of my own sort. I'd hoped I might see some kindred faces at Mass, but the congregation seemed to be evenly divided between well-to-do young families and Mexicans. Sometimes, for want of company, I'd take the twins to Wattles Gardens, down the street, which was opened to the public on certain days. The gardens were an elegant place, terrace upon terrace of flowers, shrubs and trees, rising upon the hills above Prospect Avenue. They were planted in an assortment of styles, Italian, Japanese, Mediterranean and American, divided by marble balustrades and leafy colonnades where children rolled their hoops and courting couples strolling past laughed softly and secretively as though everything – these gardens, this afternoon, this sunlight – was theirs alone to behold and enjoy.

Naturally, a great fuss was made over the twins. People would pause to look at our oversized navy blue pram and gaze in wonder at the matched pair of babies inside. By the time the boys were in their wicker stroller, almost everyone who walked regularly in the Gardens knew who we were. Gentlemen would tip their hats in our direction, and ladies would pause to chat, their own youngsters tugging impatiently at their skirts. We became acquainted with a number of them, the twins and I. There was a cheerful, vague woman named Barrett with a nose like a bran bun and four blond children dappled with freckles. Always, it seemed, the Misses Neal were walking side by side in the Gardens when we were there, dressed in sombre clothing even in the midst of summer and looking as though they'd come to a cemetery for the burial rites. Though they spoke to passersby, they rarely exchanged so much as a word with each other. When the twins toddled towards this familiar pair, they would stop in their tracks with sounds like faint canine whimpers and wait with outstretched arms to meet them, their moist dark eyes brimming.

Even at that early age, the twins were unmitigated imps, already aware of their specialness and not above taking advantage of it. At a signal between them, Andrew would run in one direction and Anthony in another, both of them giggling with glee, whilst I struggled to round them up like a regular cowboy. Once Andrew, that scamp, managed to elude me for almost half an hour in Wattles Gardens, until the Vixen found him out and brought him back. The Vixen was another who came to enjoy the scenery there. I don't remember when I first started seeing her in the Gardens, but it must have been several months before, since we were on speaking terms by then. She was a slim, shapely young woman with curls the colour of orange marmalade. Her clothing ran to shades of russet, chestnut or copper, chosen, I suppose, to complement her hair. I thought of her as a red fox, with her bright quick amber eyes and shy manner. I could picture her alone on a hill on some clear night when it was raining light, hearing the sound of human voices approaching, lovers perhaps, come to see the shooting stars, and she stealing swiftly away on padded paws without so much as a sound. I don't believe she ever spoke to anyone else in the Gardens, save the twins and me. And it was a long time before she spoke to me. When the children and I walked through the tall, iron gates to the Gardens, I would spy her, often as not, her hair aflame in the sunlight, resting on a balustrade on a high terrace, looking out over the landscape and the street below as if she were expecting somebody. No one ever came to join her. At first, she watched the twins from a distance, saying not a word, but those boys with their rosy cheeks and winning smiles could have softened a heart of Aberdeen granite. After a bit, she played little games with them. Things like 'This is the church, and this is the steeple.' When she spoke to me, it was only to be polite, to compliment me on the way the children were dressed or to comment upon the weather. I thought her one of those people more at ease with animals and small children than with the full-grown of our breed. Though she was far prettier and more stylish than I, I couldn't help feeling sorry for her, more even than for the mournful Neals.

Verna, the Prudhommes' cook, gave notice about then. Verna was a worrier. If it wasn't rats that worried her, it was the fat catching fire or the cake falling. Verna made a fuss about the telephone. She was sure it conducted electricity and in the event of a lightning storm would attract a fireball through the wires and into the house. Lately, the telephone had been upsetting all of us. It rang at odd times of day and night, but nobody spoke. By the time you'd signalled the operator, the party had hung up. Sometimes the operator knew where the call had come from. It was always a public place such as a hotel or a restaurant, but never the same place twice.

'Victor,' Mrs Prudhomme said after one of the calls, 'I wish you'd put an end to this.' She replaced the earpiece on its hook and set the telephone back on the hall table.

'What can I do? I don't know who's responsible.'

'I find that difficult to believe.'

'Ada, come into the study. It won't do to stand here in the hall talking about such things.'

I could tell by their voices that the two of them were about to exchange words. When Mrs Prudhomme emerged from the study, her eyes were rimmed with red. She went upstairs alone to her room.

Verna was sure the telephone calls were part of some sinister plan, a hoodoo plot or perhaps enemy spies. (The Great War had drawn to its close, but Verna still had her suspicions.) Now she said that she and James weren't getting any younger and this was more than a soul could take, all these eerie calls that made a body jump every time the telephone rang and anyhow, they wanted to go back to Louisville, where they had people, before they were too far gone to enjoy what little time was left to them. I don't know what James thought of this. Verna always spoke for both of them. Then, wouldn't you know, not a week before they were to leave, a mockingbird flew into the house through the kitchen door. Worse yet, the addled creature flapped furiously about the kitchen, squealing in panic, while James, waving a broom, tried to drive it back outside. Verna shut herself in the larder, shouting directions to James through the closed door. The poor bird evaded James and hurtled towards a promise of daylight above the sink, striking the window head first. With a last spasm of fluttering, it tumbled down and lay dead on the scrubbed white enamel.

It was an omen. There wasn't one of us who didn't know what it meant, and I'll admit it gave me a turn. Verna was beside herself. She was sure it was she who'd die before she could return to Louisville. She made James promise her a shiny white coffin trimmed with brass and took to sighing despondently as she moved about the kitchen, dabbing her eyes with her apron, lamenting her late self.

The night it happened, I was in my room, next to the boys', reading the *Saturday Evening Post*. I heard the sound of Mr Prudhomme's car pulling into the drive in front of the house and a woman's voice, not Mrs Prudhomme's, speaking. I thought they'd brought back guests with them from their party. I hoped that didn't mean people would be wanting to peek in on the twins. Anthony was a light sleeper and he'd dropped off later than usual. I didn't want him awakened because he became peevish without his rest.

They made quite a commotion out front, but I wasn't paying much attention, until I heard Mr Prudhomme, in his Lord of Thunder voice, declaring 'We must go inside! We cannot continue this out here.' Then the ladies began to speak, and soon after, I heard the front door close and footsteps on the first floor.

It was quiet for a while. I was finishing a serial about a handsome young married couple that had come a cropper through jealous quarrels. It was one of those stories that you know will end safely, all forgiven and everyone wiser. I guess that's why it surprised me when the voices below grew louder instead of quieter. I couldn't hear a word being said, but there was no mistaking the sound of a raging argument. I was glad that Verna and James were off for the evening, lest they get an earful never intended for their hearing. As for myself, I was only concerned that such a hullabaloo might wake the twins.

Some time later, I laid my magazine aside and turned out the light. Still the row went on, filtered through the rooms between us. They must have spent the better part of an hour like that, shouting and carrying on. Suddenly a door was flung open downstairs, reverberating against a wall, and Mr Prudhomme's voice roared through the hallway, a bewildering storm of syllables that I couldn't sort into words. It was followed by a woman crying out, hysterical, running her words together. 'You cannot-treatmelikethisIwillnotallowit!' The front door opened and closed, and someone was hammering on it and ringing the bell.

'Leave here at once!' Mr Prudhomme demanded through the closed door. 'At once! You'll not speak of this matter, do you understand? Don't forget that I could very well produce evidence of your own improprieties. Shall I send the proof to your family? Is that what you want?'

Nobody answered.

'Is it?' he asked loudly.

There was only silence.

Just then, I heard running on the stairs and somebody opening the door to the twins' room. I reached for my robe and slippers and ran into the hall.

Mrs Prudhomme was standing in the doorway to the children's room, her chest heaving, as though she'd dashed a mile. She spun about, looking startled to find me there.

'The boys are all right.' She seemed distracted.

'You mustn't wake them. Anthony didn't drift off until quite late . . .'

'Yes. Of course.' She glanced quickly into their room once more. 'I must go turn off the lights.'

I watched her down the stairs, wondering at all the fuss. After a moment, I went into the boys' room to make certain they were still sleeping. I felt the sheets to see that neither had wet. Andrew stirred, plucking at his pyjamas. I hushed him and sat him on his little chamber pot. He did his business drowsily and allowed himself to be tucked back into bed without fully awakening. I went to the bathroom, washed the pot and set it back under his bed. He and Anthony were fast asleep. I tiptoed out, closing the door behind me.

Mr and Mrs Prudhomme were talking quietly downstairs, moving from room to room, turning out the lights. They were at the foot of the stairs now.

'Did you get the porch lamp?' Mr Prudhomme asked.

'I will,' she replied, going to the switch beside the front door.

When she cried out, the sound of her voice was so sharp, so peculiar that for a second I felt myself go stiff with fear. Then I ran to the top of the stairs and saw her below, staring out of the etched glass panel set into the door, repeating her husband's name over and over again.

He came, I think, from his study, throwing open the front door, pushing her away when she tried to go with him on to the shadowy porch. 'Get back. Stay clear.'

Mrs Prudhomme retreated into the brightly lit hallway. She stood there in silence, her hands clasped tightly in front of her. Finally she cried out to him. 'What is it? What's happened?'

He didn't reply.

I went downstairs then, thinking I might be of use.

His voice came through the open door. 'Telephone Doctor Banks, Ada. Tell him I'm coming.'

She passed me in the hall as if she didn't see me.

'Mr Prudhomme,' I called into the night, 'is there anything I can do?' I ran on to the porch and started down the steps after him.

'Yes,' he answered from the darkness beyond. 'Open the door of the automobile for me. Watch your footing, Nanny. The bricks are slippery.'

I glanced down at the steps beneath my feet and saw that they were slick with blood, shining scarlet in the lamplight. I could hear it sticking to my slippers as I went down the walk to the drive. What terrible thing had happened to these people, I wondered.

I reached the auto abreast of Mr Prudhomme and opened the door to the passenger seat.

'Help me to balance her.'

In his arms he carried our Vixen. Her skin was as pale as the moon, and her marmalade hair spilled over his arm. Her mouth lay open, but no sound or movement came from her. Her arms hung limply beneath her, dangling blood-soaked tassels that were his handkerchief, his stockings, his necktie. He must have seen my expression.

'She cut herself. I bandaged her as best I could.'

I looked down and saw that he was barefoot. 'Will you be able to drive like that, sir?'

He slid into the driver's seat and started the engine. 'Go take care of Mrs Prudhomme, Nanny, and see that the bricks are hosed down.'

I never told them that I knew the red fox. In truth, I really didn't. She was only one of those who'd befriended the twins in Wattles Gardens. Roxanne Pollard was her name, rest her soul. The newspaper reports said that she'd once been employed by Mr Prudhomme, then moved to Chicago where she'd supported herself as a public stenographer. She'd returned to California wanting her former positon back and become irrational, they said, when Mr Prudhomme turned her down. That poor unstable young woman must have truly enjoyed working for him, I thought, to have gone to such extremes and then to have taken his refusal as a mortal blow. I remember that Verna and James bought several copies of the newspapers to take back to Louisville with them.

Roxanne Pollard's suicide weighed heavily on the Prudhommes, I could tell. 'A very great misfortune,' Mr Prudhomme said it was. It was a while before he shook it off and returned to being his jaunty self. His wife did not refer to it at all. She seemed to wish to push it from her thoughts. Once, though, I came upon her gazing through the glass-panelled front door at the spot where Roxanne Pollard had lain. She turned when she heard me, and for a moment I wondered if she might weep, but she only shook her head and walked sadly away.

I don't know that it was a consequence of the tragedy, the Prudhommes' deciding to leave that house. Lord knows, I all but broke into a jig when Mrs Prudhomme told me that her husband had given his permission to look elsewhere. Now that I think of it, that was when Mrs Prudhomme came into her own. It was as if she'd been holding herself in check all the while and then, by some mutual agreement, had suddenly been given free rein. Merciful heavens, how that woman charged ahead. I think her husband was quite astonished at the talents she let loose. He sometimes looked at her as though she were a genie he'd brought forth from a bottle.

She must have had the vision in her head for some time, because she knew exactly what she wanted. It was she who tracked down the land and the gentleman who designed the buildings and the gardens. Mr Prudhomme never countermanded her. Whatever she wanted, she got. Something had changed between them, though I couldn't say what it was. I'd always thought her in awe of her husband, the way she deferred to his wishes. Now the shoe was on the other foot. He as much as acknowledged it. 'Don't bother me with petty details, Ada,' he told her. 'Do as you please. Only tell me when we move, so I don't come home to the wrong house.'

For the twins, the construction site of Silverwood was like their own huge playground. They clambered about the piles of masonry, made mud-pies of mortar, hurled snowstorms of shavings at each other and played hide-and-seek about the maze of half-finished rooms. They were oblivious of the grandeur springing up about them. Indeed, I think they were a trifle disappointed when the place was finished and no longer a gigantic plaything. By then, though, they had a whole new world to explore.

Ralph Gamble

You could of knocked me over with a daisy when this beaut of a little lady comes up to me at a party for ACTS at Silverwood year before last and introduces herself as Daphne Prudhomme. I was still stuck for words when she went on and asked me, 'Mr Gamble, would it be an intrusion if I came to see you sometime at your office? I'd like to talk with you about . . .' She broke off, smiling, and motioned towards the portrait of Ada Prudhomme that hung above the crowd in the hall. 'About her,' she went on, 'and about Silverwood and what this place used to be like.'

'Sure, sweetheart,' I said, 'but I don't know what I could tell you that your Dad hasn't probably told you already.'

She looked away, like maybe I'd touched a nerve. Then I remembered what a changed person her father was from the genial guy I used to know. 'Listen,' I said, 'it's the least I can do for Drew Prudhomme's daughter,' and I told her to set it up with my secretary.

Even before she kept the appointment, she'd got me to thinking how different my own life might have turned out if it wasn't for that family of hers.

I started right after the war (that's war number two we're talking) building apartment houses here in LA. Then on to tract homes in the Valley. Mostly we sold to ex-servicemen. A lot of guys had passed through California on the way out to the Pacific, and one look at this place was enough to convince them they'd had it with Minnesota or Kansas or whatever hind leg of the world they'd come from. Those times, that's where the real money was. You couldn't put up the walls fast enough. Nothing fancy by today's standards. Two bedrooms, fireplace in the living room, two-car garage and barbecue pit in the yard. Ten thousand, landscaping included. The way the crowds came, you'd of thought we were giving them away for free. One day we sold eighty in a single hour. Even if we started construction on a hundred more daily, we couldn't keep pace with the demand. Every time someone mentions the GI Bill, I feel like crossing myself.

After that, it was easy. sailing. I could afford to build for a classier market, homes with more land, more features, developments with fancy names like Spindrift Ridge. That's one of our best, near Laguna, full half-acre homesites overlooking the ocean. Six different split-level floor plans. We kept the nautical theme throughout, street names like Anchor Lane, Harbor Road, Spyglass Drive. That sort of detail pays off.

The theme of the old Prudhomme property was prestige, pure and simple. Some of our projects are planned for people with big families or for retired couples or for the horsey set (bridle trails, riding rings, stalls, tack rooms, barns – that's Palomino Grange out by Altadena). We figured the buyers for the Prudhomme tract would be attracted by the Beverly Hills location. There just wasn't a lot of available acreage with a Beverly Hills address attached, and we knew that the ones who'd pay the price would want the world to know they'd arrived, if you get my meaning. That meant top-dollar luxury. Everything first class. Terrazzo foyers, wet bars, all-electric kitchens, marble vanity tops, olympic-size pools and iron-grated entries with remote control from indoors. Like we say in the trade, they were loaded.

We had a hell of a time, though, settling on a name for the place. We needed something real tony that spelled it all out for the prospective buyers, and the twins had made it a condition of the sale that we couldn't use either their name or Silverwood. Me and my partners, Ben Lewis and Harry Connors, would try out names on Laurel, our secretary. She went to some ladies' college in the south someplace, and genteel was her middle name. Nothing sounded right. Jesus, we were only a few months from opening and we hadn't yet got a name. Ben kept pushing Jacaranda Hills. When he still couldn't get a rise out of Harry and I, he went for Jacaranda Mesa. *Jacaranda Mesa*, for God's sake. Sounds like some Mex settlement outside Tijuana. Anyhow, half the people who read the ads wouldn't even know how to pronounce it. Harry couldn't make up his mind whether he liked Beverly Knoll or Beverly Heights better. Don't get me wrong – Harry's a good man with the books, none better, but he's got no head for charisma.

I kept thinking elegance, class. Ada Prudhomme, what kind of name would she have picked? Then it came to me. Silvercrest Estates. That was it. The vote was unanimous, Laurel included. We took out double-page spreads in the paper, showing half a dozen front elevations and a location map. The copy read: 'The address says it all. Silvercrest Estates in Beverly Hills. Homes for the discriminating buyer.' Right off, some of your best people, big names, came nosing around to take a look, and our first section was eighty per cent sold within three months. Three months! We went on to open up the second section, and the rest is history. We're still building, and they're still selling. It's a damn shame Ada Prudhomme didn't leave another hundred acres behind her when she quit the game.

Not, mind you, that she would have approved of allowing the general public to share the hallowed family grounds. She guarded Silverwood like a watchdog. She reminded me of one of those chichi hounds with the long snoots and the smooth gait. My ex-wife, Irma, has one. A borzoi. The damned thing cost a fucking fortune. Ada Prudhomme had that same kind of graceful walk and that down-the-nose way of looking at you. Come to think of it, I never met a beautiful woman who didn't have that sort of mildly insolent expression. Ada would fix you with her cool, blue-eyed gaze and start speaking in that soft kind of teasing voice like she was challenging you to mix with her. She had an upper crust accent, too. Words like 'tom-ah-to' and 'ennething.' She was the real thing, a lady, blue blood in every vein. And get this: never mind that I was thirty-six when I met her and she was over fifty – I wanted to jump on her bones like no broad I ever met. I used to think my second wife, Irma, was the sexiest woman on earth. God knows, I can't picture Ada Prudhomme doing the stunts that Irma did, but there was something about that woman that gave me a hard-on whenever I was close to her. For starters, she was a toucher. When she spoke to you, even if she was telling you in her ladylike way to go to hell, she'd let her fingers rest lightly

44

against your wrist or lay a hand on your shoulder. Sometimes, if the room was noisy, she'd lean close to you to speak and, intentionally or not, her lips might brush your ear. It was enough to drive any man crazy. Here's this aristocratic dame who acts like butter wouldn't melt in her mouth, tantalizing you with her hands and voice and eyes and you know if you make move one, she'll carve you into little pieces. Believe it or not, I've had dreams about Ada Prudhomme, about her taking down all that plaited blond hair and letting it fall loose over her breasts. I've even caught the aroma of her scent in my sleep, that rich sweet fragrance that smelled so good you wanted to lick it like a pastel bonbon from one of those fancy candy stores.

At the time I met Ada Prudhomme, social types like her were something new for me. When people ask, I tell them my father was a tomato farmer in Illinois, which, after a fashion, is gospel. He owned a string of houses around Chicago. I never got along with the old bastard. He used to beat the shit out of my brother Phil and me after my mother ran off. When Phil got pneumonia and died, I blew town before Pa could lay Phil's share of the punishment off on me. In those days, nobody asked questions. You were willing and able to work, you got hired. I was sixteen but I looked two or three years older. I picked up odd jobs on construction crews – water boy, hod carrier, you name it. I dug excavations, then became an apprentice mason. I helped plumb and paint and whatever else paid forty cents an hour. I kept drifting further west. I don't know why: by chance, I guess. Des Moines, Omaha, Denver, Phoenix, LA. I reached LA in '29, just in time to get myself situated in a job before everything hit the fan and the Okies and Arkies pulled up stakes and moved to California looking for work. I shared a place out near M-G-M with two other guys – Ben Lewis who worked with me then and is a partner of mine today, and an odd duck named Fuzzy Rickert who worked extra at the studios. He was the tightest s.o.b. I ever met. Still had the first nickel he'd earned. He'd escort some poor girl or another to those fancy studio parties and steal enough food to see him through the next couple of days. He lifted soap from washrooms. All he really cared about was being comfortable in his old age. Nearly every penny he made got invested. He was one of those guys who was going to retire early and start living it up at the age of fifty. Ben kept telling him he'd never *know* how to live it up when the time came unless he practised somewhere along the way. 'Poor Fuzzy,' Ben would say to me. 'The day he hits fifty, he's going to want to jump for joy and his ass will be stuck to the floor.' As it happened, Ferdinand Z. Rickert (that was the way they wrote it in the newspaper) jumped from the Arroyo Seco Bridge four years later, at the ripe old age of twenty-seven, having lost his shirt when the market crashed. Me and Ben have had no trouble enjoying life, not with Fuzzy in mind.

Early on, we decided to get together our own company, but we had to wait nearly ten years because the economy was in such lousy shape. Then the war came. We made up our minds that as soon as it was over and the government slacked off defence building, we'd race like hell to put up apartments for all those GIs and their brides who wanted to settle down in sunny Cal.

I remember it was on V-J day when I met Drew Prudhomme. I was with Harry who's now my other partner but who still worked at the bank then. It was early in the evening, still light outside, and hot, I remember, being August. Harry and I were hoisting a few at Musso and Frank on Hollywood Boulevard. Christ, the place was jammed. People kept bumping into this guy, and the stuff was sloshing all over his fancy clothes. I thought from the ascot and jodhpurs he was some pansy movie actor, and when Harry waved him over, I said, 'Jesus, Harry, if he so much as puts his hand on my knee under the table, I'll break his fucking wrist.'

Harry looked at me like I'd gone nuts. 'It's Andrew Prud-homme. Married to the daughter of Hale Hunt Outerbridge.'

'*Jeez, excuse* me. You didn't tell me, Harry, that you'd been rubbing elbows with the country club crowd.'

'He does business at the bank.'

That day, of all days, friendships happened fast. You'd of thought Andrew Prudhomme and me would have nothing in common. Here was a guy who'd spent the morning horseback riding with his kid, talking to two working stiffs who hardly knew one end of a pony from the other. Talking about the war and the

46

future and then, just as easily, about how Ben and Harry and I were making big plans.

'Our men.' Drew raised his drink. It was straight gin by then. 'Our men deserve the best.' He waved his drink towardss a gob who was singing the Chiquita Banana song with a pretty brunette WAC. 'To you. The best. The best of everything.' He glanced at Harry, then me. 'They gave their all for the war effort. We owe them our all for peace.'

'Well spoken,' Harry told him.

'Ditto,' I said.

'Housing's the top priority,' Harry reminded him.

'Housing,' Drew agreed. 'It's the least we can do. A roof over their heads.'

'Tiled baths and gas heat and carpeting.' I pounded the table for emphasis.

'Damned right.' Drew turned to me. 'Were you in it?'

'I was 4 F. Bad ticker. On account of rheumatic fever when I was a kid.'

'Same here,' he said. 'Bum leg.'

'Asthma,' Harry put in.

'We are deeply in their debt,' he announced solemnly.

'Ben, too,' I reminded Harry. 'His eyesight kept him out.'

'Gentlemen.' Drew rose a little unsteadily. 'My wife is expecting. She is also expecting me home sometime. Can't keep her waiting any longer.' He shook hands with each of us. 'We must discuss this further. A matter of honour.'

I figured that was that. A few friendly drinks and we'd seen the last of him. But no. Come to find out from Harry that the next time Drew was in the bank, he came over to Harry's desk at New Accounts and started questioning him in detail about our plans. Harry told him how the three of us had bought and demolished a block of old gandy dancers' shacks near Santa Monica Boulevard and how we were only waiting to get the bucks together to proceed. He wanted to arrange a meeting. That was what he said. 'Arrange a meeting!' Did he know that Harry and me and Ben would of walked over hot coals to a meeting with some guy like him who worked for Hale Hunt Outerbridge?

Connections. If I had a kid, I'd give him that word to live by.

Don't tell me those swanky boarding schools and colleges teach half of what I know. I'll tell you why people send their kids there – for the connections they make. Without connections, you're an outsider with your nose pressed to the glass, wondering what life is like in those fancy drawing rooms. And now, all because Ben hadn't got plastered with us on V-J Day and because Harry got food poisoning the day he was to meet Drew, I was the one who connected with the Prudhommes.

I knew who they were, naturally. You couldn't pick up a newspaper without reading how 'Mrs Victor Guy Prudhomme has recently returned from Cincinnati where she presided over the opening of an exhibit of paintings from her late husband's collection.' According to the papers, Mrs Victor Guy Prudhomme, the widow of the financier and polo player, was always traipsing around the country, bringing culture to the boondocks. Even the country being at war hadn't slowed her down. *Time* magazine called the exhibit 'a stirring show of great American paintings guaranteed to bring out the patriot in the art lover and vice versa.' War or no, she and her pictures went on being 'fêted' in places like Minneapolis or Santa Fe.

Irma, my former wife, used to read the society pages aloud at breakfast. I would like to say that's why we're no longer married, but the truth is she went off with a caterer she met working at the Hollywood Canteen in '44. Anyhow, she'd read about the doings of 'Mr and Mrs Hale Hunt Outerbridge and their daughter and son-in-law, Mr and Mrs Andrew Prudhomme' and how 'Lieutenant (j.g.) Anthony Prudhomme, home on leave from the United States Navy, is once more in demand as a sought-after bachelor-about-town.' Irma liked that kind of thing. Some women read movie magazines. She read the society columns. Once in a while she found Lily's name there. Lily Cantrell was Irma's half sister and eight years older. She used to be a real looker, from her pictures. Not that she wasn't still attractive in a frayed sort of way. She looked like a rag doll that had been loved a lot by some rough kids and got faded and worn. Still, she was never without a guy to pay the bills, and every so often she popped up in the society section at a party with some old duffer. According to Irma, Lily had been Victor Prudhomme's sweetie for a time.

Victor had the rep of being a player, she said. I don't know if it's true. If you believed Lily, she'd had romances with everyone from Roscoe Arbuckle to Al Jolson and Errol Flynn. Maybe she only said that stuff to impress Irma. Social batting averages were Irma's favourite dish.

The first meeting I had with Drew, he came to our office, such as it was. Me and Harry and Ben had rented a hole in the wall above a bakery and got ourselves some stationery with a letterhead printed with the firm's name, CAL-SUN QUALITY HOMES, and the address. Drew took a look around at the place – there was no janitorial service, and we weren't what you'd call neat – and he laughed aloud. 'Christ, Ralph, this looks like the kind of dive where you'd go to fix a basketball game.'

I opened the venetian blinds and swept some doughnut crumbs off the desk into the wastebasket. Drew dusted the chair with his hand before he sat down. He was wearing white flannel trousers and a yellow silk shirt open at the neck. He propped his feet up on the wastebasket.

'I'll say one thing, you guys *must* be honest. If you weren't, you'd never risk meeting me in a place like this.'

In spite of the fancy-dan clothes, he was nobody's fool. He wanted to see title papers, deed restrictions, tax records, soil tests, the works: I sat there while he took his time going over the information. Once in a while, he'd glance up from the papers in front of him to ask me a question.

'I'm not rich, in case you wondered,' he said offhandedly. 'At least not yet. My father believed that if a person inherited money early in life it blunted his ambition. He liked to talk about the dignity of work and pride of accomplishment. I can still remember those sermons of his, even though he died when I was eleven.'

'A great loss, I'm sure.'

'The point is, neither my brother nor I will come into the principal portion of our inheritance until we're thirty-five. Both of us are twenty-eight now.'

'Both of you?'

'Twins.' He lit up a Camel. 'But I do have some money set aside. That's also thanks to my father. He'd give us a dime a week for our allowance, and we were supposed to save ten per

49

cent of it, along with ten per cent of any money we earned or received for Christmas or birthday gifts. It became a habit with me. That's the first bite out of every salary or trust fund check I deposit.'

'Your father would be pleased to know he had two such sensible sons.'

Drew exhaled, coughing. 'No.' He punched the smoke with his fist. 'Hell, no. We're not batting a thousand. My brother has never been out of hock a day in his life.' He paused, examining the tip of his cigarette. 'But that's another subject.' He flicked his ash into the wastebasket. 'What kind of money do you fellows need to come up with?'

I told him, not overly padding the figures.

'And you're willing to open up the deal to outsiders?'

It was my turn to laugh. 'Willing? Jesus, Drew, do you think you'd be sitting here in these plush accommodations if we could afford to swing the deal ourselves? Harry and Ben both have big families, and me, I got alimony payments I wouldn't wish on Tojo. We were on the verge of going to scout money when you turned up.'

'Drunk and disorderly. But solvent.'

The more we talked, the more I got the idea that although Drew liked working for his father-in-law in the comfortable shade of the money tree, there was a part of him that wanted to go it alone. I think he'd of liked to be an entrepreneur, but at Outerbridge Industries there was only one of those and it was Outerbridge himself. With us, Drew became a partner who had equal say. I suppose you'd have to call his venture into the construction business a pastime, but the way he went at it, you'd of thought it was his sole bread and butter.

About his brother, he never said much after that first time. Ada Prudhomme used to say how close her sons were, but you could of fooled me. When Tony Prudhomme eloped with Nita Paris, it was all over the papers. It was spooky, seeing the photographs, how alike those twins looked. 'Your brother's gone and got himself some beautiful bride,' I told Drew.

'Asshole.'

'Pardon?'

50

'Strike that, Ralph. Yes, indeed he has.'

As far as I could see, that's how close they were. I never met Tony or Nita until the day of Ada Prudhomme's funeral when Nita bailed me out of a conversation with Dorcas Outerbridge, who was looking at me glassy-eyed, not half listening, which was no surprise since she'd arrived at the church with a breath on her.

As I recall, Drew first invited me to Silverwood on Saturday when we were building our initial fourteen units. One of his children was having a birthday party over at his own place, and niether one of us liked that ratty office because the smells from the bakery underneath drove us nearly nuts with hunger. He'd been out of town on business for Outerbridge, and I was going to bring him up to date on the project. I'm not the type that's easily intimidated, but coming up that winding drive lined with bird of paradise and catching sight of that mansion looming ahead, I felt like a kid being called up to the principal's office.

We sat in the solarium, I remember. The solarium, by Jesus. I'd never been in a solarium, in in my life. I thought they were only on luxury liners.

'Perhaps Mr Gamble would like some refreshments.'

Drew and I looked up. In the doorway stood a genuine goddess of a woman, tall, fair, with her hair high on her head like a Greek statue. She was wearing a loose dress of some rosy, light-weight stuff that moved in the breeze from the hallway. All at once, her perfume floated by me, and I began to feel what Irma used to call my Damned Itch.

'Mother, may I present Ralph Gamble?'

I could see, as she moved towards me, that she was older than I'd first thought, but that didn't stop the Itch. Show me a tall, cool, self-possessed blond, and I want to climb her like an alp.

'*Mis*-ter Gamble, how nice to meet you after hearing Andrew speak of you so enthusiastically.'

'Pleasure's mine, I assure you, Mrs Prudhomme.' Her hand felt long and smooth, and it lingered in mine for what seemed like several minutes. There was a kind of glittering look to those bright blue eyes; I couldn't make out whether she was regarding me with amusement or contempt.

51

'Well, Mr Gamble? Will it be tea or perhaps a drink?'

'Thanks all the same, ma'am, but I ate lunch late.'

'What a shame.' She smiled at me. 'It seems we can't give you anything but money. Why, Mr Gamble!' She reached out and touched me. 'Your face is flushed. Are you blushing? Or does the mention of the word money give you a warm feeling all over?'

'Ma'am?'

'It does me, I know. There's something very comforting about prosperity, don't you agree?' She sat down on the divan and took a cigarette from a small silver urn on the table next to her. From a matching urn, she picked one of a dozen or so coloured holders. Hers was red. She screwed the cigarette into it.

As I lit it for her, she clasped my hand in both of hers and held my glance with those deep blue eyes. 'Thank you. Now do sit down, both of you. Do you mind my interrupting?'

'You didn't, Mother. Ralph just finished briefing me.'

'What a pity. I'd have liked to listen.'

'I'd be pleased to answer any questions, Mrs Prudhomme.'

'You would? Well then, Mr Gamble, start from the beginning, if you will.' She exhaled and watched the smoke disappear, waiting.

If she was trying to throw me off balance, I wasn't falling. She had no way of knowing that feisty broads are my game. Sure they can be a pain, but if you know how to handle them, you'll never be bored. The thing with that type of woman is to show them up front who's boss. I flashed her my best Boy Scout smile and gave her a short history of Ben, Harry and myself. I told her what our plans were and where things stood. I skipped over the part about getting soused with Drew on V-J Day.

She waited until I'd finished before she spoke again. 'Tell me, is my son risking much with you?'

'Mother – '

'He's hardly taking any risk at all, Mrs Prudhomme.'

'Just how much of a chance is there that he might lose money by investing in this scheme?'

'Mother, this is really not your affair.'

She acted like she hadn't heard him. 'I do not wish my sons ever to find themselves over a barrel. Do I make myself clear?'

Her eyes were fixed on me like a cobra trying to hypnotize its next meal. 'My sons, Mr Gamble, must never be at the mercy of others for want of money.'

I understood, all right. I'd been there. I knew how it was to have to kiss ass to earn a bowl of red. What I wondered, then and now, was how Ada Prudhomme understood it so well.

'If I can be utterly sincere with you, Mrs Prudhomme . . .'

'Please.'

'Between you and I, if I was a wealthy man myself, there's no way I'd let Drew or anyone else in on these projects. I swear to you, there's no foreseeable chance of losing money in California real estate. Not for a decade, if you ask me.'

'You're quite impressive, Mr Gamble, when you get down to business.'

'I mean to be. I don't intend to come up a loser. Or for any of my associates to come up losers,' I added.

'Have a drink, Ralph,' said Drew. 'I'm going to. Mother?'

'Ring for Safford, dear, or help yourself. What will it be?' she asked me.

'Gin and ginger,' I said to Drew. 'Easy on the gin.'

'What a good idea. I'll have the same, dear. You know,' she told me as Drew left to get the drinks, 'I envy your being so clever with your financial dealings.'

'I'm not a clever man, Mrs Prudhomme. A party like myself just works harder than the next fellow.'

'Still, it must give one a great sense of security to know the trick of making money.'

'There's no trick to it. Like I said . . .'

'Nevertheless, you can do it, and I cannot. Imagine yourself in my position, Ralph. May I call you Ralph?'

'I'd be pleased.'

'And I am Ada.' Ah-dah, she pronounced it. 'Imagine, Ralph, as I said, how you would feel inheriting an establishment of this size and having none of the skills to ensure its upkeep. If I possessed your talent for enterprise, I should sleep much more soundly. Money disappears easily. We all learned that after 1929. It would be a comfort to know that one simply had to apply

53

oneself assiduously and it would reappear. But life isn't that way, is it?'

I'd been looking at her ankles. She had great legs, what I could see of them. I glanced up like I'd been caught with my hand in the till. 'I guess that's why a lady like yourself should have a gentleman around to rely on.'

'Exactly. Ralph, if I ever feel in need of some advice . . .'

'You got it.'

'I was hoping you'd say that.' She reached for my hand and squeezed it once lightly, smiling at me like we shared a confidence. Still, I couldn't get it out of my head, the way she'd looked at me when she was letting me know nobody better pull a fast one on her sons.

When I got up to go, she insisted on walking me to the door. At first I thought she wanted to make sure I didn't palm any of her expensive doodads on the way out. I wasn't sure she trusted me a hundred per cent, in spite of how I'd laid the facts on the line to her. But Ada was full of surprises. When we got to the door, she put her hand on my arm. 'I want to thank you,' she said, 'for giving Andrew this opportunity.' Just like that. Sincere. If she didn't have me before, she did then. The idea of the mistress of Silverwood, saying she was in debt to *me*.

'That's not necessary. I need him more than he needs me. Anybody who works beside Hale Hunt Outerbridge . . .'

'But he's still an employee. He works for Hale and for Hale's company. You're giving him the chance to do something for himself. My husband would be very glad. He was an entrepreneur of the old school.'

In my book that phrase translated to 'gentleman bandit,' but at that point I didn't give a damn how Victor Prudhomme had got the loot to erect a monument like the one I was standing in. I was just glad to have been asked there.

Now that I look back on it, Drew must really have been rankling under Outerbridge's thumb. For him to take a flier with three guys he'd barely met was, in hindsight, out of character. No wonder Ada had approached me like I was a second-story man after her famous emeralds. Throwing his lot in with Ben and

Harry and me was a rash act on Drew's part. It's just lucky we three were on the level.

'What do you think, Mother?' Drew held open the front door. 'Shall I let Father Outerbridge in on this?'

'No. First you and Ralph and your partners will make a success of this building. Then you might allow Hale and some others to invest with you. But you'll have to scramble. If Ralph is correct, everyone and his brother will be buying land and putting up houses and apartments. It's a question of getting there first with the best.'

'That part's up to Ralph and the others.'

She took my hand. Her fragrance seemed to be everywhere. 'Don't disappoint me, Ralph.'

Disappoint her? Hell, at that point, I'd have gone to war for her.

Dorcas Outerbridge

Each morning I sit here at my dressing table, looking at Silverwood. Not the way it is now, God forbid, with those hippies traipsing through the halls. No, I see it at its meridian, stately and magnificent, framed in sterling, standing behind my ivory comb and brushes beside my crystal perfume bottles. Safford, Ada's butler, snapped the photograph the last Thanksgiving we were all together. My dearest Dosie is cradling Duncan in her arms, looking down at his little face with the doting gaze of a Madonna. My other two grandchildren, Daphne and Dexter, stand in front of their parents in the picture. Daphne is wearing the lace-collared velvet dress I bought for her sixth birthday.

How peculiar that identical twins could be so different that Drew would want a wife like my Dosie, while Tony would choose to marry a Nita Paris. In the picture, Tony is close by his mother, with his new bride beside him. They'd eloped to Reno only two weeks earlier, when Dosie was in the hospital having the baby. Probably Tony thought he'd have less trouble with Ada if he presented her with a *fait accompli*. He has his arm clasped possessively around Nita's waist. She holds his hand with both of hers and wears a wide, feral smile, her head thrown back, her hair unkempt. She looks like a jungle cat with its claws clutching some careless quarry. Anyone with half an eye could see that she was the kind of woman who exploited men and then tossed them aside once their usefulness was exhausted. Tony deserved better than that. Poor Ada, putting up such a brave front, when she must have been utterly dismayed.

Hale stands next to our Dosie in the photograph, presiding over his grandchildren with permissible pride. Then, of course, there are *les juifs* from the bottom of the hill.

I can remember that day as if it were only a week ago. Safford took the picture and went back into the house, while Hale packed up the camera and tripod. Ada was admiring the baby, and I suppose Nita became jealous. She started trying to hurry us all to the table to eat, saying she was in the middle of a film and had to be home early to prepare her scenes for the next day. I don't think it even occurred to her that she was being rude.

'But you're married to a Prudhomme,' I remarked, taking her arm and leading her away from the family, into the house. 'Surely you've no need to keep doing that sort of thing.'

'I'm a star, Mrs Outerbridge. I like it. Wouldn't you?'

'Oh, I should think not,' I replied in haste. 'It's frightfully public, isn't it?'

Nita laughed as though I'd made some kind of joke. 'It is frightfully, gloriously, sensationally public, and I love every blessed minute. Think of it,' she went on, as Drew and Dosie joined us, 'how many women have the thrill of giving so much pleasure to so many people?'

'Offhand,' Drew told her with a malicious grin, 'I'd say every tart on the European and Pacific fronts.'

'Andrew!' Dosie looked embarrassed.

Nita smiled broadly. 'Vicarious pleasure. Look but don't touch.'

'Drew, would you please take Duncan up to the nursery?'

56

Dosie asked, handing him the baby. 'The stairs tire me.' She went into the dining room with Nita and I overheard her say, 'It's even more wonderful, though, to have one special someone close to you, someone you can always depend on, don't you think?'

I was so touched to hear my daughter declare her values like that, but Nita just busied herself rearranging the place cards so that she would be seated between Tony and Drew.

Movie people are not like the rest of us. I suppose they experience their strongest emotions in front of the camera and life seems dull by comparison. Or perhaps they are simply so used to posturing that they haven't any sense of life's real virtues. They are a hard lot, from what I've observed. That's why it's so appalling to think of them taking over Silverwood like an army of ants crawling over that splendid establishment, indifferent to its aaesthetic properties. Regardless of whatever problems arose between Andrew and Anthony Prudhomme, those two shouldn't have disposed of Silverwood so callously. It was an affront to the memory of their parents. I know for a fact that Victor and Ada created that house not so much for themselves as for their children and their children's children. It was their gift to future generations of Prudhommes, a family retreat that would be a gathering spot for an illustrious clan. Now, of course, the twins have seen to it that my grandsons, not to mention Daphne, can never claim their rightful place.

Drew and I no longer speak. When Hale died, Drew brought the children to his funeral but he had the sense not to appear at the house afterward. The loss of Silverwood was the least of our differences. Worse, in my heart of hearts, I still feel he was in some way responsible for what happened to my beloved Dosie, though I don't know how or why. Perhaps some tragedies are inexplicable, after all, and that makes them all the more tragic. But why, oh why, did he have to turn my grandchildren from me?

It seems to me that Hale and I met Ada and Victor Prudhomme shortly after we returned from our wedding trip. There were a number of parties in our honour, and most probably we met at one of them. Ada, I remember, struck me as more handsome

57

than pretty, due to her height. Victor was easily the more engaging of the two. He was much older than she. I'd say Ada was Hale's age, and Victor must have been in his middle forties. He reminded me of Douglas Fairbanks. He had that same urbane charm, the ready smile, the slightly receding hairline. He had the physique of a man of half his years.

We saw the Prudhommes often during the first two years of our marriage. They lived near Wattles Gardens in Hollywood, in a large two-story house with a low pitched roof that made it appear to hover close to the ground like a large hen, wings spread, brooding over her young. I can recall sitting outside the dining room in the cool shade of one of its porches, feeling very drowsy after a large luncheon, while Victor and Hale discussed business. At the time, Victor's greatest enthusiasm was petroleum, while Hale's was aviation. Victor had the advantage of having been born to money. I doubt that Ada's family's circumstances could have matched Victor's fortune, but her people were old California and very well placed. The Prudhommes were originally from New York where Victor's father had made his fortune in iron. Victor wasn't the type, however, to follow a well-worn path. He thrived on challenge and competition. There had always to be an element of daring in his ventures. He had come west to build his inheritance into his own personal fortune. He was the kind, really, that has made our country great, one of those visionary capitalists with an invincible faith in the brilliant industrial future of America. I'm sure that's why he enjoyed Hale's company and treated him as an equal, despite there being at least twenty years' difference in their ages.

In those days, Hale was working in Inglewood for Glenn Curtiss, but only a year later, he joined Donald Douglas whom he'd known before Douglas left Curtiss. In turn, Hale later left Douglas to manufacture aeroplane parts on his own – the sorts of things they call components today. It was nothing so fancy, then. Even when Hale became a great success, he never let it go to his head. I suppose we could have had a grand estate like Silverwood, but we were always content to live in comfortable, lovely homes where Hale could putter about in his carpet slippers and not think twice about putting them up on the furniture.

We didn't see the Prudhommes so often after I was in the family way. I wasn't feeling well, and after the child was born, we had a very hard time of it for a while.

At first we were grateful that he wasn't a troublesome baby, that he was calm and didn't cry a lot. I don't know when I began to think of the word 'lethargic' in connection with him. I do know that each day, more and more apprehension built up inside me, until I was terrified that I would scream out my fears in my sleep. I couldn't bear to speak my mind to Hale. I would stand over Hale junior's crib and look down into his dark eyes, praying to see some comprehension there and receiving only the mindless black gaze of a guppy.

There was talk at that time of some kind of tragedy that had taken place at the Prudhommes', but our own tragedy so overshadowed anything beyond the four walls of our home that I never did know the details. All I knew was that shortly after we gave our boy up to the nuns, I was again in a delicate condition, this time with Dosie. By the time she was born and I'd finally stopped nursing, Victor and Ada had already started the construction of Silverwood.

We rarely saw them during the three years that they threw themselves into creating their masterpiece. Silverwood was completed, to the last swag of red silk on the tented ceiling of the smoking room, in time for the Prudhommes to welcome 1923 with a New Year's Eve party.

The line of Pierce-Arrows, Lincolns, and Duesenbergs going to Silverwood stretched all the way down to Sunset Boulevard. We stopped at the gatekeeper's cottage where our names were checked off the list of those invited and moved slowly up a drive lined with tall gas lamps that glowed warmly in the black winter night. At the door, we surrendered our coats and were announced to Ada and Victor who stood receiving in the main hall, directly in front of the solarium. As Hale and I waited our turn, I spied the twins in their pyjamas and robes, peeking at the throng of guests from the upstairs balcony. I never was able to tell them apart until they were fully grown. At that time, they would have been almost six. How like Victor they looked. I glanced at the portrait of Ada that had been painted when they were in England on their wedding trip. Her motionless gaze contemplated the crowd, looking faintly amused at the stir she had created. She was wearing her pleated apricot Fortuny dress and those magnificent emeralds.

'My dears!' she greeted us as we came through the receiving line. 'How good to see you both.'

'We were very nearly late,' I apologized. 'My hairdresser had a most unpleasant *contretemps* with one of our German Shepherds.'

'I'm glad it wasn't serious enough to keep you from coming,' said Ada. 'How is that sweet little girl of yours?'

'Angelic,' said Hale.

'Aren't you lucky. My boys are such a handful. They run their poor nanny quite ragged.'

'I saw them just now at the top of the stairs. They're going to look exactly like you, Victor – dark, dashing and tall.'

He kissed my cheek. I felt the light pressure of his hand cradling my hip. 'You're much too generous with your flattery, Dorcas,' he said. 'God help them if they turn out like me. They'd be better off to model themselves after Ada.'

'But you're right, Dorcas,' Ada said. 'They're the image of their father. I can't take any credit for their handsomeness.'

'You're being overly modest,' Hale accused her.

'Yes,' agreed Victor. 'The shrinking violet role hardly suits you, my dear.'

Ada glanced at him sharply. 'I only meant to say, Victor, that since the children are carbon copies of you, it would be presumptuous of me to act as if they owed their good looks to my side of the family.'

'Now, now, my dear,' he said jovially, 'we mustn't argue over compliments. Besides, tonight you'll be taking enough bows to last a lifetime. Hasn't Ada made a superb job of the house? Do stroll around,' he called after us, as we moved on.

Guests in holiday finery drifted from room to room in shoals, like silver and rainbow fish investigating the inlets and coves of some congenial lagoon. In the drawing room an orchestra played and there was dancing under the chandeliers. Fires capered in every fireplace. The billiard room was hushed. Substantial wagers rested on the outcome of a game between two men who, between them, had erected at least a third of the oil derricks in Los Angeles. And everywhere one looked there was Victor's art collection which, in those days, he kept at home. There were Cropseys, Eastmans and Binghams lining the walls. Victor only bought American art, a choice Hale admired. 'Why subsidize some foreigner's culture when we've just as good stuff in this country?' Hale, like Victor, was very much a patriot.

In the oak-panelled library, one wall of bookcases opened to reveal a vast well-stocked bar. Hale fetched us some scotch, pausing to congratulate Benny Walsh. Benny was everybody's bootlegger, a saturnine little man with a beard so dark that it gave his face a bluish cast. He had deep circles under his eyes and wore a perpetually melancholy expression. Aside from his professional life, he was, Hale said, the most honest fellow he'd ever met. 'You've outdone yourself, Benny,' Hale told him. 'It looks as if you've drained Scotland dry.'

'And France. And Canada. And Cuba. It's a parched world out there tonight, Mr O. Have you met Mr Ferris Warburton from New York City?' He inclined his head towards the man next to him. 'He's the architect responsible for this place. Mr Warburton, may I present Mr and Mrs Hale Hunt Outerbridge.'

Hale shook his hand. 'Is this the first time you've designed a house on the West Coast?'

'Indeed. One finds great homes in certain areas of the east, such as Newport or Long Island, but they're still a rarity in southern California.'

'I expect you'd like to change that,' said Benny.

'One tries to make the best of one's opportunities. If it weren't for Mrs Prudhomme's inspiration, after all, I shouldn't be here in the first place. She was eager to contribute an establishment of lasting beauty to grace her birthplace.'

Benny gave him an admiring look. 'Mr Warburton, sir, you've got a way with words that'd put Sister Aimee to shame.'

'I thought Ada came from San Francisco.' Hale turned to me. 'Didn't she? No one here met her until Victor produced her like a white rabbit out of a hat.'

'Here she is now. Ada!' I beckoned to her. 'Didn't you say you originally came from up north?'

'I did.'

'But Mr Warburton said that you were born here.'

'Why, Ferris,' she said quickly, 'are you trying to confuse these good people?'

'I distinctly understood you to tell me – '

'Of course. It's my fault, really, for misleading you. What I must have said was that my parents *planned* for me to be born here. They were visiting Los Angeles at the time. They'd contemplated buying a ranch in the area, but they decided against it.'

'Then Hale was right. You were born in San Francisco.'

'Not precisely, Dorcas. I was born in a little town on the peninsula, though my parents moved to the city not long afterward. It's simpler to say I was born in San Francisco.'

'Are your parents still in the city? What are their names? Perhaps we know of them. Hale and I have a great many friends there.'

'They've both been dead for some time. Goodness!' she exclaimed. 'What a gloomy thing to be saying. Do let's change the subject. Dorcas, have you read the Dreiser book everyone's talking about?'

'Hale says it's much too dreary.'

The orchestra struck up 'Ain't We Got Fun.' Hale took Ada's arm. 'May I steal a dance with the hostess before she's spirited away?'

I looked after them through the drawing room door until they disappeared among the dancing couples that eddied about the floor. 'Surely, Mr Warburton, Silverwood must rank among your greatest accomplishments.'

'I can't accept full credit for it, Mrs Outerbridge. It is, you know, an adaptation of Langehurst Hall in England. Did you or your husband know the Lambtons who lived there?'

'I don't believe so.'

'Rather a sad tale, really. I gather Nigel Lambton was a school chum of Victor Prudhomme. Lambton's mother was American, and sent him to Exeter. His father made a fortune in metal products and built Langehurst Hall in the 1870's. Nigel married Lady Penelope Campbell-West, called Poppy. She was a famous international hostess in her day. Surely, you've heard of her salons.'

'I'm so sorry.'

'Ah. Well. Unfortunately, she was lost with the *Lusitania*. Her poor husband died of a tumour four years later. At present, Langehurst Hall is a warren of draughty rooms, only a dozen of which are occupied by their son, a slim, sallow chap who entertains his friends there in the style of Oscar Wilde. One could, I suppose, draw some sort of moral from the story.'

'Maybe Mrs O would like to dance,' suggested Benny Walsh.

I was relieved he'd curtailed Warburton's sorry account. In his way, you see, Benny was a gentleman. He knew better than to ask me to dance himself. He was a tradesman, and he knew his place. As luck would have it, the music stopped just as Ferris Warburton and I stepped on to the dance floor. Hale and Ada joined us, and we strolled into the main hall. 'Has anyone seen Victor?' inquired Ada.

'A moment ago,' answered Ferris Warburton, 'I saw him chatting with Elodie Swann, and then Lily Cantrell joined them.'

'There's Elodie,' I said, 'by the door to the morning room. Have you heard? She has made herself a great deal of money in the past three years, trading in real estate. She's made a small fortune, buying and selling property around Western Avenue.'

'But do any of you see Victor? Where did he go, do you know?'

'I'm sure he'll turn up presently,' Hale told her.

'You must forgive me,' Ada said as she withdrew and made her way through the crowd.

'The land boom won't last, you know. Your Miss Swann quite agrees with me,' Ferris Warburton told Hale. 'You had a similar phenomenon here sixty years ago that went bust almost overnight. This is the same sort of wild speculation, everybody and his brother taking a fling, driving up property prices to the point of absurdity. Sooner or later, the bubble will burst.'

I don't know if it was Ferris Warburton's influence or not that led Elodie to get out of the real estate marked in time, before, less than two years later, it plummeted. Whatever the case, Elodie became, and remains, a rich woman. She has weathered the

Great Depression and the ups and downs of the past years without any visible dent in her circumstances.

Ada returned shortly, apologizing for having rushed off. 'So many small details! A large party is rather like a complicated military exercise, don't you think?'

'Did you find Victor?' I inquired.

'Not yet, no. Why, do you know where he went?'

'There he is now,' Hale said, with a nod towards the far end of the room, 'standing with Austin Chase and Laurence Ward.'

Victor and the others parted, and a ravishing young woman, her wavy black hair bobbed, her lips rouged brightly and her topaz beaded dress sparkling like champagne, motioned Victor to join her.

'Would you all excuse me?' Ada asked. 'I must make sure that Victor speaks to the orchestra about the music.'

Hale looked after her. 'Who's the pip who's got Ada's antennae up?'

'Lily Cantrell,' said Ferris Warburton. 'Word has it that she was at that party that Fatty Arbuckle gave at the St Francis a couple of years ago.'

'Good heavens,' I said. 'Not that scandalous affair where the young woman died!'

'Hush. She's coming our way. Miss Cantrell,' Warburton said, kissing her hand, 'what a pleasure to see you again.'

Lily Cantrell's forehead furrowed momentarily. 'Washburn?'

'Warburton, Ferris.'

'The builder.'

'Architect. Allow me to introduce Mr and Mrs Outerbridge.'

'Charmed,' she said to Hale, 'I'm sure. Say, how does a girl get a little more of the bubbly around here?' She held up her empty champagne glass.

'Allow me.' Ferris Warburton took it from her and made off in the direction of the bar.

'Are you Victor's friend,' she asked Hale, 'or his wife's?'

Before Hale could reply, Victor appeared at his side. 'Lily,' he said, taking Miss Cantrell by the elbow, 'what do you say I find you a cup of coffee? Shall we go see if Safford has some in the pantry?'

64

'I was only making polite conversation.'

'I'm sure you were, my dear.' He smiled at Hale and me. 'You'll excuse us, of course.'

'Of course,' said Hale. A moment later, when they had gone, he added, 'With a peach like her, one could excuse damn near anything.'

Still, I thought, if Lily Cantrell was foolish enough to have designs on Victor Prudhomme, she was courting failure. You could tell, the way he'd given Ada *carte blanche* to build Silverwood, that his wife had him all sewed up. His devotion to his family was boundless. Nothing was too good for his little boys and their mother.

Bibi Prudhomme Biddeford

Everything after the age of sixty-five is thin soup. One feels fortunate to have caught the merest hint of some favourite spice, sufficient to recall to mind whole banquets swallowed with the youthful assumption that there was lots more where that came from. In my youth, as it happened, there *was* lots more. I was born in 1875, three years after my brother, Victor. That makes me a member of that curious breed with one foot daintily poised in the Victorian era and the other tapping time to the Beatles. Lately, during these past few months since Jack Kennedy was gunned down in his prime, I have taken to stirring up that soup and extracting whatever tidbits are big enough to chew upon, in hopes of not having missed a single, savoury morsel. I am eighty-nine, and let's face it, the kitchen has to close sometime. I don't want to have to quit the room with a lot of regrets that I didn't lick my plate clean.

I was brought up, as was Victor, on the loony logic that the rich are indispensable. That if they didn't see to it that the little children at the orphanage were employed in embroidering fine linens for them, the poor tykes would be working the streets for some Fagin. That if 'those more fortunate than others' (as my mother used to say) didn't hire a laundress to care for their hand-embroidered linens at a munificent ten dollars a week, the wretched young woman would be forced into a life of unspeakable sin. I was the same age as the Vanderbilts' daughter, Gertie, who was a pal of mine. I recall going to Gertie's coming-out party at The Breakers under the rosy impression that, as well as giving a smashing party, her family was performing something of a public service by keeping slews of nurserymen, vintners, musicians, seamstresses and the like gainfully employed. It was nothing for a hostess to spend a hundred thousand dollars on a party, and it was comforting to think, in those days before income taxes and government aid, that we fortunate ones so gamely shouldered the burden of providing for those less well-off than we were.

After 1912 when incomes taxes established a firm purchase on anything over three thousand a year, men like my brother searched for loopholes with the enthusiastic cunning of chess masters plotting their strategy, yet I'll bet Victor didn't bat an eye at sinking a total of some four million dollars into Silverwood. If I know my brother, he felt he was doing his duty to his community in a far more personally responsible way than by just mailing a check to a mythical Uncle Sam.

I never would have known the place cost four million if he hadn't told me. I remember almost recoiling at his words, not because of the sum but because, the way we were raised, one would no sooner discuss money than one's bowel habits. I had come west for their housewarming (as it were) not having seen Victor, Ada and the children since the boys were born nearly eight years before. In the interim, it appeared, Victor had become very western in his ways. He thought nothing of speaking of money, not in discreet allusions but, God help us, in specific sums, not to mention open discussion of what he baldly referred to as 'deals.' Our parents would have been mortified. I could only conclude that all that money talk came from California. Out there they think as little about discussing money as they do talking about their divorces or their high colonics. In a relatively new society, one's station in life is not so much a matter of background as it is a matter of bank account, and the only way to establish the existence of substance is by displaying a good deal of it. In California, the dollar wins hands down over the D. A. R.

Perhaps Victor gravitated there in the first place knowing that he needed that kind of brash, freewheeling society in which to make his mark. Had he stayed in Manhattan, he would have had to contend with the shadow of our father and an overbearing tradition as well. Victor never would have submitted to those constraints. He needed space, and California had plenty of that.

He. had changed in other ways, too. He had assumed the gregarious attitude of a Rotarian, a kind of middle-class bonhomie altogether unlike the manner of the gentry who maintain a judicious distance at first, like strange dogs sniffing out each others' pedigrees. He'd invited his bootlegger to the party, which had ticked off Ada no end. She was ill at ease with people like Benny Walsh, while Victor daily did business with the likes of wildcatters, eccentric inventors and horse traders. Victor moved with complete self-assurance in any echelon of society. Ada should have enjoyed the same liberty, but for some reason she never seemed comfortable in the presence of the proletariat. I thought this a surprising foible for one so well-bred as Ada. Actually, I thought Victor had scored a diplomatic coup by including Benny Walsh on the guest list. After that evening, Lord knows, the Prudhommes would never want for the choicest booze. I tried to jolly up Ada, but she continued to refer to Benny as 'that dismal blue-chinned troll,' a description which was fairly apt and amusing, though I'm sure Ada didn't intend it to be witty.

Ada did not have a rollicking sense of humour. Once in a while she would attempt some amiable teasing, but it came off rather clumsily, like a lioness trying to play with a salamander. She tended to take things very seriously, which must have been rough on her. Too, Ada was more given to sensibility and sentiment than she cared to let on. It was no coincidence, in my eyes, that she wanted Silverwood to duplicate Langehurst Hall. That was where she and Victor had enjoyed their greatest happiness together in the first months of their marriage. Perhaps Ada thought that the setting had been responsible for the mood.

67

I remember one glorious piece of slapstick from that first party at Silverwood. My laughter, I admit, contained a trace of malice, since neither Dorcas nor Hale Outerbridge has ever been among my favourite folk. Hale was a consummate stuffed shirt and when he deigned to be amused, which was infrequently, he'd emit a curt, harsh noise somewhere between a cough and the sound of a seal barking. My husband, Oren Biddeford, R. I. P., used to say that Hale was the only man he'd ever met who looked as if he could throw the switch at Sing Sing and then play eighteen holes of golf without pausing in between to wash his hands. Dorcas was equally full of herself but since her life had a much smaller scope than Hale's, this meant she was preoccupied with magnifying trivia until they filled every inch of her little canvas. She habitually arrived as late as politely possible at any function and always with some minor disaster on her lips, the incorrect address or a lost handbag, to let you know that she had suffered some travail in getting there. Everyone else might be hunky-dory and having a fine time, but she, brave darling, had been battling and vanquishing difficulties all the way. Maybe she thought this made her more interesting.

Anyhow, Dorcas turned up at the party looking queenly in a white panné velvet gown trimmed with white fox. It had a slight train, and with it she wore a headdress of pearls and osprey plumes. Ferris Warburton, the architect, brought her on to the dance floor where she allowed him to propel her around rather stiffly for a moment or two until the music stopped. They turned to go, and Ferris, poor man, inadvertently stepped on Dorcas' train. For a split second, she swayed ever so slightly. Then, straight as could be, she toppled – felled like a tree. Lordy, I laughed until I wheezed, though I did have the good grace to hold it until I reached the powder room. She wasn't hurt in the least. I suppose she was feeling no pain that night. Mack Sennett couldn't have staged it better. Ada never forgave me for thinking it was funny.

Ada was understandably nervous that evening, since it marked Silverwood's entry into society and vice versa. Victor wasn't much help. He enjoyed himself circulating among the crowd, leaving Ada to manage the whole affair. At one point, Victor had the twins brought downstairs where he put them through their paces, steering them from room to room, parading them in front of the guests, showing off their party manners. Ada was fit to be tied. Dinner was ready, the wine uncorked and a couple of hundred dessert soufflés stood waiting for the ovens, in imminent danger of disaster.

'Boys,' Victor was saying, 'always speak up clearly when you're introduced.' He singled out one of his guests and brought her forward. 'This pretty lady is Miss Lily Cantrell. Let's hear you give her a hearty hello.'

The twins bowed politely. 'How do you do, Miss Cantrell?' they said in unison.

She laughed gaily and patted both boys' cheeks. 'Why, I'm doing just ducky is how I'm doing. Any time I get introduced to *two* handsome devils at once, I guess I'm doing more than all right!' She winked and gave a suggestive little shimmy that set her beaded dress rattling and flashing.

That was enough for Ada. 'Victor!' she called out. 'I think it's time our guests had some dinner, and I *know* it's time our boys had some sleep.' She didn't wait for his reply. 'Go along, children,' she told them. She crossed the room and held out her arm for Victor to escort her to dinner. I thought Miss Cantrell looked a bit miffed at having to surrender the spotlight.

Actually, I was at Silverwood less than half a dozen times. The first was for that party, the next, unfortunately, at the time of Victor's death, then for a visit in 1935, for Drew's wedding three years later and last of all when Ada died. Still, between those visits and the few times Ada passed through New England, I think I came to know her pretty well.

Her father, a Mr Willson, had investments in real estate. He was a dashing type, to hear her tell it, and she had adored him. I suppose Dr Freud would have said that's why she was drawn to Victor. Her mother, as I understand it, was quite the hostess in her day, though Mr Willson's fortunes fluctuated, and the family was occasionally temporarily hard-pressed. In fact, when he died, his estate was embroiled in some sort of litigation which tied it up for an unconscionable length of time. That was why, when Victor met Ada, she happened to be working for a modiste in San

Francisco, a circumstance which, understandably, she preferred to play down, although she herself confirmed the story. Her mother passed away shortly thereafter, so Victor never had an opportunity to meet the Willsons.

I guess one of the reasons I understood Ada's life so well was that I knew Victor better than anyone else.

My brother's character was shaped by our father, or, more correctly, by Victor's feelings towards our father and the life he had given us.

Now when I think of our childhood, it appears the kind of quaint panorama glimpsed through the gilt-edged peephole of an elaborately decorated Easter egg. Lordy, but we were privileged brats. We enjoyed the best of all possible worlds. That is, if one was white, of a certain class and comfortably off. In winter, we lived at 690 Madison Avenue, a spacious, murky house decorated with heavy panelling, Oriental rugs, tapestries (among them the Flemish one that Ada later sold), plush upholstery, thick silk brocades and uncounted miles of gimp and galloon. The furniture was dark and cumbersome, and although there were lots of chandeliers, massive mirrors and shiny brass hardware, the general effect was of a big, cosy cave in which to hibernate during the cold months. It smelled, I remember, of the coal furnace, a gassy, sulphureous odour which I still associate with feeling snug and comfortable. In the front hall, staring sternly from the stair landing, was a Sargent portrait of Father which later became the first acquisition in Victor's celebrated collection of American art. In it, Father wears a dark suit and waistcoat, a white shirt and a tie with a wide maroon and grey stripe. He is a substantial figure, just this side of portly. One hand fingers the gold watch-chain draped across his waistcoat, and the other grasps what looks like a newel post. He leans forward slightly, as if impatient with posing and eager to dash off. He was a man of seemingly infinite energy, and I cannot imagine him pausing long enough in one place to be committed to canvas. His lips, framed by his neatly trimmed moustache and Vandyke beard, are pressed firmly together in a challenging half-smile. His eyes bore into the artist or the viewer as though there were some crucial contest at stake between him and the other person. It is the gaze of a man who does not intend to lose. My mother thought the portrait unflattering, but Father insisted it be hung there on the landing where it could not be missed. Maybe he wanted to pay Mother back for insisting he allow himself to be painted. More likely, being Father, it was a matter of one-upmanship, a deliberate attempt at intimidating all those who entered our house. He was the most competitive man I've ever known. In the summers, when the household moved out to Merrifields, our place on Long Island, he would seek out local boys to try to best Victor at swimming, archery, wrestling, tennis and rowing. As soon as Victor proved himself against one boy, Father would find another bigger, stronger boy to pit against him. Later, when Father took Victor out west to the Big Horn Mountains one summer, it was Victor who bagged the most game, to Father's chagrin. Father insisted that their kill should be packed off as one to the taxidermist and afterward feigned not remembering which of the stuffed and mounted bear, deer and elk were his and which were Victor's.

Merrifields was very different from the house on Madison Avenue. It was a rambling, shingled affair with large round porches and airy rooms filled with wicker furniture and light linens. It smelled of wistaria and sea breezes and, in the evenings, of wood fires. I gathered mayflowers there and collected shells along the beach below the lawn, but I think I preferred Merrifields to Manhattan mostly because one day, though it was forbidden, I had surreptitiously made my way to the fourth floor of the Madison Avenue house, where the servants' quarters were. What I found there were not rooms at all but tiny cubicles, most of them windowless, separated from each other by thin, wooden partitions which denied all but an illusion of privacy. In each, a single gas jet provided all the light and heat there was. The rooms were identically outfitted with a cot and a chamber pot, a washstand, pitcher and basin, a narrow chest of drawers and four clothes pegs. These were the dreariest, meanest surroundings I had ever seen, and I found it nearly impossible to believe that our mother, who was the soul of kindness and forever reminding us that charity began at home, could possibly be aware of the conditions in which our help lived. Nonetheless, I knew enough not to broach the subject. At least at Merrifields, the servants would be warm and their quarters would be perfumed by the same scented summer breezes that drifted through my open window.

When we were older, our parents took us to Europe each summer, to whatever spa or strand was currently the rage. Mother, her maid, Father, his valet, Victor, myself and Mademoiselle, our governess, were part of that annual migration across the Atlantic for 'the season.' It was Mademoiselle who had inadvertently given me my nickname. Though my parents had chosen Sophie Louise Prudhomme, Mademoiselle referred to me as '*le bébé*,' which Victor, who was only three, pronounced Bibi. No one could have foreseen that I would marry Oren Biddeford and wind up with a name like a chorus girl.

We were expected, on those trips, to absorb something of the culture of each place. Father would quiz us nightly about the local history and politics, the art and customs. Victor, being a boy, received most of Father's attention. I am sure there were times he wished that girls were supposed to be as smart as boys. When Victor was at Exeter, Father goaded him to higher grades with stories of how our cousin, Charles, who was four years older than Victor, had done better than he on this or that examination. Charles became Victor's bête noire. Victor despised him, though they had once been close friends. It wasn't until long after Father died that Victor learned from Charles that he had barely scraped by at Exeter. Father had trumped up those tales to force Victor to work harder.

I don't know whether Victor became an overachiever to please Father or to compete with him, as sons will. I do know that if he *hadn't* become an overachiever, Father would have regarded him as a complete failure. Father had devoted his life to excelling, to becoming what the newspapers called 'the iron lord' or, less kindly, 'the iron fist' and he expected his son to carry on in that tradition.

Father died only three years after Victor started working for him, and it became immediately apparent that Victor had no intention of marching in Father's footsteps. Prudhomme Iron would continue to thrive under its established management.

Prudhomme Iron was a means, not an end, to Victor. It was his stepping-stone to greater enterprises.

Among other things, my brother had inherited Father's vigour. The difference was that Victor cloaked his amazing energy with an easygoing, disarming charm which, like everything else, served its purpose. Whatever he undertook he tackled with an almost fanatical intensity. To Victor, there was little difference between work and play since both involved winning. What passions he permitted himself were spent upon the game. The prizes, whether they were trophies, mineral rights, women or a controlling majority of stock, rarely held his enthusiasm for long. As often as not, they merely became expedients in the next contest. The quarry mattered less than the chase. As a young bride, Ada must have gradually made this discovery, with its unflattering implications of her expendability. I've no doubt that's why she was so desperate to have Victor's children. There are some things that even a man like Victor won't trade upon. For a time, before the twins were born, Ada must have sensed the precariousness of her position. If an investment didn't bear fruit, Victor didn't hesitate to cut his losses and move on. Certainly, for Ada, there can't have been much warmth or companionship in that marriage after the first year or so. For a woman of deep feelings, it must have been like slowly starving to death, yet she never betrayed the slightest grievance. I respected her for that. Most people would have said Ada's life was beer and skittles. It takes a commitment to grace to present the kind of front that Ada showed the world.

In many ways, that explains Sam Farkas' presence later on. There was Ada, widowed, a gentile princess, the ideal blond Venus and landed gentry to boot. What Jew packing thousands of years of dislocation and humiliation at the hands of people like the Prudhommes wouldn't aspire to wearing such a prize on his arm? The difference with Sam, though, was that the fulfilment of his fantasies satisfied him. He treated Ada like a beloved consort, even though she must have exasperated him at times.

Victor could never have understood why she would be attracted to someone like Sam Farkas. Sam wrote and produced films, which made him an artist of sorts. Victor, like most men of his background, had little regard for what he dismissed as 'creative types.' Artists were suspect, having elements of the gypsy and the crackpot. In families like ours, they were seen as frivolous, self-indulgent and less than manly. They were tolerated only for as long as it took to extract their work from them and never, needless to say, invited to join one at the dinner table. In some cultures – the African, the Oriental, for example – art and life are insepar-able. To the upper-class American WASP, art is a thing apart, something created by a suspect alchemy he neither wishes nor has the ability to fathom. Victor didn't buy fine paintings because he was an aesthete. He amassed his collection because to possess objects of great value implied power; and power, not art, was Victor's greatest pleasure.

I can remember Mademoiselle taking Victor and me to galleries and museums when we were young. I became aware that Victor studied the things we saw, the sculpture, the paintings, the antiquities, with something other than the detached appreciation of the usual gallery-goer. I could see by his gaze that he silently coveted certain pieces, that he was mentally measuring this icon or that fresco, imagining where he might fit it into our parents' house on Madison Avenue and how much it might cost to ship there. It was impossible for Victor to enjoy anything he did not want to possess and impossible for him not to want to possess anything he enjoyed.

As time went on, he also possessed a prodigious number of women, beginning with one of our parlour maids who became pregnant and was summarily sacked. Not long after that, Father had to pay off an actress who had threatened a scandal. As Victor matured, he became somewhat more discreet, though he never was at a loss for companionship. Our parents were keen for him to marry, Mother because she thought him in need of the mitigating influence of a wife, Father because his vision of a dynasty demanded heirs and a wife was essential equipment in the production of heirs. There was no shortage of likely candi-dates. For several years, it was taken for granted that Victor and Honor Wortham would one day tie the knot. Like so many long-term alliances, though, it became a convenience, then a habit and finally a pretence. There were no hard feelings, perhaps no feelings at all. After that, Victor squired Justina Phillips for a couple of years. Justina would have liked to marry him. When he failed to make a move in that direction, she paraded about on the arm of Palmer Forbes, in hopes of making Victor jealous. Instead, he was relieved, and sweet, dull Palmer Forbes couldn't understand why Justina turned on him with such a vengeance. I think Victor actually came close to being engaged to Polly Van Dorn, if only because our parents had both died by then and he was as aware as anyone that if he wanted children he had better settle on a wife. But Victor had no real interest in the likes of the Misses Wortham, Phillips or Van Dorn. Their lives were cut and dried, consisting of nannies, tutors, debuts, marriage, motherhood, charitable works, visiting cards, the opera and an occasional gala ball. This was old stuff to him. Victor's entrepreneurial nature demanded that his wife be a product of private enterprise. It was a matter of personal pride for him to build his successes from scratch. I think he would even have resented Father having left him so well-off if he hadn't been able to turn his inheritance to his own uses.

What he needed, then, was a good woman to mother his children, yet who would be putty in his hands. I wonder how long it took Ada to realize that it wasn't anything she *was* that had attracted Victor to her but, rather, everything she wasn't. And I wonder how she felt when she'd figured that out.

They were married in our garden in Wellesley. Oren had taken to Ada immediately. 'She's a splendid young woman,' he told Victor. 'You're luckier than you know.' She was beautiful, of course, and carried herself well. She was clearly bright, despite a certain reticence which was hardly surprising, since she'd been virtually thrown to the lions in marrying into an old East Coast family. Cousin Charles' wife, Cornelia, who was quite deaf, loudly demanded across the dinner table, 'Just where *is* it you come from, dear girl?'

'San Francisco,' Ada replied.

Cornelia strained forward. '*Where?*'

'From San Francisco, California.'

At which point Cornelia shrugged and gave up, obviously

thinking that what she'd heard was so farfetched that she'd failed to comprehend what Ada was saying.

'Are you by chance related to President Wilson?' Charles inquired, trying to fix Ada in some familiar context.

'I'm afraid not. The President has one l, and we're the two l Willsons.'

Charles persisted. 'Where is your family at present?'

'My parents have both passed on.'

'You have my sympathy.' Charles appeared somewhat relieved to think that the Willsons were in heaven and not somewhere west of the Rockies. 'Your father – what were his interests?'

'He was a speculator.'

'Indeed.' The Reverend Holcomb, who had been quietly swirling his brandy, seemed to find this information worth contemplating.

'In real estate.'

Victor leaned close to my ear. 'It's no use, of course. They weren't anyone we'd know,' he whispered.

'Dodgy affair, California land,' said Charles.

'What was that?' cried Cornelia. 'What did you say?'

Charles patted her arm. 'Only twenty-five years ago, the bottom fell out, as I recall. Was your father affected?' he asked Ada.

'He was, but fortunately times changed for the better.'

'What did she say, Charles?'

Ada handled it very well. She seemed to understand that there was less snobbishness than provincialism in the situation. In any case, Charles was utterly taken with her. 'How does he do it?' he asked nobody in particular. 'Victor always bags the superlative, whether it's champagne, cigars or shirting. You've done it again, old man,' he told him. 'She's a perfect corker.' Cornelia, nonetheless, clung to the absurd impression that Victor had married beneath his station.

PART TWO

Elodie Swann

Once, storks flew over the coastal plain where signs on Wilshire
Boulevard now advertise Jacuzzis, Pop-Tarts and the La Brea
Tar Pits. The mammoth elephant and the sabre-toothed cat
prowled the Los Angeles basin. Some of them, at one time or
another, lured by the spectacle of a seemingly inviting lake, its
glassy surface mirroring the scudding clouds overhead, waded
instead into an asphalt pool where they were mired and sank in
the glistening black ooze, keeping eternal company with lions,
camels, mastodons and a lone Indian woman apparently felled
by a blow to the head.

Asphalt, as some people know, is a residue of petroleum, and
anyplace one discovers it seeping to the earth's surface is a pretty
good spot to drill a well. I came by this intelligence from my
father who, by the time I was fourteen, had sunk over half a
dozen producing oil wells near Westlake Park. Indeed, I could
scarcely spy a tree from our front parlour window. Our white
frame house with its tidy picket fence was dwarfed by a bristling
forest of derricks. Day and night, the air was filled with the
sounds of men and equipment. Papa occasionally slept in a tent
at a drilling site, leaving me alone at home. Back then, it cost
about fifteen hundred dollars to sink a well. If that came in, you
used the profits to drill another. By the time we moved to the
Hollywood section of the city, there were about three hundred
wells around Westlake Park, a good number of which belonged to
Papa.

We did not live grandly. Papa's people had been Quakers,
though he himself was a Methodist. Still, he disapproved of
excess in any form and was attracted to Hollywood primarily
because it was a temperance community. Our home had two

stories and a wide curved veranda. Between the house and the street were planted a dozen or so young orange trees. A lawn was a virtually unheard-of luxury. Bearing trees like citrus, walnut and olive were worth cultivating, but a lawn? My father would have thought it absurd. Hollywood was country then, a place of dusty dirt roads, browsing cattle and broad fields dotted with haystacks. We lived on Prospect Avenue, which they now call Hollywood Boulevard. From the time I was twelve, Papa and I had lived alone. My elder brother had died when he was fifteen of a burst appendix, and my mother, who always had difficulty carrying to term, haemorrhaged after yet another miscarriage and could not be saved. That left the two of us. I must have been a curiosity, a pretty little sobersides with a determined chin and the concerns of a middle-aged lady. After we moved to Hollywood, my father engaged a Mexican woman to help me with the housework and a tutor for my lessons. Still, it was I who did the sewing, mending and ironing. I was too busy to feel lonely, however, and my evenings were spent with Papa, who was the most interesting person I knew.

Marriage, when I was a girl, was almost inevitable. A man needed a homemaker, and a woman needed a provider. In my case, however, I was already a homemaker, and Papa was providing very nicely for me. I remember going to dances and church socials and the birthday parties of friends, but I cannot recall having any persistent suitors. The marriageable years, from seventeen to twenty, elapsed without my taking much notice. I became a spinster without regret.

Bear with me. Despite my advanced age, I am not one to ramble on aimlessly. I am coming to the part about Ada, but it's necessary to know who I was and how circumstances brought us together. Understand: I did not think it suitable to tell Daphne everything when she contacted me. For the benefit of my own fickle memory, however, I must keep the details in order.

I could tell that Papa was increasingly concerned that I was well into my twenties and still unmarried. 'I mustn't allow you to squander your youth on me. You must have a life of your own, Elodie,' he would feel obliged to remind me. I am sure that he actually dreaded the prospect of my leaving our home and equally sure that he felt morally obligated to urge me to marry while there was still some faint hope. I think he was looking to the time when he would pass on. He didn't like to contemplate my being alone in the world. So Hugh Cathcart must have appeared a mixed blessing in his eyes.

My memory now is like a skipping-stone flung out of my hand, touching down at random here and there, gliding over everything between. Even after all these years I cannot bear to hold on to that piece of the past for more than a few moments at a time before casting it out of my mind.

I do not recall how I met Hugh Cathcart. He was part of that group of young men who played golf on weekends at the Los Angeles Country Club on Pico Boulevard and Western Avenue. He must have played tennis also, because I picture him in the flannel trousers, striped blazer and cap that fashionable gentlemen wore on the courts. It was typical of him to cut a fine figure and to have found his way into the Country Club even though he was new to the city. Hugh had an eye for the best of everything, which, when he turned his glance towards me, I took as a compliment of the first magnitude. Men recognized immediately that Hugh was what my father called 'a bully fellow.' His attire was correct without being foppish. His rust-coloured moustache and hair were meticulously trimmed and pomaded, though not conspicuously so. His cologne was subtle, his nails buffed and his voice pleasant. He could converse on almost any subject but preferred not to be the centre of attention. Instead, he would fix a person with his heavylidded gaze and intent expression, making an occasional encouraging inquiry, and elicit from the most timid, taciturn people confessions of such an operatic nature that arias of hopes, fears, frustrations and joys would burst forth from a sphinx. It was an amazing spectacle, really. I thought him the most empathic of men. It would have been heresy for me to think that his intense compassion might also serve the purpose of deflecting scrutiny from himself.

Hugh was a surveyor by profession. When I met him, he was part of the team that was overseeing the subdivision of the Lankershim Ranch in the San Fernando Valley. Its owners, Mr and Mrs Van Nuys, had sold off forty-eight thousand acres for

81

the development of a number of residential communities. The surveyors were expected to take well over a year at their work. The job was a feather in Hugh's cap, since he'd come to California from Saint Louis only the previous year. He had established a fine reputation very quickly, and there was, as I said, something about the man that invited reliance. Maybe the solidity of his appearance played a part. He reminded me of one of Remington's bronze bulls. He was always lightly tanned due to his outdoor life and though he was not a particularly large man, he was strong and muscular, squarely built, with wide shoulders and a thick torso.

Los Angeles was a wonderful place for courting in those days. There were clean green public parks in which to picnic and lakes for boating excursions. The clear air was scented with orange blossoms. We took the red trolleys out to Venice Beach, rushing along the tracks at fifty miles an hour, past farms and lemon groves, the electric motor humming and the whistle announcing our presence. We would stroll along Ocean Front Walk, the ladies' hats quivering in the sea breeze and our sashes fluttering like pennants. We rode the scenic railroad high over the water and took gondola outings up the canals. In the evenings, we attended band concerts and musicales. Harley Hamilton was the conductor of the Los Angeles Symphony in those days. Now it's an Indian gentleman whose name I can't recall. I have always been partial to Brahms, whose lyricism renders me treacly. Hugh knew this, of course, and it was after a concert of Brahms, as we were driving home, that he proposed to me. Papa was waiting for us, and Hugh asked if he might have a word alone with him in the library. After a while they emerged and came to the door of the parlour where I was sitting in the dark. I see the scene distinctly in my mind's eye: Papa silhouetted there in the doorway by the light from the hall beyond and Hugh Cathcart drawing a leather case from his inside pocket, extracting a pair of Havanas, cutting them both with the gold cigar cutter he wore on his watch-chain and handing one to my father. The gesture joined them as equals, the men of the family, having favourably settled the future of its weaker vessel.

It was only when we began to make wedding plans that Hugh

82

confessed he was a widower. He was thirty-two to my twenty-six, and he had been married in his early twenties, he told me, to a girl he'd known all his life. She'd had heart trouble, become an invalid and died. He had tears in his eyes, speaking about it. I was content to have a quiet ceremony, since I was rather embarrassingly long in the tooth to be a bride. My father, who disliked pomp of any kind, was doubtless delighted.

If Papa was upset by the news that Hugh had accepted another job up the coast, near Monterey, he generously kept it to himself. It was a fine opportunity, to head the surveying team on a new project there, and his work in the Valley was coming to an end soon anyhow. So we were married that November of 1910 in a small ceremony at home with only a handful of people to wave good-bye as we started away in Hugh's new green Packard with its tufted leather seats and shiny brass trim. Papa was trying hard not to let me see that he was crying. Hugh and I had known each other exactly five months.

Hugh had taken a six-month lease on a small square bungalow of white clapboard with a mansard roof, set on a rise that overlooked the sea. We were some distance from town. To our right was a cul-de-sac and, beyond a fenced pasture where sheep grazed. To our left were two vacant lots, each marked with a 'For Sale' sign. Past them, on the other side of our street where it met the road into Monterey, there was, on the corner, a weathered two-storey redwood house with hollyhocks in front and a small vegetable garden in the rear. It belonged to a couple named Deems.

The husband, Rowley Deems, was a short wiry man with sandy hair and Teutonic features who walked as if someone had wound him tight. He had a peculiar stiff-legged stride, shoulders hunched, head thrust forward, that gave him the appearance of always being intensely busy. From Hugh, I learned that Deems was a barber and a local hunter of some renown. He was said to have a short fuse. Rumour had it that he'd once beaten a barking dog to death with a shovel. I don't believe I ever heard Rowley Deems utter a word. Once I complimented him on a fine brace of quail he was carrying home, but he merely acknowledged me with a curt nod and kept going. His wife, who was a good deal younger – I assumed about my age – was much taller than he, a lanky fair-haired girl, all elbows and angles. She appeared eager to make friends but too timid to do much about it. I thought her an awkward soul and felt a little sorry for her. One day I took her some roses from our yard and introduced myself. Her name was Adelaide, she told me, apologizing for her appearance. She had tripped over a doorstop and split her lip on the washtub. Despite the accident, it was easy to see that she was a beauty. She had extraordinary hands, too. They were unusually large and slender and gestured with a grace that set them quite apart from the rest of her. She presented me with a basket of squash from her garden in return for the roses. As I reached my front door, I turned back and saw Rowley Deems standing on the porch with Adelaide, gesticulating angrily in my direction. Hugh and I were new to the neighbourhood, I realized, and he probably had his reasons for not wanting his wife striking up a friendship with strangers he hadn't yet endorsed.

I waved at the Deems when I passed by their place. He nodded and so did she. When she was alone, however, she returned my salute with an enthusiastic wave. The next time I spoke to her, she came knocking at my door one morning, searching for her pet kitten. It was a calico named Dandy. I had heard her calling it in the night. It had run off and she, poor thing, had sprained her wrist badly, looking for it in the dark. Adelaide was accident-prone. She was continually apologizing for her appearance. If she didn't have a bruise on her cheek from a fall in the bathtub, it was a black eye from the corner of a cabinet door. I saw her perhaps half a dozen times before Rowley Deems died, and it seemed to me that she always bore the mark of the some calamity.

The night of Rowley Deems' death, she came pounding at our front door after midnight, crying our names, begging Hugh to come with her as 'something frightful' had happened.

Rowley Deems owned a number of rifles which, according to all accounts, he liked to keep in prime condition. That evening, he'd wanted to clean and oil some guns. He tucked one under his arm and tossed another, his favourite deer rifle, to Adelaide. 'Look alive,' he'd said. 'Catch!' The gun discharged in her hands. The charge struck him full in the forehead. Rowley Deems probably never knew what happened. It was a ghastly accident. People said you couldn't be too cautious, could you, when a seasoned hunter like Rowley Deems could make a single error that cost him his life. I wondered if it was purely the great shock of it that caused such a marked change in Adelaide. Whatever it was, after the tragedy, Adelaide was something more than careful. She ceased being accident-prone. Those things simply did not happen to her anymore. If there was any more to the story than that, I, for one, was not inclined to pursue it.

Hugh and I hadn't been there three months when Rowley Deems was shot. It was only afterward that Adelaide actively sought out my friendship. She didn't know many people thereabouts. The Deems had kept pretty much to themselves. Then too, there were the kind of rumours that commonly spring up when something like that happens. Not that the authorities didn't believe Adelaide's account of the tragedy, but she was a lovely young woman, many years the junior of her husband, and the circumstances were bound to beget gossip. Maybe that's why she was so quick to sell her house.

'Where will you go?' I asked her.

'Home, I suppose, for a while. I guess I'll spend the summer with Ma in Santa Paula. Then I'll figure out what to do.'

'You don't sound sad to leave.' We were sitting on my porch, overlooking the verdant rolling headlands and the shining silver sea beyond.

'Leave here?' she said scornfully. 'I'll say I'm not sad. Rowley and I never intended to let ourselves get bogged down in this place. We weren't going to stay here forever, you can believe that. Rowley had plans.'

'What kind of plans?'

'Rowley wasn't like these ordinary, small-minded fellows. Rowley was going to be a great man. This town wasn't big enough for people like us, he said. Someday soon we were going to move to San Francisco and buy a nickeldeon and eventually own a whole chain of them. He was trying to save some money, but things weren't happening fast enough around here to suit his tastes. His business worries sometimes made him – difficult.' Adelaide jumped up from her chair. 'My word, I've stolen a good part of your afternoon. I must be going.' She was already halfway down the walk. 'Adieu!' she sang out on her way.

That was as close as I ever came to knowing Rowley Deems alive or dead. While Adelaide never spoke of Rowley less than kindly, it was I who scoured my mind for some congenial memory of the man and never found one.

About that time, I learned that I was expecting a child. I can remember hanging out the wash one March morning, hearing the wet laundry flapping on the line against a brisk wind. Clouds tumbled across the bright blue sky. The sheep ambled about the adjacent pasture, followed by their wobbly-legged lambs bleating reedily. The air was chilly, filled with the smack of an outgoing tide. The nearby hills were gilded with flowering yellow mustard. I gazed at them, watching the grass and wildflowers undulate in the wind, making it seem as if the hills themselves were stirring from within with new life as I was. Never before or since did I feel such a sense of fulfilment, I belonging to some infinite eternal plan. I felt completely at peace, sure of the promise of summer, sure of all the myriad promises life held out to me.

I do not know why I can recall that scene in such detail as even to be able to catch the scent of the breeze, especially as I have difficulty remembering what I did last week. Perhaps some part of me still clings to it for dear life, the only precious relic of that year in which my life was so suddenly and cruelly changed.

One afternoon – it can only have been a few days later – Hugh came home early from his work, walked into the kitchen where I was preparing our supper and announced that he had quit his job and was leaving town. We sat across from each other at the kitchen table. I could hear gulls crying through the open window. Hugh never looked at me. He kept tracing the grain of the table with his thumb. He was a married man, he told me, with four children growing up in Missouri, and his duplicity had become an intolerable burden. It was as much for my sake as anyone's that he was leaving, he said. He could not bear deceiving me any longer. I remember I stood in the bedroom doorway, watching him pack. I didn't try to stop him even then. I knew there was no use in my trying.

To this day, I have no way of knowing whether or not any of it was true. It didn't matter, really. All that mattered was that he was bent on leaving me. Afterward, I thought of attempting to find out where he'd gone and whether or not the story was true, but it seemed no good could come of it. Either he had stated the facts and was a liar and a bigamist or, if he hadn't, he was a liar who had concocted an excuse for deserting his new wife and unborn child. I wanted nothing more to do with him. I no longer wanted his child. I wanted no tangible reminder of that man.

For days after he left, I wept until I vomited. I was hardly able to swallow food, much less hold it down. I kept to my bed, the room darkened against the painful light of day. I don't know what would have happened to my sanity if Adelaide Deems had not hammered on the door, refusing to go away until she saw me. I collapsed in her arms, too weak to walk back to bed. It was Adelaide who nursed me back to health, who heard the whole sorry tale and who refused to let me dwell upon my troubles.

'Done is done. You'll never solve anything if you keep looking over your shoulder at what might have been. Think of Lot's wife. You have to look ahead. My Ma says nobody ever got anyplace without a plan. Even God had to have a plan, she says.'

'I can't go home.'

'Why not? Everyone thinks you're married. Maybe you are, for all we know.'

'My father would make me keep the child. I know he would. I couldn't bear that, having to live with it for the rest of my life.'

'Why didn't you say so before? You can come home to Santa Paula with me.'

'What good would that do?'

'My Ma . . .' Adelaide hesitated. 'I have to say, Ma's sort of an unusual person. But she's a very *good* person,' she added quickly. 'She helps young ladies in trouble. Room, board and delivery and adoption.'

'But she must charge something.'

'It's not much for the mothers. The folks who come for the babies pay most of it. You'd be surprised how many people would give almost anything to have a child.'

'How long has your mother been doing this?'

She thought for a moment. 'Well, Pa left when I was twelve and she started with the neighbour's cousin's daughter a year after that. It must be five years.'

Until then, it had never occurred to me that Adelaide might be a full nine years younger than I. She was tall and capable, and I had simply assumed that we were contemporaries, especially, I suppose, since her late husband had been so much older than she. I was about to entrust my well-being to an eighteen-year-old girl. At the time I saw no alternative.

I withdrew what little money Hugh had left in our bank account, sold our wedding gifts and wrote Papa that Hugh had taken a job in Canada and we were leaving before the week was out. I might be too busy for a while to write, I said, but I promised to come home in the fall for a visit. It was my intention to go back home to Papa as soon as I was physically able.

'Santa Paula,' Adelaide told me, 'is a one-horse town. Oil rigs and orchards. Rowley said he knew when he set eyes on me that I was looking to get out of there. I was, too. He promised to take me away from Santa Paula if I'd marry him. Lord knows I never thought I'd be going back, but sometimes a person needs a quiet place to think things out. If there's one thing Santa Paula is, it's quiet.'

In spite of my circumstances, I thought Santa Paula much pleasanter than Adelaide had painted it. It was a peaceful, bucolic little place, lying in that series of fertile valleys that rambles among the foothills some twenty miles inland from the Pacific.

Adelaide's home, 'the Watkins place,' everyone called it, stood beside a winding strand of country road where the comings and goings of farm wagons were announced by plumes of light-brown dust in the distance. The house was typical of those that presided over the vast acreage of California farmlands in those days. Some of them still exist, three-storeyed white furbelowed buildings rising starkly from flat fields, closely bordered by a windbreak of tall trees. They look like stalwart dowagers in white lace, discreetly situated behind a clump of potted palms.

The Watkins place had seen better days. The apricot orchards surrounding it had long ago been sold off, and the house let run to seed. Here and there, among the darkish warren of rooms with their faded and stained floral wallpapers one came across an occasional relic of past splendour, a frayed red silk portière or a lampshade of yellowed, brittle lace.

I don't know what I had expected of Adelaide's mother. Surely nothing had prepared me for that wide-bottomed barge of a woman with a seamed, androgynous face and the sort of aggressive ebullience one associates with the elder Brueghel. 'Ma Watkins,' as everyone addressed her, possessed that kind of zealous cheer that skates on the thin edge of furious excess, an overwhelming, exhilarated jollity that all but obscures the hiss of the cutting blade. 'I am,' she announced, seizing my hand, 'God's angel.'

'We all are, Ma,' Adelaide said, unpinning her hat.

'Some are fallen. But you,' she said, looking me up and down, 'you're married, according to Adelaide's letter. Is that so? The wages of sin are suffering, you know.'

'She's married, Ma.'

'Then you needn't worry.' She cuffed me good-naturedly on the shoulder. 'You won't have a hard time of it. There's a little girl upstairs. Evangeline something. They came for the baby this morning. Land, how she suffered with that child. Still hasn't got her strength back. She'll think twice before she lets lust have its way again.'

'We're tired, Ma. We've come a long way. Could we have a cup of tea?'

Ma Watkins presided over the tea table like a chatelaine, handling the mismatched cups and saucers as though they were precious Sèvres. As she raised her cup to her lips, she held her little finger crooked. Between each sip, she pursed her lips and patted them daintily with her napkin. Over the rim of her teacup, she watched Adelaide. 'Isn't she a beauty, though?' she asked me, not taking her eyes from her daughter. 'Such refinement in that face. Addie,' she told her, 'you know you can't stay here. This is no place for a young lady of your stature.'

'It's only a visit, Ma.'

'You'd be hiding your light under a bushel, and that's not right. The good Lord meant you to shine, daughter.' She turned to me. 'These hayseeds around here can't appreciate a real lady. Now, Rowley Deems – '

'I don't want to talk about Rowley,' said Adelaide.

'I was only going to say that he knew quality when he saw it. There was a fellow who was going places.'

'Excuse me, Ma.' Adelaide rose from the table. 'I think I'll take a nap before supper.'

'Ah, well.' Ma Watkins looked after her as she went up the stairs. '"The best laid schemes" and so on. A real shame abut Rowley's accident.'

'Yes.'

'It was God's will, of course. But she's a young, pretty girl. There's nothing to stand in her way. She's a comer, my Addie.' Ma Watkins, for all that she went about brandishing the wrath of God, was a relentless optimist, and whatever twist of fate presented itself was, to her, merely another mysterious turn on the way to paradise.

What a peculiar establishment that was. The long-suffering Evangeline left soon after I arrived. Her place was soon taken by a dumpling-faced Irish girl whose eyes were perpetually red from weeping and who rarely spoke to anyone. Ma Watkins seemed to take great satisfaction from her misery. 'Tumble in haste; repent at leisure,' she would call out as she passed her room.

'You mustn't take Ma too seriously,' Adelaide told the girl. 'That's just her way.'

Adelaide spent the long sunny summer days helping Ma Watkins around the house. ('But mind you cream your hands, Addie, and put on gloves before you so much as lift a finger!') What spare time she had, she spent poring over fashionable magazines like the *Cosmopolitan* or reading romances in the *Ladies' Home Journal*. She would sit at the dining room table, long after the last dishes were done at night, bent over her mother's ancient copy of Mrs Sherwood's *Manners and Social Usages*, turning its fragile, foxed pages with a reverence usually reserved for the Scriptures.

'Why,' she asked me one evening, 'is it bad manners to cut lettuce with a knife?'

'I don't actually know. It is, that's all.'

'Have you ever used finger bowls?'

'I have.'

'Are they used at every meal?'

'Only for luncheon and dinner. Why do you ask?'

'It might be useful. Someday I may need to know these things.'

Ma Watkins stood in the doorway to the kitchen, untying her apron. 'Adelaide has a great destiny. A holy woman told me before she was born. She had the gift. She told me a lot of things I didn't believe then but that happened later. Mark my words, Addie is going to be some pumpkins one of these days.'

Sometimes I would glance at Adelaide as she sat shelling peas or shucking corn and wonder what gilded fancies illuminated her eighteen-year-old dreams just then. Rowley's name, after that first day, never passed her lips again, to my knowledge. Ma Watkins spoke no more of him, either. As the weeks passed, I sometimes wondered if I was the only one who troubled to remember Rowley Deems at all.

In the evenings, when it was cooler, I usually took a short walk. My condition was such that heat bothered me greatly. I resolved never to put myself in the way of such misery again. I loathed the increasing burden of my humiliation. I wanted only to expel the wretched thing from my body and be done with it. I could not bear to catch my reflected image, that swollen caricature of myself, with its ugly, protruding belly. I kept to the shade of the parlour during the day, where Helen, the Irish girl, sat rocking by the hour, tears seeping from her closed eyelids, cooling herself with a paper fan. At dusk I ventured out for fresh air. Once or twice, Adelaide went with me.

There is a time, no longer than a few minutes, really, when, in the clear summer twilight, pale objects reflect the last brilliance of a sun already set against a sky not yet black. That interlude between the lights is, to me, a queer and magical moment, the world luminous, poised between yesterdays and tomorrows. I can recall standing with Adelaide in silence a short distance from the house at just that time, listening as the birds grew still, gazing at the large, pale shape of the house floating in the shadowy fusion of earth and sky like a huge, tethered, white balloon. It was as quiet as eternity. Only the sky stirred, shifting colours from blue to purple to black. The house was absorbed into the night, all except for the glimmer of a lamp in the parlour window. The air was suddenly chilly. A bald moon intruded from behind the trees.

'You'll forget about this place,' Adelaide said quietly. 'You must, you know. The past is heavy baggage. The farther you intend to go, the more important it is to travel light.'

'Who gave you that advice, Adelaide?'

'I read it in a story in the *Journal*. It's true, I think. When I leave this poky little town, I shan't look back even to wave good-bye.'

'Perhaps you'll marry one of the nice young men who come to the orchards lately, harvesting apricots, and you'll settle in Santa Paula after all.'

'Me? Never. I don't want some clodhopper with dirt under his fingernails and mud caked on his boots, who doesn't even know which fork to use.'

I didn't point out to her that one fork was thought sufficient at her mother's table.

'I shall have all the finer things – a big house, a grand auto, lots of money, fine clothes . . .'

I couldn't help but laugh. 'It may take more to make you happy, Adelaide. Possessions don't guarantee contentment.'

'But don't you see? I shall be a great lady. That's my destiny, Ma says. She knows all about the finer things. She used to work in a swell house where there were crystal chandeliers and marble floors and a ballroom.'

'Where was that?'

'In San Francisco, before she married Pa. My pa was rich, you know.'

'You don't say.'

'Sometimes. He had his ups and downs. He went to the Klondike when I was small and came back with a sackful of gold. He bought me my own little pony cart, and Ma didn't have to do a lick of housework. She had a pair of Chinese for that.'

I glanced at her. Even in the darkness she discerned my doubt.

'Truly. Pa was a gambling man, though. Ma says he was the kind who'd bet on what time the next white horse would pass. Once he bought a silver mine in Nevada but it flooded and caved

in and he never did find out if there was any silver there.'
Adelaide shivered and started back towards the house.

'What happened to your father?' I asked, watching our twin
shadows bob along the path.

'Ma didn't mind his prospecting or speculating, but she drew
the line at out-and-out gambling. I honestly don't think Pa saw
the difference. He couldn't understand what upset her so. I guess
his bewilderment sort of defeated him, and he had to get away.
He used to send letters. He knew better than to send Ma tainted
money, but sometimes he'd mail me a little something.' She
shrugged. 'That was a while ago.'

'What are you two doing out there at this time of night?' Ma
Watkins called from her chair on the veranda.

'I was telling Elodie about the time we lived in that nice house
in San Jose.'

'The one that burnt down?'

'Don't say it like that, Ma.' Adelaide went up the steps and sat
on the edge of the hammock.

'Burnt like hellfire.' Ma Watkins stared into the night as if she
could still see the glow. 'That's what it was, too. Hellfire.
Devilment burning.'

'You set it on fire, Ma.'

'It's the Father within us does His works.'

'You did it, Ma.'

'Vengeance is the Lord's affair. God punishes. I'm only a
servant of the Almighty.'

'We could have sold it.'

'And profited from a den of iniquity?' Ma's wicker chair
squealed like a bat as she thrust herself from it and stalked into
the house, banging the screen door.

'That's the sort of thing,' said Adelaide, inclining her head
towards the door, 'that Pa couldn't understand. Ma set fire to the
place because she found out he was running a poker game in the
attic. After that, he never gambled at home, but we never had
such a nice home again, either.'

They must have been a pair, Ma and Pa Watkins, each
pursuing visions of glory from opposite directions, bound for
collision. And now their legacy of wishful thinking had been

handed down to this rangy girl who smelled of laundry soap and cabbage and dreamt grand dreams of casting off the past and sailing to success on winds of wishing.

I did not think, for a moment, that Adelaide had a prayer of achieving her lofty desires. To me, she was an adolescent daydreamer, bound to have her hopes dashed to the ground sooner or later. I felt rather sorry for her. I thought she should get away from Ma Watkins, who was continually reminding her of her splendid destiny. 'Adelaide,' I asked her, 'have you any money of your own? Did Rowley leave you anything at all?'

'I've a little. With luck I'll be able to make do until I have a diamond wedding ring on my finger.'

'Lots of people are content without being rich, Adelaide.'

'You don't understand.' She sounded disappointed in me. 'It's not just the money. It's that I mean to someday be a great lady, and you can't do that without the finer things.'

'What does a great lady do, exactly?'

'She sets an example.'

'I see.' I sensed that a great lady, in Adelaide's lexicon, meant something more than was intelligible to me just then. Much later, I understood what she had been unable to explain at the time.

It was Adelaide's innocent notion that nobility meant just that. She wholeheartedly believed that those in high places must be high-minded, that they exercised high standards and represented humankind at its finest. It was a remarkably naïve assumption, even for a young girl like Adelaide; yet, like her mother, she held fanatically to her own peculiar vision of the world. I don't believe she ever let go of it, even long after she had realized her ambitions. She was right, thinking I had missed her point. I had heard the noun and not the verb. She had clearly said she meant to *be* a great lady, in her eyes an honourable and worthy calling. And if the pursuit of this virtuous estate required sangfroid and a selective memory, Adelaide was willing.

I have managed to block from my mind my last weeks in that place. I had great discomfort towards the end. I longed for the degrading business to be over and done with. I found the process as revolting as it was painful. The infant was healthy, a boy. He had fair hair. Ma Watkins knew of just the home for him, she told me. I have never regretted putting the entire episode behind me.

I went home to Los Angeles and told Papa what Hugh had said but not when he had said it or what had happened afterward. Papa took it hard on my account. I think he felt he'd rushed the match for fear it would be my only chance at marriage. I took Adelaide's advice and did not speak of Hugh again, except to say we were divorced. I used my maiden name of Swann.

As time passed, memory jarred me less frequently. There were occasional nights, though, when a gale gusted hard from the west, making the clapboards of the house creak, the loose shutters bang and the dogs bark. The wind carried with it the unmistakable smell of the ocean, though the ocean was miles away. It rushed among the palms and yucca and the brittle manzanita, redolent of tidal pools and sea smack and spindrift. And then, though the wind continued, the aroma would disappear, as though it had been sucked thirstily out of the air by the dry fields and hills and consumed without a trace. Suddenly, without my wanting it to happen, I would be reminded of the circumstances that had wrested me from the cosy bungalow overlooking the sea and thrust me into the limbo of that dry, hot valley. Over the next two years, I occasionally wondered if Ma Watkins and Adelaide might still be there, sustaining themselves with their grandiose ambitions for her.

Soon enough, I realized how greatly I had underestimated Ada.

Tony Prudhomme

I was about six years old when we moved to Silverwood. The only thing I remember about our previous house was that everyone seemed glad to leave it. Everyone, that is, except my father, who would have been content to be quartered in a hotel. As long as the food was good, the mattress hard, the service efficient and the place convenient to his office, his accommodations weren't of much concern to him. Subsequently, my mother concocted a romantic scenario in which the two of them had recreated the site of their honeymoon, Langehurst Hall, to keep alive the memory of their happiness there. She told the story so often that I'm sure she came to believe it. I remember, though, the day we moved to Silverwood and how my father stood at the top of the marble steps in the foyer, taking in the fourteen upturned faces of the staff assembled in the lower hall as he handed the butler his hat and said quietly to my mother, 'All right, Ada, here it is, signed, sealed and delivered. All this and a pound of flesh, too.'

For a second, I thought Mother had lost her balance. She swayed slightly. Her hand flew to her mouth. Her eyes watered, and two bright spots of colour appeared on her cheeks. Young as I was, I believed he had scared the living daylights out of her in a teasing kind of way. 'A pound of flesh' sounded like something out of a werewolf story, and for a long time I equated the scene with my father having crept up behind her and saying 'boo!' Some years afterward, when I learned the meaning of the phrase in school, I decided that Silverwood had been some sort of payoff my mother had extracted from Father. I told my brother about it.

'You left out the rest,' Drew said. I was surprised that he, too, had remembered. 'Mother looked at him like he'd slapped her right there in front of everyone. She whispered, "My God! How *dare* you say that, when we both know it was *your* fault!"'

'Mother said that? I didn't hear her say it.'

'I did. I'd never heard her swear before. That's what made me prick up my ears.'

'What did you make of it?'

'I figured that Father had killed some rich relative in an auto accident and inherited the money to build the place. You know what a daredevil driver Father could be.'

'But nobody in the family ever died in a car accident.'

'I know that now. You were asking me what I thought at the time.'

So neither my brother nor I ever made sense of the incident.

Once we were settled at Silverwood, Father readily took to the place. And no wonder. Mother had considered his every whim. There were great expanses of wall upon which to mount his paintings, stables for his horses and his own private gymnasium. There was a trophy room for the silver cups and platters his polo team won. Next to his dressing area was a pressing room for his valet. There was even a small steambath adjoining his gymnasium. Though Mother was the one who liked swank, it was typical of her to have racked her brain to think of everything that might please Father.

My mother was a born wife. Even as a child, I understood that our Father was foremost in her affections. She was a wife first, a mother second. Looking back, I wonder if she would ever have had children if not to please him. Some women, my late sister-in-law among them, are at ease with kids, and motherhood comes as naturally to them as breathing. My mother, on the other hand, always seemed at sea and a little panicky when called upon to exercise her meagre maternal aptitude. She might as well have been the bewildered recipient of a pair of untrained seals. She liked my brother and me, and in some ways we occasionally delighted her. Still, it wasn't until we were verging on adolescence that I knew any closeness to her, and perhaps it was not closeness but sympathy I felt, prompted by Father's death.

Our father was a different story. He would have enjoyed being one of those Arabian monarchs with several wives and dozens of royal children. Gruff and unsentimental as he was, he genuinely loved kids. He was a light sleeper, and sometimes rose in the night to slip into our rooms, careful not to arouse Nanny. He'd tell us stories about places he'd travelled and things he'd seen and done. He had no flair for invention, but he was a good reporter with a memory for detail.

I recall that when we first moved to Silverwood I used to wake in alarm in the middle of the night, thinking that strangers were gathered outside in the dark, hurling things at the house. On one such night, Father, coming into my room in the small hours, found me sitting upright, listening, rigid with fear. He scooped me into his arms and padded downstairs. Pausing in front of Mother's portrait, he muttered, 'Just once, Ada, can't you look the other way?' He set me down by the front door, took my hand firmly in his and led me outdoors where, in the moonlight, we collected handfuls of the eucalyptus pods that pelted the house when the wind blew.

'See?' My father threw his pods on to the roof of the porte cochère, producing the sound that had, minutes before, filled me with apprehension. Buoyant with relief, I flung mine high in the air. A scattering of them rattled against the panes of Mother's bedroom window. A lamp flashed on upstairs. Father chuckled and put a finger over his lips. After a bit, the light went out and we crept back to our rooms.

Another time, he spirited Drew and me out of the house on a hot night and the three of us swam naked in the pool, silent as sharks lest we be discovered.

Once, when he brought home an Eakins painting of a man in a scull, Drew and I expressed interest in rowing, and Father found us oars, a pair of boats and a local lake on which to try our skill. I don't think we went more than once, since we were only ten and not quite up to mastering the sport.

When he bought a Catlin of some buffalo hunters, Drew asked him if the three of us could go hunting sometime. Father had often told us he and his father had hunted together.

'Absolutely not!' Mother cried before he could answer.

'Now, Ada – '

'I won't have them playing with guns! Think of the risk.'

'In the first place, Ada, it's not play. A young man has to learn respect for firearms. Secondly, I'd be with them. You don't think I'd let anything happen, do you?'

Mother looked as though she were on the verge of tears. 'It's too easy.'

'What's too easy?'

'All it takes is a second. Some of those things have hair triggers. You take aim, and before you can even make up your mind whether or not to shoot, the thing goes off. Then where are you? You'll never be sure if you really meant to fire, but it's too late, isn't it? Would you want your sons to have to live with that?'

'Ada, stop rattling on so. What do you know about guns?'

Mother turned her head away. 'Nothing.'

All the same, we were never even allowed to go trapshooting.

Mostly, though, Father had his way. When Pop Grauman's famous Chinese Theatre was completed, it was said to be the most ornate and exotic movie palace in the west. Every kid we knew wanted to get inside for a glimpse of the mysterious Orient, transported to Hollywood Boulevard. 'Buzz Mooney says his grandfather can get him a free pass,' I told my parents, hoping to strike a competitive chord in them.

'What sort of name is Buzz Mooney?' my mother asked.

'That's what everyone calls him.' I addressed my father. 'I told Buzz you could get Drew and me into the premiere. I bet him we'd see Grauman's before he did.'

'Really, dear,' Mother said, 'it's not our kind of thing at all.'

'How much did you bet him?' Father wanted to know.

'A buck.'

'One dollar,' corrected Mother.

'Thank you, Ada, but I understand the language. Tony, is it all that important to you?'

Drew spoke up. 'I said you could pull strings. I told him you could do all kinds of things that other people couldn't.'

My brother always had a knack for politic phrases.

'Did you make a wager, too?' Father asked him.

He shook his head, 'No.'

That also was typical of Drew.

'Well, I don't see what harm it could do to scour up some tickets.'

'It's bound to be a pointless rout with a lot of tawdry people pushing and shoving their way about.'

'Then that settles it, Ada. You needn't go if you don't want to. I'll take Nanny and the boys.'

I was amazed to see how many movie people recognized my father and made a point of coming over to shake his hand and be introduced to us. I had thought my parents knew nobody in films. What impressed me even more than Mr Grauman's pagoda roof, moon gates and gilded Fo dogs was the number of gorgeous dames who called Father by his first name, bussed him familiarly on the cheek and left their calling cards in lipstick. I had always sensed that my father was someone to be reckoned with, but that night I realized that in the eyes of these glamorous people, my father possessed no small degree of glamour himself.

Mother, though she enjoyed handsome surroundings, was leery of glamour. She was beautiful, dressed well and could charm the bark off a tree if she cared to make the effort, but it was Father who held the monopoly on charisma. Now that I think of it, maybe she was a little flustered by his magnetism. It must have inadvertently atttracted all sorts of random types into his orbit, and my mother, who was not by nature gregarious, would have been hard put to cope with that. This, however, didn't occur to me until I gained some distance from my childhood and began to see my parents and their marriage in greater perspective.

Elodie Swann

If memory serves me, I met Victor Prudhomme through my father, with whom he had some brief business dealings. Though we liked each other at once, Victor was quick to see that, unlike most of the women he knew, I had no interest in marriage. It was with some relief on his part that we became and remained great friends.

In the autumn of 1912, Victor was embroiled in a liaison with Katherine Cameron, whom everyone called Kiki. The Camerons were San Franciscans who came often to Los Angeles to visit friends. I suppose that's how Victor met them. Kiki's husband was elderly and lame and seemingly indifferent to their affair. Chivalrously, he removed himself to a spa in France, well beyond the range of gossip and humiliation. Kiki reacted by accusing him of desertion and hiring a lawyer. About then, I would have expected Victor to hear the hounds and bolt. Imagine my amazement when he began to talk of settling down and raising a family. It was time, he said, to put his life in order. Victor was in his forties by now, and I suppose it had occurred to him that if he hoped to have children, he'd better attend to it. If that was what he wanted, it was fine with me. All I cared about was that his bride not be Kiki Cameron, someone I regarded as a callous, cunning, carnivorous little shrike who would make Victor's life thoroughly miserable, especially if given the opportunity to bear his children and hold them for ransom. Of course, I dared say nothing to him.

As it happened, Papa and I spent six weeks in San Francisco that year. He was negotiating some oil leases, and when his work was done, decided to stay on for a vacation. I was delighted. I had some friends there and was warmly embraced by the city's society, which was far livelier than what Los Angeles offered me at the time. I soon exhausted my wardrobe; but Papa, seeing how much I was enjoying myself, allowed me to order several outfits from a stylish modiste across the street from our hotel.

The modiste was always delighted to see a cash customer. 'Mademoiselle Swann! All day I have been hoping you would come in. Blanche! Marie!' she called. 'Bring me the beige duster with the fur collar. *Quelle coincidence!* It is your colouring exactly that I see when I design this. In my head, I see you in a fine automobile, wearing my driving coat.'

'Actually, Madame Ninette, I was shopping for a tea gown.'

'No matter. You will try on the coat, too.' She took it from the girl who brought it and held it open for me to put on.

'Madame?'

'Yes? What is it?' She turned towards the voice as I regarded my image in her large gilt-framed mirror, trying the collar up, then down.

'There is a woman at the rear door who wants to show you her beadwork.'

In the mirror, I could see the speaker – a tall, fair-haired figure standing in the passageway that led to the dressing rooms.

'I am busy. Ask her if she will please return at six this evening.'

'Yes, Madame.' She retreated into the area at the back of the shop.

'Madame Ninette,' I asked, 'who was that young lady?'

'Mademoiselle Willson, my manageress. I will introduce you when she returns. Blanche,' she ordered the salesgirl, 'fetch Miss Swann the blue silk gown on the figure in my workroom. Ah, Mademoiselle Willson, come here. You must meet Miss Swann.'

I knew before I turned around who it was, but I am afraid I gaped anyway.

'Ada Willson,' she said, extending her hand. She pronounced the first name with broad a's.

I shook her hand.

She regarded me with an even blue gaze as cool as a glacial pond.

'Madame,' called Blanche, 'would you come here for a moment?'

102

'Excuse me.' Madame Ninette left the room.

'Ada?' I tried the name on my tongue.

'Yes. Ada.'

'Willson?'

She nodded.

Gone was the gangly, awkward girl of two years ago. In the time since I'd last seen her, her beauty had come into its full bloom, and she carried herself with a grace that could only come from a sense of supreme self-confidence.

'You're married then?'

She shook her head. 'But Willson sounds so much nicer than Watkins, don't you think?'

'You never looked better.'

'I know. Isn't it lovely?' Her voice had a mellowed timbre. It was richer and sweeter than I had remembered it.

'And your mother?'

For a moment, she hesitated. 'Ma's not with us anymore,' she said finally.

'Your mother is dead?'

'To all intents and purposes.'

'Adelaide!'

'My name is Ada.'

'For pity's sake. . . .'

'My mother is in the county hospital, Elodie. It's seven months now. Sometimes she knows me and sometimes she doesn't. She's not unhappy. She talks to God all the time.'

'What happened?'

'Who knows? One day she saw Beelzebub and had to kill him, she said. She took a pillow off the bed and smothered him. Only it was a two-day-old baby. Sit down, Elodie. Shall I get you some water?'

'No, thank you.'

'The lawyers used up every nickel I had. I sold the house, too, not that there was much money in it. Ma had it mortgaged to the skies.'

'I'm sure it's been difficult for you. I'm sorry.'

'Not for me,' she objected. 'I'm Ada Willson.'

I realized she was serious. She was that prgamatic. She had

103

simply reinvented herself rather than allow her past to hinder her. That was always her greatest talent. Her life, both then and later, was a series of catastrophes which she breasted like a mermaid. Each time, she emerged from the waves baptized anew. First, she had been Rowley Deems' wife, until the shooting when she had cast off all vestiges of that identity and returned to being Adelaide Watkins. Now she had conveniently rid herself of Adelaide Watkins and become Ada Willson. I am not waxing overly dramatic when I say she gave me a chill.

'Elodie, my dear, is that you? Fancy finding you so far from home!'

I had not even seen Victor enter. Ada excused herself as Madame returned. 'Monsieur Prudhomme! *Je suis enchantée de vous voir.*'

'*Merci, Madame.* I came to collect my gift for Mrs Cameron. Is it ready?'

'But certainly. Miss Swann, if you will follow me to a fitting room, I have a very special gown to show you. Monsieur Prudhomme, I shall return in a moment with your parcel.'

'Elodie,' Victor called after me, 'I'd like to see you in that very special gown. Will you model it for me?'

'If you insist.'

When I stepped from the fitting room, Ada was standing in the hallway. 'I want you to introduce me to that man.'

'I beg your pardon?'

'That man you were speaking to just now. I want to meet him.'

'That's Victor Prudhomme.'

'I know who he is. He's been here before.'

'He's a dear friend of mine.'

'Are you going to introduce me to him or not?'

I gazed at her for a moment. 'Of course,' I said. 'Come along.'

'I'd rather you didn't say that I'm employed here. He seems to think I'm one of Madame's patrons.'

'Are you trying to put words in my mouth?'

'What I meant,' she told me, 'is that it simply wouldn't do for either of us to divulge every little detail we know about each other.' She gave me a slow, deliberate smile. 'Would it, Elodie?'

All right, I thought, Victor could take care of himself, and surely this wasn't the first cheeky young woman to arrange an introduction.

I had no inkling until several weeks later that my cursory introduction had 'taken,' as they say. I didn't see Victor during that time, though I did hear that he was no longer with Kiki Cameron. I was flabbergasted when I found out that he'd invited Ada to Los Angeles and put her up at the deluxe new Beverly Hills Hotel. Ada was admittedly a beauty, but so were all his women. Beyond that, I couldn't imagine what attracted him. He was, after all, very worldly, and Ada was hardly a sophisticate. It couldn't possibly be serious.

My own feelings were mixed. True, I thought Ada a girl with an eye to the main chance, but compared to someone like Kiki Cameron, she was quite innocuous. I could see that Victor took immense pleasure in his protégée, and that made me happy for his sake. For a long time it had seemed to me that he was merely going through the motions of acting the man-about-town because it had become expected of him. His enthusiasm for Ada was the real article. Still, knowing Victor, I didn't think it would endure for long.

It was Victor who told me in his unsentimental way that they were going to be married. He wanted a family, and Ada had happened along at the right time. What could I say to his choice of a wife? I wondered if he knew about the Watkins. Had she told him her father was an adventurer and her mother a madwoman? I knew better than to step between Victor and something he wanted. Moreover, I was mindful of what traditionally happened to the bearers of bad news. If Ada had already told him about the Watkins, Rowley Deems and how she'd been forced to work for a living, he'd be within his rights to regard me as nothing more than a meddlesome gossip. I kept my thoughts to myself. I admired Ada's diamond ring and gave her my best wishes. We were at the theatre, I remember, and Papa had drawn Victor aside to discuss some oil investments.

Ada thanked me for wishing her well. 'You're not going to try to stand in our way, are you, Elodie?' she inquired, smiling.

'Why do you think I would do that?'

'I wasn't sure how you'd feel.'

'I wouldn't dream of it.' I recognized, as did she, that we each knew far too much about the other. It was ironic to think we were bound together by a past we both wished to deny. Our friendship, if it was ever wholeheartedly that, was a kind of symbiosis. We were forced to trust each other whether we liked it or not.

'It's not what you think, you know. Just because Victor put me up at the hotel doesn't mean I'm a kept woman.'

I quickly hushed her.

'Being a widow, I felt a chaperone was unnecessary. Besides, I made it clear I would not be compromised. And Victor is a gentleman above all.'

'He's everything you've ever wanted, sure enough.'

'He's more than that. I love him, Elodie. Believe me. It's Victor I love, not simply the life he can afford me.'

'Then you're fortunate indeed, aren't you?'

'You don't believe me, but you will one day.'

I guess I finally did, come to think of it, but the actual reason that I chose to remain close to them was my friendship with Victor. I was Victor's only real friend, in the sense that I was the only person he knew who was loyal to him without ever wanting anything from him or making any demands upon him. He recognized this, and he trusted me. I was aware, for example, that Benny Walsh, the bootlegger, also supplied Victor with introductions to pretty girls. Maybe Ada suspected. I know she never liked to have Benny Walsh around. Victor's affairs were common knowledge, yet he knew that of all their friends, I was the least likely to betray him to Ada.

There was, of course, the mess about Roxanne Pollard, the girl who killed herself after Victor had given her the gate. It was hushed up quickly, but not in time to spare Ada the full brunt of that particular catastrophe.

There was one thing about it, though, that I never did understand. While Victor wasn't flagrant about his peccadilloes, he didn't make any great effort to conceal them. I suppose they added to what would nowadays be called his 'image,' and he must have secretly enjoyed that. So I had known about his affair with Roxanne and known when it ended, too. She'd quit her job as his stenographer and moved to Chicago. Why, I couldn't help wondering, would she reappear in Victor's life nearly *three years* later for what appeared to be the sole purpose of making him a party to her death? Regardless of how she may have pined away for him in the meantime, it still seems strange to me that someone would undertake to travel halfway across the United States only to commit suicide.

True to form, Ada surmounted the tragedy and in so doing propelled herself onward and upward. She insisted that they move from that house. The next thing I knew, Victor had bought her some four hundred acres in Beverly Hills, and Ada was hiring people right and left to build herself a mansion the likes of which this area had never seen. My guess is that Victor felt guilty about the whole mess and was appeasing Ada. She had, after all, given him the children he'd longed for. No expense was spared on behalf of his sons and their mother.

During those early years of their marriage, Ada was still learning. At parties or in public, I would watch her eyes sweep back and forth over the room, moving from person to person, fixing some of them now and again with that bright gaze like the gleam from a pair of blue diamonds. She assessed, compared, reassessed. She was continually appraising her own situation, too, taking inventory of the gentry around her, weighing its merits, counting its assets and – God forbid – liabilities.

I distrust those who want desperately to belong. Whether they want to belong to the D.A.R. or the Elks or the Bohemian Club, the greater their drive to belong, the deeper their venality. I've always thought, by the way, that Tony's wife, Nita Paris, being the same type, scented this in Ada, even after all those years. Though Ada might look down on her, Nita sensed that deep inside they both had the same weakness. They were matched antagonists.

Ada learned quickly. Moreover, she had either the wisdom or the intuition to know that if she assiduously acted her part, sooner or later it would come naturally, out of habit. Ada exemplified those traits of the beau monde she so admired. She was gracious, dignified, principled and charitable. Sometimes I thought her a bit heavy-handed in her characterization, but then, my viewpoint was unique.

She and Victor did not entertain people 'in trade,' she told me, evidently having forgotten that she and Rowley Deems had once wanted nothing more than to own a chain of nickelodeons. She was given to pronouncements like 'You can always tell a lady by the impeccable condition of her shoes and gloves,' or she'd use a phrase like 'seated below the salt.' She never learned that at Ma Watkins' table.

If there was the slightest remaining intimation of Ada's origins, it was implicit in her dealings with the staff. She was never wholly at ease with servants. She addressed them with a kind of detached civility that underscored whose was the upper hand. It seemed to me that she felt it necessary to dissociate herself from that class and to predominate; a reaction, no doubt, to Ma Watkins' once having worked in a 'swell house,' as Adelaide had told me.

Telling it now, it sounds as if Ada was an insufferable snob, but those were different times. Before the Second World War muddled the arrangement, it was expected that the lower classes knew their place, that the superiority of the aristocracy was unassailable and that the twain would never meet. Ada was simply doing what was expected of her.

All she ever wanted, I suppose, was to be worthy, a Somebody. She gave good value in return for this. And if I took such things for granted or never gave a hang for them, who's to say which of us was right?

Nanny Beale

The main house at Silverwood had a staff of fifteen including the cook, two scullery maids, the laundresses, the upstairs maids, the parlour maid and under parlour maid, two footmen, Mrs Prudhomme's personal maid, Mr Prudhomme's valet and Mr Safford, the butler. From the first, the twins had every one of them charmed. The cook, Mrs Weir, made them armies of gingerbread men and the footmen, Alfred and Burt, would allow them to slide down the long, winding banisters when neither Mr Safford nor myself was looking. We got along famously, all of us, despite Mrs Weir being a devotée of Sister Aimee Semple McPherson. 'The staff,' Mr Safford used to say, 'is the spine of a great house. It wouldn't do to have it out of alignment.' He was a stern taskmaster, but nobody complained. He stayed with Mrs Prudhomme until her death, when he retired. He once told me he'd never seen a hostess turn a table as skilfully as she. That was high praise indeed. Mr Safford had previously been employed in two titled households.

We were aware, all of us, of the distinction of belonging to the finest estate in southern California. The newspapers had made a great to-do about the Fairbanks' place, naming it Pickfair and carrying on like it was Balmoral Castle, but now that Silverwood was completed, there wasn't an establishment within a hundred miles to compete with it. None ever did.

Outside the house, there were the gatekeeper, the handyman, the caretaker, the staff of Japanese gardeners under Mr Yamada, the chauffeur and the stable hands. The children each had a little Shetland pony, to begin with, and later a pair of chestnut geldings. Mr Prudhomme sometimes kept one or another of his polo ponies at Silverwood, if it needed special tending; otherwise they were stabled out near Santa Monica where the gentlemen played.

It was a children's paradise. The boys swam in the vast turquoise pool, rode the gentle hills in the care of the groom, Brian, and were allowed by Mr Yamada to potter about the kitchen gardens (never his formal gardens) planting their own small patches of vegetables. They had a beagle dog, named Bingo after Cracker Jack's pup, and a family of cats that prowled the grounds, keeping the rats and gophers scarce. They played croquet with their own miniature mallets and balls, and as soon as they were big enough to hold a racket, took tennis lessons three times a week. Mr and Mrs Prudhomme favoured badminton.

The boys were close in those days. They had between them that special bond that twins possess. Sometimes they didn't have to exchange a word to share their thoughts. It was eerie, in certain ways. If one developed a mole on his right shoulder, the other would be sure to have one on his left. When they fought, which thank the dear Lord was rarely, they battled so savagely that you'd have thought they were trying to kill one another. Maybe they were. I dare say every child wants to be thought singular and to be loved for himself alone.

Despite their obvious similarity, they had their differences. Anthony was poetical, a dreamer. He invented an imaginary family, the Kippins, who had a pet pigeon named Kooloo, though where he came by those names none of us could fathom. Andrew was the practical one. He cared nothing for tall tales. He only wanted information he could use, and the moment the details exceeded his use for them, his attention wandered. Anthony would read fairy tales aloud for the sheer pleasure of the way the words sounded, while Andrew had no patience for pretty phrases and read only what he wanted to learn. I suppose Anthony might have been the scholar of the two, given his love of books, were it not for that tendency to daydream which he never quite outgrew. He would spend his school days staring out of the window, more preoccupied with fantasies of adventure than with spelling it. So it was Andrew who fared better with his lessons. He took it upon himself to learn what was necessary to bring home a respectable report card, no more. He learned how to use people to advantage,

110

too, biding his time until Mr Prudhomme was in a particularly jolly mood before he'd attempt to wheedle a new tennis racket or a trip to the auto races out of him. Anthony was more impulsive. He said what he felt when he felt it, for good or ill. He was ruled by his emotions, that boy, and he was as truthful as the day is long, while his brother was capable of being a wee bit devious if it suited his purpose.

They were good boys, though, despite being indulged by their parents and the staff. They weren't above a little devilment, mind you. They'd switch clothing to try to fool me or change places at table to confuse their playmates. They were full of energetic enthusiasm which their mother called 'rambunctiousness.' That was one of her favourite words. 'Boys!' she would say. 'Don't be so rambunctious. Don't run up the stairs. Gentlemen take their time. The world will wait for a gentleman.'

They made friends easily, each according to his tastes. Andrew tended to choose his companions with deliberation. He would bring home the kind of boys who had summer houses at Coronado or Santa Monica Beach, knowing full well that their friendship might mean a vacation at the seashore. Anthony brought home the walking wounded, the misfits; bespectacled, tongue-tied lads, a boy lamed by poliomyelitis, another with one withered arm and once, to his mother's consternation, an Oriental. That was the first time I heard his parents discuss the possibility of sending the twins back east to boarding school.

'Anthony,' I told him, 'use your poet's ear. Listen to the children's names. There's a wealth of information there. Your brother brings home friends like Parker Winthrop and Bradford Bromfield, and you bring home boys with names like Harry Quong and Ike Musgrove. And mark the bone structure, too, Anthony, and the complexion. A well-bred young person doesn't have thick ankles or a face that's as shapeless and spotted as a bowl of plum-duff.'

They weren't sent east, not then at any rate.

On weekends, Mr Prudhomme would motor out to Santa Monica to play polo on the fields in Rustic Canyon. Mrs Prudhomme rarely went with him. She thought the game dangerous. 'It's a young man's sport, Victor,' she insisted. 'You've no

111

business playing polo at your age.' He was then in his fifties, but he paid little regard to his years or to his wife's objections. Sometimes the twins and I went with him to watch the games. What a handsome spectacle they were – bronzed gentlemen in white shirts and breeches astride galloping mounts thundering the length and breadth of the bright green fields, hurtling towards the goal, wheeling about, racing past in a blur of motion; men and mallets, animals and turf flying by with a clamour, hammer of hooves and heart. Then they would change horses, mop their perspiring faces, take deep draughts of water, spit them out, take to the field again on fresh ponies that pranced and pawed the ground and, at the sound of the horn, switch sides and be at it again. The boys loved the hurly-burly of the matches, but their mother didn't want them getting ideas about playing polo, so our outings to Rustic Canyon were infrequent. I didn't tell her that Brian, the groom, occasionally allowed them to charge about the riding ring at Silverwood on their horses, brandishing croquet mallets for practice against the day they would be allowed to learn the game.

It was his love of the sport that killed Mr Prudhomme, just as his wife had feared it might. An accident, it was, two horses colliding and him thrown on to the broad green field never to rise up, brush the dirt from his clothes and laugh it off as he always had before. Praise God for His mercy, the end was swift. Knowing Mr Prudhomme, I suppose he might even have wanted to go as he did, with his boots on and his spirits high. Even in death, he was a stylish gentleman.

It was then, when Andrew and Anthony's father died, that I saw how their twinship protected them. No one, of course, could ever be closer to these two identical boys than they were to each other. That was a fact of life. Their intimacy was an exclusive thing. No one could completely breach it. It insulated them in its mysterious way against the tragedies of the world. No matter what happened, they had each other. Everyone else was expendable. Twins know they are remarkable from the first, but now I could see that Andrew and Anthony, observing their mother's grief, began to understand that, in ways they had not yet considered, they were exempt from the full intrusion of life's

112

troubles. The usual rules did not apply to them. Twins are a law of their own.

At the end of the following summer, when the boys were twelve, they went off to Exeter Academy, back east. Mr Prudhomme had studied there in his day, and it had been his wish that his sons follow in his footsteps. Now, with their father gone, Mrs Prudhomme felt the twins needed the companionship of men and boys. I dare say she was right. In any event, they were outgrowing their need for me and it was time to be on my way. Mr and Mrs Outerbridge, friends of the family, knew of a young couple in San Francisco that was looking for a nanny for their three small children.

A meeting was arranged. We liked each other. I was engaged by the Clifford Thaxters with the understanding that I would join their household a week after Mrs Prudhomme and the boys left by train for the east.

The twins promised to write and for a while they did. I kept up a correspondence with Mrs Weir, the cook, until she left Silverwood a few years later. Sometimes I missed Silverwood as keenly as though it had been my own home, never for a moment dreaming that I would one day go back there.

Mr Thaxter belonged to a shipping family that had interests in Hawaii. In 1937, after I had been with them six years, the Thaxters, their three children and I moved lock, stock and barrel to the Islands.

Dorcas Outerbridge

In my mind, gilded summer afternoons at Silverwood shine through memory's swift stream like elusive, glistening fish scudding through dark waters. I glimpse white-painted lawn furniture on a smooth carpet of green, a float of pale silk dresses, clusters of crimson leopard lilies and the gloss of sunlight all over, as though it had spilled from the great blue bowl of sky overhead and splashed everywhere. The air is warm and sweet and thick like honey. The scents of jasmine and gardenia come to me. I hear water trickling from a fountain, a mockingbird echoing its own melody, the occasional chirrup of insects and laughter, much laughter. Hale's laughter is deep and robust. Elodie Swann's is a clear, soprano arietta. From the swimming pool behind the hedge, the sound of the young people laughing reminds me of the playful yipping of a litter of pups. Ada, for some reason, rarely laughs aloud. Victor has a hearty, staccato laugh that sounds like a seventeen-gun salute.

At length, the birds' singing becomes *lento*. The serried shadows of the poplar trees crowd the light from the lawn. In that attenuated mauve dusk of summer the earth seems for a time to turn more slowly. The last diehard tennis players on the court fly about in shadow like large moths. The grass grows cold underfoot. We gather up our reading and needlework. The men put away their cigars, tobacco pouches and pocket lighters. No one wants to admit that something beautiful has gone.

Ada and Victor fit into that setting to perfection. They, the house, the grounds, were all of a piece, unlike some couples who live grandly but whose finery never quite becomes them.

I can recall one period during our friendship when Victor was particularly kind to me. It was shortly after he and Ada had moved to Silverwood and given their gala housewarming. Try as I might, I had not been able to extricate myself from the terrible guilt and sorrow that had overwhelmed me after Hale had decided that we must give up our baby. I felt such a failure. I had failed to give Hale a healthy son. I had failed to cope with having a child who was hopelessly retarded but was, nonetheless, my baby boy. The circumstances filled me with such anguish that now I wasn't fit to be a wife, either. Neither the passage of months nor years alleviated my misery. I knew how unhappy I was making Hale, but I couldn't help myself.

'I'll never understand you women,' he would say, shaking his head.

'But Hale, the boy bears your name. Haven't you at least some interest in knowing how he's being treated there?'

'I looked into the place thoroughly when we first sent him.'

'He'll be four on his next birthday.'

'All the more reason to put it behind you. See here, woman, you've a perfectly healthy daughter. Look after her. When I make investments, I don't throw good money after bad. Instead, I concentrate on what stands to prove rewarding. It's a sound principle and just as profitable mentally as financially.'

'It's not that easy.'

'Why do women want to make everything so complicated? Carrying on doesn't alter the facts. Dorcas, you must give up this Sarah Bernhardt business once and for all.'

I tried desperately to do as he said. Sometimes, though, just when I thought I had my life under control, I would see a boy the age of our own and be suddenly dashed to the depths of despair by his innocent little face. One weekend, some friends of the Prudhommes brought their son with them to watch a badminton game at Silverwood. Victor came upon me weeping in the wistaria arbour where I had fled before Hale could see my tears.

'May I help?'

I looked up with a start.

'Don't worry. I'm alone. I saw you leave and wondered where you were going by yourself.' He took his handkerchief from his pocket and handed it to me.

'I'm so sorry. I didn't mean to take you away from your other guests.'

'If one of my guests isn't happy, neither am I. I'm especially unhappy if she's a lovely woman.'

'It has nothing at all to do with the company. There isn't really anything you can do.'

He reached out and clasped my hand. 'Try me.'

'It's that little boy. So like ours. I left because I didn't want Hale to see that it bothered me. You have to understand Hale,' I explained. 'Hale is such a sensitive soul. He can't even bear to acknowledge what's happened. He wants to bury it. He's never so much as once brought up our baby's name since we gave him away. It upsets him dreadfully when I become teary. I suppose he can't stand to see his wife in pain. It upsets him so much, in fact, that he has to withdraw. He shuts himself away from me, in his study. He's that deeply sensitive, you see. I don't know what to do.'

'How fortunate Hale is to have you for a wife, my dear,' Victor said. He raised my hand to his lips and kissed it.

I have not forgotten how caring he was towards me that afternoon. I never told anyone this, but I once spied on Victor Prudhomme, quite alone, without being observed. What happened was that I was visiting an elderly aunt of mine named Felicia Moncada. My mother's family, the Moncadas, were one of the oldest families in southern California. My Aunt Felicia had a house near Rustic Canyon, not far from the place where Victor and his friends played polo. I had driven out there alone to pay a courtesy call, only to find that my aunt hadn't yet awakened from her afternoon nap. I decided to take a walk to pass the time. It was a misty day in April, and the woods smelled of green and growing things. The leaves were heavy with moisture. Clear beads of condensation rolled off them like occasional raindrops. I wasn't aware of approaching the polo field. I heard the sound of hooves in the distance and wondered who might be racing at a gallop on such a quiet grey afternoon. Suddenly I found myself at the edge of the woods with only a sparse stand of trees separating me from a wide, level field of closely-cut grass. I recognized the place immediately. Through the silvery fog I made out a lone rider on a slate-coloured horse hurtling across the green turf, turning, galloping the length of the field and back. He swung his polo mallet as they went, practising smooth, clean strokes that swept the ball through the haze ahead of him. The pony's legs were wrapped with blue bandages, its mane clipped and its tail plaited. The rider wore sleek brown boots and white breeches. He had on a brown leather belt. He wore nothing else. He was stripped to the waist, his body wet and shiny with sweat and mist. His black hair was slicked to his skin. They thundered by, unaware of my presence, man and horse joined like a single heaving, glistening creature. I caught the gamy, animal scent as they passed. I am not sure how long I stood hidden there among the moist and dripping trees. Perhaps it was only for a few

116

minutes, but it was long enough for me to recognize Victor, to begin to turn away out of modesty and then to turn back to stare at the sight of him. At Victor Prudhomme, half-naked, perspiring, his muscles taut, his face fierce and rapt, making a wide arc of his arm, slamming his mallet unerringly against the ball, sending it flying. I still cannot imagine my doing something so furtive. It was quite out of character. I remember my aunt was very annoyed that I had kept her waiting after she arose from her nap.

Bibi Prudhomme Biddeford

Victor was Prince Charming personified. Ada – or any woman, for that matter – would have been utterly defenceless once he'd set his sights on her. Here was a handsome, successful, socially prominent bachelor offering her the world on the half shell. It would never have occurred to her that she might be of interest only as a means to an end, a mechanism in the Prudhomme line of succession.

If she hadn't been quite so bright, she might have held his interest a little longer. As it was, Victor dictated the style in which he wanted to live, and Ada catered to his every wish. He told her what to wear, whom to entertain in their home and what he wanted on the table. He taught her to distinguish between Eakins and Homer and even chose the books she was to read.

Unfortunately, as I say, Ada was a quick study. No sooner had she become the embodiment of her husband's designs than he turned his attentions to other projects. She wanted desperately to please him, but she didn't understand that as long as she pleased Victor, as long as she complied with his wishes, she presented no challenge to him. On the other hand, I suppose, had she failed to please him or become contentious, he would have dropped her without a backward glance. Ada was stuck with Hobson's choice.

Only her anatomy stubbornly refused to conform to Victor's will. If the twins hadn't come along when they did, I've no doubt she would have been put out to pasture. They saved her marriage, and she knew it.

God knows, she had guts. Given Victor's nature, I can think of few things more demoralizing than being married to that man. Worse still, she loved him passionately. How it must have puzzled Victor to be an object of passion. Certainly it was not a familiar element in our set. Passion, in our crowd, was regarded as something inherent in the lower classes, the less evolved of the species. If, by some atavistic quirk, it reared its head among us, it was regarded as an unfortunate weakness, a freak of nature like strabismus or a cleft palate. Worse, to give in to the affliction was tantamount to a betrayal of one's rank. It was nothing more than self-indulgence. To witness such a display was as disturbing as seeing one's elderly grandmother drunk and disrobed. Like most embarrassments, one tried politely to ignore it. Victor must have been baffled, not to say a trifle irritated, to be the focus of such emotions.

I thank the Lord I had the dumb luck to marry Oren Biddeford, who, due no doubt to an Italian infiltration on his mother's side, was a man of great feeling. We had a nifty marriage, if I say so myself, twenty years that sped by like a cannonball. Oren, bless him, died suddenly at the age of forty-six. He simply slumped over in his chair one afternoon at the Boston Athenaeum, dead of heart failure while reading D. H. Lawrence, not that I think there's any connection.

Victor was a great help to me and Oren junior. He corresponded almost daily with young Oren at Exeter. I think it helped the boy a great deal. As for me, I felt like an aerialist wire-walking without a safety net. Until then I had never so much as written a check or purchased a railroad ticket on my own. Oren had done it all. If it hadn't been for Victor giving me a crash course in financial management, I would have fallen to shivers. Whatever else breeding produced in Victor, it also produced a sense of family responsibility. The word 'duty,' to men like my brother, meant something very fine. Perhaps they were at their best when living up to their duties as they saw

118

them. I only know that when times were rough for me, I could count on Victor.

It wasn't even two years later that Oren junior died. He was a senior at Exeter the year of the Spanish influenza. Half a million people succumbed, and one of them was my son, a brown-eyed blond, nearly six feet tall, a champion swimmer, editor of *The Exonian*, crack hockey player. We couldn't get him into a hospital. There were no empty beds. You had to wait for someone to recover or die. His fever lingered at 105° for three days. When it began to rise higher, he hadn't a chance. One could almost *see* death rushing full tilt at him. We were all virtually as helpless as he was, lying there. As for me, I might as well have been struck head-on by a speeding truck. It took me years to recover, and even now I sometimes find myself unexpectedly drawing in my breath sharply with the pain of it.

How manifold the ways in which we humans respond to tragedy. I don't know how I expected Ada to react to Victor's fatal accident, but whatever I might have anticipated, I was unprepared for what she made of it.

By the time of Victor's death Ada was aware that he had long ago placed her on the shelf with the rest of his trophies. She was yesterday's news. The future lay with his sons. If Ada hadn't cared about him so much, she might have managed to remain oblivious of his attitude. But she did care. I often think she showed more concern for Victor's state of mind than he did. She was overly sensitive to his every mood. It's ironic, but I guess it was part of her intense desire to please him that forced her to be continually aware that a series of other women were fulfilling that function. She mentioned it only once. It seemed, at the time, an attempt to save face and to reassure me that she not only understood Victor but remained devoted to him. It was only a few days before the twins were born. It must have been a very trying time for her. The two of us were seated in front of the hearth in my living room, having tea. Ada stared into the fire in silence for a while. I thought her face the saddest I had ever seen.

'Don't think I'm a fool, please, Bibi,' she said quietly, still gazing at the flames. 'I'm not stupid or unfeeling or indifferent. I've known since the day it first happened that Victor would never be satisfied with me, that he had to have other women. I'm aware of everything. I even know when his affairs are going sour or when he's discovered someone new. He did promise me that he would never become involved with anyone from our set. You see, it's not that he wants to humiliate me. . . .' Only someone who loved deeply could forgive as much as Ada forgave my brother.

On reflection, you could say it was a blessing that Victor died doing something he loved and that he was spared the paralysis that would have been his lot had he survived. Still, you are never prepared when death plays the burglar, slinking into your life behind your back while you remain caught up in the disarming illusion that God's in his heaven and all's right with your world. That was how it was when my husband, Oren, died. Heaven knows what I was doing, laughing perhaps, merry as a lark, when death stole him from me.

So it was in June of 1928 when I was visiting Ada and Victor at Silverwood. June in that part of the country, I discovered, is likely to be damp and dismal, muffled in mists that are only now and then penetrated by wan, whitish sunlight that appears and disappears like a wraith. It was Sunday, and Nanny had the afternoon off. The boys were lying on the floor in front of the fireplace in the library, poring over the comic pages of the *Times*. I was comfortably settled in a large wing chair by the hearth, reading the account of Amelia Earhart's Atlantic flight, only vaguely mindful of Ada's presence outside, beyond the closed French doors. She was moving slowly along the tall row of rosebushes that grew there, pausing occasionally to snip off a blossom with her shears and lay it in the wicker basket that hung from her arm. In the silence, the logs hissed on the grate, and I heard the sound of Safford's footsteps in the hall, trotting up the marble steps with that brisk, businesslike gait that meant he was answering the door.

A few moments later, as I turned the pages of my newspaper, he came into sight outdoors. Ada stopped her cutting and laid her basket on the lawn. Safford disappeared from view, and his place was taken by someone I didn't know, a figure in riding boots, white breeches and shirt, with a bright green neckerchief knotted at his throat. I turned my attention back to my reading. Presently, as I folded the paper, I glanced out at the two figures beyond the glass.

Something about their posture seized my attention. The visitor was standing stiffly, his arms at his sides, his body pitched forward slightly towards Ada. He stood poised there in that odd stance as though a Gorgon had turned him to stone.

Ada looked straight ahead, her eyes averted from him, her gaze seemingly fixed on the wisps of fog that curled about them. She might as well have been an alabaster statue standing motionless on the grass, its face glistening with mist, the moisture running in rivulets down its indifferent cheeks.

I knew then what had struck them numb. God knows how I knew, but I did. 'Boys,' I said abruptly to the twins, 'gather up the paper. I feel like playing Mah-Jongg. Are you game? Ready, on your mark! Last one upstairs to the playroom is a rotten egg!' I knew that sooner or later, after she had composed herself, Ada would come to find us there.

Victor's death had come so unexpectedly that it was a few days before the initial shock abated. It was only as we were leaving the church on the way to the cemetery that I began to observe what it had done to Ada. She was walking towards the limousine on the arm of Laurence Ward, Victor's polo-playing buddy. Tony, Drew and Nanny Beale were behind her, and I followed. Laurence opened the door and stood ready to help Ada in. Suddenly, without warning, she stepped back and raised her gloved hands in front of her, gesturing as if to push the car away. 'Leave me alone!' she cried. 'Let me do it my way!' I suppose Laurence thought she was merely understandably upset. He murmured something solicitous and attempted to ease her into the limousine. 'No!' Ada pulled away from him. This time, Laurence took her quite firmly by the elbow and steered her towards the open door. Ada raised her arm and brought her hand down full force against his face. Laurence went reeling. The twins looked panic-stricken. Nanny hustled them into another of the waiting automobiles.

'Bibi!' Laurence called to me when he'd caught his breath. 'Can't you help? Can't you reason with her?'

121

By this time, Hale Outerbridge and some of the other pall-bearers had grouped around Ada. She acted as though they weren't even there. She pressed through the crowd to where the funeral director was standing. 'I'll walk,' she said.

That's what she did. She walked behind the hearse for the mile or so to the cemetery. She refused to allow anyone to go with her. I can see her now, a tall, black-clothed figure, striding doggedly along, the tears streaming down her cheeks, strands of fair hair catching the sunlight about her head, looking for all the world as if she were giving off sparks. Now that Victor could no longer deny or belittle her feelings for him, her passion flared unchecked, incandescent as a Catherine wheel.

Nobody who witnessed her explosion ever mentioned the incident again, to my knowledge. I doubt they knew what to make of it. I stood next to her at the burial rites, and she appeared to be regaining control of herself. Afterward, back at Silverwood, she presided over the gathering with complete aplomb, politely appreciative of all the words that people rattled off, useless as pebbles to comfort her.

One thing alone seemed to console her. That evening, as I kissed her goodnight outside her bedroom door, she said softly. 'He's mine now, Bibi, isn't he?'

I suspect that's the main reason Ada always considered marriage to Sam Farkas out of the question. She had paid dearly for the privilege of being Mrs Victor Guy Prudhomme, an honour which had been about as comfortable as a crown of thorns. Only after Victor's death did she derive a full measure of gratification from it, and she was not about to relinquish that. Perhaps it *was* superficial, nothing more than a role she chose to play, but then Ada had learned to be a good actress. She'd had plenty of practice in the fifteen years she was married to my brother. Who was I to deny Ada her consolation, especially since she made it apparent that she regarded the Prudhomme name so highly?

Tony Prudhomme

Even after Father died, he remained for several years the central figure in my mother's life. Like a mortician plumping up and retouching a cadaver, Mother put a flawless face on his image.

'I'll never forget the day your father gave me those emeralds,' she said, gazing at her portrait and touching a hand to her throat. 'We were staying with Nigel and Poppy Lambton at Langehurst Hall. It was – '

'I know, on your honeymoon,' said Drew.

'On our wedding trip. Your father came up behind me as I was sitting at my dressing table – '

I knew the rest. 'And slipped the necklace around you.'

'I saw it in the mirror. And then – '

'He gave you the earrings.'

'And the bracelet. Don't forget the bracelet.' She held her wrist close to its painted, bejewelled likeness and seemed pleased that the resemblance held up. 'How your father loved that portrait,' she said. 'He was always so glad that Nigel and Poppy had talked him into having it commissioned.'

I had never heard him mention anything of the kind. I guess it was about that time, when Mother began slathering on the paint, that I began to outgrow my innocence. 'Your father,' she would remind us by way of reproach, 'was a gentleman.' This was supposed to shame us into everything from taking our elbows off the table to letting our guests choose what games to play. I wondered what she'd have made of the pair of scorched photograph albums Drew and I had found by the incinerator in back of the greenhouses. We had recognized them immediately.

'Those are the books Father had way up high on the top shelf of his trophy room.' Drew slid off his horse. He stuck his riding crop into the ash pit and poked about to see if it was still smouldering underneath.

I tied my horse's reins to a tree and joined him. 'How did they get here?'

'I don't know, but I saw Safford up there on a ladder yesterday. I thought he was polishing Father's trophies.'

'There used to be half a dozen albums. Polo pictures, I guess. What happened to the rest?'

He reached into the charred litter and extracted the blackened spine of another. 'Gone, it looks like.'

'That's not fair.' I blew the cinders off the two he'd salvaged. We hunkered down and laid them on the ground. Gingerly, I raised the seared leather binding of the one on top.

'Jee-zuz!'

'Yeah.'

'Holy smokes!' Drew let out a wild cackle.

I felt a self-conscious grin spread across my face. 'Where do you think they came from?'

'They were the old man's, stupid. Sonofabitch, will you look at the pair of jugs on that broad?'

'Hey, Drew, you don't suppose he took these pictures himself, do you?'

Drew looked incredulous for a second. Then he burst out laughing. 'I don't know. Maybe he did.' He pulled one loose and examined it. 'Look.' He handed it to me.

On the back side of the photograph, in Father's script, was written 'Roxanne.'

'This one's Lily.'

'Who's the blond one playing with herself?'

He turned it over. 'Nadia.'

'Take a look at Irene!'

'Cripes, she must have been a contortionist.'

We were both giggling like a pair of crazies. 'What the hell are we going to do with them?'

'I don't know about you, but I'm keeping these.' He began removing photographs from one of the albums.

I started on the other. 'Safford would piss in his pants if he knew he hadn't burned them all.'

'Safford! What about Mother?'

'Oh, shit, you don't actually think she knows.'

'Are you kidding? Our perfect gentleman of a father? The light of her life? She'd die if she found out.'

As I said, that was when I began to shed my innocence. Not only was our mother's word fallible but our father, that paragon of impeccable aesthetic taste, collected obscene photographs of sluts on the sly. What was worse, having discovered his secret, I was now an accessory to his betrayal of our mother's dogged delineation of his virtues. As if that didn't make me feel guilty enough, the more she embellished his memory, the more I thought she was a fool. It never occurred to me that she might have been trying to persuade herself more than anyone that Father had truly been all the things she wanted him to be.

Whatever twinges of guilt I felt didn't stop me from my own carnal enjoyment of Father's photos. When the time came to go away to boarding school, I carefully prised loose the lining of my steamer trunk, tucked them inside and glued the edges back into place. Drew, I learned, had slipped his behind the snapshots in his own photgraph album which he carried by hand on to the train.

Much of our early popularity at Exeter was ill-gotten, a direct result of peddling pornography for friendship. Even after some little prick turned us in and the pictures were confiscated, we had established a reputation for sophistication and daring that far outstripped the facts. It gave us a lot to live up to.

So far, my sexual experience had been confined to whacking off. Though I owned a packet of condoms, it was only for show. I had no notion as to how one might try to interest a girl in intercourse. Once, I remember, at a dance with some young ladies from another school, a well-developed brunette kept allowing her velvet-upholstered tits to graze my shirtfront. I waited until I was pretty sure it was deliberate. Then I led her outside to the porch for some air, under the benign surveillance of our chaperones. We made small talk for an eternity, while I tried to figure out how to approach the subject. Finally, forcing a casual air, I took the plunge. 'Say,' I inquired, 'have you tried the great experiment yet?'

'I beg your pardon?'

'You know. The limit. The big thrill.'

'Fucking?'

I nodded.

'Sure. With your brother.'

God knows what I said. I found out afterward that she'd lied, but she'd won her point. After that first clumsy endeavour, it was a while before I made another attempt at seduction.

I managed to lose my virginity the following summer, with very little effort on my part, to a girl named Rosalie Hill who boarded her horse at our stable. She was two or three years older than I was, and the word was out that she had hot pants. There were a number of popular jokes about 'climbing Rosalie Hill.' As it was, Rosalie climbed me in the high grass above the vegetable gardens. Despite my fear of being stumbled upon by Mr Yamada, it was an experience of such sublime ecstasy that I can still recall the scent of the sun-dried grass mingled with the yeasty odour of Rosalie Hill's perspiration.

I was in love. When we weren't furtively fucking, I was gently, if persistently, interrogating Rosalie, trying to discover what misfortune had turned her into a nympho. I was certain that given my understanding and devotion, she would gladly forswear her promiscuity and we'd be as happy as Joan Crawford and Doug Fairbanks, Junior.

Eventually, I guess, my implicit disapproval irritated her, because Rosalie systematically laid every last one of my friends, including my brother. I was forced to come to grips with the fact that she was hopelessly perverse. I took up smoking and wore my bitterness like the hash marks of a veteran. Finally, I even forgave Drew for fucking her. Rosalie was, admittedly, irresistible. The one thing I neglected to learn from the experience was that my brother had no loyalty to anyone other than himself. A lot of years passed before I grasped that lesson.

PART THREE

Elodie Swann

When my father died in 1920, he left me sufficiently well-off from his oil investments to indulge in a bit of speculation on my own. At the time, nearly any fool with a dollar could make a profit in real estate, and I considered myself no more of a fool than the next person. A hundred thousand people a year were moving into Los Angeles. Building permits tripled, then quadruped. Tracts with names like Longacres, Beverly Wood and Carthay Center were promoted with brass bands, stunt flying and barbecues, not to mention the requisite movie actress to cut the ribbon. Carthay Center was advertised as being only fourteen minutes from the heart of the city via subway. Nobody seemed to care that there was no subway. I jumped aboard the prosperity express with a lot of company. The bean fields I bought near Western Avenue for seventy dollars the front foot sold virtually overnight for twenty times that amount. The occasional tract lot I bought almost as a bagatelle at six hundred dollars or so went for ten times as much in six months. Overnight, fantasies were fulfilled and fortunes made. The very air seemed perfumed with money, and nothing was too good to be true. There was, however, a giddiness about the boom that heightened daily, until it bordered on hysteria. What had at first seemed wholesome optimism became an intemperate frenzy that was as repugnant to my sensibilities as public drunkenness. I knew Papa would have frowned upon my being swept up in such a rage, and I began to feel guilty that it was his money that allowed me to be a party to this festival of greed. I won't deny that I was thrilled at my success, but I began to view the furore through my father's disapproving eyes. Lucky for me, I should say, because I extricated myself in the nick, after three heady, profitable years. The bonanza dried up as quickly as it had appeared. Hopes and fortunes vanished, and I, who had entered the market as innocent as any lamb being led to slaughter, would awake in the night, moist with perspiration, from dreams in which I had failed to sell in time. The panic of those dreams was so intense that I have never since been tempted to speculate.

The urge to gamble is a tenacious thing. When the real estate boom petered out, those who had money simply turned their attentions to the stock market. Men like Victor, who were knowledgeable, were suddenly amazed to find that their brokers were handling the accounts of shoe salesmen, typesetters and postal clerks who were, thank you kindly, doing very well indeed in Wall Street. It was thought to be almost unpatriotic not to take a harmless plunge on a sure thing like General Electric or US Steel. Faith in the market was faith in our country. This is something I wanted Daphne to understand when she wrote her history of Silverwood. It is important to place events in their proper context. As it was, Victor encouraged Ada to have an occasional fling which he rendered foolproof by offering her a choice from several stocks that he knew to be safe investments. He divulged this device to me in confidence. Victor persistently – and quite misguidedly – believed that since I had made such a financial killing I was a reliable confidante in business matters. Ada would pore over the market reports and follow their progress for a month or two before making her decision. It gave her a feeling of knowing something about trading. She actually knew very little, but half the people in the market were in the same boat, and often as not the postman's guess was as good as his broker's.

At first, I wasn't fully aware of the degree to which Ada had been bitten by the bug. After Victor died, her main enthusiasm beside her home and children seemed to be The Victor Prudhomme Foundation for the Arts. Once in a while, when the subject of Wall Street came up, as it inevitably did at any social gathering, Ada would join the rest of the self-styled authorities in singing the praises of Allied Chemical or Otis Elevator. She had started smoking Chesterfields and wearing a freesia perfume, too. Victor had disliked women who smoked or wore scent.

Primarily, as I say, her professed interest was the Prudhomme Foundation which Victor had set up the year before his accident. I knew something about that, because one of Victor's lawyers, Austin Chase, was my lawyer also, and from time to time they'd discussed plans for the Foundation in my presence.

Victor not only endowed the Foundation with his entire art collection but he provided the wherewithal to generate sufficient income to allow the better part of the collection to travel continually to various museums and exhibition halls, usually in small cities that couldn't afford to attract such a splendid collection on their own. It was a very philanthropic gesture and met with great success. Victor stipulated that after the collection had been touring the country for twenty years, the Prudhomme Foundation should be terminated and all its assets turned over to the Metropolitan Museum of Art in New York City where he'd been born and raised. Victor's paintings are there now. They must have gone to the Museum in the late forties because Victor died in 1928.

He'd created a trust fund for the twins, too, I knew. It was one of those discretionary trusts, worded so that the trustees paid the beneficiaries sufficient income from the trust as they deemed appropriate for their support, maintenance and education until they reached twenty-one, when they'd receive the income monthly. Only when they reached thirty-five would Andrew and Anthony have access to the principal. Victor didn't want his sons deprived of anything, including ambition, so he thought this a sound arrangement. As he said to me, 'I don't want the boys to be slugged senseless by wealth. I can think of a few fellows I knew at Exeter who never recovered from pater's last will and testament.' I thought Victor very wise.

Ada, naturally, inherited everything that wasn't tied to the Foundation or the trust. Silverwood and its collection of antique furnishings, Victor's stock portfolio, several hundred acres of undeveloped land outside San Diego and a respectable amount of cash became Ada's when he passed on.

When Ada emerged from the prescribed period of mourning, everyone was buzzing about the Lindbergh–Morrow marriage, the newly invented Technicolor film and whether *Lady Chatterley's*

131

Lover was literature or smut. The pervasive topic, however, remained the stock market. Investing was a grand game. People discussed it endlessly, like inveterate anglers holding forth on favourite streams and lures. For the few of us who weren't in the market, I confess, the table talk could be quite tedious.

By the time Ada had given up the crepe, I realized, she'd accumulated quite an extensive portfolio. This wasn't sheer hubris on her part. Everybody had complete confidence in the market: Hadn't Evangeline Adams, the celebrated astrologer, said, 'the Dow Jones could climb to heaven'? Like all the other optimists, Ada bought on margin heavily.

If there was, that autumn, some faint seismic ripple foretelling disaster, I was oblivious of it. The Teapot Dome scandal was in the courts. Papa had been in the oil business with some of the men involved, so I was more interested in their fate than in anything else in the newspapers. When at last the whole structure of the Great Bull Market began to shudder in its death throes, I still thought the stories quite overblown. I was so used to the exaggerations of the trading crowd that headlines shrieking 'Stocks Dive' or 'Billions in Limbo' seemed to me the stuff of standard melodrama, after which everyone would clap each other on the back and pretend not to have been nervous at all, like small boys coming out of the Saturday suspense serials on to the humdrum, homely and suddenly sublime pavements. After all, if men with names like Whitney and Rockefeller continued to believe in the market, despite its reverses, how long could these problems possibly continue?

Good sportsmanship was more important then than it is nowadays. Ada even manged a wry smile when she told me she'd had to sell the San Diego land to put up more margin. I guess that was when I began to sit up and take notice. If she'd had to part with the land, that meant her cash had gone first. I offered to help tide her over, but she just thanked me and laughed it off. It was all part of the game, she said. 'Besides, I always have the emeralds for collateral.'

As time went on the laughter dwindled, and some of the best sports, born with sterling spoons, put revolvers in their mouths instead and blew their heads off. The worst had indeed happened.

The country was in ruins, financially, and people were so stunned by disbelief that they hardly knew where to begin picking up the pieces.

Regardless, the next time I saw Ada she was done up to the hilt. It was at the premiere of a movie, of all things. She was on the arm of Austin Chase, looking the picture of elegance and gaiety, despite her professed distaste for Hollywood parties. It was the opening of *Hell's Angels*, and ten blocks of Hollywood Boulevard had been roped off for the festivities, while two hundred fifty searchlights turned the night sky to silver. 'It's spectacular, isn't it?' she said to me. 'So vulgar and gorgeous. You must point out the famous faces for me. I don't know these people.' Just then a girl ducked under the police barricade and dashed up to Ada, asking for her autograph. With a look of dismay, Ada allowed Austin Chase to lead her off through the crowd. One evening not long after that, I happened to attend a dinner party at the new Guggenheim house. There on the fifty-foot wall of the drawing room was Ada's huge Flemish tapestry. I asked my hostess how on earth she'd persuaded Ada to part with it. 'My dear, Ada Prudhomme is doing over Silverwood. Haven't you heard? From top to bottom, I'm told, though I've never seen the place myself.' I rationalized that Ada couldn't be hard up, if she was redecorating Silverwood, and as she herself had said, there were always the emeralds.

I hadn't set foot inside Ada's home since Victor's death, and I'll admit I was curious as to what she was making of the place. I cut an armful of Dorothy Perkins and took them over to her. Ada grew roses herself, but for some reason my Dorothy Perkins always fared better than hers, and they were Ada's favourite. Safford came to the door and opened it slightly.

'Miss Swann?' He allowed the door to swing all the way open. 'Goodness, I could barely make you out behind that bouquet. Let me take those.'

I stepped inside. The foyer was precisely as I had last seen it, the portrait of the twins on one side, the portrait of Ada in her splendid emeralds on the other. 'Is Mrs Prudhomme at home?' I asked.

'No, ma'am. She went to attend a reception in her honour in Savannah, Georgia. She's due back by train tomorrow.'

'Then the roses will be a nice welcome. Let me show you where I want you to put them, Safford.' I started down the marble steps to the hall.

'Please, ma'am.' He came after me and reached for my arm. 'Mrs Prudhomme doesn't wish anyone in the house until she's done with her decorating.'

'Oh, come, Safford. I'm an old friend of the family, aren'tI? I'm eager to see what changes she's made. You needn't worry; I'll make allowances for its not being finished. I understand these things.' I headed for the library with Safford close behind. 'I think the flowers would look their best in that large Chinese vase on the Duncan Phyfe table. That way she'll see them from her desk.'

'Ma'am. . . .'

The room was almost bare. Not even its magnificent pair of coromandel screens remained. I glanced at Safford. He appeared to be at a loss for words. I went into the drawing room. Gone were the damask-covered camelback sofas, the Chippendale armchairs; even the ormolu clock on the mantel had disappeared. I think there were a couple of chairs under dust covers by the far windows and a needlepoint bench at the hearth. 'Mr Prudhomme must be turning in his grave,' I told Safford. 'How could she part with it all?'

'I believe Mrs Prudhomme wishes to have the house appear somewhat less formal, ma'am, to bring it up to date. That's what she indicated to me.'

'But why hasn't she replaced her furniture?'

'She's been travelling a good deal. If I may say so, ma'am, these things take time.'

'Yes, so I gather.' The vast, echoing room seemed overwhelmingly dreary. I turned and walked back down the hall. 'I suppose the Bechstein piano went, too,' I said with a nod towards the music room. I didn't bother to look inside.

'Yes'm.'

'I do wish she'd offered it to me. She knows how much I admired it.'

134

'I believe she engaged a gentleman from San Francisco to oversee disposing of the furnishings she didn't wish to keep.'

'I find it a disheartening sight. As far as I can see, the only room she's left intact is the foyer.'

'Yes, ma'am.'

'Well, I don't want to carp. I shan't tell her that I burst in and thought the place a disaster.'

Safford looked relieved. 'I'll put the roses upstairs on her dressing table.'

'Thank you, Safford.'

'You're quite welcome.' He held open the front door for me. 'If I may ask, Miss Swann, have you any Richfield stock? I only inquire because I've heard you mention that your late father was in oil.'

'Richfield? No, I haven't any. Why do you ask?'

'The stock seems to be in a tailspin. I wondered if you had any information.'

'Have you been badly stung in the market, Safford?'

'No worse than most, ma'am.'

'I'm sorry I'm no help to you. Perhaps times will take a turn for the better soon.'

After seeing Silverwood, I couldn't decide whether Ada was truly in trouble or merely being capricious. She called to thank me for the flowers and seemed in high spirits, full of her gala welcome in Savannah where she had gone to the opening of a show of early American portraits from Victor's collection. Redoing Silverwood was taking an age, she said, and she had only a few weeks at home before she had to be off to Indianapolis for an exhibit of landscapes. After that, she'd fetch the boys home from school for the summer.

She mailed me some newspaper clippings from Indianapolis, society page articles about a banquet in her honour and a rotogravure photo of the mayor presenting her with a floral spray. I learned from other people that Ada often did this. It was her way of remaining in touch with her friends although she was away from home. We kept track of where she toured for the Prudhomme Foundation and read about the festivities that greeted her everywhere she went. She was becoming quite celebrated through her championship of art. I didn't have to worry about Ada. She was something more than a survivor. She not only landed on her feet but proceeded to dance the Charleston as well. While half the Wall Street crowd were being fed at soup kitchens, Ada was still dining on filet mignon.

David Farkas

I don't believe I ever completely lost my awe of Ada Prudhomme. It would have puzzled her, perhaps even hurt her, to know that although she had extended every possible kindness to me, I remained intimidated. She and Silverwood were, in my eyes, part and parcel of each other, and behind the mortal and womanly form of Ada Prudhomme loomed a vast establishment that represented a way of life that both fascinated and frightened me. On the one hand, the Prudhommes were a living testament to the American Dream. Men could and did make fortunes, which was a proper and worthy pursuit, according to the Reverend Horatio Alger. On the other hand, my father had seen to it that I was made keenly aware that, at the same time, educated men were selling apples on street corners or standing in breadlines and boys my own age were going to bed hungry. In this light, Silverwood seemed the symbol of something hard and dangerous. On the one hand, its grandeur was straight out of the kinds of films that starred Leslie Howard or John Barrymore, movies in which smart, elegant people bantered their way through life's misfortunes and complications, never once losing their poise, their gaiety or their altruism. I was enough of an idealist to want to believe that that world might actually exist. If it existed anyplace, surely that place was Silverwood. On the other hand, I was no stranger to the magic of make-believe. I had gone with my father to enough movie studios to know that the opulent mansions on the back lots were nothing but false fronts, that the panelled interiors on the set were just plywood painted to resemble wood grain and that the grand curved staircases led only to the dusty gloom of the lighting grid overhead. Probably, if I hadn't been so ambivalent, I wouldn't have been so intrigued.

Shortly after we met Mrs Prudhomme, my father bought me a horse. In those years, I was captivated by anything western and had looked upon our move to California from New York as nothing less than a miracle with my name on it. Some of my new friends had horses, and I learned to ride western-style almost before I learned the way to school and back. I wanted more than anything to be a straight shooter like Tom Mix. I must have badgered my father unmercifully until he relented and found Gypsy, an ageing, gentle veteran of several western films. The horse was boarded at the Silverwood stables. Although the twins had gone away to school, their horses were still in the care of Brian, the groom, who ran the place. Several other people in the neighbourhood also boarded their animals there, so I was rarely at a loss for company, although often as not I chose to ride by myself, entertaining elaborate fantasies of my exploits as a rough-and-ready cowboy.

It was on one of these occasions that I first felt something more for Ada Prudhomme than the shyness her presence usually engendered in me.

I was riding Gypsy alone on the dirt road that bordered the farthest reaches of the estate, beyond the grape arbour and the garages, where, I was sure, only my vigilant mounted patrol kept horse thieves, bandits and entire gangs of desperadoes from overrunning the place. The road curved up a wide knoll and continued along its ridge, overlooking the vast vegetable gardens, until it gradually descended to the greenhouse area. Below me, I could see Mr Yamada and another gardener working in the asparagus beds, cutting the green stalks with quick, deft motions and laying them in boxes in the back of their truck. I reined in my horse, dismounted and crept quietly to the brow of the hill for a better look, in case the two were not gardeners at all but members of some robber band, Oriental Youngers or Jameses, bent on villainy. But no, even from the top of the knoll I could hear Mr Yamada going about his chores as he always did, his lips pursed, inhaling and exhaling with a tuneless whistle that sounded like the last wheezings of an expiring canary. Just then there was a noise in the underbrush to my right. I stiffened and held my breath. Who was concealed there, spying on the gardens? Could it be that some outlaw was hiding until the truck was fully loaded, when he would spring up, brandishing his weapon, and make off with the spoils like one of the Dalton boys attacking a train? There was a sudden burst of sound – squalling, scrambling, rustling – and with a flash of white, one of the ubiquitous Silverwood cats took off after something I could not see, dashing out of the bushes and down the hill. I let out a relieved sigh.

'David? Is that you?'

I whirled about, embarrassed to have been discovered at my clandestine pursuits. Mrs Prudhomme was guiding Pirate, Andrew's chestnut gelding, along the hilltop towards where I stood.

'Is everything all right? There's nothing wrong with Gypsy, is there?'

'No, ma'am. I was just giving her a rest.'

She looked down at the gardens and the two men working there. 'Thank God we sell all the sasparagus we can grow.'

'Ma'am?'

She seemed flustered. 'Well, it wouldn't be right, would it, to keep it all for ourselves, especially with the twins away at school and hardly anyone to eat it. We grow so many good things here that it's our duty to take them to market so that people without gardens can buy them for their dinner tables.'

'Yes, ma'am.' I stuck my foot into the stirrup and mounted my horse.

'Wouldn't you like to learn to ride an English seat like this one?'

I tried to disguise my aversion for such tenderfoot trappings. 'Thank you, Mrs Prudhomme, but I like a western saddle.'

'As you wish.' She looked back at the gardens. 'They're done,' she said, as Mr Yamada, noticing her, doffed his sola topi, bowed and gestured towards the truckload of asparagus.

'Very good!' she called.

He bowed again, replaced his hat and climbed into the cab of the truck with his partner.

The motor coughed and roared, and over it I heard Mrs Prudhomme cry out or exclaim something – or perhaps she only made a sharp sound that carried to my ears over the noise of the engine. I glanced at her. She was staring down at the lower road where a cloud of dust was settling in the wake of the departing truck. There was something in the road, some indistinguishable mess of red and white, clearly visible under the dwindling veil of dust.

'What is it?'

She reached over and grabbed Gypsy's halter, turning both our horses back toward the stables. 'A sack of berries. One of them must have dropped a white paper bag full of strawberries and the truck ran over it. Shall we have a canter, David? Come!'

It was the white cat. She'd lied to me – I was sure of it. What surprised me was how much I liked her for it. It wasn't simply that she had tried to shield me from something gory. That was decent of her, of course, but the fact was, I was glad to have caught her in a lie, because it meant that she was fallible and therefore somehow more approachable than I had thought.

That summer, I met the twins. I'd gone to the stables early one Saturday, and as I approached, I heard Brian's brogue at a roar, shouting to 'git the divil out o' here with them things before y' set the place afire.' Out the door ambled an identical pair of boys, each with a cigarette adroitly suspended from a corner of his lips. They were the most gorgeous young men I had ever seen. I could not have imagined any males being that beautiful without appearing effeminate, yet they were the epitome of unmistakable, self-assured masculinity. What a spectacle they made, those two – tall and lean, with hair straight and black as Indians, high foreheads and prominent brows, dark eyes, aristocratic noses, generous mouths and the firm, square jaws of the handsome smokers in the Chesterfield ads. They sized me up.

'What do you want?' one of them asked.

'I came to get my horse.'

'Who are you, anyway?'

139

'I know,' said the other. 'He's the Fark from down the hill.' He and his brother exchanged sly looks and laughed.

I must have sensed that if I didn't win their respect right then I never would. and at that moment nothing seemed quite as worthwhile as being accepted by these paragons of manhood. I stuck out my hand to the one who identified me. 'You win,' I said, faking nonchalance, 'I'm David Farkas.'

'How old are you, kid?'

'Nine.'

'You come on strong, for a little kid.'

'They all do,' said his brother. 'They come by it naturally.'

'*Chutzpah*,' I told him.

'Gesundheit.'

'What's that mean, anyhow?' the second asked me.

'It's the Jewish word for nerve.'

'All right, laddies.' Brian emerged from the stable, leading their horses. 'Be on yer way, now. And stamp out those coffin nails or I'll be tellin' yer mother, y' hear?'

One of them took the stub of his cigarette between his thumb and forefinger and flicked it expertly at Brian's feet. Brian stepped on it without comment. With a sublimely casual motion, the other twin tossed his butt into the puddle beneath the spigot on the side of the building. They swung into their saddles and were off at a brisk trot. I watched them go, straight-backed as princes leading their court across some legendary plain.

Brian spat on the dirt. 'Don't be lettin' those hellions git yer goat, Davy, or they'll never let go, mark me. They're not bad boys, y' understand, but they're used t'havin' their own way.'

He needn't have worried. Tony and Drew seemed oblivious of my presence most of the time. I expect, being much older than I, that they considered me nothing more than a pipsqueak, if they considered me at all.

Now I was torn. While part of me still wanted to fill the boots of Tom Mix, playing cowboy suddenly seemed childish. The twins were smooth, sophisticated, young men of the world. I wanted to toss off phrases like *infra dig* and *comme il faut* with the same nonchalance as the Prudhommes, although I hadn't any idea what they meant. Drew and Tony smoked and drank and

140

drove like Barney Oldfield at Daytona, although, naturally, they took pains to see that Ada was not privy to their escapades. They hinted at a profound and intimate knowledge of the female anatomy. A beautiful girl back east named Cissy Bostwick was supposedly carrying a torch for Drew, but he seemed not to care. 'She hasn't got enough sex appeal for me.'

'She pets with damn near anyone,' Tony argued.

'But not well.'

We were sitting by the swimming pool. There was a heat wave on, and Ada had telephoned Tilly, our housekeeper, to ask if I might like to use the pool. I sat on the steps at the shallow end, trying not to make a ripple. The more unobtrusive I was, I figured, the more I might learn.

'You could have dipped it in Brenda Doyle, I bet,' said Tony.

'N. O. C. D.'

I knew what that meant. One of the kids at school had told me. It meant 'Not our class, dear.'

'So what?' replied Tony. 'You aren't afraid of catching something, are you?'

'Not if it's worth it, but I wouldn't do it for Brenda Doyle. She wears cheesy cologne.'

I longed to be suave and experienced like the Prudhomme twins.

'No,' continued Drew, 'the one I have my eye on is closer to home.'

'Not Peggy Talbot. I've already invited her to the picnic next week. She's a real duzy, if you ask me.'

He shook his head. '*Chacun à son goût*. I'm after Dosie Outerbridge.'

'She's no pushover.'

'She's the second richest girl in Los Angeles.'

'How do you know?'

'I overheard somebody saying that her old man is the second richest guy in the county.'

'Who's the richest?'

'He didn't say.'

'Dosie Outerbridge is a honey of a girl, Drew, but she's not the type to be swept off her feet.'

141

'Oh no? What do you suppose would happen if I got her just a little bit ossified and then moved in for the kill?'

'How do you plan to do that? You know Safford keeps the hooch under lock and key unless Mother wants it served.'

'I know a way to get a few bottles.'

'How?'

'You want to go along?'

'It depends. Where to?'

'Up above Malibu.'

'What's all the way out there?'

Drew sat up and wrapped his arms around his knees. 'You remember my friend, Knox Fairchild?'

Tony nodded. 'The one who lives at the beach in Santa Monica.'

'Used to. They moved away. Anyhow, last summer he worked for Benny Walsh. I went with him once.'

Tony let out a low whistle. 'No fooling? What doing?'

'Just keeping an eye out, sort of. Benny would call him when he was expecting a shipment near where the Fairchilds lived. I guess he figured nobody'd question two nice-looking, polite boys who were studying astronomy.'

'Astronomy?'

'We had to have some kind of excuse for sitting on a cliff in the dark together, didn't we?'

'You could have pretended you were a couple of fairies.'

'Very funny. Well, are you with me or not? It means we get to split a case of whatever kind of booze we want.'

'You know that Mother won't let us take a car at night unless we're chauffeured. We'd have to borrow one.'

'I have an automobile,' I offered casually. My heart was in my throat.

Both twins looked startled. I guess they'd forgotten I was there. 'You?' Tony laughed.

'It's my father's, but he's on location in Phoenix. I could lend it to you, maybe.'

'You probably don't even know where the key is,' scoffed Drew.

'I do, too. I could tell Tilly a friend of my Dad's is borrowing it.'

142

Drew gazed at me. 'What do you think?' he asked his brother.

'Let me guess what the catch is.'

'I want to go with you.'

Tony sighed. 'I figured that.'

'Jeez, you're a nine-year-old child! We're talking about rumrunners!'

'I'm a nine-year-old boy with the key to a Studebaker.' I rose from the pool and went to get my towel from a lounge chair.

'Any other ideas?' Tony asked Drew.

He shook his head. 'Anyway, I'd have to get in touch with Benny Walsh to see if he could use us.'

'You really think it's worth all this just to try to get into Dosie Outerbridge's pants?'

'Listen, once I show her my style, I'll have her in the palm of my hand. She'll never say no to me. Hell, she'll marry me if I want her to.'

'Baloney. You're not even in college yet.'

'She'll wait for me, I tell you.'

'Unless, of course, in the meantime you're lucky enough to make the acquaintance of the *first* richest girl in Los Angeles County.'

Drew laughed. 'Hey, kid,' he called to me as I collected my things, 'we'll let you know if we can use you.'

That night, there was only a sliver of moon visible now and then between the clouds. I swallowed hard as I slid into the back seat of my father's car and handed the key to Drew. My mouth felt dry. My stomach seemed to be located right below my Adam's apple.

Drew started the motor and we slid out of the garage and down the driveway before he turned on the headlights. I looked back at the open window of my bedroom. God forbid Tilly should wake in the night and discover my absence. Tilly and my father trusted me, and here I was sneaking away in the car like a thief. I tried to persuade myself that what we were doing wasn't exactly *wrong*, just a little racy.

'Step on it,' Tony told Drew. 'It's almost ten, and it'll take us over an hour to get there.'

'He needs us in position from twelve to two.'

I peered out the window. The dark trees were loosely wrapped in a fine mist. 'What are we going to say if the police find us?'

'*You* are going to say nothing.' Tony raised a large red can from his lap. 'Anybody asks, we ran out of gas on our way home from a beach party, and I'm just back from walking to find enough to get us to the next filling station.'

'They'd want to know if they could notify our parents that we were all right.' I was proud of myself for thinking of that.

'I telephoned home when I got the gas. They're not worried.'

I kept quiet most of the rest of the way. After we passed Malibu, the road climbed slightly. To the right, I could discern the shadows of the mountains. On the other side, below the brushy cliffs, lay the ocean. We drove for what seemed like a very long time. Few cars were on the road.

'Keep your eyes peeled,' Drew said. 'It's the second unmarked dirt road on the left past a wagon wheel on the right that says "Strickland Ranch."'

'Go slow,' Tony told him. 'It's hard to see much of anything out there.'

We found the place and turned in. 'What now?' Tony asked.

'A quarter-mile ahead there's an open grassy meadow on the right. It's at the top of a sixty-foot cliff, so don't take any walks. We're to pull off and stay there.'

'That's it?'

'Unless the police or federal agents come along. If that happens, we turn on the headlights. That's the signal.'

Despite my guilt and fear, my spirits were exalted. I had never done anything so daring. And to be treated by Drew and Tony as almost their equal was an honour so heady that I all but ignored my discomfort as the night grew colder.

'Hey, kid, your teeth are chattering. Take this.' Tony tossed me the plaid throw my father kept in the car.

I wrapped it around me like an Indian chief. The three of us looked out at the sea below the black, irregular rim of the cliff. We could hardly make out the phosphorescent signature of the breaker line. Just beyond it lay a thick bank of fog, billowing silently like the white, windfilled sails of some ghostly armada. The only sound was the rhythmic rumble of the surf.

144

Tony jabbed Drew with his elbow. 'Well?' he said.

'Yeah, yeah. Say, kid – Dave – you warm enough now?'

I nodded. 'Thanks.'

'Tell me something about your old man, then.'

'Like what?'

'Like, for instance,' Tony said, 'is he divorced or separated or what?'

'My mother died. My father's a widower.'

'How many times has he been married?' inquired Drew.

'What?'

'How many wives has he had?'

'My mother, that's how many. What did you think, for pete's sake?'

'Take it easy,' Tony said. 'Where did you live back east?'

'New York.'

'Where in New York?' demanded Drew.

'Roslyn, Long Island.'

Tony and Drew exchanged glances. 'Not bad,' allowed Drew.

'Why are you asking me all these questions, anyhow?'

'Research,' replied Tony.

'And I wouldn't mention our asking them, if I were you,' Drew told me pointedly. 'Unless you wanted the world to know you'd given us the keys to your father's car. By the way, how'd your father make his money?'

'He's a writer. He writes movie scripts.' I was trying to figure out why the Prudhommes had set me up like this. Why had they put me on the spot to ask me a bunch of stuff about my father under the seal of secrecy?

'Jeez!' whispered Tony. 'Will you look?'

At first I could scarcely see what he was pointing at. Then, as I stared hard into the darkness, I made out the long, pale shape of a boat pulling through the churning combers of the breaker line.

'The tide has to be high,' said Drew, 'otherwise they can't get the booze close enough to shore to be picked up.'

There were more – two, then three, then still more behind those.

'Lobster dories.'

I watched in wonder. I could see the lobstermen now, nearing the beach, their gunwales perilously close to the water, their boats laden with packing cases. 'Where did they get the stuff?' I wanted to know.

'A cargo ship,' Tony explained. 'It's out there in the fog.'

There was movement on the sand beneath the cliff. Out of the shadows came several men, running to the water's edge to help drag the boats in. 'Where did they come from?' I asked Drew.

He shrugged. 'Go take a look, but don't go too near the edge.'

Tony went with me. As we lay on our bellies on the chilly, moist grass, the figures below unloaded the boats one by one, forming a chain of men to pass the heavy cases up the beach from the shore to the base of the bluff where they disappeared from our view.

'David?'

'Yeah?'

'Does your father go out with a whole lot of women?'

'Listen,' I whispered angrily, 'how come you're giving me the third degree like this?'

'All I meant was, does he play the field? Is he one of those Hollywood movie types that strings the dames along or is he the sincere kind?'

'How would I know? Do you think he'd tell me things like that?' This whole adventure was beginning to sour. I felt like I was a patsy, but I didn't understand why. Tony and I watched in silence for a long time until the last boat had been relieved of its cargo. Tony smothered a yawn and stood up.

'Evening, boys.' A harsh, metallic snap followed the words.

I scrambled to my feet. About two yards away stood a large man in dark clothing and tall rubber boots. He held a Winchester rifle aimed steadily in our direction.

'Benny sent us,' Tony said quickly.

'What's your name then?'

'Prudhomme.'

'Right.' He lowered the rifle. 'It won't be long now.' He turned at the sound of a motor starting up. It was an old chain drive, a Reo, I guessed.

Slowly, from the bottom of the cliff, up a tortuous, uneven

trail, lumbered half a dozen trucks, their loads carefully concealed under canvas covers. The man with the Winchester waved them past.

'Go get yourselves some branches with plenty of leaves and brush away those tracks. Start by the beach and work your way up.'

Below, the lobstermen were securing their dories to chains embedded in the rocky wall of the cliff. They tied down tarps over their boats and, without exchanging a word, walked off down the sand and were gulped into the night. By the time Tony and I had made it to the top of the trail, not even the man with the rifle remained. Drew opened the car door and gestured towards the back seat. 'Hop in, kid. Just shove the Seagram's over.'

As we reached the highway, Tony turned around, pulled himself to his knees and leaned into the back seat. 'Come on, kid. Give me a hand opening this case.'

I'd had whisky before, a taste of my father's highball or the diluted remains in the glasses of guests gone in to dinner, but I wasn't prepared for the jolt of a swig of straight Seagram's. I tried not to choke. My eyes teared up. I gasped for breath, feeling the liquor travel down my gullet and into my stomach.

'Easy does it. That stuff's the real McCoy.' Drew reached over and took the bottle. He helped himself to another swallow and gave it to Tony.

'Easy does it yourself,' Tony told him. 'It'd be a helluva note if we got stopped for drunk driving.'

'M. Y. O. B. I can handle myself.'

I felt warm and relaxed for the first time in hours. It was the whisky, I knew. I took it gladly when Tony handed it back to me.

'David,' Drew began, 'about your father – '

'Ah, lay off,' Tony told him. 'He doesn't know any more than we do.' He reached for the bottle and took another swig.

'How're y'doin' back there?' Drew inquired sometime later.

'All right,' I murmured.

'You didn't ask *me*,' said Tony.

'How're y'doin', brother?'

147

'I am,' he announced, ' a wee bit spifflicated. Hey, kid, you want any more of this?'

'Better not,' Drew said.

'Only a little.' My voice sounded kind of funny. There was a ringing in my ears, and I felt a little dizzy. I took a deep breath.

Tony turned to look at me. 'Jeez, kid, you look awful. You're not going to upchuck, are you?'

I shook my head. That was the last thing I remembered.

When I woke, I was in a strange bedroom with pink wallpaper and cretonne curtains at the open windows. I felt poisoned and halfway dead. My head throbbed and I was desperately thirsty. The daylight hurt my eyes. All I could see was the bed and a dresser. There was no other furniture. Two pale rectangles on the wallpaper marked where a pair of pictures had once hung. The room was hot and my sheets were damp with perspiration. I pushed them off me. I wore only my underdrawers. I wondered what had happened to my clothes.

'You're awake. Good.'

I was mortified. Ada Prudhomme stood in the doorway. I grabbed the sheets and quickly covered myself.

She set down a breakfast tray on the dresser. The odour of the food nauseated me.

'I trust you've learned a lesson.'

I nodded. My throat felt too dry to speak.

'I telephoned your father and Tilly. You'll have to answer to them for this.'

'Yes, ma'am,' I whispered.

'It was a stupid, stupid thing to do, not to mention illegal and unsafe. I blame the twins for getting you involved. You're only a child, after all.'

I felt worse than ever.

'Yet the car, as I understand it, was your idea.'

'Yes'm.'

She shook her head. 'I had always thought your father was lucky to have such a good son. I cannot imagine why you would betray his trust for some idiotic lark that could have put you in real danger. Have you no judgement? Don't you care for your father's feelings?'

She was right. Miserable, I tried to blink back the tears.

'It's too late to cry, David. You should have thought of the possible consequences earlier. There, now.' She handed me a fragrant cambric handkerchief embroidered with her initials. Her scent on it was like a balm. I blotted my face and gave it back to her.

'I have dealt with Drew and Tony. Their horses will be sold as punishment. At least they had the decency to bring you here, instead of frightening Tilly out of her wits.'

I wondered morosely if they would hold it against me for getting them in Dutch. If they hadn't had to deal with my passing out on them, the whole escapade might have gone unnoticed.

They didn't, though. Neither one of them spoke about the fiasco, and while they didn't have much to do with me for the rest of their vacation, they didn't make a point of avoiding me, either. My relationship with the Prudhomme twins was one of those puzzles that I was sure only confused me because I wasn't an adult. It wasn't until after they had gone back east that I began to get a glimpse of why they had set me up that night to squeeze me for information.

I came down with measles shortly after school began in the fall. I didn't feel so terrible, but I was stuck in bed, contagious and bored, with my father away in New York on business and only Tilly for occasional company. I can remember lying there in the late afternoon, more than a little sorry for myself, lonesome for my friends who were out playing tennis or touch football or riding in the hills after school. Another day had passed by, leaving only a quiet, dusky vacuum in which some few restless birds still cried out fitfully, their sounds growing fewer and fewer. The scent of the eucalyptus outside my window was suddenly made more pungent by the evening damp. It was a time of day that filled me with melancholy and still does.

I heard a tap at the open door to my room and glanced up. There stood Ada Prudhomme with an armload of books.

'May I come in?'

I drew my bathrobe around me and smoothed the bedcovers. 'Yes'm. Would you like to sit down?'

She drew my desk chair to the bedside. 'I expect you must feel

149

like a prisoner, all alone here in your room. I thought you might enjoy some of the twins' books. I brought some Mark Twain and some Jules Verne. Would you like me to read to you for a bit?'

I was astonished that she had even known I was ill. 'Yes, ma'am. Are you sure you want to?'

'I always feel rather forlorn right after the boys leave for Exeter. I thought we might keep each other company until you're better.'

Each morning and each afternoon for nearly a week, she returned. I would lie there, my eyes half shut, inhaling her perfume, listening to her as she read. Despite my indisposition, I was as close to rapture as most small boys can get, to think that this tall, golden, sweet-scented goddess would lavish her attention upon me.

The day after I returned to school, recovered, my father arrived home. Once again the house was filled with the comforting aroma of the Latakia that emanated from the study where he typed at his trusty Royal, a pipe clamped between his teeth.

My father kept an office at the studio, but he preferred to work at home when he could. He loved his work but not the kind of dog-eat-dog competition that sometimes went on at the studios or at Hollywood parties. Once or twice a week he went out to play poker, but only rarely did he attend any of the gala events for which the film colony was famous. That was why I was surprised when he told me he was escorting Mrs Prudhomme to a charity ball. They struck me as being as mismatched a couple as anyone might imagine. It was one thing for Ada Prudhomme to keep me neighbourly company and another for her to be waltzed about by my father. She was not his type. The women in our family were all brunettes. Anyhow, what could be more incongruous than Ada W. Prudhomme (I remembered her initial from her handkerchief), that elegant *shiksa*, born with a silver spoon in her mouth, on the arm of Sam L. Farkas, born Shmuel, son of Yussel and Chana Farkas, immigrants both. Not that I wasn't proud of our family, but it sure wasn't your Social Register crowd.

My father had been the only boy-child in a family with three daughters. This meant he received all the educating. It was thought that he'd be a professional man, a professor of English

150

maybe. In such sons were vested the hopes and responsibilities for the future of the clan. His older sister, Ruth, married a rabbi at the age of seventeen and died only last year. The two younger girls went to work to help support their parents and put their brother through college. Jenny, who was fourteen, got a job packing blouses with a clothing manufacturer. Molly, at twelve, joined her there, snipping loose threads from the finished garments. The place where they were employed was at Greene Street and Washington Place in Manhattan, close enough for them to walk to work. It employed well over a hundred girls. The doors were locked when they came to work at seven-thirty in the morning and opened at eight or nine that night to let them go. For this, they made a dollar and fifty cents a week, no overtime, no conversation please and no singing on the job.

One Saturday when my father was in his senior year of college, only a few months from graduating and still living at home, he came back to the apartment to find the door wide open and his mother, my grandmother, gone. His father, he knew, would be spending the day at Ruth's as he always did after temple, discussing religion with his son-in-law, the rabbi. His mother, a neighbour called to him, had gone to the fire on Greene Street.

What he remembered from that day was not the tumult of the firemen, horses and equipment, nor was it the terrible stench nor the horrified crowd. What he remembered were the charred bundles that he took for rags on the pavement, until he saw a policeman turn one over with his boot, exposing a blackened human face.

Of the hundred and forty-six girls who died in the Triangle Shirtwaist Company fire, two were my young aunts, Jenny and Molly. They were found together, among a pile of bodies wedged against a locked emergency exit.

After that, nothing was the same. My grandfather decided it was God's punishment for his allowing his daughters to work on *Shabbes*. He withdrew to studying the Torah and the Talmud and seemed, my father said, like a man sleepwalking. My grandmother wasn't herself anymore, either. She came down with a series of ailments that gradually debilitated and destroyed her. My father, who had hoped to earn his doctorate in English, set his ambitions aside to care for his parents. He found work writing scenarios for the Vitagraph Studios in Flatbush. My grandfather was dismayed. Moving pictures were nothing but a fad; no matter what, my father must become a professor. Had his sisters been killed for nothing? My grandfather passed away before my father could share his success with him.

In his own way, my father repaid his debt to Jenny and Molly as best he could. The labour movement, in his eyes, was a holy cause. He wrote tracts for the International Ladies' Garment Workers Union. He wrote films that documented the plight of the labourer at the hands of an unfeeling management. Later, he helped organize the Writers' Guild of America. One of the first rules of behaviour I learned as a toddler was never, never to cross a picket line. Never mind that my father, in later life, wore silk shirts and custom suits; there wasn't a film that came out of his typewriter or bore his name as producer that didn't carry his message of compassion for the average guy pitted against the big shots.

After my mother died, we moved to California. The work was there, my father told me, and it was a healthy place for kids. Privately, I guessed he wanted to start over someplace, leaving his grief behind, because after a while he said, 'There's just as many sick here as back east. The difference is they're all so suntanned a person can't tell.'

He had a difficult time negotiating with Mrs Prudhomme's lawyers to buy the piece of land she was selling at the bottom of her drive. It was pretty clear that they didn't want to sell to a Jew. My father heard they were going to let it go, for less than he'd offered, to an insurance man named O'Rourke. He raised hell about that. They said that Mrs Prudhomme didn't like the idea of the movie crowd's loud parties so close by. My father corralled a bushel of character references, including one from a priest who'd been a technical adviser on one of his pictures, and promised the lawyers they'd never hear the end of it if he didn't get that land. He got it, of course, but they made him pay her full asking price, which, for those days, was well above the market value.

That was why, despite the courtesies that passed between our two households, I had continued to think of my father and Mrs Prudhomme as being polite adversaries. Now it seemed they had mended their fences when I wasn't looking. Not that I could picture either my father or Mrs Prudhomme casting sheep's eyes at anyone. Anyhow, the stately Mrs Prudhomme was my friend, not my father's. She had tried to spare my feelings when the white cat was killed. When I'd got into mischief with the twins, she'd opened the doors of her castle, taken me in and cared for me herself. She'd even descended from her hill to visit me when I was ill. Hadn't she confided in me? She'd said something about wishing Drew and Tony wrote home more often. Then she'd said, 'But I've never actually been terribly close to the twins. Isn't that queer? There was never much room for me in their lives. They had each other.' I thought she sounded sad.

I wasn't sure why the pairing of my father and Ada made me uneasy, except that they obviously had almost nothing in common. The image of my father whirling about on a dance floor with Mrs Prudhomme in his arms was, to me, inappropriate, if not ludicrous. I was clearly my father's son in that I didn't want my old man to be the laughingstock of the upper crust. To be wholly truthful, too, I didn't want to think that Ada Prudhomme would lay him open to ridicule like that. In my mind, she was a little like the Almighty; I stood in awe of her, yet I wanted like crazy to have my faith in her justified.

Within a few months, it had become clear to me that her deeper feelings were for my father, not me. I was incredulous. He was a wonderful father, sure, but what could *she* possibly see in him? Nobody seemed to care how I felt about this alliance. She'd come sailing into our lives, exuding charm from every pore, capturing my halting admiration, and now she had enthralled my father. I didn't know which of them was the more disloyal, though I held my father less culpable. After all, Ada Prudhomme was pretty strong stuff. It was a while before I forgave them for being only human.

Drew Prudhomme

In the months following my father's death, it was Safford, our butler, who became for me the man of the house. As a small boy, I had imagined Silverwood a great ship with my father its captain. Safford was the first mate. Now it was he who'd taken the helm and who kept the place gliding smoothly before the wind, on an even keel. I admired the calm, deft way Safford ran things. I was a willing member of his crew. 'Master Andrew,' he might say, 'chewing gum is not appropriate for a young gentleman.' I would swallow my gum and damn near salute. Safford's criticisms consisted of variations on the theme of 'Appropriate.' With that one word, he kept my brother and me in line. It's not surprising that Safford's sangfroid made him a hero in my eyes. Even my father, suave as he was, had been more flappable than Safford. Now that Father was gone, the stability of Silverwood and our family lay vested with him.

One hot summer day, I came into the house, padding barefoot along the cool, marble floor of the hallway, to swipe some cookies from the pantry to take back to the pool where Tony and I were swimming with friends. I could hear quiet voices. I didn't know from where. With the house nearly empty of furniture, sounds bounced eerily from every surface. As I passed the half-open door of the music room, I heard Mother say, 'I'm sorry you fared so badly with your Richfield stock. I feel it's my fault. It was I who recommended it to you.'

'Not at all, ma'm.' Safford's voice replied. 'The decision to buy it was my own.'

'Still, I had no business giving gratuitous advice.'

'If I may say so, you might one day recommend that I go fly a kite, but. . . .'

154

'Would you?' Mother sounded as if she was smiling now.

'No, ma'am. I would not.'

I stood there, outside the door. I had never before considered that Safford might have funds of his own, investments of his own, interests of his own or, for that matter, any life at all except our life.

'I am not unaware,' Mother went on, 'that I owe you almost six months' salary.'

'Yes'm.'

'You do realize that if it were possible. . . .'

'Certainly.'

'Safford, I shall understand completely if you feel you cannot afford to remain at Silverwood. You need only give me sufficient notice.'

'For the time being, ma'am, I shall stay.'

'Of course, the moment things ease up a bit I'll make it up to you, to the penny.'

'I understand quite well, Mrs Prudhomme.'

'If worse comes to worse, I shall take the jewels out of the vault and pawn them.'

'Your emeralds. . . .'

'They're virtually all I have left. If I have to sacrifice them to keep Silverwood. . . .'

I didn't wait to hear the rest of it. At a dash, I fled down the hall towards the pantry and seized as many cookies as both my hands could hold.

I didn't tell my brother what I'd overheard. I'd always looked on Tony as being more vulnerable than I. I made a point of trying to protect him, not that I ever saw any evidence of gratitude on his part.

From that time on, I had nightmares and by the time I returned to Exeter I'd developed a spastic colon. My brother was preoccupied with fantasies of hookers in Scollay Square, while I was sick with anxiety over the likelihood of my mother and the two of us penniless, homeless and consequently friendless. My grades fell. I didn't dare explain to Mother when she asked why.

It must have been about then, while we were away at Exeter, that Sam Farkas made his move. My brother and I stayed away

155

that whole school year. We spent vacations with Aunt Bibi and twice were joined by Mother when she came east for exhibitions of Father's collection.

When we returned to Silverwood the following summer, the place looked more livable. It was only sparsely furnished, but it was obvious that things had improved. For the first time in nearly a year, I slept well and my stomach stopped acting up. In retrospect, though, I'd have to say that those ten months made me goddamned certain that if I had anything to do with it, I'd never again be put in the position of having to worry about money. I was smart enough to realize that this would require some compromises on my part. What I failed to see was that my mother had already made a bargain of her own in order to save Silverwood for my brother and me. Looking back, the irony is enough to make you wince.

Mother and Sam were an item, as they say. Most everywhere Mother went, he went too. She opened doors for Sam that otherwise would have remained firmly closed. My brother and I were of an age that made much of sex. It was never far from our adolescent minds. The thought of our mother having sex with anyone, much less someone like Sam Farkas, was, nonetheless, appalling. I was already aware, though, that sex, like everything else, could be a negotiable commodity.

My brother Tony's ambitions were limited to his own amusement. He was always trying to wangle an advance on his allowance or coming to me to borrow ten bucks so he could show some little skirt a good time. When he flunked out of college, he owed half the guys we knew. I loaned him the dough to square things so Mother wouldn't find out. He had some grandiose vision of developing a system to beat the roulette wheel. So instead of getting a job, this prince of velleity spent all his time playing the tables and chasing tail. Mother finally put her foot down. Sam found work for him at the studio. Naturally, Tony went wild jumping on every little starlet and secretary he could corner. For a while he was even screwing some waitress from the commissary, some Greasy Gracie who could scarcely wrap her tongue around the king's English. My brother, for chrissakes, would fuck a coatrack.

156

In spite of everything, I doubt the poor sonofabitch ever knew what it was to be really in love with a girl. He was always looking over her shoulder for the next conquest. Not me. I knew what I wanted, went after it and wouldn't take no for an answer.

Dosie, bless her soul, was the perkiest girl in our crowd. Christ, but she was full of beans. She had a cute, round face, a turned-up nose and skin as pale and smooth as milk. When she was amused, she broke into a peculiar, downturned smile that made it look as if she were apologizing for enjoying herself. Her eyes had that slightly myopic look of well-bred girls who know that the farther things are from the centre of their world the less likely they are to be of much consequence to them. One incident, early in our romance, still stands out in my memory. We had gone out to dine with her parents. At the restaurant, the doorman let Dosie out of the back seat and then reached inside to help her mother out of the car. Dosie skedaddled ahead in that bouncy way of hers. I was some distance behind her. She was trotting straight towards the door of the restaurant with nobody there to open it. I made a dash for it, but just as she reached the door, at the precise moment she would have lifted her foot over the threshold, it was opened from the inside by a couple on their way out, and she went in without a millimetre's variation in her stride. What impressed me was that it never occurred to her that the door would not open for her when she expected it. She was a girl for whom doors opened automatically. I knew then and there she was first-rate.

Girls like Dosie are born with certain prerogatives and they know it. With her mother, Dorcas, it was the privilege of always arriving last, like royalty. With Dosie, it was losing personal articles. She mislaid gloves in restaurants, umbrellas in taxis, compacts in the theatre. 'Oh, Drew,' she'd say, 'I've gone and done the daffiest thing. . . .' And when you had crawled on a dusty floor, between the feet of irritated strangers, to find her fallen earring in some dingy nightclub, you knew you had paid her the kind of homage she understood.

I don't want to make it sound like she was one of these dames who makes a guy jump through hoops for her. She made you feel like protecting her. She expected men to be strong and dependable, like Hale, her father. It would have broken her heart if her daddy had ever failed her. Dosie was a tender soul. She trusted men to run things capably and keep her little world from harm.

Hale Hunt Outerbridge was the toughest gent I ever knew, and I looked up to him as I would have to my own father. Hale had a physique like a tank and damned if he didn't give the impression that shrapnel would bounce off him. Like most powerful men, he moved deliberately and without haste. He was an independent cuss. It was his nature to be objective and impartial. His detachment led some people to call him cold. I remember his eyes as being slate-coloured. He would fix you with this rather opaque gaze and you'd wonder if he'd heard anything you'd said. Then, without mincing words, he would come back at you, stripping the excess from your argument and seizing the essentials. 'Don't feed me the entire effing smorgasbord, fella,' he'd say, 'just give me the meat and potatoes.'

God only knows how he put up with Dorcas, but whatever she wanted, Hale gave her. Her clothing bills alone would have financed a revolution. She had only to admire an automobile, a hunk of jewellery or a fur coat and it was hers. Hale spoiled her unmercifully.

Dorcas was still a beautiful woman when I met Dosie, but already she'd developed the habit of collecting injustices, real or imagined. With little or no provocation, she would trot them out to be examined, noting each minute detail of their construction, like an art historian sharing his appreciation of some treasured piece.

Dosie and Hale managed to overlook her weakness for the bottle. The way they acted, you'd have thought Dorcas was a prize package. They handled her with kid gloves. If you ask me, she could have used a swift kick in the ass, but the most she ever got was a whispered, 'Mummy dear, please, you *promised*. . . .' Half the time it was Dosie who was the maternal one.

My wife was the sweetest little mother you ever saw. Christ, but she adored the kids. The only thing she never could do was lay a hand on them. She was incapable of hurting anyone. She was as close to a goddamned saint as anyone I ever met. She never said a mean word about a living soul, and when someone else did, she'd look at him in that nearsighted way of hers, as if she didn't want to examine the remark too closely, and ask, 'Are you being wicked?'

How the devil, I mean seriously, how in hell could you find fault with someone like that, even if she wasn't perfect? Nobody's perfect. Dosie was conservative, if you know what I mean. She wasn't the sophisticated swinger type. That was part of her charm. I wouldn't have changed her for the world. 'Maybe I'm just goofy, honey,' she would say with that apologetic, upside-down smile, 'but that stuff isn't very attractive to me. It's a little sordid for my tastes. We're not animals, after all.' She liked the lights turned out. I guess you could say she had delicate sensibilities. She set great store on decency. God knows, I wouldn't have wanted my children to have any other kind of woman for their mother.

Men are different. Men are hunters and explorers by nature. We want to push things to the limit, break the sound barrier, sometimes only for the hell of it. It's got nothing to do with loving your wife and kids. That's just the way we are. It's no bed of roses. There are hundreds of dames out there, wiggling their cute little asses, and it takes a helluva lot of intestinal fortitude not to react. It's a matter of self-discipline. But, to repeat, nobody's perfect. We all make mistakes.

Tony Prudhomme

The summer after my second year at Exeter was a strange time. My mother had written us at school, saying she was redecorating the house and we'd have to be patient if it wasn't finished before we came home for summer vacation. If I'm not mistaken, it was more like two years before it was fully furnished again. Meanwhile, our house was stark, hollow and unremittingly bleak. Even the summer sun slanting across the bare floors served only to illuminate the depressing emptiness of the place. I had not realized, until then, how much I had appreciated the antiques my father had amassed. Now it was too late. Even my parents' matched pair of canopied French beds had been dismantled and spirited to San Francisco to be sold. My mother slept on a mattress on the floor. Drew and I lived out of our trunks. The bureau in my room and the armoire in his were gone. The only room left intact was the foyer. No visitors were allowed to venture further. We greeted our guests there, but that was all they were permitted to glimpse of the house. We were encouraged to have picnics by the pool or the tennis court by way of entertaining. The weather that summer must have been much like any other summer, but in my memory it remains uncomfortably cool.

Given my mother's penchant for putting a fine face on things, I was uneasy. Some of the boys Drew and I had known at Exeter had not returned the previous year. Not much was said, but everyone knew what had happened: The market crash had brought their families down. The tuition was beyond their means. I wondered if Mother was as well-off as she acted. I lay awake nights, trying to think of some way to approach the subject subtly, but I couldn't think of one.

'Are we broke?'

My mother started visibly. 'Where did you hear that?'

'I didn't. I just wondered.' We were in her dressing room. Mother was cleaning out her closets. Her personal maid, Stella, had departed along with the furniture.

'Don't you dare even *say* such a thing!'

'It was only a question.'

'That's how rumours get started.'

'We could stay home and go to state school this fall.'

'Absolutely not. Your tuition is already partly paid.'

'I thought maybe we didn't have enough money.'

She turned to look at me. 'Oh, Tony, darling! You mustn't worry!' She put an arm around my shoulders. The scent of her perfume mingled with the tang of the cedar-lined closets. 'Honestly. Your father has provided very well for you boys.'

'But the house is nearly empty, and over half the servants are gone.'

'What would I do with a big staff, now that you're away at school most of the year? They'd be at loose ends with only me to wait on, and they'd probably get into mischief as a result. As for the house, I'll have it redecorated before long.'

'Everybody says times are bad.'

'Are you having such a hard time of it?'

I shook my head.

'My word! If I believed everything people said!' She shook her head, smiling. 'Let me tell you a story: When I married your father, a rumour spread that he was marrying a seamstress he'd got in the family way. Imagine! And I can barely sew a stitch, not to mention that the rest of it was just as absurd. The truth of it was that your grandfather Willson's will was being contested by some business associates, and his estate was tied up. In the meantime, I was helping out a family friend who had a smart shop. I was managing her business affairs. But imagine me a seamstress! Unbelievable! So you must take hearsay *cum grano salis*, my dear.'

Only my mother would have tried to dismiss the Great Depression as hearsay.

I hadn't mentioned my concern to Drew, but I wasn't surprised when he brought it up. It was typical of our thoughts to run a similar course. It was also typical of him to approach the subject from his own angle.

'Mother, would you say we were wealthy?'

'That's a distasteful word, wealthy.' She closed her eyes briefly as if its unpleasantness were visible. 'It's used by the same sort of people who refer to draperies as "drapes." Either say "comfortably off" or, if you must, "rich."'

'Are we rich then?'

'Comfortably off.'

'You know Ted Thayer, the boy who's captain of our football team?'

'I believe you pointed him out to me when I visited.'

'I got a letter yesterday from someone who lives on Cape Cod in the summer, next to the Thayers. He said Ted's father has gone flat bust. Mr Thayer tried to kill himself in his automobile so the family could collect the insurance. Except before he could do it, the police arrested him for driving drunk.'

'Poor man,' she murmured.

'That couldn't happen to us, could it? Could we go flat bust?'

'Perish the thought! You children will never want for money, thank heavens. Your father saw to that. Besides,' she leaned forward and whispered confidentially, 'there are always the emeralds.'

'Would you have to sell them if things got bad?' I asked.

'I wouldn't dream of parting with them! I'd use them as collateral for a loan. Of course,' she said, dismissing that eventuality with a curt wave, 'Hades would likely freeze over before it came to that.'

'How much do you think they're worth?' Drew wanted to know.

'I wouldn't have the slightest idea. Hundreds upon hundreds of thousands, I suppose.'

'Where do emeralds come from?' I asked.

'Mine came from South America, Colombia to be precise. They belonged to a Spanish noblewoman at one time. Your father bought them through a dealer in London when we were staying with the Lambtons. He had them reset according to his own design.'

'How come you don't wear them?'

'Oh, I don't know. It's an effort to get them from the safety deposit box. Besides, I haven't been dressing up much since your father died.'

'Still,' I said, 'I'll bet you're glad you have them. Just in case.'

She looked from me to Drew. 'Boys,' she told us, 'this concern with finances must be put to rest once and for all. It's a dreadful thing for a child to be anxious about money.'

'When you were young, didn't you ever wonder if there was enough?'

'What a question! Do you think my mother and father would have allowed me to be unnecessarily upset? We were very

162

comfortable.' She thought for a moment. 'I do know, though, of some little children not as fortunate as I who lay in bed scared and sick-feeling because they weren't even certain they'd have clothes for school. Or shoes. Not even a pair of good shoes to walk to school. And how the other children would tease if your feet were poking through at the toes.' Her eyes looked beyond us, gazing into the past. 'Children like that never know a moment's peace, even in good times. The boom can always fall out of things. That's what they remember.'

I could hear Safford winding the grandfather clock in the foyer. The rhythmic, metallic chirring of the cables sounded somehow reassuring. Time ticked its appointed way around the clock. Safford went methodically about his duties as usual. Everything was in order.

'So!' Mother sprang out of her chair. 'We shan't ever speak of this gloomy subject again. Come along. I'm taking you two to C. C. Brown's for ice cream sundaes. We'll put the top down on the Chrysler and pretend we're the Romanian royal family on a tour.'

'I'll be king,' announced Drew.

'They just deposed him,' I said smugly.

'You see?' he told Mother. 'It even happens to kings.'

It wasn't long afterward that my mother sold the Chrysler for a Chevrolet, but I took her word that it wasn't for reasons of economy. Since my father had died, Mother had discovered, among other things, that she enjoyed driving. She had dismissed our chauffeur and tooled merrily about as though her car was a favourite toy. For as long as she lived, she persisted in calling the accelerator the 'exhilarator.'

Mother was spreading her wings in other ways, too. Wherever Father's collection travelled, Mother went as an honoured guest. She managed to make it plain to the directors of each of the host museums that the presence of the collection in their city would be enhanced by having a real live Prudhomme in their midst. Her letters to them were worded in such a way they could scarcely afford to turn her down, lest she use her clout with the trustees to cancel the exhibition. Consequently, she would receive a ticket to Rochester or Charlottesville or wherever, be put up in the home of someone on the museum's board and reign as the toast of local society at the opening festivities. She was not above clipping the newspaper accounts of these events and posting them to the *Los Angeles Times* where they received respectful acknowledgement. It was her way, she insisted, of seeing that Father's philanthropy never faded from the public's memory.

'They must be made to understand what a splendid man he was! I want them to know how much it meant to your father to give them a collection like this. How, year after year, he searched out and negotiated for the best. These things didn't drop into his lap! People must grasp the magnitude of his gift. They must understand how much of his very heart and soul he put into it. I want him to come alive for them! It's my function, you see, to make sure they fully appreciate your father's generosity.'

It was a nice speech, but I know now that my mother was not wholly motivated by love, loyalty or altruism. As long as she assiduously burnished Father's image to a high gloss, she basked in that lustre herself.

Her postcards and clippings reached us at school. We would get a scenic view of Springfield with a few hasty words on the back or an envelope full of items from the Portland papers, morning and evening, occasionally including a photograph. In her newspaper pictures, Mother invariably looked the part of the great lady whom *noblesse* obliged to modestly endure the social spotlight. It was a swell act.

Meanwhile, the house remained empty for another summer while she trouped about the country with the Prudhomme exhibits. I don't know exactly when it began to dawn on us that Mother had manoeuvred herself into a position of celebrity. When Father was alive, his personality had eclipsed our mother's. Now that she was a solo, she obviously enjoyed every minute of it. I guess her fame scared Drew and me a little. We were jealous, perhaps. Anyhow, we got a little bent out of shape, as they say nowadays, and we began to turn into real hell-raisers. Maybe we thought it was the only way we could get her attention. By this time, the house had been empty for three summer vacations. I dreaded returning to its echoing rooms. I hated not being allowed to let friends beyond the foyer. Drew must have felt the same way.

I don't know whether it was resentment or what that turned us into incipient delinquents. We stole a carton of Luckies from the drugstore and got pinched. After we squared accounts and got a lecture from the cops, we were sent home with a warning. We climbed a fence on to the back lot of M-G-M, tipped over a warehouseful of detached staircases, inadvertently started a brushfire and barely escaped being caught. Then we got mixed up with bootleggers because Drew wanted to get Dosie Outerbridge looped and screw her. Mother really hit the roof, largely because we'd borrowed Sam Farkas' car and let David, who was nine, get stinko. Sam Farkas had bought some land from Mother the previous year. Drew and I had begun to suspect that his attentions to her were something more than neighbourly. We resolved to protect Mother, but try as we might, we failed to turn up any proof that Sam was other than the decent chap he appeared to be.

Gradually, Silverwood was redecorated. I didn't know what had finally goosed Mother into action. It didn't occur to me that Sam Farkas' presence had anything to do with it until, at Christmas time, Drew and I had some friends in and were playing 'sardines.' My real aim, as I recall, was to hide in a dark place, allow some girl to find me and remain hidden with her long enough for some heavy necking. I crawled under the paisley skirt of a large round table in the bay window of the library. It was one of Mother's new acquisitions. While I waited there for one of the girls to happen by, my eyes adjusted to the dark and I noticed a sticker on the underside of the table. On it was printed 'M-G-M Prod. #462, set: Mimi's Apt. stg 5. Hold.' Beneath that, someone had pencilled in longhand, 'Charge to S. Farkas.'

'Oh, yes,' my Mother replied when I asked if the table had come from the studio. 'Sam Farkas rented it to use in one of his movies. He liked it so much that he bought it for himself. He's storing quite an assortment of furniture here. I don't mind, really. Heaven knows there's more room in our house than his. Under the circumstances, it would be ridiculous for him to have to pay to store it somewhere else. I expect he'll take things away now and then when he wants to use them on some film set. He has very good taste, actually. I rather enjoy having some of his pieces around. Besides, it saves me the trouble of a lot of looking. I merely mentioned that I was searching for a suitable refectory table for the living room, and presto! Sam said he had one he didn't know what to do with. Isn't that nice?'

I began to take even more notice of Sam. He was compact and spruce, with greying hair, bright blue eyes and an air of weary, amused resignation about him. He moved quickly and with surprising agility. I thought of him as a feisty, middle-aged bantamweight in tailor-made suits, smelling faintly of lime aftershave and pipe tobacco. Unlike most adults, he never made sappy comments about how much I'd grown, and when he asked me a question, he actually listened to my answer. Sam had a soft spot for kids. In that respect, he reminded me of my father. He wasn't like any other of Mother's men friends, who tended to be big, bluff, hearty types with thick skins and a capacity for gin.

By the following year, when we graduated from Exeter, Sam and Mother were, according to Louella Parsons, 'inseparable companions.' Winchell shortened that to 'a twosome.' It was true that they dined together two or three times a week and Sam and David had become part of the weekend group that came to play tennis or swim at Silverwood. Still, Mother travelled for the Prudhomme Foundation and Sam was often away on location, so that it took a long time before I realized the Farkases had become a fixture in our lives. In the meantime, I was busting my butt to impress the coeds at SC, and Drew was hustling to become a big man on campus so that he could do a snow job on old man Outerbridge. Neither one of us was what you'd call an intellect, so Mother viewed Hale's influence on Drew as a godsend.

I don't like to think about Dosie. She was a sweet girl. Christ, but 'sweet' is a half-assed word. Still, that's what she was, and lousy as it sounds, it's probably the nicest thing I can say. My mother, naturally, was nuts about her. Little blond Dosie with her retroussé nose, her canine devotion to Drew and her impeccable background. She must have been the answer to Mother's prayers.

What dreary snobs we boys were, now that I think of it. There were people you met and wouldn't dream of bringing home, those you would bring home only with a large crowd, those you'd bring to a buffet but never to a seated dinner and a select few whose manners and breeding made them Mother's pets.

'Tell me,' she would say at the mention of some new acquaintance, 'who are his parents?'

'The Stewarts. I think his father's name is Bill.'

'William K. or William van D.?'

'What's the difference?'

'One's Pasadena, and the other is Hollywood.'

Needless to say, one of the fringe benefits of Sam Farkas' advent into my life was that Mother stopped making a fine point of such distinctions.

Drew, on the other hand, was a social retriever after Mother's own heart. At the beach or a party, he could almost instinctively sniff out the sons and daughters of money and power. He'd invite them to Silverwood and present them to Mother for her approval like a well-trained Labrador. While I had nothing in particular against our social set, it was, to me, like a book I already knew by heart – devoid of mystery, adventure or discovery.

About the time Drew and Dosie started getting serious, I was quietly seeing a young lady by the name of Rose Hipps, whose act included a lot of pink ostrich feathers. On impulse, I had sent her an orchid backstage with some overblown sentiments about it not comparing to a Rose. She had allowed me to drive her home. Period. Rose, bless her, was a Good Girl, and what she did on stage was no more a part of her private life than what Jack Dempsey did in the ring was part of his. Still, those sinuous movements, those bumps and grinds, held great promise, and I was determined to prove myself worthy of her intimate attentions. When my mother inquired who kept me out so late every weekend, I made up some charming young thing from La Jolla whose parents were teachers.

At the same time, I recall, Rose was questioning me about my family. I said I had a brother. For some reason, I didn't feel like telling her he and I were identical twins. My father was dead, I told her.

'What's your mother like? They say men always marry their mothers in some funny kind of way. Is she anything like me?'

167

'She's a small, white-haired lady who wears lavender and lace, walks with a cane and collects Meissen china.'

'Jeepers, what a weird combination. My brother had a white rat once, but – '

I bent forward to kiss her before I could laugh. She was adorable, dumb and, finally, nowhere nearly as uninhibited in bed as onstage.

It turned out she was a little paranoid about men who admired her talents, and we broke up.

Granted, Rose was a bit of a ninny but next to the Dosies and the Bootsies and the Missys, she was a breath of fresh air. Dosie was one of those girls who had been raised to think that hers was the best of all possible worlds. It went without saying that the Outerbridges' values and traditions were the modus vivendi next to which all others were found wanting. The great pitfall of self-satisfaction, of course, is that it brooks nothing new or unfamiliar. The defenders of the status quo are smug, static and dull. Dosie might as well have been a fly in amber. It wasn't all her fault. Hale Hunt Outerbridge was a portly, overstuffed gent who perpetually looked as if he'd caught a faint whiff of something malodorous. Doreas – oh, God, sad little Dorcas was like some kind of gussied-up doll. Hale chose her wardrobe. She wore ruffled outfits and lots of bows and polka dots and fluffy fur collars and cuffs. She was never so much dressed as costumed. It was precious and pathetic. I doubt that Hale ever paid much attention to anything beyond the wrappings.

Given our upbringing, I can't say why Drew and I differed in our social pursuits as much as we did. I'm pretty sure that the reason Drew never warmed up to Sam was that old man Outerbridge never approved of him, and Outerbridge was Drew's bellwether. I can still see Hale's face when Mother told him she'd sold her land to Sam Farkas.

'Sam Farkas?' He said the name as if there were something unpleasantly oily on his tongue.

'He writes screenplays and produces them, too, I believe.'

'I hope to hell he's not going to erect one of those damned Frank Lloyd Whosis eyesores. Movie types go for the avant-garde stuff.'

Now that I think of it, that exchange explains Dosie as well as anything.

Bibi Prudhomme Biddeford

No matter what they say, Ada Prudhomme was not the keeper of the family flame. Whatever flame there was, whatever light it cast, was hers. Believe me when I say Ada was the keeper of the dark.

Take the matter of money. I knew jolly well that Ada had lost it all. She concealed her circumstances so cleverly that I doubt even her lawyers were fully aware of her situation at the time.

Unlike most people who played the market in the twenties, I never bought on margin. I expect this had something to do with my upbringing. In our circle, a lady didn't purchase anything she couldn't pay for in full upon demand. Perhaps this convention was intended to protect the weaker sex from fiendish exploitation. Whatever the case, I have always laid my greenbacks on the barrelhead and closed my ears to the blandishments of those who would furnish me with charge accounts, credit cards and real estate loans obtained by dialling one easy-to-remember telephone number. My CPA thinks me an old fool, but I notice he smokes three packs a day and has a pronounced facial tic. I shouldn't be surprised if the poor fellow curls up before he's half my age, due in no small measure to fancy debts being the modern way of life.

When Victor died, the stock portfolio he left Ada was much like my own, since it was he who had advised me on such matters after Oren's death. At the time the market took its dive, for example, both Ada and I held Eastman Kodak and General Electric. Each dropped more than forty points overnight. Ada had Union Cigar which fared even worse – it fell from $113 to $4 in a single day. Montgomery Ward, Safeway, Simmons, US Steel, names that today ring solid as brass, sounded Ada's financial ruin. She hadn't sufficient cash to meet the margin calls, and the stocks which Victor had left her outright continued to diminish in worth with every passing week. Finally, she had to sell her entire portfolio at market value to cover her losses. After that it was the land Victor had willed her, then the Stutz, the Duesenberg, the Chrysler and her jewellery. When she wrote me to say she was considering selling the Flemish tapestry that had once hung in our Madison Avenue house, I knew things must be grim indeed. For Ada to dismantle any part of Silverwood must have been as painful to her as an amputation. In the end, she did that, too, lopping off a piece of land below the house and offering it to the highest bidder.

As I say, I was the only one who was privy to the whole picture. Ada understood very well that in California one's social currency was dependent upon one's bankable currency. Here on the East Coast, in old houses with draughty rooms and creaking floorboards, the presence of threadbare Oriental rugs and ancient, scarred tables laid with mismatched silver from the dowries of departed ancestors proclaims at once that here is a Good Family. Money, or the lack of it, is secondary. Out west, however, the words 'genteel' and 'poverty' are rarely uttered in the same breath. Poverty is suspected to be a contagious disease and a danger to the common good of the uncommon rich. Had Ada not kept up appearances, she and her boys would have become social outcasts, and Ada was determined that her children should not bear the brunt of her misfortunes.

To the casual visitor, Silverwood appeared unchanged. Fresh flowers from the gardens still filled the tall vermeil urns in the foyer, and Ada's and the twins' portraits gazed calmly down from the panelled walls. Visiting cards were placed on a sterling salver on the console table by Safford, whose white gloves remained immaculate. Only the inmates, as I called them, were permitted beyond the foyer. The occasional interloper was given Ada's cock-and-bull story about redecorating. For a couple of years, she and the children slept on mattresses on the floor amid odds and ends of furniture that had failed to bring a price. The staff was pared to a minimum, and whatever vegetables from the gardens were not consumed at home went to market. Despite her economies, the question remained in my mind as to how Ada managed. One can't, after all, support an establishment like Silverwood by scrimping and saving. Meanwhile, Ada managed to insinuate herself into the forefront of every gala opening of a Prudhomme exhibit. Her name was one with the social and artistic prestige of the Prudhomme Foundation. It was a brilliant job of public relations and gave the impression that she was the hostess of these festivities. Nobody doubted that she was still in the chips. To hear her talk, one never would have suspected a thing. I remember Ada quizzing dear, deaf Cornelia, cousin Charles' widow, about some chum of Andrew's at Exeter. 'Douglas Peabody,' said Ada loudly. 'Do you know the family?'

'Old Salem,' replied Cornelia. 'His mother was a Talbot.'

'One of the Baltimore Talbots?'

'How's that again?'

Ada leaned closer. 'The Talbots,' she enunciated. 'Baltimore?'

'Oh, no,' Cordelia corrected her hastily. 'Ours.'

'From Boston?'

'The North Shore. They're Myopia Hunt Club.'

This satisfied Ada, as well it should have. Moments later, when Cornelia had left, Ada asked me, 'Do you think five dollars enough to take this boy and the twins to dinner? I've only my train tickets and a little pocket money to see me back to California.' She was living that close to the bone.

Call it shallow if you will, yet I admired what Ada did. In those days we were brought up knowing that whatever fate dealt you, you were expected to acquit yourself with style and grace. In doing so, you learned to rise above circumstances. Maintaining appearances produced the salutary side effect of teaching resiliency, self-discipline and cheerfulness. If that's superficiality, I'm for it.

171

Dorcas Outerbridge

I dare say that *au fond* the world is no worse than it ever was, yet a lack of the slightest regard for tradition, decorum or the basic niceties makes it appear to be in a state of advanced deterioration. These days, one can't turn on the television without tuning in to a dreary exposé of human excess. I do not wish, please God, to be made privy to any more personal accounts of unwed motherhood, extramarital sex, sit-ins or dropouts, drugs or going topless. Discretion derives from discipline, and in my youth if one made public one's peccadilloes it was regarded as a further lapse of self-control and thus indicative of a character weakness. There are no new sins; we simply dealt with ours discreetly. Ada Prudhomme, who was every inch a lady, knew the rules, played by them and expected no less of others.

The way my generation was brought up, men and women did not embrace or fondle each other in the presence of others. Though we were married for years, neither Hale nor I would ever have allowed our daughter to witness our more intimate moments. So from the start, as might be expected, Ada and Sam Farkas never gave any overt indication that their relationship was progressing past the ordinary cordiality of two who lived in close proximity to each other.

Nonetheless, the advent of Sam Farkas was, in itself, surprising. There he was, with no advance notice, walking across the lawn towards us, acting for all the world as if he belonged there. I kept waiting for someone, most likely Ada, to tell us why Mr Farkas had come to join us that afternoon. I imagined there must be a specific reason for his presence. When I mentioned this later to Hale, he gave me an exasperated look. 'Good gravy, woman,' he said. 'There's no mystery. It's the same old story. Victor's been gone five years now, and the woman still hasn't got used to sleeping alone.'

'You *don't* think – '

'Sure as you're born. Farkas saw that she was vulnerable and zeroed in on her.'

'Elodie told me Ada was upset by a windstorm, and he came to her rescue.'

'Wind or no, he'd have found an excuse eventually. Hell's bells, he's probably already counting her silverware. I'll have a talk with Austin Chase. Someone has to see to it that Ada isn't played for a pigeon.'

'Surely she wouldn't marry him!'

'Stranger things have happened.'

The irony of the situation was that I know Ada never intended for Sam Farkas to buy that land in the first place. She had put the price very high especially to deter the riffraff and to allow her to choose her neighbours. What she did not take into account, unfortunately, was that the crash had laid low some of the nicest people, while at the same time creating celluloid millionaires. Hollywood flourished despite hard times or, more accurately, because of them. Films offered cheap diversion to the general public which went in droves, making fortunes for the likes of Sam Farkas. With the old guard too debilitated to protect the bastions of society, the walls tumbled down and the *nouveaux riches* were everywhere. They threw their money about like confetti. It was typical that Sam Farkas would spend an exorbitant sum for a small piece of Silverwood property as though its precincts conferred some sort of *cachet* upon the new owner.

For some reason Ada tolerated the rather proprietary attitude he adopted not only towards her person but towards Silverwood as well. He took it upon himself to be her equerry – and, if Hale was correct, heavens knows what else – as well as giving orders to Safford as though he were the head of the household. Ada seemed not to notice. One Christmas at Silverwood, he erected a tree of such theatrical garishness that the humble manger Child must have gazed down upon it in shock. That was the same Christmas that he presented her with the gigantic Georgian crystal and silver epergne which thereafter ostentatiously occupied the centre

173

of her dining room table. I overheard him telling Ada, 'Miss Joan Crawford had her eye on that, but I discouraged her. Luckily I have a script she wants to do. I told her I knew a lady of such classic elegance that no other owner would be suitable for a piece of that calibre. I think she was jealous.'

'Of my gift?'

'Of your elegance, my dear. Antiques can be bought.'

'You didn't mention me by name.'

'You know me better than that, darling.'

That was when I realized that everything Hale had said must be true. Not long afterward I saw a newspaper photograph of the two of them together in San Francisco where Ada had gone for the opening of a Prudhomme Foundation exhibit. This seemed to many of Ada's friends to imply a public imprimatur on her affair with Sam. I wondered what the twins were making of the situation. My heart ached for those boys. First they had lost Victor, one of the noblest men I shall ever know, and now their mother was under the spell of a movie person by the unlikely name of Farkas who read *Variety* at the Silverwood pool and spoke of 'rushes' and 'dubbing' and 'rough cuts' in that arcane language of theirs. Odder still, Ada seemed to understand what he was talking about. The twins must have felt quite alone in the world. I have often thought that was part of the reason Andrew was so keen to marry and begin a family of his own.

My Dosie had known the Prudhomme boys since she was thirteen and had gone to Miss Olga Shoup's Friday Get-Togethers where children from some of the nicer familes were taught not only to dance but how to comport themselves in various social situations. They learned the fox-trot and the waltz, how to order in French restaurants, how to tip on shipboard and the finer points of making conversation. It was virtually *de rigueur* for any girl who wished to make her debut to have attended the Friday Get-Togethers which the young people all called 'the Gets.'

By the time of Dosie's coming-out party, Andrew had already staked his claim on her affections. All the same, Hale and I felt it was important that she make her debut and meet a number of new and eligible young men so that she might have some basis for judgement when the time came. But Dosie took after her

174

father. Like Hale, she was unyielding in her views. She had eyes only for Andrew Prudhomme. Not that either her father or I disapproved. We merely felt that both Dosie and Drew were too young to become serious about their romance. Dosie's debut, if I do say so, was the *succès fou* of that season. All winter long, the country had been reading *Gone With the Wind*, which won the Pulitzer Prize that year. There wasn't a single woman who didn't imagine a trace of Scarlett in herself. For Dosie's party, we erected an immense double marquee on our rear lawn and decorated it with a small forest of azaleas and magnolia trees in full bloom. We rented Victorian chairs and tables, swagged Confederate bunting all about and hired two dozen Negro waiters in crisp white jackets to serve the guests mint juleps and champagne. In her off-the-shoulder gown of white tulle with its appliquéd silk magnolia blossoms, Dosie could have stepped straight out of Tara or Twelve Oaks. I had never seen our daughter so utterly radiant. No wonder, I thought, that Andrew Prudhomme is smitten with her. Every so often during the evening, Hale had to cut in on Dosie and Andrew to remind her that she mustn't appear to be playing favourites. I remember Drew standing in the stag line, watching her doing the lindy hop with some young man. When the music switched to 'Red Sails in the Sunset' and the mood on the dance floor turned romantic, I saw Andrew hastily make his way through the crowd, cut in on Dosie and the young man and whirl her away in his arms. He was taking no chances. I knew then that it wouldn't be long before he presented himself to Hale as a prospective son-in-law. Mothers sense these things. Dosie was only eighteen, and Andrew still had another year of college ahead of him. Both Hale and I thought they ought to take things slowly, but Dosie knew very well that I had been engaged to Hale when I was eighteen, so we hadn't a leg between us to stand on. Ada also felt the matter should be let alone to take its course. I expect she simply wished both of them to be completely sure that marriage was what they wanted. Andrew was eager to announce as soon as Dosie's season was over, after Christmas. The two had made plans between them to have the wedding immediately following his graduation from SC. They were so in love that it seemed impossible to deny them anything.

Andrew reminded me very much of his father. He had a splendid head for business and he took to it like a sport. His taste was impeccable, even as a young man. He was unfailingly courteous. He was gallant and charming to ladies of every age. He made you feel, as Victor had, that his was a shoulder a woman could lean on. (Not, of course, that Hale Hunt Outerbridge wasn't as fine a specimen of manhood as any woman might wish!)

What a pity that Andrew changed so much from that fine young man, the very embodiment of his father, who married my Dosie. I don't suppose I shall ever know what finally caused his character to change so drastically that he turned away from me, from his brother and from Silverwood. Certainly there wasn't a single smudge on the horizon that sparkling summer day when they were married in our garden. Dosie wore the lace mantilla I had worn when I married Hale. She looked like a Botticelli Madonna. She was so beautiful that I found myself blinking back tears as I was ushered down the aisle between the rows of gilt chairs to my seat. Andrew and Tony, who was his best man, waited stiffly at the altar, both nervously flexing their fingers. The moment Dosie appeared on Hale's arm, I saw Andrew become motionless. He stood transfixed, feasting his eyes on her loveliness. His brother had to nudge him gently when the minister spoke to him. What a glorious day that was! It seemed then that nothing could ever diminish its joy and promise. The union of a Prudhomme and an Outerbridge was a match made in heaven. I was so blissfully happy for those two that I hardly gave a thought to losing my dear little girl.

'Oh, Mummy,' she said as she was slipping into her going-away outfit, 'what shall I do without you to talk to every day?'

'You'll have Andrew!' I laughed. 'Here's a box with a bottle of champagne and some wedding cake in it for later.'

'But Drew doesn't want to talk about fashions or Brenda Frazier or what happens on *One Man's Family*. He wants to talk about Mr Chamberlain and Hitler and whether or not Howard Hughes can break the round-the-world speed record.'

'Then you'll call me on the telephone. No, dear, don't carry the box. A lady never carries parcels. Put it in your suitcase.'

'Mummy, everything will be so different now. Nothing will ever be the same again.'

'Nonsense. You're our daughter first, last and always. Promise me you'll phone, dear. If you truly love Mummy you'll call her every day.'

'Of course I will! Mummy, dear – ' She swallowed a sob.

'We mustn't get weepy. Daddy and Drew wouldn't like it. I'll go tell Drew that you're ready to leave.'

'Say a prayer for me, Mummy. I want to be such a good wife to him. I want us to be just like you and Daddy.'

Bless her heart. She was all the wife a man could want.

Elodie Swann

I hadn't seen Ada for some time when I heard from Austin Chase that she wanted to sell the odd-shaped piece of land that had been created when the gatehouse had been built several years before. The lot was almost an acre in size and lay between the driveway and the road parallel to it as though someone had tacked it on to the estate as an afterthought. 'I wish her luck,' I told Austin over cocktails. 'Is anyone buying land these days?'

'People will always buy land. As Will Rogers repeated to me the other day, it's not as though there was more being made. The point is, Ada doesn't want to hold a mortgage. She wants cash for the property.'

'Do you think she'll get it?'

'Eventually. She's had one offer, but she doesn't want to deal with that element.'

'Show people?'

'And the worst sort, at that. Ada's jacked the price up considerably in hopes of avoiding the issue, but you know how persistent that type is.'

'She sold the big tapestry in the hall to Mrs Guggenheim. I saw it in her drawing room.'

'It's one thing to sell a tapestry and another to have them practically on the premises.'

'Yes, quite. Imagine having an Einstein or a Mahler for a neighbour. Do you think she'd be obliged to speak to them or could she just wave in passing like royalty?'

'You've made your point, Elodie.'

I hate to think what Sam Farkas paid for that property, though today it would be worth a small fortune. Immediately, he set about building a home there, an attractive brick Georgian place. Then, somehow – unlikely as it was – he and Ada became friends. I spied them together first at some sort of benefit, a ball, I believe, for an orphanage or hospital. Ada was dancing with someone I'd never seen before. He had bright blue eyes, dark hair going to grey at the temples and a dandy tan. He wasn't handsome, but he cut a fine figure, I must say. His black, satin-striped trousers were pressed to a cutting edge, and he sported onyx studs and matching cufflinks in his shirt. The monogrammed handkerchief in the pocket of his dinner jacket looked so crisp it might have been cut from letter paper.

'Who is that with Ada?' I asked Austin Chase.

'That's your Mahler, my dear. The neighbour.'

'Really? How amazing. You have to admit, Austin, he's a spiffy dresser.'

'Sharp. And a fast worker. It's clear what he sees in Ada, but what could she see in him?'

'I don't know, but I intend to find out. Let's go say hello. Do ask her to dance, Austin.'

I noticed that Sam Farkas' eyes followed Ada as she left the table on Austin's arm. 'Have you known Ada long?' I inquired.

He thought a moment, as though it surprised him to realize how little or how much time had passed between them. 'It will be a year next month, in December.'

'I see you're a man with a good memory.'

178

'And you, have you known her long?'

'Longer than either of us would care to recall.' I studied Farkas out of the corner of my eye. He was gazing at the dance floor, searching out Ada, I guessed. There was actually something quite attractive about him. He had the look of someone in whom tragedy or pain had bred an extraordinary compassion. I noticed he was wearing a wedding ring. Ada wouldn't be out with a married man. Sam Farkas was a widower, then. 'You're Ada's neighbour, I'm told. You must have met her when you were building your house.'

'Some time later. The winds bother her.'

'The winds? The Santa Anas, do you mean?'

'I remember the wind roared like high surf breaking over the house. We had two or three nights in a row like that. You could hear trees toppling in the darkness, and the power would suddenly go out.'

'I remember. It was the second week in December of last year. I lost a large fir in one of those storms.'

'I could see from my bedroom that someone in the house at the top of the hill would light a lamp and pace all night until it was daylight. I stood at my window and watched the long shadows splash against the wall of an upstairs room. I wondered who it was, besides myself, who couldn't sleep. The room was large, so it wasn't one of the servants. One night, a sound brought her to the window, and I saw that it must be Mrs Prudhomme.'

I couldn't help smiling. 'A damsel in distress, as it were.'

'Ada told me later that on nights like that she would grow afraid that Silverwood would be torn apart around her and she'd find herself, when the sun rose, alone among the ruins.'

'Ada said that? I've always though her utterly fearless.'

'She's not fearless. She's plucky in spite of herself. That's the point. She's quite a valiant lady, actually.'

He'd fallen headlong for Ada Prudhomme. I wondered what it was that had gained her three such unlikely conquests as Rowley Deems, Victor Prudhomme and now Sam Farkas. Perhaps she was that kind of woman who simply attracts males in general. Such women almost never appear flirtatious. With no conscious effort, they send out a signal as soundless to other women as a dog whistle, and the men rally round, hoping to be singled out. If this was the case, I doubt that Ada recognized it. In fact, I think she didn't, because I believe she would have pressed her advantage if she'd been aware of it.

I hoped poor Farkas wasn't thinking of asking her to marry him one of these days. I knew Ada well enough to be certain she'd never exchange the Prudhomme name for Farkas and reconcile herself to some five thousand years of prejudice in the same breath.

He rose as she and Austin returned to the table. 'My dear Ada, watching you dance gives me almost as much pleasure as dancing with you myself.'

Ada glanced at him, and for a split second their gazes locked. The silent space of that moment was so far from the crowded room that it seemed to have been flung off the face of the earth, hurled past the Milky Way to some expanse beyond the breath of the solar wind, boundless and timeless as infinity. I felt sheepish and guilty to have witnessed it. 'Dance with me, Austin,' I said quickly.

I realized in a flash that Ada had fallen as hard as Sam. This threw a new light on her, which is not to say I was likely to overlook everything I knew about her. I couldn't figure out, though, why she had picked Sam Farkas over the more conventional and acceptable choice of someone like Austin Chase.

It must have been precisely the difference between them that had attracted her. To Sam, she was the epitome of everything he must once have thought unattainable. You could see that he looked upon Ada with absolute wonder that this paragon should be at his right hand. There was no danger of Sam treating her affections as cavalierly as Victor might have. Victor, for all his dashing charm, simply hadn't Sam's depth of feeling. With Sam, she was safe from the kind of pain that Victor's intrigues might have caused her. Too, Ada didn't have to jump through hoops for Sam as she had for Victor. Sam Farkas thought she was just fine the way she was. She relaxed with him. She lightened up.

Sam's devotion might have appeared fawning had it not been for his obvious affection for her and the fact that Sam Farkas was nobody's fool. He was wise as well as smart, which is rare. He wasn't one of those chaps who makes a pretence of disavowing his success all the while he's resting on it like a podium. Sam got a real kick out of his accomplishments. I remember hearing him say how much he wished his parents had lived to see his office bungalow at the studio, which was bigger than any apartment they'd ever lived in. I never heard him mention his wife except as David's mother, and even at that remove, a slight shadow seemed to fall just behind his eyes.

Ada and Sam began to be seen together regularly. Perhaps she was testing the invincibility of her social standing. Evidently, it was solid as silver and safe from tarnish, because after a while even people like the Outerbridges took it for granted that where Ada went, Sam went also and vice versa. What a feeling of triumph that must have given Ada. She had not only got where she aimed to go all those years ago in sleepy Santa Paula but had so established herself there that she was free at last from the strictures that her own ambitions had imposed upon her. I pictured her pitching Ma Watkins' tattered copy of Mrs Sherwood's *Manners and Social Usages* into the fireplace in her drawing room and watching it burn.

By this time she had finished her redecoration of Silverwood. It was, like Ada herself, a good deal more informal. It required less staff than before, which made the place easier for her to manage alone. Obviously she hadn't taken much of a beating in the market crash. I don't know whether or not she'd had to lay her emeralds on the line to keep Silverwood going. I do know that if it had been necessary, she would have put her very life on the line for Silverwood. It was as much a part of her as any of her vital organs.

I have noticed that there is a watershed in the middle years that divides us according to our character. We either fulfil our potential or default to our greatest weakness. It is a time when some men leave good women for floozies, and their wives turn to drink. Others enjoy peace of mind, and their women grow old as gracefully as tulips. There doesn't seem to be any golden mean.

Sam Farkas marked the watershed in Ada's life. I had observed firsthand the facility with which she doffed one identity and donned another. I had seen her tailor the past to suit her, with

181

shears so sharp I thought them dangerous. All the time, she was shopping for something that would fit the measure of her dreams. Now she had found it. I waited to see what would happen.

Mind, I don't think Ada loved Sam with the same kind of blind devotion she had summoned for Victor Prudhomme. The great irony of her marriage had been that Victor gave her everything she wanted, except himself. Now as keeper of the Prudhomme family flame, she still had it all, and she had Sam, too. If theirs wasn't a heated affair, it was one that gave them both a measure of contentment which, in the long run, can make passion look like so much tinsel.

Often as not, coming face to face with the realization of one's dreams is a little like staring into the sun. It ruins one. Not Ada. I don't think she was ever happier than in those years when her boys became men, Andrew produced another generation of Prudhommes to live at Silverwood and Sam Farkas was beside her.

I first realized Andrew and Dosie were interested in each other during one of Ada's famous Christmas parties. Somewhere, during those years, Ada had got into the custom of giving a large party at Christmas time. We four, the Outerbridges and I, drove up at the same time. Hale was wearing the red and green petit point waistcoat he always wore for the holidays and which smelled of the camphor he kept it in the rest of the year. Dorcas had a corsage of mistletoe and holly pinned to her lapel. 'Daddy says that's so Mummy can only kiss gentlemen who are shorter than she,' piped Dosie, giggling. 'And there aren't any!'

'Nobody ever accused your father of being a dimwit,' I replied. 'You're looking very grown-up all of a sudden, Dorothea.' She was a buxom young woman, apple-cheeked, blue-eyed, her wavy blond hair parted on one side and clasped with a single gold barrette.

'She'll be making her debut in June,' Dorcas told me, nodding to Safford as we entered.

'Ye gods, will you look at that,' exclaimed Hale.

In the foyer was a Christmas tree, standing two storeys high between the staircases to either side of it. It was a shimmering tower of splendour. Silvery scintillas sparkled from its branches

182

and showered the room like starlight. Every possible inch of the tree was decorated with dazzling stones. Clips and brooches, earrings, bangles, necklaces and bracelets were fastened or draped among its branches like ice crystals. A pair of small spotlights was fixed on the tree from the top of the hall.

'It's a bit much, don't you think?' murmured Dorcas.

'Oh, Mummy, I think it's utterly nifty!'

'Confess, Ada,' Hale said as we joined her in the drawing room, 'you're an international jewel thief, isn't that it?'

'They're only paste, I'm afraid. The tree is Sam's contribution to the party. He sent one of his set decorators over from the studio. The clever fellow thought of costume jewellery. It's quite spectacular, no?'

'*Typique*,' Dorcas said when we were out of Ada's hearing. 'I knew Ada never would have done anything so flashy herself.'

'Good evening, Miss Swann, Mrs Outerbridge.' Andrew presented himself and shook hands all around. 'Merry Christmas, sir. Hi, Dosie.'

'Hi yourself.'

'Tony and some others are in the music room putting carols on the player piano. Want to come along and sing?'

Dosie glanced at her parents.

'My wife tells me that at Avis Hamilton's *thé dansant* last week, to which you took my daughter, the lights mysteriously went out for several minutes.'

Andrew reddened and looked at Dosie, whose cheeks flushed an even deeper crimson.

'I wouldn't like to hear of such a thing again.'

'No, sir.'

'When you take my daughter anywhere, I hold you responsible for her well-being and reputation, is that clear?'

'Yes, Mr Outerbridge.'

'Go along, then, and behave yourselves.'

Dorcas looked after them. 'I wouldn't be surprised if his brother was the culprit. Anthony is too much of a cutup for his own good. I hear he's on the verge of being asked to leave college. Tony always was scatterbrained and unreliable. Andrew, on the other hand, has tremendous resolve. Don't you think he and Dosie make a sweet couple?'

'Puppy love,' Hale told her. 'They'll outgrow it, Dorcas.'

'Yes, dear,' she agreed a little wistfully.

Hale took some champagne from a tray and handed it to me. As Dorcas reached for a glass, he touched her lightly on the wrist. 'Do be careful, my dear.'

'But it's Christmas!'

Poor Dorcas. He treated her like a precocious child. She was petite, dimpled and cute. Hale saw to it that she was dressed by Adrian or Don Loper. Her appearance was a testimonial to his success. No compelling thought, however, was to trouble her mind, and if one did chance to invade that territory, Hale gently banished it. 'Now, Dorcas,' he would, say, 'don't bother your head with that. That's for me to think about, not you.' Despite the fact that she was nearly forty, she still clung to the girlish mannerisms that must once have pleased him. Her gestures were diminutive and coy. Her voice, which had once had a flighty, playful ring to it, had with time fallen out of tune, becoming querulous and edgy, as though she were always on the brink of tears or hysterical laughter. She had a nasal, whinnying delivery that made my name sound like Elodie Swine. I had to suppress the urge to correct her.

'Merry Christmas, all.' Sam Farkas raised his glass by way of greeting.

'And a happy holiday to you,' I replied.

'Damned if I can pronounce yours, though,' said Hale genially.

Dorcas looked acutely uncomfortable and gave him a slight nudge.

'Chanukah. You have to roll the "Ch."'

'I shouldn't bother with Hale,' I told Sam. 'He's an irredeemable gentile.'

'I never would have suspected.'

'I say, Sam,' Hale went on, 'I'm somewhat surprised to see you here tonight. I'd have thought you'd be on your way to join the International Brigade. Surely you're not one of those leftists who's all talk and no action.'

They were about to get into it, I could tell. Ever since the

Spanish Civil War had heated up, Sam and Hale had squared off whenever they met. Sam was outspoken in his support of the Loyalists. Hale thought 'the Hemingway bunch,' as he called them, were, in his words, 'a lot of poetic bleeding hearts who didn't know gazpacho from garbanzos' when it came to the politics of Spain. 'Hell, you're thousands of miles away. All you hear is the propaganda those reds choose to feed you. You're no better equipped than Dorcas here is to judge the truth of the situation.'

It was Sam's turn to look uncomfortable. He avoided looking at Dorcas. 'There's a small dinner party at the Gershwins this coming week to raise money to buy ambulances,' he told Hale. 'Being a humanitarian, I'm sure you'll want to be included.'

'How in blazes do you know they aren't using them to transport weapons and ammunition under a flag of immunity?'

'By George, Hale!' Sam seized his hand and pumped it enthusiastically. 'What a capital idea. Leave it to you to come up with something like that. I'll bring it up at the dinner, you may be sure of it.'

'No politics,' cautioned Ada as she joined us. 'Not tonight.'

'You're too late,' I told her.

'I believe I'll have another glass of this excellent champagne,' Dorcas said, turning to pursue one of the servants carrying a fully-laden tray. 'After all, it is a special occasion.' Hale excused himself and followed her. Sam's boy, David, caught his eye and beckoned him across the room.

'You just missed round one of the evening,' I told Ada. 'Sam landed one that Hale never even saw coming.'

'Underneath it all, you know, Hale is a good soul. He's immensely charitable. It's just his fear of being taken advantage of and made the fool that causes him to appear pompous.'

'You're overflowing with the holiday spirit, my dear.'

'Not so. Sam keeps reminding me that we can afford to be generous.'

I glanced at her.

'I don't know what I would do without Sam anymore,' she said, half to herself. 'He's made such a difference in my life.'

185

'I understand he's made some very profitable investments. I dare say he's given you some excellent tips.'

She looked at me, taken aback. 'That's not what I meant at all!' she protested.

It was an odd moment. She fully expected me to accept her exactly as she saw herself that instant – artless, uncomplicated and, from her attitude, maidenly. I had to suppress a smile. Her sincerity was beyond doubt. 'Tell me, Ada. Are you happy now?'

'Why, yes.' She looked at me as though the question were daft.

I studied her face. She had either to be stubbornly ingenuous or remarkably controlled. 'I don't believe I've ever known anyone who was so absolutely certain.'

'How sad,' she said, and she meant it.

Aside from observing the fulfilment of Ada's dreams, something I don't wish to belittle since she's probably the only person I ever knew who lived to enjoy it, the only other memorable incident of the evening was that both Dorcas and young Tony Prudhomme got half seas over and danced a tango the length of the marble hallway. Everyone but Hale was mused.

If the world was ever anybody's oyster, it was those boys'. Perhaps Tony was a little self-indulgent, but I was fond of him. Drew, I thought, was a trifle obdurate and inclined to be a bit of a snob. Tony, for all his faults, had something of the poet manqué about him. He tended to wear his heart on his sleeve. I don't think he was aware of it, but he had a habit of whistling to himself tunes that were a dead giveaway to his state of mind. I would hear him absently whistling 'Easy to Love,' and know that lightning had struck him yet again. He fell in love with each new conquest as fervently as if it were his first and then, just as impetuously, he would turn his gaze elsewhere, and I'd hear him whistling 'But Not for Me.' He was a dyed-in-the-wool romantic. Perhaps, given a different background, he might have become a writer or a musician, but being a Prudhomme, such things were out of the question. In any event, shortly after Drew and Dosie's engagement was announced, he was expelled from college for a combination of failing grades and misconduct. The twins were twenty at the time. Tony had shinnied up a drainpipe to break into a girls' dormitory and further demonstrated his athletic

186

prowess by chinning himself on some pipes in the hallway, which had come crashing down, flooding the building with water. After a time, Sam gave him a job as a production assistant. I am sure he meant it as a favour to Ada, though putting Tony inside the gates of a movie studio was like loosing a fox in the henhouse. It was inevitable that he should begin to acquire a reputation that troubled Ada and embarrassed Drew. Andrew was trying manfully to match the staid, conservative disposition of Hale Hunt Outerbridge in order to prove himself worthy of his daughter and he all but visibly winced at the mention of Tony's well-publicized flings in the netherworld of saloons and gambling clubs, always in the company of some beautiful girl. The more Tony's name was bandied about as a playboy, the more sedate Andrew became.

Years later, after Ada was dead, I heard a rumour that the twins were at odds with each other. I don't know whether their rift was serious or merely a temporary disagreement. I do know that when Drew became engaged to Dosie and Tony was forced to leave college, the bond between them began to disintegrate. Having watched them grow up together, I can remember thinking that something very special was being allowed to perish. It had to happen, I suppose, given time. I wonder if it might actually have been necessary for those two to break with each other at some point in order for each to feel he was his own man. Whatever the reason, I still think it was a shame.

As for Ada, though she plainly approved of Drew and took great pride in his accomplishments, it was my impression that she cared more intensely for Tony than she liked to let on. While Ada must have understood Drew's aspirations as well as anyone, I believe she saw in Tony those fires which she herself had had to bank in order to realize her own ambitions. Though she was quick to criticize his way of life, I think she envied it a little.

Tony Prudhomme

About the time Dosie and Drew announced their engagement, SC gave me the axe. I'd been wasting my time and theirs. I hadn't the haziest idea what I wanted to do in life except have a ball. To hear Mother talk, you'd have thought I was hellbent for skid row. I'm sure Sam offered me a job only to put Mother's mind at ease. God knows I had no visible aptitude for anything.

I was given some transparent title like 'Assistant to the Producer' which translated to 'gofer.' I ran errands, checked that Sam's orders were followed, listened to complaints and acted as a liaison between the executive office, the production and the postproduction work. Looking back, I can't think of any better way to learn the movie business. At the time, though, I was giving the job less than my full attention.

Those were the days of the big contract rosters at the studios. Of the twenty or thirty performers on the payroll, only a handful might turn out to be moneymakers. Meanwhile they were groomed, coached, trained and given larger and larger roles until they either washed out or became stars. Almost any pretty girl could last at least six months under contract before the front office decided she was a worthless investment and dropped their option on her.

Vonda Craig was a contract player when I met her. She was the first actress I ever dated. I was intimidated by the knowledge that she made fifty dollars a week to my thirty and that she doubtless knew I was near the bottom of the studio's pecking order. She lived in a small bungalow court near Gardner Junction in Hollywood. It must have been summer when I first went there, because all the windows were open. I remember hoping that if I got lucky Vonda wouldn't turn out to be a screamer. I rang the bell and stood waiting outside, aware of the airborne voices of 'Amos 'n' Andy' and the smell of fried chicken coming from the surrounding apartments.

Vonda opened the door wearing a floor-length white fox coat over a silver lamé evening dress that fit like a second skin.

It must have been my expression that made her giggle. 'It's the studio's stuff. They even did my hair and makeup for tonight. They want me to look like another Harlow.'

'I was hoping maybe we could drive out near the ocean for some seafood and a walk on the beach. The moon's almost full.'

'Listen, Tony, the studio will never know I didn't wear these clothes so long as we don't go anyplace grand and get seen. Come inside and make yourself comfortable. I'll only be a sec, okay? I'll change into slacks and a blouse.'

Vonda was a swell girl. She had a face like a kewpie doll. She was shy, thoughtful and scared stiff that the studio would force her to exchange her real personality for another that wouldn't fit. Already her name had been changed twice. She'd been born Wanda Clegg. Warner Brothers had changed that to Wanda Craig before they'd dropped her. Paramount had changed her first name to Vonda because they already had a Wanda under contract. Both Warners and Paramount had let her go after the first six months. She'd been piecing together a living as an occasional day player until she'd landed another contract on the strength of a faint resemblance to Jean Harlow. I'm not sure which frightened her more, the possibility of striking out a third time or of becoming some manufactured stranger she couldn't live with.

She never did either. She killed herself with an overdose of chloral hydrate. One of her girlfriends at the studio told me that the casting director had threatened to see that Vonda's option wasn't picked up unless she put out for him. I'd have liked to kill the sonofabitch. I was twenty years old and not yet resigned to corruption. For a long while afterward, every time I heard the song 'All of Me,' my eyes would tear up because it had been Vonda's favourite. I was in Sam's office, I remember, a couple of weeks after she died, and I heard that melody coming from a piano in one of the rehearsal rooms across the way. I must have looked kind of strange because Sam shooed his secretary out, closed the door, came over to where I was sitting and put his arm around my shoulders.

'It's a goddamn shame, I know.'

I hadn't realized Sam knew about me and Vonda.

'She was a nice kid. I gave her a bit as the gangster's moll in *Gotham Holiday*. She always called me sir. At first I thought she was kidding. She wasn't. She was being polite.'

I took a deep breath. 'I read it in the trade papers, how's that for a helluva note? You know what it said in *Variety?* "Casting exec Vince Furino hailed her as one of his studio's most promising talents."'

'Don't think about that slimy little putz. He's not worth your time.'

So Sam had heard the story, too.

'What kind of business is this where a guy like Vince Furino can get away with leaning on some frightened girl? It stinks, Sam.'

'Sometimes it does. A few lousy things go on in almost every business. They make us ashamed. Maybe they even make us work harder to prove the whole system isn't made up of Vince Furinos. There are decent and kind people in this business, Tony. Word gets around who they are. Word gets around about guys like Furino, too. Sooner or later he'll get his.'

Sam thought like that. If virtue was its own reward, so was evil. I remember one time when he thought the unit publicist was padding his expense account. 'Roy,' he said to him, 'if these charges are legit, I have no quarrel with them. If they're not, you've proven that a person can indeed be cheated. The trouble with that is: You're a person. Ergo, you can be cheated. Knowing how easy it is, you'd never have any peace, would you, wondering if you were continually being had. Sounds like a lousy way to live, Roy.' The charges diminished, and nothing more was said. Sam kept Roy on the picture.

Sam never discussed my girlfriends with Mother. She must have figured they weren't the kind I could bring home, since I rarely took anyone to Silverwood. It wasn't only my mother's feelings that I was protecting. Most of the girls I liked would

190

have felt awkward and ill at east there. Why would I have taken Gracie Higgins, for instance, who was an improbably russet-haired waitress from the M-G-M commissary, and served her up to people like the Outerbridges to be sliced into little pieces?

It drove my brother crazy that I took out girls like Gracie. She was a terrific dancer, and we'd bumped into Drew and Dosie someplace where we'd gone to dance to Benny Goodman's band. Gracie did a helluva double take when she saw him. I guess I hadn't mentioned I was an identical twin. She got a big kick out of sitting between us.

'Who the devil was that broad you had with you?' he asked me on the phone the next day.

'I thought I introduced you. She's Grace Higgins. She works at M-G-M.'.

'Another actress?'

'Waitress. In the commissary.'

'Jesus. You really don't care who it is, do you?'

'She'd be disappointed to hear you say that. She thought you were a nice guy.'

'Tony, be serious. How does it look for a Prudhomme to be acting like a common alley cat?'

'You live your way, and I'll live mine. Let's not make an issue of our differences.'

'You're not thinking of trying to bring her to the bridal dinner, are you?'

'I wasn't aware she was invited.'

'She's not. Dosie has you seated between her mother and Faith Halliburton.'

'Fine. I can count the hairs in Faith's little blond moustache.'

'And don't be a cunt, either.'

The bridal dinner was one of those subtly hysterical affairs where a lot of tension is. released as gaiety. Such tribal rites invariably become wayposts by which we judge the distance between our dreams, past and present, and the reality of our lives. The greater the span, the more uneasy we feel. Drew, who was aiming to fill a pair of shoes the size of Hale Hunt Outerbridge's custom-made elevens, had more reason than anyone to be anxious. He'd fortified himself in advance with a couple of belts and laughed often and loudly and, as the evening went on, more unaccountably than anyone else. Dosie cried at the toasts, then rose to read a poem she'd written to her parents. She broke into sobs halfway through, and Mother finished it for her.

When the liqueurs were passed, Dorcas requested a double bourbon. 'Those sweet drinks always upset my tummy,' she said. 'Tony, perhaps you'd be good enough to go tell Hale I'd like to dance.'

'I'd be delighted to dance with you, Mrs Outerbridge.' I rose.

She tugged at my sleeve and pulled me back down to my chair. 'We'd better not. Hale thought we made a spectacle of ourselves the last time.'

'You mean the Christmas party when we did the tango?'

She laughed and touched her fingers nervously to her lips. 'I thought we were almost as good as Fred and Ginger, didn't you?'

'Mummy.' Dosie approached from the direction of the powder room, still wiping away her tears. 'That drink in your hand is the color of mahogany. Do be careful.'

'I didn't say I was planning to finish it.' Dorcas took a swallow and set the glass on the table beside her evening bag.

'Hey, babe!' Drew shouted from the dance floor. 'Let's do the Big Apple!' He raised his arms and waggled both index fingers in the air as he stomped. 'Truck to the right. Re-verse! To the left!' Turning, he all but collided with Elodie Swann and Austin Chase.

'Oh, crumbs,' moaned Dosie. 'He's blotto. Tony, can't you do something?'

I was none too sober myself. I don't recall how I manoeuvred Drew out of the place before either one of us could disgrace himself. I do know that he insisted on driving, and I kept my eyes closed all the way home. By the next morning when we left for the ceremony, he wasn't in much better shape. He was still so numbed that I had to give him a sharp jab in the ribs when it was time for him to step into place next to Dosie at the altar.

Four or five months later, Dosie announced she was pregnant. You could tell how it pleased her. She would sit contentedly, smiling to herself, her arms folded over her belly, embracing the baby inside it. She had one of those wide-hipped peasant bodies

192

built for breeding. I think she was happiest when she was pregnant, regardless of the discomfort.

My brother was pretty pleased himself when Daphne was born. I think he liked the picture of Andrew Prudhomme and Family established in their Monterey colonial-style home complete with Nanny, the housekeeper and a Scotty named Moxie. He was playing the patriarch and squire, damning Roosevelt and the WPA and warning sagely that nothing in Europe could compete with German air power. He had Hale's rather dour view of affairs. I, like so many others, was tap-dancing as fancy and furiously as I knew how, as though if the world could be proven to be enough fun, nobody'd want to blow it up.

I spent nights I can't count or remember boozing, chasing tail and playing the tables. When the mayor closed the gambling clubs in LA, we took to the sea. For a quarter, Tony Stralla's boys would ferry you out of Santa Monica, beyond the three-mile limit, to his square-rigger, the *Rex*, for an evening of chemin de fer or roulette. On shore, guys like Artie Shaw, Glenn Miller and the Dorseys were making the world swing. It was a noisy, nonstop carnival, as far as I was concerned. Unlike Drew, I was in no hurry to be middle-aged. I was as carefree as only a supremely self-involved hedonist can be.

The first, distant rumblings on the Western Front marked the end of my hayride, though it was nearly two years until I got the message. Despite my brother's dark predictions, Europe still seemed very far away. It was Sam who caused me to sit up and take notice. After Russia and Germany signed their nonaggression pact and Joe Stalin toasted Hitler's health, Sam took to calling Stalin a motherfucker. Not that Sam didn't curse; what surprised me was how much he seemed to care. True, he had supported the Spanish Loyalists, but I'd attributed that to Sam's usual affinity for the underdog. I hadn't known he had a heated interest in international events, yet he was as angry as I ever saw him. Betrayal, I realized later, was not something Sam took lightly.

Betrayal became epidemic in the months after that. Quisling became a common noun, and Mussolini declared war on France and Britain. Roosevelt made his speech about Italy having plunged a dagger into her neighbour's back. By the time the

President signed the bill for the draft, seventeen million registered in a single day. I didn't want to wait until my number was called. I was itchy to enlist. It was the white hats against the black hats. We were still young enough then to believe in a clear distinction between good and evil and the obligation of every man to do his duty. Righteousness, I guess, is something one tends to outgrow. We were never again so innocent.

PART FOUR

Nanny Beale

Some people call the Hawaiian Islands a paradise, but as I confessed to young Daphne in reply to her letter, I could never be happy there. To my mind there is something unwholesome in so much lush, sinister greenery that would, if you didn't beat it off, entwine itself about your flesh. It always seemed to me that the creeping vines and that monstrous foliage were only waiting for the day when the entire population would be destroyed by hurricane or volcano or tidal wave and the derelict vegetation could run riot over the land. I was discontented there for other reasons, too. The Thaxters' staff was mostly Japanese. They kept to themselves, not that I would have intruded. What it boiled down to, I suppose, was that the life there and I were not compatible. I stuck it out for over a year, trying to get myself acclimated, but it never happened. After my second Christmas and with the New Year coming, I decided to make a clean break. I gave the Thaxters notice and took the liberty of writing to Mrs Prudhomme at Silverwood to see if she knew of a family on the mainland that might be looking for someone like myself.

That was how, on Good Friday of 'thirty-nine, I came to be standing at the front door of a Spanish-looking house near Griffith Park when Mr and Mrs Andrew returned from the hospital and laid little Daphne Prudhomme in my arms.

Andrew had graduated from his university the previous June and married a month later. In the opinion of the senior Mrs Prudhomme, he was marrying far too young, but his choice of a wife left her no cause for complaint. The Outerbridge girl was, in Mrs Prudhomme's opinion, an ideal match. Andrew and she had grown up together and moved in the same circles. In fact, her father had offered Andrew a position at Outerbridge Industries

197

before it was even settled that he was going to marry Miss Dorothea.

Andrew (and of course Anthony) looked like his father come to life all over again. To be sure, he was a robust young man, not quite as lean as Mr Prudhomme senior, and hadn't his receding hairline or his grace of movement, but there was no doubting he was his father's son, cut from the selfsame cloth.

Mrs Andrew was a sweet soul, modest and soft-spoken and as devoted a mother as I've ever known. Her family was her life. Her children (there were to be three), her husband and her parents were the be-all and end-all to her. Now that I think of it, she hadn't any close friends. I suppose her mother, Mrs Outerbridge, was her most intimate lady friend. Sometimes Mr Andrew would poke a bit of fun at her lack of interest in worldly matters. 'Dosie thinks Franco is a kind of sausage and the Abraham Lincoln Brigade freed the slaves.' Mrs Andrew would laugh shyly at herself along with the rest of them but she never protested.

Anthony showed no interest in settling into marriage or any other earnest undertaking. His life, according to his brother, was a constant festival in which nothing was to be taken seriously.

'Drew, dear, Tony dropped by half an hour ago,' Mrs Andrew was telling him.

He hushed her. 'In a minute.' He came to the doorway of the living room and took his daughter from my arms. Each evening, when he arrived home, little Daphne was brought to him. Mrs Andrew would serve him his cocktail, and he would sip it, talking with her about the affairs of the day, his baby girl on his lap. They were the handsomest family you could imagine.

'Now what's this about Tony? What did he want?'

'A couple of hundred dollars. He said he was taking Eloise Martin out to the *Rex* tonight and he'd forgotten to go to the bank. What sort of a club is the *Rex*?'

'It isn't. It's that gambling ship off Santa Monica that Governor Warren has been trying to scuttle. Did you give Tony the dough?'

'I couldn't. You had the checkbook.'

'Just as well. Mother says he's spending too much time and money on those floating casinos.'

'I'll bet he didn't tell her he was going with Eloise Martin, either.'

'Who's she?'

'An actress. We saw her in that movie with Franchot Tone and Ida Lupino.'

'The moon-faced blonde?'

She nodded. 'Mama told me she's married. Separated from some bandleader but still married.'

'How did your mother know about it?'

'She was here to see Daphne when Tony came.'

'Then Mother's bound to find out. It was bad enough when he was seeing Alice Boyd, but at least she wasn't an actress.'

'Drew, Alice Boyd is a divorcée and at least five years older than Tony.'

'Honest to God, Dosie, can't my brother find one single decent companion in this entire city? Why is it always a starlet or a divorcée or some playgirl? Where's his taste, anyhow? Dammit, people are always confusing the two of us. His shenanigans affect *my* name, too. I'm going to speak to him. Surely he can choose more appropriate company.'

'You know very well what he'll say. He said it the last time you brought up the subject.'

'You mean about Mother and El Farko.'

Mrs Andrew glanced in my direction. 'I think Nanny wants to take Daphne back upstairs now, Drew.'

So that was all I knew of that conversation. It was the first time I'd heard Mr Andrew refer to Mrs Prudhomme's friend, Mr Farkas, and I wasn't sure whether he'd called him what he did out of affection or distaste.

Mr Farkas, you see, was a Jewish gentleman who had somehow, in the time I'd been away, become a friend of Mrs Prudhomme. He wasn't the loud kind. He was a quiet, bespectacled, pipe-smoking man with keen blue eyes, a prominent nose and full lips. His neck was kind of scrawny, so that it looked not quite up to carrying his head about. He was a natty dresser, even at his leisure. Every crease was pressed sharp, and his shoes were always polished to a conspicuous sheen. His fingernails shone, and he smelled faintly of some sort of citrus scent. He had an unassuming manner, and he acted like regular gentry. He was so constantly solicitous of Mrs Prudhomme that it finally dawned on me that they might be more than friends.

On Saturday afternoons, there was usually a small crowd at Silverwood: Mr and Mrs Andrew and Daphne, Mr Anthony, perhaps with one of his lady friends, the Outerbridges, Miss Swann, Mr Farkas and his son, David, and various other friends and acquaintances, some with their children. There were tennis and croquet, lawn bowling, badminton, swimming and special games for the youngsters, which were my responsibility. Mrs Prudhomme saw that there were enough players on hand for each sport and that everyone had sufficient food and drink. There was always a long, white-draped buffet table filled with little sandwiches, cookies and cakes, cheeses and crackers, ripe fruits and various kinds of cocktails and juices.

As for Mr Farkas, he made it a point to see that she managed to enjoy her own party. 'Ada,' he would call out, catching up with her between the swimming pool and the tennis court, 'you mustn't overdo. Come sit in the shade and relax a bit.' Or to someone else, he would say, 'I want Ada to hear this story. I know she'll appreciate it. I'll go find her.' When the sun dropped low in the sky, Mr Farkas would disappear into the house without a word and return with a wrap which he would drape over her shoulders before she could feel the chill.

It was his nature, I think, to be kindly. I guess that was what laid him open to the kind of ideas that finally got him into trouble. He was one of those people whom children, for some mysterious reason, love on sight. Daphne would run to him on her chubby little legs and leap on to his lap. I think it irked Mr Outerbridge that she didn't find her grandfather's lap as hospitable as Mr Farkas'. Several times Mr Farkas gave me passes to see his films. There wasn't one I didn't like, though *Shadow Flight* was my favourite. That was about refugees escaping from the Fascists in Europe. I liked *Cartwheel*, too, and the three sequels that came after it. They showed how a pair of ordinary, hardworking police detectives exposed the crimes of powerful, corrupt bigwigs and their socialite cronies. There was always a surprise twist to the ending of the picture that made you feel warmhearted and glad that goodness won the day. I guess that Mr Farkas put a lot of himself into his movies. He was that kind of man.

The only time I ever heard him disagree with Mrs Prudhomme was when Mr Anthony wanted to enlist. He – Mr Farkas – said it 'might do Tony some good' to be in the service. Mrs Prudhomme was aghast.

'You mustn't let him hear you say that! It's a silly, savage idea.'

'Serving his country?'

'America is *not* at war, Sam.'

'Yet.'

'Don't be so pessimistic. Besides, it's frightening.'

'Face it, Ada, we can't stay on the sidelines forever.'

'And why not? This isn't Europe. Do let's drop the subject, please. Here comes Anthony.'

That was another of the changes I noticed in Mrs Prudhomme since I'd come back. She was very self-assured. In the past, she'd always deferred to the Mister. Now she stood up for her opinions. I suppose if it's an ill wind that blows no good at all, it could be said that Mr Prudhomme's passing had made her quite independent. She did not discuss her loss. She had closed the door tight against her sorrow, put on a brave face and stepped boldly into the future. She was a mettlesome lady.

There were other changes. The Silverwood staff had been pared down, since she didn't entertain as much as she had when Mr Prudhomme was alive. And her hair, if I'm not mistaken, was a shade lighter.

Mr Anthony continued to talk about joining the Navy all that summer. Mrs Andrew didn't like the subject either. It worried her that her husband might get the same idea, and she was expecting again in October.

This time it was a boy. They had a bit of dispute over the name, Dexter, which Mr Andrew called 'corny.'

'For Pete's sake, Dosie, we sound like the Seven Dwarfs or some broken-down vaudeville team. "And now, folks, here they are, Dosie, Drew, Daphne and Dexter!'

'But you promised I could choose this one.'

'But why Dexter? It's not in either of our families.'

'It means right hand.'

'So? It's still too damned bloody precious for comfort.'

'But you promised,' she repeated. 'When I was in labour, you promised me – '

'Ah, Christ.' He threw up his hands. 'Who can argue with that? Go ahead, Dosie, name the poor little bugger anything you want, but don't blame me if he grows up with a complex.'

Mr Andrew was irritable, I think, partly because of his brother's talk about enlisting. That same month, two of our American destroyers were torpedoed by German U-boats. The war seemed to be closing in on us like some sort of sly, blood-thirsty animal that prowled invisibly in the darkness, putting everyone on edge.

December was the worst month. The Japanese bombed Hawaii, and I had no way of knowing whether or not the Thaxters and their children were safe. Then the Germans declared war on the United States. Worst of all, not a week before Christmas, I heard that my brother Sean had been killed in an air raid on London. What shocked me most was how they could kill a boy like Sean. He was the youngest of all eight of us children. I had to remind myself that he was thirty, impossible as it seemed. Still I can only see him as an amiable, towheaded boy of three, waving good-bye to me when I left for the States, looking puzzled at the grown-ups' tears. And now I cried for him, feeling empty and cheated, not so much because he'd gone with God but because the murdering Nazis had robbed me of ever really knowing him.

I suppose it's foolish of me, but that month, in my memory, marked the beginning of the end of Silverwood as we had all known it. The groom, Brian, joined up and then the one remaining footman, Alfred. And Christmas Day, just as we were all, myself included, preparing to go into the dining room, Mr Safford took Mrs Prudhomme aside.

'Wait a moment, Daphne.' I picked the child up in my arms. 'Let your grandmother lead the way.' Being almost three, it was the first Christmas she had really understood.

'Here, darling, see the ribbon necklace Mama made for you.' Mrs Andrew slipped it over her head.

'What do you say to your mother, Daphne?' I reminded her.

'Oh, God!'

When I heard Mrs Prudhomme say that, all I could think of was the night long ago when the red-haired girl had died. It was something in her voice.

'Mr Yamada's wife just telephoned. Mr Yamada won't be coming to work tomorrow. His father poisoned himself. He couldn't live with the dishonour of his people.'

'Too bad there aren't more like that,' Mr Outerbridge said.

'Daddy!' cried Mrs Andrew.

'Well, you know what I mean, Dosie.'

'It's perfectly clear,' said his wife, 'that the Japs have no conscience at all. Otherwise, Pearl Harbor never could have happened.'

'Mother Outerbridge,' argued Mr Andrew, 'I don't think the Yamadas constitute a threat to Beverly Hills.'

'We mustn't let this ruin our Christmas dinner,' she told him. 'Lead the way, Ada.'

'Where's Tony?' asked his brother.

'He dashed upstairs rather suddenly,' Mrs Andrew answered.

He made a sound between a laugh and a snort. 'Probably to telephone one of his dollies.'

I put Daphne down when we reached the hall and held her hand as we walked to the dining room.

'Have I missed anything?'

We all looked up. There, halfway down the curved staircase, under his mother's portrait, stood Anthony in the blue and white uniform of an officer of the United States Navy. Mrs Prudhomme covered her face with her hands and began to weep. Mr Andrew bounded up the stairs and threw his arms around him, jubilantly pounding him on the back.

'Hey!' He laughed. 'Take it easy! It's only a costume. I talked Sam into letting me borrow it from the studio. But you'd better get used to seeing it. I'm in. As of yesterday. I'm to report to Long Beach next week to begin officers' training.' He trotted down the stairs, grinning as if he'd pulled off a great trick. As he passed me, he stopped and took my hand. 'I'll pay back the Jerries for your brother, Nanny.' I think I thanked him. I don't remember. I was feeling so many things at once.

'I'd like to kill Sam Farkas for being a party to this,' his mother told him.

Mr and Mrs Outerbridge exchanged looks.

'Don't, Mother. I only went to Sam after the fact. Come on, everyone! Where's our holiday cheer?' He hoisted Daphne on to his shoulders. 'How about letting your old uncle give you a lift to the table?' he asid, as she squealed with delight.

Mr Andrew went to Mrs Prudhomme and put his arm around her shoulders. 'Look at it this way, Mother, at least the Navy has some prestige. And he'll have a commission. It's not as if he was going to be a common foot soldier.'

'Cold comfort,' she replied. 'I don't think the Japs or the Germans draw such fine distinctions.'

We muddled through Christmas dinner as best we could. Once or twice I caught Mrs Andrew gazing at Mr Anthony in his uniform, her eyes filled with apprehension. I knew she was afraid for her husband. The twins had never been separated for any length of time. It just wasn't their nature. What was more, it wasn't like Mr Andrew to allow his brother to seize the initiative in any enterprise. He had always been the more aggressive of the two, with Mr Anthony at pains to catch up with him. They were competitive, no mistaking it, and Mrs Andrew had good reason to be anxious. I'll wager her husband would have eventually signed up, if it hadn't been for his accident preventing it. Poor Mrs Outerbridge was so affected by Mrs Andrew's distress that she became rather tipsy at dinner and had to retire from the table.

Two months later, the gardening staff – Mr Yamada, his son-in-law Kawaguchi and the others – were rounded up and interned at the Santa Anita race track. Mrs Prudhomme hired some Mexicans to take their place, but they were a shiftless lot and elderly into the bargain, most of the young ones having enlisted. The gardens never really recovered from the war. Mr Yamada passed on in detention. After it was all over, Kawaguchi and the rest came back gladly. It wasn't easy for Japs to find jobs then. Unfortunately, he hadn't his father-in-law's great talent, and though he kept up the grounds well enough, they lacked that fine edge of excellence that had once made the place seem to me like Eden before the fall.

Dorcas Outerbridge

Life was good to Dosie and Andrew in those first years of their marriage. What a handsome, wholesome pair they were. They sailed together and played mixed doubles with the young crowd. They bought a pretty Spanish house in the hills and brought Nanny Beale back from the Islands to look after Daphne. Dosie was a born homemaker, and Andrew liked to entertain. It seemed that every weekend there was a dinner or a barbecue or a party for charades or bridge or just for the pure fun of it.

Hale always said he had hired Andrew at exactly the right time. With the rumblings in Europe and Asia, the aircraft industry had taken off like a firecracker. Outerbridge Industries was deluged with contracts. When the war with Germany began, the number of Hale's employees tripled. Of course, now that young men had to sign up for the draft, Hale even employed a good many women. He could scarecely keep up with his work. He counted himself lucky to have Andrew at his right hand, never too tired or too busy to do what Hale required of him without a murmur. They worked seven days a week. Poor Dosie, when she was in labour with Dexter, had to drive herself to the hospital because I was out of town with Hale on business, Nanny hadn't a licence and Andrew couldn't leave the plant. Yet Dosie never complained about Andrew's absences at work. The only thing that upset her was the prospect that he might take it into his head to enlist, especially after Tony joined the Navy. Hale was ready to pull whatever strings were necessary to convince the brass that Andrew Prudhomme was doing more for his country at Outerbridge Industries than he could in the service. Still, I believe Tony's enlistment almost swayed Drew to the point of signing up. At that time, to be young, healthy and not in uniform made a fellow feel unpaatriotic, regardless of whether or not he had family obligations or was indispensable to the war effort. Andrew would eventually have followed Tony into the Navy, I'm sure, if it hadn't been for his accident.

It was in March of 1942, only a few weeks after a Japanese submarine shelled the Ellwood oil fields near Santa Barbara. There was a strict blackout in effect. The evening it happened, Andrew had worked past ten in his office for the fourth night in a row. It was raining and the streets were slick, and the blackout made the night even darker. He started to doze off, jerked himself awake and misjudged his direction. His car swerved off Franklin Avenue, struck a stone gatepost and came to rest half in the street and half in a private drive. He had two cracked ribs and some cuts, and his right leg had been badly fractured. The first Hale and I knew of it was when someone named Riskind woke Hale in the middle of the night, calling to tell Hale that Andrew had crashed in his driveway and an ambulance was on the way. Mr Riskind had pulled Drew from the car, conscious but bleeding badly. Drew had asked him to telephone Hale. We immediately called Dosie and Ada and met them at the hospital. Andrew's leg was broken in three places. Two of the breaks were compound fractures and had pierced his skin. It was a long night for us, with the doctors working over him to try to set his crushed leg to rights. Mr Riskind very kindly called Hale the next day to inquire after Drew. He was a theatrical agent, we learned *en passant*. He seemed most solicitous. He even visited Drew in the hospital.

The accident left Andrew with a slight permanent limp and no chance of joining the service. I think Dosie was relieved. It had been a nasty experience, but surely better than a gold star in the window.

We all did our bit. I was involved with Bundles for Britain. Dosie was a volunteer at the USO. Ada made bandages for the Red Cross, and Sam was an air raid warden. With Mr Yamada and his staff rounded up and interned, Ada's formal gardens were converted to victory gardens. Gone were the larkspur, Sweet

William and begonias, and in their place were corn, carrots and pole beans.

Everyone made sacrifices, great or small, without hesitation. Boys in the bloom of youth volunteered to defend us and were sent back in boxes draped with flags. I had to learn to be by myself for the first time. As a girl, I had gone straight from my parents' home to my husband's. Now, with Hale so often away fro hush-hush meetings in Washington and other places, I was alone in an empty house with only an elderly cleaning lady for company twice a week. Lots of people were lonely then, and some were scared, too. Young men on furlough married girls they'd met only the night before. It didn't matter that they might live to regret it. To live at all was sufficient. In a world that was blowing up beneath us, it seemed terribly important to reach out and make contact with someone, if only for a moment, before the war separated you. It was a noble and a foolish time.

Hale and I closed our large house in town the summer after Pearl Harbor and took a small place at the beach for the warm months. It was large enough to accommodate Dosie's family on weekends, and it provided a relaxing atmosphere for Hale and Andrew. We spent our days on the sand or in the sea. In the evenings we closed the blackout curtains, listened to Lowell Thomas' news and read or played cards. When Hale was gone I played countless games of solitaire, night after night. Sometimes, if there was a bright, bomber's moon outside, I would turn off all the lights, open the curtains and sit gazing out at the surf and the beach, deserted save for the Coast Guard Auxiliary on patrol. I wondered what I would do, alone there, if the Japs attacked. They had already shelled the oil fields not far up the coast. Back east, our planes had sunk one U-boat offshore, and another U-boat had landed Nazi spies on Long Island. We lived on the edge, even those of us on the home front, and life on the edge caused some of us to do unusual things.

Though I was by myself a great deal, I found the shore a friendly spot. On any given day, you could go out for a walk on the beach in the morning and garner half a dozen invitations for drinks or luncheon or dinner before returning home. Hale and I had never been ones for casual socializing, and I found this atmosphere surprisingly pleasant. It provided an antidote to my solitary hours. I recall quite vividly a couple named Blair whose home was two removed from ours and who seemed to be hosting a continuous open house. From their deck above the sand, they would hail friends and strangers alike to join the party. I can still see Morgan Blair, spying a lone naval officer in uniform gazing out to sea from the water's edge, seizing a megaphone and shouting, 'Don't do it! You've got your whole life ahead of you!'

The young man turned, shaded his eyes and looked back at the row of houses fronting on the sand, searching for the source of the voice.

'You've embarrassed the poor guy, Morgan,' his wife Betty told him. She took the megaphone from him. 'The martinis are cold,' she called. 'Care to come up?'

He waved and began to walk towards the house, his shoes and socks in his hand.

It wasn't until he came up the wooden steps to the deck that I recognized Ensign Anthony Prudhomme of the United States Navy. 'Tony!' I embraced him and introduced him to the Blairs and their dozen or so guests. 'What on earth are you doing here?'

'I'm on leave. I was looking for Drew and Dosie. I went to your house, but there was nobody home.'

'Dear me, didn't Drew tell you? They stayed in town this weekend. They were running short of petrol coupons. Besides, Drew has to work all weekend because Hale's away on business.'

'I left a package for Dosie at your door. Cheers,' he said, accepting a drink from Betty Blair.

'Here's to our boys in the service,' somebody replied, and we all raised our glasses.

'Are you still stationed at Long Beach?' I asked.

'Yes, but I'll be going to sea shortly.'

Tony didn't say much about his training, and nobody pressed him for information. We were all aware that loose lips sank ships.

'Who's ready for a refill?' asked Morgan Blair.

Tony held out his glass.

'Be careful, Tony,' I warned him. 'Morgan's martinis are notorious.' I was already feeling a little tiddly myself.

'Mrs Outerbridge. . . .'

'Call me Dorcas, please, Tony. After all, you're an officer and a gentleman. I can't have an officer and a gentleman addressing me as if I were positively elderly.'

'Dorcas, may I ask you a rather personal question?'

'My goodness, just how personal?'

'What size stockings do you wear?'

'Nine. Why?'

He lowered his voice. 'The package I left for Dosie – there are five pairs of nylons in it.'

'Nylons!' I whispered. 'Tony, how marvellous!'

'Size nine. Why don't you take a couple of pairs for yourself?'

'You are wonderful, that's what you are.' I blew him a kiss. 'Dosie will be furious that she wasn't here to thank you herself. Tony, are you hungry? It's almost lunchtime, and I have some cold chicken and potato salad at home. I bought it for Drew and Dosie and the children, and now they're not coming. We can't let food go to waste in wartime.'

We had a couple more drinks and finally left the party. As we walked along the beach together, I couldn't help but think how the years between us seemed to have disappeared. I was forty-four. Tony was twenty-five, yet here we were laughing together like old friends of the same vintage. He had Victor's laugh, I remember.

We laid out the food, and Tony made a green salad. I fetched a bottle of Chablis from the ice box. 'Here,' I said, handing it to him. 'Hale's favourite French wine. Heaven knows when we'll see any more of it.'

'Should we drink it, do you think?'

'Nothing is too good for our men in uniform.' I gave him the corkscrew. 'Especially if they come bearing nylons. I have three bottles on ice, and you may drink them all if you like.'

As it was, we drank two. After lunch, Tony put on Drew's trunks and went for a swim. I had a shaker of chilled martinis waiting for him on his return. We rubbed each other with cocoa butter and sat outside, sunning on the deck.

'I've barged in on you and made myself quite at home. I hope you don't mind.'

'Not at all,' I told him. 'You're good company. I'm probably keeping you, though. You must have a date waiting for you.'

'Actually, I wasn't planning to see anyone in particular. I was just going to prowl around a few bars by myself.'

'Do you do that a lot? Go pub crawling by yourself?'

'Now and then.'

'But you don't usually go home by yourself.'

He shook his head.

'I thought as much.'

We must have talked a long time. I remember we both got hungry again and made sandwiches, and I spilled the potato chips all over the kitchen floor. We picked them up together, laughing like loons over something that now slips my mind. We laughed a lot all that afternoon and into the evening.

'Where is Mr Outerbridge?' he inquired at one point.

'I don't really know where he is this weekend. His company is involved in so many top-secret projects that he sometimes goes away without notice and can't tell me when to expect him back. I think the Army Air Force is testing something Outerbridge Industries produces. Perhaps that's why he went away.'

'It must be lonely living here by yourself.'

'There's always someone to talk to on the beach. Besides, I'm learning to enjoy solitude. I like to watch the ocean from this room. Especially at this time of day when the sun is setting on the water.'

'What do you think about when you're watching the ocean all alone?'

'Think about?'

'Yes.'

'Oh. Hale, Dosie, the children.'

'Do you?'

I don't know why his questioning made me feel uncomfortable. 'Yes, naturally. What else would I think of?'

'What about yourself?'

'Me?'

'You.'

'Let me refresh your drink.' I took his glass into the kitchen

210

and mixed the gin and vermouth. 'Tony, would you please draw the blackout curtains? It's getting dark.'

I heard him moving through the house, drawing the curtains. When he came back, he turned on the radio and found some music.

'Here.' I gave him his glass and touched it with my own. 'You said you were shipping out soon. I shan't ask any questions, but you know I'll be thinking of you.'

'Here's to the ladies that we're leaving behind us on the home front.'

'How very gallant. And here's to your safe return.'

I think we drank to almost everything we could think of.

'To your perfect martinis, Dorcas.'

'Stirred, never shaken. Here's to my nylon hosiery.'

'Let's see it.'

'You want me to model it?'

'Did anyone ever tell you that you have great legs, Dorcas?'

'I'll be livid if I put a run in my new stockings.'

'I'll buy you some more.'

'You'd do that? How sweet. Wait here.' I went into my room, took off my slacks and panties and put on a garter belt and a pair of Tony's nylons under a cotton skirt. I slipped into my shoes and went back to the living room. I raised my skirt an inch or two and struck a pose in the doorway. The radio was playing 'White Cliffs of Dover.' Tony was singing quietly to himself. I joined in. '"... There'll be love and laughter and peace ever after. ..."' He looked up, rose and came towards me, and we began to dance.

'You're a sensational dancer, Dorcas.'

'And you lead wonderfully.' I was breathing in the scent of him as we moved. He smelled of maleness and salt water and cocoa butter.

From the radio came the strains of 'The Last Time I Saw Paris.' We both began to sing quietly. I guess we were feeling the wartime blues. I felt the roughness of his sun-dried trunks as he held me closer and the strength of his body against my own. I remember his mouth closing over mine. I felt myself give way in his arms and begin to fall. He collapsed with me on to the carpet.

211

He slipped my blouse from my shoulders and unbuttoned my skirt, sliding his long, strong hands down over my stomach. I heard myself whimpering like a puppy. I couldn't have stopped. Something had overtaken me. I heard him using words to me that my husband never would have dreamt of speaking. He did things to me that Hale had never done. He taught me things about my body that I had never known. I remember the soft, black whorls of hair on his chest. Hale's hair was sandy and coarse. I don't know if I was asleep or awake when I raised my eyes and saw Tony above me, bronzed and glistening as a young sea god riding the waves astride a dolphin. The pounding of the surf rang in my ears. When we awoke we had carpet burns on our skin. We went into the bedroom, but we didn't sleep. When the dawn patrol droned overhead, we were still together.

Thinking of that weekend, I am still appalled and ashamed and something else I cannot quite name. It was one of those *coups de foudre* that happens in wartime. It was better for both of us to pretend that it had never occurred. The next I heard of Tony, he had been promoted to lieutenant (j.g.) and was serving aboard a destroyer escort, the USS *Simon Browne*, somewhere in the Pacific.

The *Browne* went down in the spring of 1945 off Okinawa. Tony was picked up by another ship and returned home shortly after V-J Day. I suppose he must have met Nita Paris almost immediately. They were married less than three months later. Even though he was out of the Navy by then, I still think of it as one of those precipitate wartime marriages. Duncan, Dosie's third child, had just been born, and I was visiting her at the hospital one evening when she told me the news. Neither one of us knew what to make of it. 'Who on earth is she?' I asked Dosie. 'I mean, I know who she is, but who is she really?'

'You know as much as I do. He met her at the studio, they say. Tony's working for Sam Farkas again. He's an associate producer now. They're in preproduction, whatever that is, on a film called *Sunday and Monday*.'

'Is Nita Paris in his picture?'

'I don't think so. Here, one of the nurses brought me this photograph of Tony and Nita from the newspaper. It was taken right after the ceremony in Reno.'

'She's quite dark, isn't she? Or is it the photo?'

'Someone told me she had a Brazilian father and a Canadian mother.'

'An Eskimo, perhaps.'

Dosie giggled. 'Mummy, aren't you wicked! She's awfully striking, don't you think? She looks like some kind of lush tropical flower.'

'Striking' was a good description of Nita Paris. I would not have called her beautiful, because I have always believed beauty must be more than a matter of superficial appearance. Obviously, Nita knew the tricks of her trade. She was skilful with makeup, and her wardrobe was stunning. She wore her black hair in the peekaboo style that was popular among glamour girls like Rita Hayworth and Veronica Lake. I don't know how she could abide it falling over her face like that and forever having to brush it back, but I dare say she thought it gave her an aura of mystery and sophistication. The real mystery, however, was what she was doing in the Prudhomme family. Anyone could see that she was not a domesticated animal.

I doubt that Andrew approved of his brother's choice, though I certainly wouldn't have broached the subject to him. He never actually put his opinion of Tony's wife into words. It was just a feeling I got from him. Andrew had become very closemouthed. Perhaps it was the effect of all the wartime secrecy at Outerbridge Industries. He seemed to have developed a reticence that lingered even in peacetime. Despite the fact that the war had ended, Andrew was still absent from home for much of the time. He kept to himself about his work, and it was only from me that Dosie inadvertently learned that Andrew was no longer working at the plant on Saturdays.

Needless to say, I hadn't any intention of causing trouble between them. When I realized what I'd done, I wanted to leave their house immediately.

'Absolutely not, Mummy. Drew and I have no secrets. Or until now, I *thought* we hadn't. Drew!' She called across the lawn to the pool. 'May I speak with you, please?'

I glanced at young Daphne who was reading her alphabet book to Dexter. '*Pas devant les enfants,*' I whispered to Dosie.

'Daphne, Dexter,' she said, 'please find Nanny and have her get you ready to go to Silverwood for Sunday dinner.'

'Andrew,' I told him as he came on to the lanai, towelling himself off, 'I seem to have committed a *faux pas*. Believe me, it was unintentional.'

'Mummy says you're not working for Daddy on Saturdays anymore. You haven't been working for him on Saturdays for months.'

Drew gave her a quizzical look. 'I never said I was.'

'But I thought you were still at the plant every Saturday.'

'I guess I forgot to mention it. I've been involved in a project with three fellows named Gamble, Connors and Lewis.'

'What kind of a project?'

'Oh,' he said tiredly, 'I'd rather not go into it now.'

'They're not competitors of Daddy's, are they?'

Drew laughed. 'Of course not.'

'Then why are you so secretive?'

'Dosie, darling,' I put in, 'perhaps you two should have this out in private.'

'Mother Outerbridge, there's nothing to "have out," as you put it.'

'There is too, Drew!' argued Dosie. 'If these people are above-board, why can't you talk about what you're doing?'

'I didn't say I couldn't. I said I didn't feel like it right this minute.'

'You're not having an affair, are you?'

'Dosie!' I was aghast.

'That's all right, Mother Outerbridge – '

'It is *not* all right,' I retorted. 'Dorothea, I'll thank you to remember your breeding! Ladies do not discuss such personal matters.'

'Well,' said Drew, 'If anybody cares, I'm not.' He rose, ran briskly across the lawn and executed a perfect dive into the pool.

Eventually, Andrew let us all in on his real estate dealings with Ralph Gamble and his other associates. I suspect he wanted to show Hale that he could be successful without the aegis of his father-in-law. Actually, Hale was delighted for him and success-fully invested some of his own money with them, though neither

214

one of us thought much of Mr Gamble's personality. He was one of those people whom the tides of war had swept into our lives like flotsam. The war had demolished social barriers, ostensibly for the duration. To be sure, one was as grateful for the heroism of Okies and Arkies as one was for that of young men with background, but once those distinctions had been donated to the war effort they were, unlike silk, steel or petrol, never fully restored afterward. Hence the presence at Silverwood of someone like Ralph Gamble, with his abrasive speech and star sapphire pinky ring. It was easy to see how impressed he was. He lavished flattery upon Ada in spite of the fact that she was almost old enough to be his mother. It was really rather amusing to see how both Ralph and Nita Paris curried favour with Ada, though I don't believe the two ever met until Ada died. If they had, it would have been quite a contest.

I never found Nita a warm person, although she clearly tried to create the impression of what Hale called 'a hot number.' I found her charm to be a glossy veneer behind which there was a substance of adamantine density. I hadn't the patience or the interest to analyse it. Nita had a way of getting on my nerves. She seemed always to be on stage. At a party, surrounded by men, she would play up to Tony outrageously, as though he were only a vehicle for her to display her charms. It was a shameless ploy. Poor Tony. In the bosom of the immediate family she became as wholesome and ingenuous as Andy Hardy's Polly. With Dosie's and Andrew's children she was the doting, solicitous Auntie Nita. To me, these performances were not entirely flawless. Though Nita spoke with the studied inflections of someone who has deliberately improved herself, she had a vulgar, guttural laugh like the last gurglings of bathwater being sucked down the drain. And she hadn't the delicacy to wholly conceal her ambitions, either. She called people by their Christian names well before the courtesy was offered – something which Hale could not abide – and made no secret of her acquisitiveness. 'Dorcas,' I can recall her saying, 'Dosie has very sweetly offered to let me borrow that beautiful sable coat that Drew gave her for Christmas, but I'd never forgive myself if someone spilled something or dropped a cigarette on it. What do you think I should do? I must have something grand for the premiere of my picture next month.' Tony, of course, was sitting not five feet away and supposed to take the hint.

'Can't you borrow a fur from the studio?' I said. 'I thought actresses could do that.'

'But those things never look quite right. If I had my own, we could probably write it off as a business expense.'

'We?'

She cast a smile in Tony's direction. 'Did I say that? Imagine, we've been husband and wife less than two months, and already I sound like an old married lady. It must be love.' She waited, still smiling, for Tony to raise his eyes from his newspaper. When he merely turned the page, she pursed her lips and rose impatiently from her chair. 'I don't suppose anyone would like to play backgammon.'

At this, Tony looked up. 'I thought Drew said he'd play when he got back.'

'I'm bored. Won't you play until he comes?'

'What about Hale?'

'Hale left with Drew and Dosie.'

'Oh, all right.' Tony folded the paper and followed her into the other room.

It was embarrassing to see how she led him around by the nose. He wasn't the old Tony at all; even Hale had mentioned it. But then, after that holiday season, we were all changed, and Tony and Nita were the least of my cares. When I think back on it, I see a tableau like the ones inside the hollow, round glass paperweights that once were sold in five-and-dime stores. There is snow, shaken up and drifting down. There are fir trees and ice-spangled houses and the figures of brightly scarved people. Suddenly, without warning, some superhuman hand seizes this shining bauble and dashes it to pieces.

Ralph Gamble

After that first time I went to Silverwood and made the acquaintance of Ada Prudhomme, Drew and I would meet there regularly.
He'd set aside time on the weekends, and we'd get together to go
over the week's business. Ben and Harry both had families, but I
had spare time on Saturdays and Sundays. As for Drew, I had
the impression that his kids got on his nerves and he welcomed
the break. Also, I guess he didn't want his wife listening in until
he could show her old man how he'd brought home the bacon.

Within a matter of months after we became partners, we had
our first fourteen units finished and renting. We were ready to
roll on some acreage we'd seen in Van Nuys. 'What about letting
my father-in-law in on it?' Drew asked the three of us.

'That's up to you.'

'Say about five o'clock on Sunday at Mother's. How about
allowing me do the talking? Think you can trust me with the job,
Ralph?'

'Shit, yes. I was never big at elocution. You don't need me
there at all, Drew.'

He glanced at us. 'One of you should be there to corroborate
information and correct me if I go wrong.'

Harry shook his head. 'We're going to Arrowhead for the
weekend. Won't be back until late Monday night.'

'You take it, Ralph,' said Ben. 'I don't move in those circles.'

I didn't remind him that until recently I hadn't, either. The
truth is, I was beginning to like pulling into the motor court and
having Safford open the door and say, 'Good afternoon, sir. Mr
Andrew is waiting for you on the south terrace.' That kind of
thing is easy to get used to.

So I wasn't thrown for a loop when I walked in that Sunday

afternoon and found Drew had invited half a dozen other people to hear his spiel.

It was Ada, though, who commandeered me and took me by the arm to meet the others. That was her way of giving me her stamp of approval. I knew it, and they knew it.

She introduced me to the Outerbridges first. I was surprised to find that Hale Hunt Outerbridge was my height. I'd thought he'd be taller, a big man physically as well as financially. His eyes were a little bloodshot, and his razor had missed a place right under his lower lip. He'd of looked like any ordinary bozo if he hadn't of been wearing expensive clothes.

'Pleased to make your acquaintance, sir.'

'Fine, fine.' He clapped me on the shoulder. 'Andrew says you're a real go-getter.'

'Where, exactly, are you from?' his wife wanted to know. She reminded me of one of those little white fluffy poodles, the kind with a jewelled collar.

'Chicago, ma'am.'

'Not now, Dorcas,' her husband told her. 'Have you met our daughter, Mr Gamble? Dosie, dear, come here.' He beckoned her away from Drew.

'How do you do?' She smiled shyly and shook my hand.

I guess I'd envisioned Drew's wife as being the sophisticated type, seeing how she came from wealthy, high-type people. Whatever it was I'd expected of her, this wasn't it. Dosie was one of those passably pretty women with wide hips and a docile way about her. She looked kind of soft and pliable and bland, like angel food cake. Nine chances out of ten, she'd have a weight problem before she was forty.

As it was, she died only a month or so later. Lost in a blizzard or some freakish thing like that. Too bad she wasn't the spunky sort like her mother-in-law; maybe she would have survived.

'And this,' Ada manoeuvred me to a chair by the window, 'is Miss Elodie Swann. Elodie knows a good bit about real estate investments.'

'Did.' Miss Swann corrected her. 'Once upon a time. Mr Gamble, is it? A name well suited to your calling.'

'Yes'm.'

'Being in the real estate market is rather like being a houseguest. The greatest knack is knowing when to leave.'

She was in her sixties, I guessed, a peppery old broad, the kind who could hold her own in any company.

By now I'd worked my way around the room to where Drew stood. 'Ralph, may I present Sam Farkas?'

He was a short guy, pipe-smoker, fifties, big nose, a tired look around his eyes. The name rang a bell.

'Are you the Sam Farkas who made *Shadow Flight* and *Victory at Dusk*?'

'The same.'

'Say, this is an honour.' I gave him a hearty shake. 'Those were the two best movies about the war. The part in *Shadow Flight* where the refugees are in the cemetery and the Nazis – ' I caught sight of Dorcas Outerbridge out of the corner of my eye. She was giving me a look of such contempt that it bordered on pity. Here I was, making a fuss over some kike movie producer when Hale Hunt Outerbridge was cooling his heels, waiting to hear what me and Drew had to say. 'Anyhow, it was a terrific picture.'

'Kind of you to remember it. Thanks,' Farkas said. 'Drew, are you ready to enlighten us? Should we sit down?' He laid his pipe in a silver ashtray on the table beside him, opened a drawer and took out a pipe cleaner. He seated himself in a big armchair and began to ream out his briar. That surprised hell out of me. Obviously, Sam Farkas felt quite at home.

Afterward, Farkas and Outerbridge both invested some dough with us. They both made money, too. I guess it was a drop in the bucket for Outerbridge, but his name as an investor was almost worth more to us than the cash.

Like I said, Drew's pitch was a success, and our projects kept expanding. By the next year, though, Drew began to withdraw from our group. I'd still call him to ask if he wanted in on this deal or that, and he'd usually mail a check just on my say-so. He made a lot of money that way, over the phone. By that time, though, his wife had been found dead, and the tragedy had made him a changed man. He looked burned out. All the spark had gone from him. Even his movements were different, slower, like

219

an older man. He became a loner. He spent all his spare time at home. He wasn't so much a part of things anymore.

But I used to see Ada out and about. One time, she was with Sam Farkas at a charity premiere. She kissed my cheek and introduced me and my date to Gary Cooper and his wife. Like I later told her granddaughter, Daphne, I thought Ada was one swell dame. She had a way of, whenever she saw you, making you feel like you were the one person on earth she'd been wanting to run into. She'd demand to know how you were, and she wasn't just making conversation. She acted like it mattered to her. She listened to what you said. How many dames do that? The thing with Ada Prudhomme was, once she'd sized you up as a square shooter, she treated you like you were on equal footing, irregardless of whether you were an Outerbridge or a nobody.

The morning after the premiere, Ada phoned me. She'd never done that before. She wanted me to know, she said, that I'd made Drew independent. That he knew now that he could make his way in life even if he didn't have a trust fund on his job with Outerbridge Industries.

'There's a marked change in him,' she told me. 'It's clear that he's his own man now. If it hadn't been for you, Ralph. . . .'

'It would probably have happened sooner or later, Ada.'

'Perhaps. Perhaps too late.'

What a class act she was, thinking to call me to say that. I knew Ada Prudhomme for only a few years, but I think of her like a good friend. It shocked hell out of me when she died so suddenly.

She left almost four hundred acres of prime Beverly Hills real estate. It never occurred to me that the Prudhomme twins would sell it, especially after I heard they were both living there, Drew with his three kids and Tony with Nita Paris. I figured Silverwood for one of those family mansions that gets handed down from father to son. So naturally, when I heard some time later that damn near the whole thing was on the market, I could of kicked myself for not having made an offer before the fact. The truth is, though, that I wouldn't of had the brass. Drew and Ada and that bunch had treated me like one of their own, and I couldn't of summoned up the nerve to make a fast grab for Ada's estate with her not yet cold in the grave.

But over a year afterward was another thing. I got hold of Drew and told him me and my partners wanted in on the bidding.

'Whittaker and Wyndham have an exclusive on the property. We're talking big numbers, Ralph.'

'I figured. You can't scare me off with that. Ben and Harry and me are doing great. Besides which our credit is tops. And we've got a new partner, Corning Merritt, Jr. You know him?'

'Junie?' He laughed. 'Hell, Ralph, Junie's got more money than Fort Knox. I went to school with him at Exeter. I remember him arriving with a trunkful of silk sheets. Is he still a big drinker?'

'Not very,' I lied.

'Listen, Ralph, right now the bidding is wide open, so feel free. I'll send you the brochure on the property. Don't hesitate to call me with any questions.'

'If you don't mind me asking, how come you decided to sell in the first place?'

'Ah, well, staffing it – finding help and all that,' he said.

I didn't press him. 'Your brother's all for it, too, then.'

'What matters is that my brother's wife is all for it. And my brother is for whatever keeps her happy.'

'Sounds like he's nuts about the dame.'

'Just nuts. Period.'

Like I said before, Drew got prickly as a hedgehog on the subject of his brother and sister-in-law. To hear Nita tell it, there was no love lost among the three of them by the time they quit Silverwood. I ran into Nita at the carwash a few years ago and we made a date for dinner. I took her out that one time only. As soon as we sat down at the table, she started bellyaching about how lousy Ada had treated her and what a prick Tony could be when he wanted and a few other details about the Prudhommes, which, if you believed them, were better left unsaid. Even if none of it was true, the Prudhommes sure had themselves one bitter enemy in Nita Paris. Whatever the case, the evening left me with a bad taste in my mouth, and I never returned her phone calls.

As for Silverwood, it took nearly a year before all the details of

221

the sale were worked out. A year after that, we opened up the first section for construction. We'd divided the property into fourteen sections with about thirty homesites each, and our projections were to open only one section per year, so as to maintain the value and prestige of the place. We've handled Silvercrest Estates like De Beers handles diamonds. The last section is open now, and like I said before, would to God that Ada had left even more land.

I live in Silvercrest Estates myself, in a Hawaiian modern complete with projection room, sauna and a Rolls in the driveway. Every year I take a table for ten at the annual ACTS benefit. I always get a charge out of telling my guests what the place was like in its prime. It's a real kick, being able to say I was there in the good old days. Like having been Hearst's guest at San Simeon, someplace that's history now. I can see that some of them don't believe me and some others are 'trying not to look surprised that a regular joe like myself was received at Silverwood. The fact is, I tell them, I wouldn't be where I am today if it weren't for the Prudhommes. They gave me my start. It was a lucky break for me, meeting that crowd. And like I always say, half the fun of being lucky is spreading it around. It's a rule of mine to give as good as I've got. Even Ada Prudhomme herself couldn't take it with her, right?

Nanny Beale

Mr Anthony came back from the war unscathed, through the grace of God. By the time he returned, he'd been gone four years in all. Mr Farkas gave him a job as an associate producer on a movie he was making called *Sunday and Monday* about a pair of servicemen who came home to sad times. It won two Academy

Awards. I remember I wept so hard in the theatre that I was afraid I'd be asked to leave.

No matter that the fighting was over and our troops were coming home; staff was hard to come by. Mr Safford said it was the war effort at fault. Parlour maids had put on trousers and snoods, learned to use welding torches and thought themselves fit to have afternoon tea with Mrs Roosevelt. Nannies like myself had abandoned their youngsters for defence jobs, not so much out of patriotism, if you ask me, but so they could drive convertibles, wave twenty dollar bills about and assume the airs of their betters. Young men didn't mind taking orders from a sergeant, but nobody wanted to have to say 'Yes, ma'am' to the lady of the house. A number of the upstairs rooms were closed off. Mr Safford made do with a staff of four, where there had once been fifteen, and of those four, two were bumpkins who needed to be trained from scratch and supervised every waking minute. No wonder Mr Safford's hair went quite white.

It wasn't only the character of Silverwood that changed. The twins had been growing steadily apart ever since the war separated them. I suppose Mr Andrew resented being forced to sit out the fighting due to having a bad leg from his accident. It embarrassed him to have people mistake him for his brother and congratulate him on his return to civilian life. Occasionally someone, noticing his limp, would inquire as to where he'd been wounded. I don't like to say it, but he was envious of Mr Anthony in certain ways. Mr Anthony had served his country and been welcomed home like a hero. He was handsome and footloose, and the young ladies made much of him, you may be sure of that.

We, Mr and Mrs Andrew's household, had settled into a larger home by then. It was a wide, white pillared house on Mansfield in the Wilshire district, almost around the corner from Mr and Mrs Outerbridge. They took a keen interest in the young Prudhommes. Mrs Andrew was, after all, their only child and hers their only grandchildren. Their closeness, not to mention the fact that Mr Andrew worked for Mr Outerbridge, circumscribed his life. There was his brother, cutting up in the society pages and making a name for himself in the movie magazines as a man about town, while he and Mrs Andrew stayed at home awaiting their third child. He was too much of a gentleman to let it show, but I'm sure he must have felt restless now and then. He was only twenty-eight. His mother's admonition about marrying so young must have repeated on him like a heavy meal.

The child was another boy. Mrs Andrew named him Duncan. If Mr Andrew objected to this name like the last, he didn't trouble to say so, at least within my hearing.

His brother chose that time to marry. I remember it well. Mrs Andrew was still in hospital with the new baby. It was a rainy, dark afternoon, early in November. I heard Mr Andrew come in, shake out his raincoat and call up the stairs for the youngsters, as he did every evening. Dexter, who was four, dashed down and threw his arms about his father's knees. Daphne ran after him, waving her book of *Just So Stories*, begging to be read to. She was her daddy's darling, no denying it. He gathered them together on the sofa in the library and began to read. I stepped out into the kitchen to listen to the six o'clock news with Mrs Morrill, the housekeeper. We could hardly believe our ears when we heard the announcement of Mr Anthony's elopement. I knew very well that Mr Andrew hadn't been aware of it or Mrs Prudhomme either because she would have called to tell him. I looked in amazement at Mrs Morrill who was just as surprised as I.

'"Bless us and save us" cried Mrs O'Davis!' she said. That was her pet expression. 'Mr Anthony and Nita Paris! We've a movie star in the family! What do you make of that, Nanny! Why, I saw her in *The Saracen Oath* and *The Silver Blade*. Merciful heavens, but she's a glamorous lady. Do you suppose Mr Anthony will bring her here? I wouldn't know what to say to her, would you?'

'Is she the one who was in *Gypsy Daughter* with John Hodiak?

'That's her. What should we call her, do you think, Mrs Anthony or Miss Paris?'

'Mrs Prudhomme isn't going to like this.'

'I read in *Photoplay* where her mother was from Istanbul and her father was some kind of Spanish diplomat. She must be a real woman of the world.'

'Do you think I should break the news to Mr Andrew? It's almost time to collect the children.'

224

Mrs Morrill shrugged. 'It's no secret, is it?'

I said I guessed not, since it had been on the air. I went in and told the children to scamper upstairs and begin undressing. Dexter begged for 'just one more page,' as usual, but his father looked relieved to close the book.

'Do as Nanny says, kids. Off you go. I'll come up later to say good-night.'

'I'll be there in a moment,' I told them. 'I want everything hung up or folded neatly, please.' I waited until they were well on their way up the stairs. Mr Andrew was pouring himself a drink at the bar. 'There was some news just now on the radio about Mr Anthony.'

He turned, the bottle in his hand. 'Nothing's wrong, is it? He's not in any kind of trouble, is he?'

'He's gone and got married. Eloped, they said. With Nita Paris, the movie star.'

Perhaps it was something in his face or the way he was holding the neck of the bottle in his fist, for I know that just then I thought without a doubt that he would hurl the bottle across the room. I cannot now imagine why I would think such a preposterous thing.

'Thank you, Nanny,' was all he said.

Mr Andrew never did take to Nita Paris, although she seemed to like him well enough. As for Mrs Andrew, I think she was a bit put off by all that glamour. I don't think she ever quite knew what to make of the sudden appearance of this exotic creature in the family fold. Poor dear, perhaps if she'd only had more time they might have become friends. Not in our darkest dreams could we have foreseen that Mrs Andrew had less than two months left upon this earth.

I don't know what happened. I guess no one ever will. The twins and their wives and Mr and Mrs Outerbridge had gone to Sun Valley for a holiday over New Years. As luck would have it, both Daphne and Dexter came down with whooping cough right after their parents left. They were mild cases. The doctor and I both told Mrs Andrew not to worry; the children were receiving good care. Then the worst happened. Little Duncan, who wasn't yet two months old, caught the disease. We had taken pains to

225

isolate him from his brother and sister, but somehow he contracted whooping cough anyhow. Dear God, what a worrisome time that was, hearing that tiny boy choking and gasping for air. I telephoned his mother and told her she'd best come home. By the hour, I knelt beside that poor lamb's crib, saying I don't know how many Hail Marys.

By the time Mrs Andrew stepped off the train, thank the good Lord, my prayers had been answered. The crisis had passed and we knew he would recover. Still, she would have stayed with the youngsters, I'm sure, had it not been for Mrs Prudhomme senior insisting she rejoin her husband. How that fact must have haunted Mrs Prudhomme. 'Dosie, my dear,' I can recall her saying, 'I won't hear of your staying an extra day! There's no reason for it. Andrew's holiday will be quite spoiled without you. Nanny and Mrs Morrill will take care of everything here. Go and enjoy yourself.'

She never returned to us. I'm told she reached Sun Valley at the onset of a blizzard. It snowed for two nights and two days, they say, without letting up. She went to the lodge, of that we're sure, because someone saw her leave again. Nobody knows why, but she went to a cocktail lounge and sat there by herself until well after dark. Maybe she was expecting to meet a friend. It wasn't the sort of thing Mrs Andrew was accustomed to doing. She drank very little, perhaps a sherry or two before dinner. The others, Mr Anthony and the Outerbridges, were skiing, and Mr Andrew was lying down in his room. He didn't ski because of his bad leg. He'd been tobogganing and taken a tumble that wrenched his back, so he was resting. Mrs Anthony, Nita Paris, had gone skating.

What I'll never understand is why Mrs Andrew, who was such a levelheaded young woman, should suddenly do something so unaccountable. She was too prudent to have done what she did, yet she did it. She went out into the storm for a walk. Walked out of the cocktail lounge into a blinding blizzard in the dark of evening, as if she were taking a stroll along Malibu Beach on a midsummer day. There's no sense to it. One looks at it from this way and that, holding it up to the light, turning it over and over, shaking it, testing the weight and the feel of it, looking to

226

recognize something comprehensible. Still there's no explanation. They found her the next day, a short distance from the village, wrapped in the fine fur coat Mr Andrew had given her for Christmas, lying under a covering of snow, frozen to death where she had fallen.

It all but broke my heart. Having to tell the little ones, Daphne and Dexter, was the hardest, saddest thing I've ever had to do. It was worse, far worse, than when Mr Prudhomme senior died. Mrs Andrew was so young, only twenty-seven, and with a newborn who would never know his mother's love. Daphne, who was nearly seven, understood. Dexter tried to be a brave boy, but night after night for almost a year, he'd wake sobbing from nightmares, crying out for his mother.

Mr Andrew wasn't the same after that. He sometimes drank too much and fell asleep in his chair after dinner. I'd hear him making his way unsteadily up the stairs to his room in the small hours of morning. He seemed not to stand so tall and straight as before, as if now he shouldered a great and terrible weight. His mind tended to drift off a subject, and if you caught him unawares, he'd be gazing at nothing at all with a kind of puzzled, pained expression. There were lines of strain about his eyes and a rigid set to his jaw. All at once he looked several years older than his twin brother.

He didn't want to stay in that house after Mrs Andrew's death. Having her parents' home so nearby didn't help matters. Mrs Outerbridge would drop in without notice to see her grandchildren and she persisted in telling them stories about their mother as a little girl, the sorts of charming, funny little snippets that all parents cherish about their young. In this case, though, it seemed she was not doing it so much to amuse Daphne and Dexter, but rather to keep Mrs Andrew alive by repeating her loving litany over and over again with a kind of fierce intensity that frightened the youngsters and myself alike. I was as glad as Mr Andrew when he put the house up for sale. Even though it would mean another jolt for the children, I was beginning to think they'd be better off away from Mrs Outerbridge.

I don't think he was prepared for how quickly it would sell. He hadn't found another place to live, and heaven knows what we

227

would have done if Mrs Prudhomme hadn't suggested that all of us, Mrs Morrill included, move to Silverwood for the time being.

Mr Andrew was relieved, I think, not to have the task of setting up a new household. Mrs Prudhomme should have been in her element, opening up those musty, sealed-off rooms and refurbishing them for a new generation of children. Instead, I dare say, it preyed on her that she had sent Mrs Andrew to her death as it were. All she could think to do now was to gather the family close and help her loved ones recover from the tragedy.

Carpenters, painters, paperhangers and upholsterers paraded in and out in a carnival of industry. Mr Andrew paid the bills quite as uncomplainingly as his father had before him. Mrs Morrill and Mr Safford got along swimmingly, and for a time the house seemed to function almost as it had in the old days when the twins were growing up there.

We had one peaceful, happy year at Silverwood, thank God. Fifteen months, to be exact. A brief respite, it was, in the midst of miseries.

Nita Paris

The first time I laid eyes on Prudhomme, it was across a crowded commissary. I was making some tits-and-sand epic, either *Sahara Diary* or *Mark of the Asp*, one of those things where I wore filmy harem pants and a bunch of veils and said things like, 'The desert nights can be cold, sire. The sultan has sent me to see to your comfort.' Fade out. Anyhow, I had a terry robe thrown over my costume, and I was lunching with Hedda Hopper, which was something my agent had been trying to set up for months. Hedda wasn't about to waste her time on just anyone, so the interview was a fair indication that I was on my way upward, out of the B-pictures and into the biggies. The studio publicist sat watching me like a stage mother. ('Nita, perhaps Miss Hopper would be interested to hear how you overcame polio as a child.') I was laying on enough sweetness and light to send Hedda into a diabetic swoon. Then, over her shoulder, I spot this knockout guy standing in the doorway, looking around the room. I see him catch sight of someone and I'm trying to peer around this huge hat which Hedda has on, so I can follow him across the room. He looks like a taller Bob Taylor, but his expression is more outgoing, and he moves as smooth as a dancer, weaving around tables, dodging busboys, waving to people he knows. It's making me nuts, trying to see who he's sitting with. I'm craning this way and that, and finally Hedda looks over her shoulder and then asks me if I'm trying to get somebody's eye. I thought the publicist would choke on his chicken salad. For the rest of the lunch, I make nice to Hedda like a good little girl, and by the time we stand up from the table, my Adonis has left the room.

A few weeks later I was with DeWitt Mowbray, the director, at the polo matches. The day was hot, and I was holding a big red umbrella to keep the sun off my face. It was between chukkers, and the teams were coming off the field. I guess it must have been the umbrella that made one of the horses skittish. I remember it shied and pranced all over the place and its rider was mad as hell. I said I was sorry. He wheeled the horse around, and I could see he was ready to tell me off. Instead, he took one look at me and his eyes made a quick tour, head to toe. He gave me a broad smile. He had beautiful white teeth. 'If you spook my horse again, I'll make you pay for it,' he said, still smiling. With a flick of the reins, he trotted away.

It was the same guy, my Captain Handsome from the commissary. I turned to DeWitt. 'Do you know that man?'

'Never saw him before.' He asked the fellow next to him who it was.

'He's one of the Prudhomme brothers.'

I had to let it go at that. DeWitt was directing my next picture, and I didn't want to get his nose out of joint. I'd learned early that it pays for an actress to have her director at least a little in love with her. In DeWitt's case that was difficult because he was partial to boys, but he kept that under wraps. He liked to wear

229

me on his arm and call me 'my glamour girl' and hint that we were having a big romance. Actually, it worked almost as well as the real thing for me because he played his charade to the hilt. He had my role expanded and gave me some great close-ups.

I asked around about the Prudhommes, and somebody told me they were high society. It seemed there were two brothers, an Anthony and an Andrew. I still didn't know which one was the good-looker, but I was occupied with a certain stuntman just then, and the question somehow slipped my mind.

After the war broke out, I made a quickie foreign intrigue picture called *Ticket to Tangier*. They'd wanted Hedy Lamarr, but she wasn't available and I got the job. The picture turned out to be a sleeper. It was a real break for me. The studio renegotiated my contract and began putting me in big-budget productions. I got the sultry parts, the woman of mystery or the good bad girl. I was riding high, getting a couple of thousand fan letters a week. Between pictures, a bunch of us would go around to the local Army camps and make personal appearances. The boys went gaga at the sight of a dame. I could have stood there and told them Santa Claus was dead, and they would have whistled and clapped like wild men. The thing I didn't like, though, was to go to the hospitals when they were sent back. You'd see some gorgeous guy lying there in his cot – you'd start to say something, and he'd roll over and you'd see the other half of his face had been burned away. There were young fellows with no legs and urine tubes dangling from their wheelchairs and pale boys who just sat there and shook so hard they couldn't speak. Christ, I hated that, mostly because I felt lousy, trying to con them into believing everything would be peachy and I thought they were just fine the way they were, when what I really wanted was to run away screaming.

After one of those mornings, I drove back into Beverly Hills and headed straight for the Polo Lounge for a stiff drink. It was barely noon, but I didn't care who caught me. As it happened, it was my agent, Joe Riskind, who spotted me tossing back a neat scotch.

'Nita, you don't think it's a little early for – '

I started to tell him where I'd been all morning when I

saw, coming up behind him, my Mister Marvelous from the commissary and the polo field. Only this time he had two canes and was walking with a limp and looking like it hurt like the bejesus for him to move. It wasn't precisely the time to confess that I hated being around wounded soldiers.

'Hello,' I said, and gave him a big smile.

'How do you do.'

He'd answered politely enough, but you'd have thought he'd never laid eyes on me before. In those days I was, let's face it, a memorable item. This guy just sort of gives me a cursory nod and looks to Joe to make the next move.

'Drew, meet Nita Paris. She's currently on loan-out to Twentieth, starring in *Lone Star Law*.' Joe never passed up a chance to hype a client.

'We've met,' I said, 'but we haven't been properly introduced.'

'May I present Andrew Prudhomme. He and I were about to have lunch. Are you waiting for someone, Nita, or would you care to join us?'

I glanced at Prudhomme again. He still didn't remember me. It annoyed me that he was so cool. What kind of high mucketymuck did he think he was, anyway, acting like I was hardly there? Especially after the once-over he'd given me at the polo matches. I decided I'd teach the stuck-up stiff a lesson he'd never forget. I'd lay on enough sugar and spice to make Nimitz's whole Pacific Fleet go AWOL, and then, just when he thought he had a chance with yours truly, I'd peel him off and make my exit.

We sat at a banquette in one corner of the room. I hung on his every word, pretending to be fascinated. I was minding my p's and q's, not doing anything obvious. I let it look like he was the one with all the charm, and I just couldn't help but melt. When he lit my Parliaments, I'd bend down to the flame before he could raise it to the cigarette, giving him a nice glimpse of cleavage. I'd reach out to steady the light and just barely graze his hand with mine. I'd inhale and look up, giving him a real intimate smile, as if we were the only two people in the place. Then I'd sort of catch myself and pull back, acting like it had all been quite involuntary. I was really going to haul him over the coals.

231

'You must tell me,' I said to him, 'how you and Joe met.'

Joe gave a short laugh. 'By accident.'

'I fell asleep at the wheel. Joe heard the crash, pulled me out and phoned for an ambulance. I figured the least I owed him when I got out of the hospital was a decent lunch.'

'What a dreadful thing to have happen,' I told him, although after what I'd seen earlier in the day it seemed more stupid than anything else.

'Now,' Prudhomme said, 'you tell me how *we* met. I find it difficult to believe I could have forgotten.'

This blasé act of his had to be a crock. 'We bumped into each other at the polo matches last summer. Before that I saw you in the commissary at the studio.'

'Ah. But I didn't play polo last year. I was too busy. And I've never been to a studio commissary.'

'How – '

'That was my brother.'

'Your brother?'

'Tony. He's in the Navy now. People often confuse the pair of us. It's a natural mistake.'

'But you two look – '

'We're twins. Identical.'

'No joke? Identical twins?'

'I hope my brother didn't create too bad an impression, Miss Paris. I wouldn't like to think he'd prejudiced you against the Prudhomme family.'

'No, nothing like that.'

'That's good.' There was a pause. 'Isn't it.'

He knew the answer.

All the time I'd been stalking him, he'd been stalking me. I turned to face him. His eyes met mine. He didn't have to say a thing. The deed was as good as done. He gave me a long look, then broke into that wide white-toothed smile I'd remembered. 'What do you say we order? Who knows when we may need our strength?'

Joe Riskind had an appointment, so he excused himself early. Prudhomme walked me to the door and waited with me for my car.

'Miss Paris – '

'Joe's gone. You don't have to be so formal.'

'When am I going to see you again?'

'That's up to you.'

'This evening? I could stop by for a drink on my way home from the office.'

'I'm busy tonight.'

'Maybe sometime next week, then. But it would only be for a drink. There's some brass in town from Washington and I'm booked every evening for dinner.'

'We'll see.' I wrote my phone number on a scrap of paper and handed it to him.

He called several times before we finally got together. I remember I answered the door in a pair of red silk lounging pyjamas by Adrian. Silk was hard to get because of the war, and I'd been saving them for a special occasion. I was wearing a red chenille snood with sequins scattered over it.

He was walking with only one cane, though he still had a noticeable limp. He stood there on the threshold and gave me the once-over. 'That's some outfit.'

'I hope you mean that as a compliment.' I pointed him towards the bar.

'Definitely. I'm sorry I'm looking so inelegant. It's been a long day. Am I right in remembering you like scotch?'

'On the rocks, please.' I sat at one end of the sofa. 'Actually,' I lied, 'I have to make an appearance at a business function later.'

He handed me my glass. 'You'll take their minds off business, and that's a fact. Cheers.'

'To you.'

He kept looking at me as he drank.

'You're embarrassing me. Why do you stare?'

'As to the first: I doubt it. As to the second: You know damned well you're a specatacular woman. I was trying to figure what chemistry could create a creature like you.'

'My mother was from Hawaii. My father was born in Argentina.'

'You don't say. How in the Sam Hill did they get together?'

'He was travelling. He'd planned to go from San Francisco to the Orient, but he went to mass one day in Honolulu and met my mother. After they married, they moved to Texas. He'd seen a spread there that he wanted to buy.'

'You don't sound like a Texan.'

'The drama coach at the studio would be pleased to hear that.'

'And where are your parents now?'

'I was very young when they died. They were in a hotel fire in Chicago. I was brought up in a convent near San Antonio. I became a photographers' model. After I moved to LA and started acting, the studio changed my name from Anita Del Campo to Nita Paris. My real name was too much like Dolores Del Rio, they said.'

'That's an interesting story. Anything else?'

'What do you mean?'

'Is there anything you want to add to it – dates, details, embellishments?'

I put my glass on the table. 'I don't understand.'

He swallowed the rest of his drink and set it down. 'Didn't Joe tell you anything about me?'

'I didn't ask him. I keep my private life private.'

'I see. I'm vice-president of an outfit that has a lot of government contracts. High priority, top-secret stuff. Our employees have to have security clearances. I have some close contacts in the FBI and the Treasury Department.' He rose and went to refill his glass.

'What does that have to do with me?'

He added a couple of pieces of ice and turned. 'I have plans for us. Don't tell me that comes as a shock to you. As things are, I can't afford not to know something about you. If I'm going to get caught by the g-men with my hand in the cookie jar, there better not be any surprises at the bottom.'

'You're awfully damned sure of yourself, aren't you?'

'So,' he continued, 'I had my friends run a check on you.'

'Jesus! You've got one hell of a lot of crust, you know that?'

He raised his glass in my direction. 'The same goes for you, Miss Nita Paris, the Texas Tornado.'

'That was some dumb gimmick the studio dreamed up when I

first signed my contract. The publicist who got the idea has since been given the heave-ho.'

'We were born the same year, you and I. You may originally be from Texas, for all I know. By school age, though, you were living in La Mesa, California, where your father was a house painter. Your mother was nowhere to be seen. In your teens, you posed for an illustrator in San Diego, left school and travelled with him to New York. After about eighteen months, you left him and moved in with a handbag manufacturer. By the time that ended, you were calling yourself Nita Paris. You got a job as a fashion model. A studio talent scout saw your picture in *Life* magazine, and off you went to Hollywood. That was almost four years ago.'

'Bastard.'

'Your real name is nothing as fancy as Del Campo. It's Anita Maria Sanchez.'

'I had it legally changed.'

'My felicitations. You are also known to be quite a greedy girl.'

'What the hell is that supposed to mean?'

'You like men a lot.'

'That's my business.'

'Evidently not entirely.'

'Listen, I don't rumba with just anyone. I'm the one who chooses my dancing partners.'

'Okay. The choice is yours. I'll stay or I'll go.'

'Jesus! I never came across anyone like you before!'

'That's good news. Here, let me make you another scotch.' He took my glass to the bar.

'Are you trying to get me loaded?'

'Whatever it takes.'

'How do you know I'm not going to throw you out?'

'Because you would have said so already. Let's get one thing straight, Nita,' he said, handing me the drink. 'When I make up my mind about something, I can be very stubborn.'

'But not exactly romantic, I notice.'

'You want flowers? Perfume? Nylons?'

'It wouldn't hurt.'

He was still standing over me. 'Put your glass down.'

'Who are you to give me orders?'

'I'm the guy who's going to be sending you all the flowers and perfume and nylons you want. Maybe even some champagne. Now get up.' He slid his hands under my arms and raised me to my feet. Before I could say another word, his mouth was on top of mine. 'That red thing you have on. I'm going to peel it like a tomato.'

I'll say one thing for him, he may not have been a romantic, but he was the goddamnedest, most inexhaustible, inventive stud I ever met.

After a week or so, I got busy shooting *North to Burma* and I didn't see Drew for a while. Our schedules never meshed. To tell the truth, I had a short flirtation with the producer of the picture, but compared to Prudhomme, he was flat beer. The trouble was, I couldn't break it up until after the picture was cut, or he might have messed around with my part.

When Prudhomme and I came together again, it was late in the fall. Eisenhower had landed troops in North Africa, and what remained of France was under German occupation. The war effort had been stepped up, and Drew was working all kinds of oddball hours. At first he was evasive about what kind of work he did. Then he told me that it had mostly to do with planes. By that time, I'd seen the ID he carried with him for security clearance. He would toss his billfold on the dresser in my bedroom; once his ID had fallen out, along with a list written on pale pink paper, which said 'Gas coupons, meat stamps, Colonel's fudge, corsage for Colonel's wife.'

I picked it up and handed it to him. 'I'll bet your secretary is some rich college girl.'

'Why do you say that?'

'The handwriting. See how she makes those prim, squat letters. They look more like printing than script. Rich girls write like that.'

'I never noticed.'

Sometimes Drew would phone me from his office as early as seven in the morning or as late as midnight. I took him at his word when he said he had to be at the beck and call of the government. It was important to him to do his part. After all, his

236

twin brother was a Naval officer, and he was only a pencil-pusher. I think the real reason he used a cane for so long after the accident was to make it plain why he wasn't in uniform.

He kept his comings and goings pretty mysterious. I assumed it was part of his job. We'd only been seeing each other for about a month this time, and I didn't want to back him off with too many questions. Besides, we didn't do a helluva lot of talking when we came together. Jesus, it was crazy. We couldn't keep our hands off each other even if we tried.

There was this one morning he was stopping by for breakfast on the way to his office. I went out and picked up the paper and put it on the table. Prudhomme was late, so I started thumbing through it.

'Pictured above: Mr and Mrs Andrew (Dorothea Outerbridge) Prudhomme offer their greetings to General William Becker, principal speaker at the War Bond rally held Saturday on the grounds of Silverwood, Mr Prudhomme's family home.'

At first I wanted to believe it was some stupid mistake and the photo was of his brother with someone else, but I knew better. I felt like I'd been punched in the stomach. I kept blinking back the tears because crying would make my mascara run, and I didn't want him to find me looking like a raccoon. The worst of it was, when I thought about how bad it made me feel, I knew how deep I was into this thing. Drew Prudhomme was everything I'd always wanted, and as I watched him through the window, coming up the walk, I didn't know whether to slam the door in his face or fight for him. I swear, I didn't know which I was going to do even when I stood there in the doorway and looked into his eyes.

'Here.' I gave him the paper.

'I saw it already.' He tossed it on the sofa.

'At the risk of sounding foolish: You never told me you were married.'

'I never said I wasn't. I assumed everyone knew.'

'Oh.'

'You really didn't?'

'No.'

'Well, what do you suggest we do?'

237

'I don't know.'

The next time I saw him, I'd recovered my wits enough to ask a few questions. I still wasn't sure how I was going to handle it.

'Dosie and I will have been married five years next June.'

'I suppose there are children.'

'Daphne is three, and Dexter is one.'

'Jesus.'

'What?'

'Nothing.'

'Not to belabour this thing, but I can't stay long.'

'So?'

He inclined his head towards the bedroom. I figured I might as well make a few points while I decided what to do, so I went along with him.

He was getting dressed, tucking his shirt into his trousers. He glanced at his watch. 'What time do the stores close?'

'Five.'

'Damn. I've missed the boat. I meant to buy my wife's Christmas gift.'

'What is it?'

'A washing machine. You know how hard those things are to get with a war on. There's a salesman holding one for me.'

That did it. I mean, what kind of dumb Dora would want a goddamned washing machine for Christmas? And what kind of lacklustre marriage would prompt a husband to give the little lady a fucking laundry appliance, for Christ's sake? If things were that dull at home, I had better than a fighting chance. I'd use every trick in the book. I'd have him, hook, line and sinker, before he knew what had happened.

Cuckoo, isn't it, how we kid ourselves. After a while, you realize it may take a little longer than you thought. You chalk it up to the children. I mean, if this guy is the prince you believe is, he's going to think twice before he leaves his little boy and girl regardless of how dismal his marriage may be.

At home, he says, he's just going through the motions. The only time he feels really alive is with you.

You remind yourself that he's involved in essential war work for Outerbridge Industries. If the damned Axis would surrender,

238

then he could cut himself loose from the Outerbridges, one and all, and have his pick of jobs any place in the aircraft industry.

His wife, he complains, smells of baby powder and is getting heavy in the fanny. All she talks about is the children. He wonders if she even knows that Omaha Beach is not in Nebraska.

You tell yourself that by next winter (or next Thanksgiving or next baseball season) you'll be enjoying life together someplace.

Then I found out I was pregnant. It was in December of '44, the week before Christmas. Drew came over to help me trim the tree. I waited until we had hung the last of the ornaments and he had put the star at the top. I poured him a drink and told him.

'Oh, sweet Jesus.' He kneaded his forehead with his fingers.

'My feelings exactly.'

'Honey, this couldn't have happened at a worse time.'

'For me, too. I'm supposed to start a picture in three weeks.'

'I'm not at liberty to go into details, but it looks like the war can't last another year. I'd be the cause of a major snafu if – for any reason at all – I had to leave Outerbridge Industries when we're in the home stretch. It would be tantamount to sabotage. And believe me, if the story got out about us, there's no way my father-in-law would have me under the same roof. At the moment, there are more important things at stake than how you and I feel about each other.'

'Drew, a girl can't just ring up her doctor for a quick fix. It's illegal.'

'There are people who do that sort of thing. Can't you inquire around?'

'Who do you suggest I ask? Hedda? Louella?'

'Sarcasm won't help. What about whatshername, your hair-dresser at the studio?'

'Cripes, she goes to church every day, and her sister's a cloistered nun.'

'Ask your girlfriends then.'

'And have some ambitious bitch go running to the head of the studio and spill the beans? There are morals clauses in our contracts, you know.'

'But baby, something has to be done.'

In the end, it was my agent, Joe Riskind, who came through.

He put me in touch with a girl who used to be his secretary. She'd got knocked up and had it taken care of by some guy who made house calls. She gave me his phone number.

I don't think he was a doctor. He was wearing an old trenchcoat with deep pockets, and he had this little Chihuahua in one of the pockets. He was maybe fifty, so fair and pale that he looked almost like an albino. He asked me for five hundred in cash, and I gave it to him. He counted it twice, then stuffed it in the pocket with the dog. He went into the bedroom, and he took a syringe and some shiny instruments out of his other pocket, along with a bottle of brownish liquid. He put the coat on a chair, and the dog climbed out and sat on top of it, watching us. This man asked me if I had a rubber sheet. He said if not, a shower curtain would do. We took down the curtain, and he laid it on my bed and put some old towels on top of it. The dog kept making noises. I guess it wanted some attention. The man ignored it. I didn't have any rubbing alcohol, so he rinsed his instruments in the bottle of stuff he'd brought along. He made me lie at the edge of the bed, draw up my knees and open my legs. I remember he hadn't put on any kind of surgical gloves. His hands were plump and feminine. He filled the syringe from the bottle and told the dog to pipe down. Then he opened me up and injected this stuff inside me. The dog kept whining. I couldn't help but think how this was the same bed where Drew and I were so happy in each other's arms. When it was over, I was bleeding and the dog was yelping loud enough to bring the neighbours. The man didn't stay but a minute longer. He let himself out. I thought I was going to faint. I was crying and shaky and bleeding like I was never going to stop. For a while, I was afraid I might die from it. You hear those stories.

I wonder why it is that I can't even recall the colour of the roses Drew sent me afterward, yet every time I see a Chihuahua dog I feel like I'm going to be sick to my stomach.

Drew told me how much he appreciated the sacrifice I'd made and all that. He couldn't give me any guarantees, he said, or even promises, but he'd try to find ways to repay me. For Christmas, I got a fox coat, and a month later, for my birthday, diamond earrings.

Worse than ever, the situation was getting on my nerves. Here

240

I was, the pinup of fifty thousand GIs, and the guy I was in love with didn't care enough to make a move in my direction. While I had to show up at trade functions with beards like DeWitt Mowbray, he and his wife were hobnobbing with socialites, senators and statesmen.

Twice I tried to cut loose. I played around briefly with an actor and a writer, but I was too far gone by then. I was hooked on Prudhomme, and he knew it. He gave me a high like nobody else could, a pitch of intensity that made me feel turned on and hot as an arc light. If he wanted me to wait until the war was over, I'd play it his way. I'd wait.

By May, when the fighting ended in Europe, Drew was involved in a real hush-hush project. I found out later that Outerbridge Industries had designed some kind of an instrument for the Enola Gay. He begged me to be patient. He had too many things on his mind, he said. It would all be over soon.

I waited until a week after V-J Day. I mean, how the hell patient was I supposed to be? We'd been together over three years at that point. In two more years I'd be thirty and on the downhill side of my career.

The way Drew looked at me, you'd have thought the idea had never before entered his mind. 'Divorce?'

'The war's over, Drew.'

'I know, yes, but – '

'But what?'

'There are other considerations.'

'Such as?'

'You can't ask me to suddenly – '

'It's not sudden. And I have every right to ask.'

'You don't understand.'

'Try me.'

'There's the situation at home.'

'Which, to hear you tell it, is pretty dreary.'

'It's not that.'

'Then what is it, for Christ's sake?'

'Dosie's pregnant.'

Goddamn him. I wasn't going to let him see me cry, no matter how it hurt. I turned my back and walked away. I stood looking out the window. The day was hot. There was no breeze. Nothing moved. The stillness roared in my ears.

'I guess I should have told you.'

'How far along is she?'

He came to the window. 'Six months.'

Jesus wept. Six months, and Drew never said a word. I felt his hands on my shoulders, but I didn't turn around. Talk about a double standard. His wife gets pregnant, and he doesn't want to leave her side. When I told him I was carrying his child, he washed his hands of the whole thing and left me alone to deal with it. 'I think maybe you ought to leave,' I said.

'Now? I just arrived.'

'Now.'

'See here, Nita, don't go off the deep end about this.'

'I need some time to think.'

'Whatever you say. I'll call you later tonight, honey.'

I took the phone off the hook. The next day, I left for four days on location in San Francisco. When I got back, I didn't bother to return his messages.

The studio was throwing a party for some of the stars who'd returned from active duty. I went with Russ Hardwick. He was touted as being a young Ty Power. Maybe he would have made the grade if it hadn't been for the grain and the grape. Anyhow, I was feeling pretty good. I had on this slinky black satin sheath with a slit up the front. Over it, I wore an Eisenhower jacket covered with black sequins. My hair was parted to the side and kind of fell over one eye.

I must have known when I saw him that he wasn't Drew. He was in uniform, after all. Still, I remember I drew my breath in so sharply that Russ asked me what was wrong. I said nothing was and excused myself to go to the powder room. When I came out, I motioned Russ to the far end of the bar. I didn't want to have to come face to face with Drew Prudhomme's twin.

Did you ever notice how cats will seek out the one person in a room who can't stand cats? They seem to do it instinctively, like they want to put them on the spot. It was that way with Tony Prudhomme. I must have moved around that room four or five times to avoid him, yet every time I turned around, he'd be right over my shoulder. Finally, I guess, it was curiosity that made me stop running and let him catch up with me.

. If I'm not mistaken, his face was slightly less broad than Drew's. He was more soft-spoken than his brother and smiled more often.

'I don't expect you to remember me, Miss Paris – '

'But I do. The polo field. Four years ago.'

'You had a red parasol. It frightened my horse.'

'How did you know who I was?'

'I'm a fan.'

'*You?*' I started to laugh.

'Why is that so funny?'

'It is, that's all.'

'We had your photograph aboard the *Browne*. Unfortunately, the Japs scored a perfect hit amidships. I'm afraid you're full fathom five now.'

'I can swim.'

He smiled. 'Can you dance?'

I nodded. He took my arm and led me on to the dance floor. I knew it was only a matter of minutes before he'd ask me for a date. What's more, I knew I was going to say yes.

It was a while before I saw Drew again. 'Jesus Christ, Nita.' He took off his jacket and tossed it on the sofa. 'What's this hard-to-get routine you've been practising recently? It's a little late to be coy, isn't it?' He went to the bar and mixed himself a drink.

'I've been busy.'

'I realize you've been working.'

'That too.'

'How's it going?'

'Not good. *Frisco Venture* is beginning to smell like a flop. The comedy pacing isn't there. They hired the wrong director and they're stuck with him. Listen,' I told him, 'you can't stay. I have to dress for dinner. I'm going out.'

'Don't give me such a fast shuffle. We haven't seen each other in nearly two weeks.'

'I told you. I have a date.'

'Break it.'

'No.'

243

'Who's so important?'

'Tony. Your brother.'

For a split second, he looked at me like a whipped dog. Then he took a deep swallow of his drink and set his glass down hard on the bar. 'How the fuck did this happen?'

'I like the type.'

He reached for his jacket. 'You goddamned well better make up your mind.'

'Or what? Don't tell me you're going to go public, not after all this time and all those fancy excuses of yours.'

'Just watch it, Nita.'

A couple of days later, the *Times* ran a picture of Tony and me at some charity event. On Winchell's Sunday broadcast, he said, 'Naval Lieutenant Tony Prudhomme of the very social Prudhommes is sending up smoke signals in the company of Hollywood lovely Nita Paris. Lucky man.'

I knew sooner or later it would start getting to Drew. Meanwhile, Tony was fun. He wasn't the bedroom acrobat his brother was, but he knew how to give a girl a good time. I figured he wasn't exactly getting shortchanged, either.

I could tell Drew was pissed off. He didn't even bother to remove his jacket. I asked if he wanted a drink. He acted like he didn't hear me.

'You're beginning to look like a slut, you know that?'

I burst out laughing. 'Says who? I thought nobody knew about you and me.'

'Don't you care what I think?'

'Drew, has it ever occurred to you that *you* have two women?'

'That's different. Dosie's my wife.'

'Like hell it's different. Listen to me, Drew: There's only one way you can make me give up your brother, and that's by giving up your wife.'

'You know damned well I can't leave her now. She's due to deliver next month.'

'I'm sick of excuses.'

'That's not an excuse. It's the truth!'

'Do you want me to marry him?'

He shook his head. 'You wouldn't do that.'

244

'The subject has come up.'

'Stop trying to blackmail me. It won't work.'

'Drew.' I put my hand against his cheek and turned his face to mine. 'Do you still love me? Do you still find me attractive?'

'You know very well that I'm in love with you. It's only that _ ,'

'Then, baby, you'll adore having me in the family where you can see me almost every day. And you'll see a nice, big smile on your brother's face, too.'

'You bitch.'

'Leave her, then.'

He walked to the door. 'I'll tell him about us. He'll never marry you.'

'Do that. In return, I'll see that your wife and your exalted father-in-law know everything.'

He slammed the door before I'd finished.

If Drew had only given so much as an inch, for God's sake, if he'd only come out and promised that as soon as the baby was born he'd get a divorce. If he'd done anything else but make more excuses, I never would have gone through with it. I would have waited forever for Andrew Prudhomme.

I was so tired of being on the outside, of reading in the society pages about the Prudhommes and the Outerbridges and their swell set. I'd paid my dues. I wanted to belong to that crowd, to wear the Prudhomme name. In the movie business, you're only as good as your last picture. The public forgets fast. If you're high society, though, the maitre d' never forgets your name. I knew *Frisco Venture* was a turkey. What's more, the damn studio had me typecast now as nothing more than an exotic-looking clothes horse. I wanted to bust loose, to get the kind of meaty roles that went to Joan Crawford and Barbara Stanwyck. As soon as Tony got out of uniform, he was going back to work for Sam Farkas. That wouldn't hurt a bit. There were plenty of reasons for me to say yes to Tony Prudhomme, not the least of which was that he seemed like he was a decent guy. God knows, he was treating me better than his brother ever had.

Whoever said everything's a question of timing sure said a

mouthful. I remember Tony and I were having dinner at the Brown Derby. The waiter was just delivering our cocktails.

'We have something to drink to tonight,' Tony said.

'Don't we always?' I gave him a smile.

'Something new. My brother's wife gave birth to a boy this morning.'

I got this godawful queasy feeling, like I wasn't going to be able to keep anything down, but I raised my glass and touched it to his.

'They've named him Duncan.'

What a case of the cutes they had. Their bloody Christmas cards must have loooked like season's greetings from Santa's reindeer, Drew, Dosie, Daphne, Dexter and Duncan.

For a while, it seemed I couldn't stand the sound of my teeth grinding together as we ate. Then, between the cocktails, the wine and the brandy, we both got pretty mellow. We went up to the Café Gala afterward, to listen to some piano and have a nightcap or two. Judy Garland was there with a bunch of people, and we kept ordering drinks, hoping that if we stayed long enough she'd get up and sing. We must have been really juiced by the time we left. All I recall beyond that point is that we decided to start for Reno in Tony's car, and we had a helluva time getting gas. I think we stayed drunk for three or four days. Somewhere in there we were married by an elderly JP with a wife who looked like Dame May Whitty and played 'My Shining Hour' on her parlour organ. The two of us had trouble keeping straight faces.

It was a crazy, giddy spree. I guess I thought maybe I deserved a good time after Drew's making me suck hind tit for three and a half years. All I know is, Tony and I didn't come to earth until some reporter tracked us down by phone and asked if we'd pose for a picture to go out over the UP wire.

I knew I had to call the studio but quick. Not that they wouldn't approve, but the front office liked to control any press releases concerning their stars. I couldn't afford to antagonize them right then, since I was in the middle of my struggle against being typecast.

We both had hangovers that should have happened only to Hitler. The phone was ringing off the wall. By the time Tony got through to his mother, she'd already heard the news on the radio. I could tell she was furious from the expression on his face. I should have figured right then and there that I was going to have big problems with Mrs Victor G. Prudhomme.

'It was a spontaneous thing,' he told her. He held the phone away from his ear while she went on. 'Mother – ' He gave me a resigned smile and shrugged his shoulders. 'Mother, dear, if you'll only give me a minute to – '

She gave nothing, that one.

'She's here beside me, Mother. I know you'll want to say hello.'

I shook my head frantically, but he handed me the phone anyway. 'Mrs Prudhomme?'

'My dear.'

The way she said those two words, they sounded like someone saying, 'Take this,' and slicing you with a sharp sword. She could do that. She could smile and say all the right things and Christ Almighty if you didn't feel like she was skewering you with every syllable.

I don't remember what else she said or what I said to her. Tony took pity on me and reached for the phone.

'Mother, it may seem we've got off on the wrong foot, but – ' There was a pause. 'Yes, I know I should. Sure. When did you say it was? Okay, Mother, it's a deal. We'll be there.'

'What was that all about?'

'She pointed out that I'd be remiss if I didn't introduce you to the family and our friends. Not that it should be a wedding reception – '

'Why not?'

'Because we eloped. People don't give a formal reception under those circumstances.'

That was the first time I came in contact with what 'people' or 'we' did or didn't do. 'How come? Can't we do as we please?'

'It's not done, that's all. It would be considered inappropriate. Mother had the bright idea that we could take advantage of the charity party she's giving a week from tomorrow. She'll send out telegrams telling everyone who's coming that we're the honoured guests.'

Mrs Prudhomme, I observed, was a take-over lady. 'What kind of gig is it?'

'Something to do with resettling DPs. Mother's helping raise funds. She allows a few favourite charities to hold parties at Silverwood.'

Mrs P. was also no dummy. Parties like that kept her in the limelight and probably gave her a tax break to boot – all without her coughing up a dime.

'Mother said my brother's boiling. I guess we should have called them before they could hear the news from anyone else.'

That was the first I knew of Drew's response. I wasn't sure whether it was that or the hangover that made me feel nauseated. I was suddenly frightened to have him angry with me. I felt like a little kid who'd done something terrible and was scared to face her daddy. I should have realized from my reaction right then that I'd go to any lengths to patch things up with Drew. But what the hell, I'd have plenty of time to worry later. Meanwhile, Tony and I were having a ball. Everywhere we went, we were comped. Our suite was paid for. We were wined and dined. The management gave us chips to play the tables. Our elopement had given the hotel the biggest publicity break it had had all year.

We stayed on in Reno a couple of days, then went to San Francisco and finally back to LA the day before Mrs P's party. Jesus, how I dreaded it. I was afraid of meeting her, sure, but the prospect of facing Drew frightened me more. I didn't know whether I could carry it off or not. I had nightmares about coming apart at the seams and throwing myself at him in front of everybody.

I was damned if I'd let any of the Silverwood set fault my appearance. I'd play it understated and ladylike. The Irene Dunne look. I decided on a simple ivory crepe gown with a high round neck and capped sleeves. It had this beautiful draping at one hip, very classical, like the draping on a statue. I didn't put on any jewellery, just an orchid corsage from Tony. I wore my hair in an upsweep.

At the last minute, I added the diamond earrings that Drew had given me.

Drew Prudhomme

I don't know what caused it, any more than I know what causes an earthquake. We at Outerbridge Industries were under extreme pressure for the duration. Our war work was essential, even if we didn't get any medals pinned on us. Maybe we weren't out there on the front lines, but the goods we manufactured were. It's a wonder nobody broke under the stress. There was my brother, strutting around in uniform, and I was stuck behind a desk doing what looked to everyone like a cushy job. I would have thrown it over in a minute if it hadn't been that Hale needed me at the plant and Dosie had just given birth for the second time.

I did a lot of biting the bullet in those days. Tony always turned up on leave at Silverwood in the company of some poor stiff who'd be struck speechless by the surroundings. Once he dragged home on Okie named Dwayne Detmers who'd never seen an ocean before he'd enlisted. We had artichokes for dinner, I remember, and you could tell this guy had never laid eyes on one, much less tried to eat it. How that yokel became a naval officer I'll never know. Tony had this peculiar penchant for slumming. It was nine-tenths self-aggrandizement, if you ask me. To the Greasy Gracies and Dwayne Detmers of the world, he looked like a big cheese. Meanwhile, I looked like a goddamned draft dodger.

After the accident, it was almost worse. I'd be asked, 'How'd it happen, soldier?' Half the time I'd make up something rather than say I'd cracked up my frigging car.

Not that I have any excuse for getting tied up with Nita. It was no big thing, really. I'd drop by her place maybe twice a week, and we'd both enjoy a little exercise. It was playtime, a way to get out from under the pressure.

She was the kind of dame who knew how to give a guy his fun. She'd had plenty of practice, from all reports. Odd, but the only thing that sticks in my mind after all these years is her smile. Nita had this blazing smile, that was how I thought of it. There was an element of danger in it, as if she could turn it on some poor chump and incinerate him on the spot. Like everything else, she used it to her advantage. That's not to say we weren't each getting what we wanted out of the situation. I pulled some strings and kept her in champagne, steaks and a few other commodities that were supposed to have marched off to war along with Lucky Strike green. After a year or so, I slipped her cash monthly to pay the rent. If it had been anyone else, she'd have been content with the arrangement, but Nita was insatiable. She started dropping hints about wanting more time together and bitching about being single. She imagined her looks were fading and her career was slipping away. She started putting pressure on me. She had me by the short hairs and she knew it, though there was never, believe me, any likelihood of my divorcing my wife to marry her. I may be a lot of things, but I've never been crazy. Marrying Nita would have been like walking into a blast furnace. Then, as if by God to prove my sanity, the cunt turns around and tries to use my brother as leverage to force me to marry her. At that point, I figured he was in more trouble than I was. Tony never was discriminating to begin with, and Nita knew how to play a guy like Nero played his fiddle. I tried to warn him, but when it came to cooze, Tony was a pushover. Add to that the fact that he thought he was God's gift to women, and you realize he never had a chance against a determined broad like Nita Paris.

It was a real slap in the face for Mother, Tony's running off and marrying Nita on the sly. He must have known how much it would hurt her. Here she'd dedicated her entire life to making the Prudhomme name stand for something, and along comes this dame, common as crabgrass and affecting refinement as if she were auditioning for a part. Tony had one hell of a nerve foisting her on our family. Mother tried to put a good face on it, but she must have been crushed.

Dosie, God bless her, typically looked on the bright side. 'You just wait,' she said to me. 'Once Nita settles into the family, she'll turn into a real homebody and start having babies.'

'She's not exactly the type, sweetheart.'

'I don't think Nita's anywhere near as hard as she seems, Drew. She's had to be tough to get where she is. She never had the advantages we did. Look at Ralph Gamble. He's a rough diamond but underneath he's really very sweet.'

I thought about what she was saying and decided that even if she knew the facts, Dosie would be taking more or less the same attitude towards Nita. Forgiveness was her middle name.

'What's that? Why are you humming?'

'I wasn't. I was thinking what a swell girl I married.'

'You were *so* humming. You were humming "South of the Border."' She began to sing, '"South of the border, down Mexico way. . . ."'

'Is Nita a spic, do you think?'

'Andrew! Don't you dare let the children hear you use a word like that! Anyway, she told me her mother was Polynesian.'

In a pig's eye. Nita was a hot female, *olé*, from spicy Mexico.

Our life, Dosie's and mine, was just about as peaceful as anything you could imagine, until Nita came into it. Sure, sometimes we were annoyed with each other, but it was never serious. When Dosie was ticked off at me, she'd put on her little-girl pout and busy herself examining the charms on her bracelet. That was my signal to ask why she was so preoccupied.

'Why is it, Drew, that you always kiss the children before you kiss me? You never kiss me first.'

It was stuff like that, nothing major. I can't recall our ever having a real argument. Of course all married people get on each other's nerves occasionally. I remember in Sun Valley, how she'd jump up from the breakfast table, 'Come on, everyone! Time to rise and shine and hit the slopes!' Finally I made some remark about her sounding like an over-age cheerleader, and it made her cry. I felt lousy about that.

I try never to think of my wife's death – not that I didn't love her to pieces, Jesus, no. It's just that I didn't want my kids ever to think that their mother's death left their father in any way maimed or wrecked. Kids need to know they have someone strong

251

in their corner. It was important for them that I not give in to my emotions when it happened. It was important to play for time, to bear up, until time worked its repairs on them. Strange, though, that her death, instead of leaving me with the feeling that I'd lost so much, left me with the peculiar sensation of having *gained*. I mean actually, physically gained weight, as if I was heavier by twenty or even thirty pounds. I have never been able to shake that sensation of being overweight. I've been on every damn diet in the books, and nothing works. I still feel like I'm lumbering along under a heavy load. For all I know, it's pure coincidence that I first noticed the feeling around the time of Dosie's death, but it sticks in my memory that that's when it came on. It's a peculiar kind of reaction, Christ knows, but I guess there's no accounting for how different people are affected when tragedy strikes their lives.

Hale took it like a Spartan, naturally, but Dorcas went down for the count. She harangued the kids with laundry lists of their mother's virtues. Half the time she acted as if she was jealous of her own grandchildren, as if nobody had a right to suffer as much as she. She competed with their grief. She'd accuse them of not caring enough. One day Daphne came home reeking of booze, and it turned out she'd helped herself to a splash of Dorcas' 'perfume' behind the ears. Those crystal bottles on her grandmother's dressing table were filled with straight bourbon. At that point, I decided we lived too close for comfort. I packed up the kids, and we moved to Silverwood.

Mother was a godsend. She was determined to pick up the pieces and put our family to rights again. She waged a real campaign to draw the children out of their grief and gradually bring them back to normal. I had to hand it to her for all the affection and patience she showed my kids. You could tell, too, how much she loved having Daphne living there with her. The two of them became as thick as girlfriends. I got a kick out of seeing the two of them, tall and short, inseparable as Mutt and Jeff.

Maybe I shouldn't have moved in with Mother so readily. God knows, she had enough on her mind already. First she'd been stuck with Tony's choice of a wife. Then there had been Dosie's death. Now Tony and Nita had taken to bickering in public so that it was a strain to be around them. The worst was still to come. A little more than a year later, Sam, the one person Mother believed she could rely on, pulled the rug out from under her with no warning.

Tony Prudhomme

A lot of us, coming back from the war, married the first girl we fell in love with. Marriage, under any circumstances, is an act of faith. At that particular time, with Auschwitz and Hiroshima fresh in mind, maybe it seemed imperative to show some faith in the human race and its future.

I'd returned stateside the week after V-J Day, to San Diego, and more or less filled odd jobs until the Navy decided it no longer required my services. Even before I was discharged, Sam Farkas asked me back as his associate producer. I dropped by the studio occasionally on leave, to thumb through scripts or sit in on production meetings, trying to get my land legs back.

I must have met Nita only a week or two after I came home to California. The first time I saw her, I remember, was in a crowd of people at a party. I caught sight of her face, so familiar to me, with no sense of surprise at all. There wasn't a feature of it that I didn't know from memory. Her left eyebrow was a little fuller than her right. Her smile curved slightly higher on one side than the other. Her lower lip turned outward when she laughed. It was a few moment before it hit me that it was actually she and not the photograph that had hung between Betty Grable and Jane Russell aboard the USS *Simon Browne*. When I finally manoeuvred my way to an introduction and guided her on to the dance floor, I felt like someone who had dispatched the dragon and claimed the princess. The war was over. Nita Paris was in my arms. I remember thinking I was claiming that dance for all the poor s.o.b.'s from the *Browne* who'd never get the chance.

I had never met any woman so completely uninhibited in her sensuality. Nita was a born voluptuary. She was one of those women who always looks invitingly tousled, whose cheeks are faintly flushed, whose face has a bright sheen to it as though she were in a perpetual state of arousal. The aroma of her Chanel Number 5 mixed with her own scent, a heavy, sweet fragrance like melon ripened in the sun. There were pale smudges of excess under her eyes and midnight bruises on her thighs. She was instinctively tactile. It was only natural for her to touch the object of her attention. When she spoke, her voice had a salving quality, a smooth, soothing sound. When she laughed, that low, mischievous, throaty effervescence, she had the habit of running her tongue across the edge of her upper teeth as though she wanted to trace the extent of her pleasure. It was like watching a woman touch her own breasts. I never saw her do it without wanting to lay her then and there.

To me, there was something about Nita's earthy spontaneity that seemed more genuine by far than the immaculately polished style of the women my mother might have wanted me to marry, women who, in my eyes, were refined to the point of insipidity. That was my first mistake, confusing Nita's lack of restraint with honesty.

Now I wonder whether Nita was capable of telling the truth about anything at all. I wonder whether she was capable of any considerations above and beyond her own gratification. Her lies, her evasions, her omissions were all part of that same self-serving nature. Whatever felt good, she liked. Whatever wasn't comfortable, she ignored.

According to her, as I hear it, the Prudhommes gave her nothing but hard times. My mother never accepted her, my brother and his wife snubbed her and I refused to help spring her from her studio contract (which, I might add, was a hell of a lot more remunerative than my own).

The truth is that I never saw my mother treat her less than graciously, Dosie especially went out of her way to make her feel she belonged and I hadn't the means to help her out of her golden chains until Silverwood was sold. At that point, she found a sympathetic judge who awarded her nearly everything but my car and my clothing.

At the time, though, I thought she was the most exciting thing since nuclear fission. That was one of the few occasions on which I should have listened to my brother, but I had no way of knowing his view of Nita was, shall we say, privileged.

I remember the subject of Nita came up one night at Drew's and Dosie's house. I had planned to bring her to dinner, but at the last minute she'd had to work late and begged off.

'I've been counting,' Dosie said with a smile, 'and that's six times you've mentioned Nita Paris in the last half hour.'

'This isn't serious, is it?' Drew asked.

'Could be.'

'Christ, buddy, you only just hit the shore. What are you, one of these sailors who wakes up the next day with a tattoo and a couple of dependants?'

Dosie giggled. 'I've heard stories about you sex-starved seamen.'

'They're true,' I told her, 'every word.'

'Button up,' said Drew. 'Here comes Daphne.'

She was a shy six-year-old. She and Dosie were dressed in matching mother and daughter outfits, red sandals and blue cotton smocks with white Peter Pan collars. She climbed on to Drew's lap and listened solemnly to our conversation. Then Dexter, who was four, came and tried to settle on Dosie's lap, which was next to impossible since she was eight months pregnant.

'Maybe Uncle Tony would let you sit with him,' she suggested, and Dexter reluctantly switched places.

For the first time, a home and family had begun to look good to me. Here was Drew, the proud paterfamilias, surrounded by his pretty wife and cute kids, his future secure thanks to his stock in Outerbridge Industries. This was the American Dream, the thing we'd been fighting for.

I wasn't besotted enough to think it was perfect, by any means. Dosie's innocent, relentless adoration of Drew tended to be cloying. She praised him excessively and acted as if the mere

255

sound of his breaking wind were music to her ears. You could see sometimes how she embarrassed him, yet at the same time he seemed relieved to have married this myopic, undemanding soul who left him free to dance attendance on her daddy. It was Hale, of course, who really ruled that roost. Outerbridge Industries came first. Dosie and the kids ran a not-so-close second. Still, there was something about this picture of permanence that looked better than anything else I'd seen in the past few years, something about the comfortable dependence of husband and wife, the cosy familiarity of married life, that looked inviting if not ideal.

After Nanny had put the children to bed, Dosie excused herself and retired early. Drew poured a couple of fingers of whisky into a pair of tumblers.

'Confidentially speaking,' he said, 'you're not really getting all that thick with Nita Paris, are you?'

'Why not?'

'She's an actress, that's why. Soda or water?'

'Neat.'

'How are you going to contend with her career, buddy-boy?' He handed me my glass. 'Answer me that.'

'Cheers.'

'When it comes down to it, the heft is on the other side. She owes her allegiance to the studio and the public. Hell, nobody can compete with that.'

'I didn't say I was going to marry her.'

'You're not, for chrissakes, are you?'

'What the devil, maybe I will, if she'll have me.'

'Are you out of your mind? How long have you known this broad?'

'Six weeks.'

'It doesn't strike you that marriage is a pretty drastic method of getting acquainted with someone?'

'I just spent three and a half years fighting for things you take for granted, my friend. Besides which, my ship was blown up under me, and I damned near drowned getting washed off that fucking raft again and again. I'm allowed to make up for lost time.'

256

'True.' He saluted me with his glass. 'But you can't act like some horny gob on liberty.'

'Why the hell not?'

'You're a Prudhomme, that's why. What's Mother going to say if you drag home some showgirl and install her in the family portrait?'

'Watch it, Drew. Be careful what you say. You've never met Nita.'

'As it happens, I have. Only in passing. It might have been at some party Sam asked us to. She wouldn't remember me. I thought her fairly attractive in an obvious sort of way.'

'A stunner. Admit it.'

'It's in the eye of the beholder, pal. What I'm asking, all I'm asking, is that you think twice and keep a foot on the brake pedal. This is our family, remember, not some after-hours club.'

I'd stopped listening to Drew's advice a long time ago. I'd always thought his bluenose sentiments had a green tinge to them, and I figured this was just more of the same. Besides, I was already too far gone to see anything further than Nita Paris' fingertips.

'Oh, Tony, Tony,' Mother lamented over the telephone. 'Couldn't you have waited and done it *right*?'

'We didn't want a circus, Mother.'

'But eloping like this looks so shady. It looks as if you felt you had to slink away to marry. As if there were something shameful about it.'

'That's not the case, and you know it.'

'But what about the rest of the world? Don't you think they'll wonder why you had to sneak off and marry behind everyone's back?'

'It wasn't our intention to embarrass you, Mother. We thought we'd enjoy it more this way, that's all.'

'Your brother is devastated.'

'Why, for chrissakes?'

'He feels you went back on your word. You misrepresented the facts, he said. He feels you played him for a fool.'

'In the first place, I never promised him a goddamn thing. I told him I was nuts about Nita. He didn't want to listen.'

'That's for you two to straighten out. I suppose I should give my best wishes to the fortunate bride. Put her on, dear, would you?'

Mother was disappointed, to be sure. I'd let her down by not behaving according to Prudhomme standards. I was counting on Nita's overwhelming allure to charm Mother as thoroughly as it had captivated me.

'I don't blame you,' Mother told me later. 'She's quite impressive. I only hope for your sake that it works.'

'And why wouldn't it?'

'She's a career girl, dear. I don't have much faith in divided loyalties. One's family must come first.'

'Especially if it's the Prudhommes, right, Mother?'

'And what's the matter with family pride, if I may ask?'

'Not everyone feels impelled to face Silverwood and salaam five times a day.'

'Please don't be sarcastic, dear. It's quite unkind. You know perfectly well I only want the best for you both.'

'Quit looking worried, will you?'

'It is going to be a very difficult adjustment for her.'

Maybe Mother was more perceptive than I knew. Perhaps she saw at once that Nita was incapable of thinking of anyone but herself. Their relationship was pointedly cordial. Each of them was trying to win the other to her point of view. Neither was conceding an inch. But what the hell, I figured that given enough time things would become copacetic between them.

Meanwhile, I was as happy as only a fool can be. I was married to a movie star. Both Sam and I were convinced we had a hit on our hands with *Sunday and Monday*. On the strength of that optimism, I bought a house, and Nita and I moved from her apartment to two acres on Mulholland Drive, high above the lights of Hollywood.

It's tough to say why grown men become makers of puppets or doll houses or movies. It's a living, sure, but so are accounting, plumbing and police work. In the long run, they're sometimes more lucrative to boot. There are cynics in any business, the type who do the job just well enough to advance themselves without any regard for ethics or integrity. Then there are those like Sam

Farkas who spill themselves heart and soul into the business of making magic out of a strip of film. All those hard-nosed arguments over budget, promotion and bookings serve only to protect the fragile dream that fires them. It's more than a stubborn adherence to childhood games of make-believe. It's a faith in the fundamental communion of humanity, the kind of ingenuous conviction that leads the tribal storyteller to think that, as he begins 'Once upon a time,' he can perform the holy trick of enlightening, entertaining or at least making his people forget the hunger in their bellies. Sam, of course, would have roared with laughter at such a suggestion and gone back to calculating his grosses. As for me, I wouldn't presume to put myself in the same league with Sam Farkas.

Sam was old school. Deals were made on his word or his handshake. He was a believer, an idealist, even at the last, when he was frail and ailing yet confident he'd be able to reopen all those doors that had been slammed against him.

I thought of Sam as a kind of uncle, though I'd long ago come to grips with the fact of his being my mother's lover. Now that I am able to see it with a little more distance and objectivity, I guess that Sam Farkas' love for my mother probably says more in her favour than all the charity bazaars she ever organized, more than her precious heap of stone, Silverwood, and God knows, more than my brother and me.

The stuff that I thought was pettiness and pomp, Sam viewed with his characteristic generosity.

'Christ,' I complained to him, 'Mother's harping on her familiar noblesse oblige theme, trying to get Nita to play along.'

'So?' he asked. 'What's wrong with a little Christian charity, you should excuse the expression.'

'It's not the charity, Sam. It's all the claptrap surrounding it. You know Mother and her silly social conceits.'

'My boy,' he said, lighting his pipe and puffing at it ruminatively, 'she's vulnerable, you know.' He raised his eyes to me over the bowl of his briar. 'Some people require acceptance more than others. I've seen that need make men so venal they'd compromise their own families.'

'What's that got to do with Mother?'.

'Only that what you see as pride and foolishness, I see as a fairly innocent need for approval in return for which your mother gives good value. It's an honest transaction, even if there is a measure of folderol involved.'

Sam, you see, had the vantage point of an outsider. When Mother or Drew rubbed me the wrong way, Sam usually saw things from a different angle.

'The way Drew talks, you'd think Hale Hunt Outerbridge was some kind of frigging oracle.'

'Have a heart, Tony. Pity the poor bastard. How'd you like to be a yes-man for Hale? How'd you like to have a life where the challenges were only vicarious? It's hand-to-hand combat with challenge that keeps a fellow alive.'

Sam, for all that he enjoyed his success, distrusted the good life. Anything that looked too easy or smacked of complacency made him suspicious.

'Come on, Sam,' I kidded him, 'What about that red convertible you bought for David?'

'A graduation present. Besides, David doesn't have to worry. For a Jew, every day is à challenge.'

'What makes you think you hold the monopoly? All at once I'm juggling house payments and an expensive wife.'

'Tony, you're not getting in over your head, are you?'

'You know me, Sam. Always treading water but never quite drowning. Last week I tried to prise loose some of the capital Father left, but that trust of ours is tighter than Lana Turner's fuzzy sweaters.'

'Does Nita still expect you to buy her way out of the remaining four years of her contract?'

'In time she'd repay me. Trouble is, I can't get my hands on the money. Then there's the New Year's holiday. Dosie wants us to join them in Sun Valley.'

'Don't worry about the trip. I can always advance you enough for that.'

I guess it was fortunate, after all, that we tagged along. Drew went nearly out of his wits with grief after Dosie was found dead. Hale was so stunned that he fumbled about like a punch-drunk prizefighter. Dorcas seemed to feel that God had deliberately

260

taken aim at her to inflict a mortal wound. She was hurt and outraged to have been singled out for such an injustice. After a few drinks, she tended to become rather nasty. Drew was at pains to avoid her, and Nita and I had our hands full, keeping the two of them apart on the train ride back. Hale sat in the baggage compartment by the hour, staring dazed and dry-eyed at his daughter's coffin.

It seems to me that Dosie's accident marked a turning point in all our lives. It's odd that I have that impression, since, when she was alive, she was the least remarkable figure in our family. Maybe it was coincidental that things began to become unstuck after her death. Still, when her simple innocence went, our dreams began to die, too. But perhaps I am exaggerating in an effort to bring some sort of comforting order to unrelated events.

Nita Paris

I'd seen photos of Silverwood. There had even been an aerial view of the grounds in the paper one time, so I had a fair idea of the scale of the place. Still, I'll admit that, nervous as I was, it was some thrill to ride up that driveway sitting next to Tony. Whether anyone liked it or not, little Miss Anita Maria Sanchez from a tin-roofed bungalow in a neighbourhood where they called us greasers and threw stones was about to waltz into one of America's grandest homes like she belonged there. And I did.

Maybe it was that feeling that pulled me through. That, and knowing how elegant I looked. There's a whole lot to be said for superficial appearances. Most people take you at face value, which gives you something safe to hide behind.

The butler, Safford, white gloves and all, opened the door. I felt like I was in one of those George Cukor pictures. Maids in little starched caps took the coats. There was a string quartet playing on the balcony overhead between the two staircases. A full-length oil portrait of the mistress of Silverwood looked down on the crowd of arriving swells like she was counting the house. Everyone seemed to know everyone else. There was a lot of waving and blowing kisses among the women, and the men pounded each other on the shoulders and clasped hands like they were consummating major deals.

'Allegra, my pet! Where's Aubrey?'

'He's coming with the Underwoods, darling. Don't fret.'

No joke, they actually talked like that. I half expected to see Hepburn and Grant take centre stage. In a funny way, the scene made me feel relieved. I'd seen those films and I knew how the girl's part was played.

'Mother,' Tony said.

The crowd sort of parted like she was royalty. For the first time I was aware of people looking at Tony and me. I was gazing straight ahead. I could feel my smile quivering.

'Tony, dearest.' Ada Prudhomme put a hand to his face, and he bent to kiss her cheek.

'Mother, may I present your new daughter-in-law, Nita.'

'How do you do, Mrs Prudhomme.'

She didn't look at me until after I'd spoken. When she turned, her expression was as bland as bread pudding. Only her eyes gave her away. She was looking at me like a fighter coming out of his corner, sizing up the other guy. She took both my hands in hers. I kissed her cheek like Tony had and stepped back, waiting for her to say something.

'Nita. Is that a nickname? I'd much prefer to call you by your full name.'

'It's the only name I have, Mrs Prudhomme.'

'Then Nita it shall be. Let me introduce you to our guests. Tony, do find Drew and Dosie. I think they're in the music room.'

My hands went clammy. Not one of the names Mrs Prudhomme spoke registered with me.

'Darling.'

Tony's voice had come from behind me. I felt his hand on my arm, turning me towards him.

'This is my brother's wife, Dosie.'

I tried not to look anyplace else. I smiled down at her, surprised she was so short. She sort of wriggled like an excited puppy, then gave a little jump and kissed me.

'Oh, I think it's marvy about you two! Now I shan't feel so outnumbered by Drew and Tony. Drew,' she went on, 'do give your sister-in-law a big hug and welcome her to the family.'

She stepped aside, and there he was. As our eyes met, I saw he wasn't enjoying the moment any more than I was. I wondered if that was a good sign, but I knew I shouldn't get my hopes up.

He gave me a cool, correct kiss on the temple. 'My congratulations and best wishes to you both.'

'Thank you.'

'Come along.' Mrs Prudhomme steered me towards the hall. 'You've many more people to meet.'

Of the lot of them, I recall only a few from that day. Sam Farkas I'd met a long time ago at a screening. God knows what he saw in Madam P. She struck me as one of those icebox cookies who wouldn't even work up a sweat in a sauna. I never did understand that pairing. I know the subject made Drew uncomfortable, and Tony simply shrugged it off without going into it.

To my mind, Hale Hunt Outerbridge had as tight a grip on Drew as his daughter. He was someone I was prepared to dislike, but he turned out to be a jovial old fart who wasn't above copping a feel if he could slip an arm around you. That blond wife of his, Dorcas, was something else. She looked at me like she was a palomino pony smelling fire in the stable. For a minute, I thought she knew the score. My mouth went dry. Dorcas turned away from me and threw her arms around Tony.

'What a lucky girl she is!' she cried. 'She's such a lucky girl to have you!' She stepped back and lost her balance momentarily. Hale caught her by the elbow.

'That's very kind of you, Dorcas,' Tony told her. He looked embarrassed. 'Nita, what do you say we dance?' He ushered me in the direction of the orchestra in the next room.

'Is the illustrious Mrs Outerbridge drunk?'

'As a skunk,' he answered.

'I don't think she likes me.'

'She probably doesn't, not that it's any fault of yours. Poor Dorcas. I guess she's a little upset tonight. I haven't seen her for a few years. The last time I laid eyes on her, we tied one on together and went a bit too far, I'm afraid.'

'You *what*?' I couldn't help laughing.

'We drank like there was no tomorrow. Christ, we got fried. Dorcas was as playful as a kitten. Lonely, too, and hungry for attention. My God, but drunks will do crazy things.'

I looked back at Dorcas Outerbridge, standing unsteadily in the doorway to the library. 'I find the whole thing difficult to picture.'

'This is between you and me. It wouldn't do anyone any good to have it known.'

'I'll say.' I glanced around at the panelled walls, the carved marble, the crystal chandeliers and the cream of society stepping lively to the tune of 'Rum and Coca-Cola.' 'Tony, I know I'm not going to recall half these people's names.'

'Never mind. There's plenty of time. Look.' He nodded towards the far side of the dance floor. 'There are Drew and Dosie. Let's double-cut. You should get to know my brother.'

Before I could say anything it was done. Drew and I danced in silence for a few moments.

'I think we ought to look like we have something to say to each other.'

'Drew – '

'Nice dress.'

'Thank you.'

' – If you think white is appropriate for the occasion.'

'It's ivory, actually.'

'Somewhat less virginal then.' He gave me a thin smile.

'Don't, Drew.'

'Don't what?'

'Make it any worse. It's difficult enough – '

'Damn you. What makes you think it's not hard on me?'

'I thought you didn't care anymore.'

'Don't talk like an idiot. You never heard me say that.'

'But you wouldn't *do* anything about it.'

264

He smiled across the room at someone who hailed him. 'Listen to me, Nita. You're a great mistress, make no mistake, but I'll lay odds against your being a success as a wife. The two don't mix. You made a big mistake, pushing things too far like this. I don't want to see Tony get hurt.'

'So? That makes two of us.'

'Do you know how difficult it's going to be? You should have let well enough alone.' He gave the orchestra leader a wave as we danced by. 'Will you be at the studio Monday?'

'For wardrobe fittings on the next picture.'

'I'll phone you in your dressing room at lunchtime. We need to talk, and this isn't the place.'

'I forgot to congratulate you and your wife on your new arrival. Who does he look like?'

'Damned if I can tell. He's smaller than the others were. He has red hair. Lord knows where that came from. I suppose Tony told you he's named Duncan.'

'Your mother is motioning to me.'

'She probably wants to trot you around some more.'

'Drew, she doesn't seem too pleased to have me in the family.'

'No?' He laughed. 'Well, my dear, maybe there's something to the theory of maternal instincts after all.' He escorted me to Ada Prudhomme's side. 'Here she is, Mother. I'm told on the best authority that to know Nita well is to love her.'

'How nice.'

You know how sometimes when you touch something icy you feel like it burns? That's how Ada made me feel. She was cold as ice, but you felt like it was a cold that could sear your skin. God knows, though, I kept pretending she was charm itself.

'You must be pleased at such a big turnout for charity, Mrs Prudhomme.'

'Good deeds make for a good name. You must start thinking about selecting a charity to sponsor. It's expected of a Prudhomme wife.'

'I'll ask the studio to recommend one. They're very particular about tie-ins.'

'About what, did you say?'

'Endorsements. An actress has to tie in with something that enhances her public image.'

'And in your case, the Prudhomme name.'

'Of course.' I sensed a lecture coming and changed the subject. 'Please, tell me about the beautiful jewels in your portrait.'

'Yes, indeed, my emeralds. You did notice them, I see.'

'I never saw gems like that, except maybe on Bette Davis in *The Private Lives of Elizabeth and Essex*. There must be an extraordinary history attached to them.'

'Actually, now that you mention it, their provenance is fairly interesting.' She smiled slightly. 'The conquistadors were the first to bring Colombian emeralds to Europe. They are the finest, I'm happy to say. The ones in my parure come from Muzo. Emeralds from the Muzo area are famous for their brilliant colour.'

'You bought them in South America?'

'No, my dear, in London. They had been handed down through a titled Spanish family for generations. For some reason, they became available. My late husband bought them for me and had them reset as you see them there.'

'They're truly magnificent.'

'The necklace alone contains approximately forty-two carats in emeralds alone. I don't know about the surrounding diamonds.'

'Dazzling.'

'Quite. My husband attended Oxford, you see, and on our wedding trip we visited Nigel Lambton who'd been with Victor at Exeter Academy and also Merton College. Nigel's wife, Poppy. . . .'

'Ye gods, Mother.' It was Tony. 'You're not going to give Nita the story of our lives, are you?'

'But I'm interested, Tony. I want to learn more about the Prudhommes.'

'Tony's right,' his mother said. 'Another time, perhaps.'

She gave me a chummy pat on the cheek and moved away. What a phony Ada Prudhomme was. She was going through the motions of receiving me into the clan, but I sensed I was about as welcome as a case of the clap. It was all right for her to have Sam Farkas on a leash, but her precious sons weren't supposed to

266

bring anything into the family that didn't have a pedigree a mile long.

'I hope,' Ada said later that evening, 'that you're not rushing to have children right away.'

Dosie looked hurt. 'Why, Mother Prudhomme, I thought you adored your grandchildren.'

'Nita has a career. Perhaps if she were to decide to give it up. . . .'

'Why, Mother Prudhomme,' I said with my sweetest smile, 'that's up to Tony. Whatever he wants is what I want, too.'

'What Tony wants,' he said, coming across the room, 'is to go home and hit the sack.'

'Really, dear,' Ada told him, 'you might find a more attractive way to phrase it.'

Drew brought Dosie her wrap and put it over her shoulders.

'Drew, darling,' she said, 'do let's have Nita and Tony for a sail next weekend. Do you sail?' she asked me.

'There's a first time for everything.'

'We have a little sloop, a thirty-footer, named the *Merry-Andrew*. We'd love to have you and Tony join us for the day on Sunday. I'll pack a picnic.'

'We'll supply the beer,' said Tony.

'Super. You fellows can work out the details. 'Night, Mother Prudhomme. 'Night, Nita.'

'Goodnight, Nita.' Drew's lips brushed my cheek.

'I'm so glad to have met you both.'

Drew paused in the doorway. 'I'm sure we'll be seeing a great deal of each other.'

He didn't call Monday. I didn't hear from him all week.

Sunday, when we went out on the boat, I kept glancing at him, looking for some sign. Tony was dressed in his bathing trunks, lying in the sun up near the bow. Dosie had gone below for a nap after lunch. Drew didn't seem to want to talk to me. I stretched out in the cockpit, across from him. I was wearing a white nylon shirt and matching shorts. My legs and feet were bare. I lay there, arms folded behind my head, watching him steer the boat.

'What are you trying to do?' he finally asked.

'Nothing. Why?'

'Lying there like that.'

'Drew?' Dosie's voice came from the cabin. 'Did I hear you say something? Would you like a beer, darling? I'll bring one right away.'

I stood and started to make my way up towards where Tony was lying. I don't know if Drew had something to do with it or it was an accident, but all of a sudden, the boat listed, and I lost my balance and fell overboard. I came up splashing and spitting sea water. Drew brought the boat alongside of me. He and Tony pulled me aboard.

'Oh, goodness!' exclaimed Dosie. 'I'd better find you a blanket.'

If Drew had done it on purpose, it served him right. I just happened not to have bothered to put on any underwear that day, and the wet white nylon was clinging to me, advertising everything he liked best. For a moment, I saw his eyes fasten on to me and his jaw go slack. Then he turned away and grabbed the tiller so hard his fist went white.

The next day he phoned me.

'Are you alone?'

'My stand-in is just leaving.' I waved her out of my dressing room.

'You staged that semistriptease yesterday.'

'I thought it was your fault.'

'Like hell.'

'Is that why you called? To scold me?'

'You know the Spinnaker at Malibu?'

'Sure.'

'Can you be there at five?'

'I have wardrobe tests this afternoon. Make it six. Shall I meet you in the bar?'

'We can't talk there. I booked a cabin.'

'Drew. . . .'

'I said it was for Tony.'

We went at each other like two rutting, snarling animals. It was all mixed up. Desire and hurt, fury and ecstasy, all compounded and indistinguishable. It was almost like we were beating on each other. Even when it began to become painful, we couldn't stop. Nothing could satisfy our need until we had drained each other dry. We lay there in each other's arms, spent and salty with sweat.

'What did you tell Tony?'

'I said I'd be working late and I'd spend the night in my dressing room at the studio.'

'He won't call?'

'He knows I need my sleep when I'm shooting.'

'Dosie thinks I'm en route to Texas. I'll call and tell her my plans were changed and I'll be home in a couple of hours.'

'I'll bathe while you phone,' I said and left the room.

When you have a passion that powerful, it's like being addicted. Neither one of us was strong enough to quit. Nothing seemed to matter much, except to satisfy our craving for each other. Queer, how your perspective gets warped. Everything else, everyone else, seemed secondary to that. I'm not trying to make excuses. I'm saying how things were.

Dorcas Outerbridge

I don't think we'd been in Sun Valley a week when Nanny called to say that the baby, Duncan, had caught whooping cough from the older children. He wasn't yet two months old. Dosie was frantic with concern. She packed immediately. Hale and Andrew took her to the train. Hale and I had given the trip to Dosie and Andrew as a Christmas gift. At the last minute, Nita had persuaded Tony that they should join us.

Dosie called from Los Angeles to tell us that Duncan was out of danger and recovering. She said she'd stay for a few days to catch her breath and then rejoin us in Sun Valley. That was the last time I ever spoke to my daughter. I wish to God she had never left there.

269

The first I knew of her return was when Andrew telephoned, inquiring if she was in our suite.

'Is she here?' I asked. 'In the hotel? I didn't know she'd arrived. She didn't say when she was coming.'

'I can't find her anywhere,' Drew said. 'She took the hotel station wagon from the depot. I spoke to a couple of people who were in the car with her.'

'You mean you haven't seen her at all?'

'Not yet.'

'How peculiar. Did you call Tony and Nita?'

'She's not with them.'

'She wouldn't have gone skiing, would she? It's snowing quite hard.'

'They've cleared everyone off the slopes. They say it's a blizzard. Never mind, Mother Outerbridge, I'll locate her.'

'We're dining at eight. Will you join us?'

'Dosie's probably exhausted. I didn't sleep well last night, either. My back's been bothering me since I took that spill yesterday on the toboggan run. You'd better not count on us.'

'Have her stop by or call, Andrew, will you?'

I gave it no more thought. Hale, Tony and I had been skiing on the mountain all day, and I was pleasantly tired. Andrew didn't ski because of his bad leg. Nita preferred to skate, which was fine with me. The day had started out to be fair and breezy and then, very rapidly, grown darker until at dusk a fine, stinging snow had begun to blow hard across the slopes. We had called it quits, bathed and dressed for dinner. Hale and I kept glancing up from our food, hoping to see Dosie and Drew come into the dining room. Tony and Nita were nowhere to be seen either.

'Tony said he was bushed. They probably ate in their rooms,' said Hale.

I folded my napkin and laid it on the table. 'Shall we have a nightcap before we go up? Maybe they're in the bar.'

Nita was in the lobby. She looked puzzled and a little cross, as though she might have mislaid something. 'They came in and left again. I got tired of sitting in my room. They've had no luck at all.'

'What are you talking about?'

270

'Tony and Drew. Dosie. They found a bartender down the street at the Happy Time who said she'd been there. They thought she must have come back here, but nobody's seen her. They went out again just now.'

'I don't understand,' Hale said to her. 'What's the problem?'

'Nobody can find Dosie. Drew's getting concerned for her. The weather's not fit for a dog tonight. Could anyone else use a drink?'

I think we waited until the twins came back again before we called the police. I am not sure. The sequence of events is lost to me now. I can remember only my feelings. I remember being merely mildly anxious for a time. I can still feel my anxiety being slowly displaced by a dread so heavy that it seemed my heart could scarcely pump under the weight of it. By daylight, we knew something terrible had happened to Dosie.

'Do you think it might be amnesia?' Nita asked. 'Could she have slipped and hit her head? Perhaps she's perfectly safe but she can't remember a thing.'

Andrew glowered at her, and she stopped her prattling.

'I wish,' I said, 'that she hadn't been quite so ostentatiously dressed. The sable coat – '

'For God's sake,' Hale interrupted. 'Dorcas, if there's been any foul play it was probably committed by someone who wouldn't know sable from squirrel.'

'Still, she was wearing her engagement ring. It's quite a large diamond.'

'Let's agree,' Tony suggested, 'not to think of the worst. It won't help Dosie, and it certainly isn't doing any of us any good.'

'Hear, hear,' Drew said.

Nita glanced at her watch. 'It's almost time for the noon news. Maybe the radio will have a report on the storm. It has to let up sometime soon.'

Two children found her. As soon as the snow had stopped, they had gone out to play as children will after a snowfall, making angel prints in the immaculate landscape, building forts and tunnelling under the fresh white drifts. She lay beneath a snow-drift, wrapped in her sable coat, like a princess in an alabaster tomb. We took her home to Los Angeles. I remember almost

271

nothing of the train ride. What I do remember was how it rained all day the day of the funeral, as though the world were weeping with us.

After the service at the cemetery, we went back to Silverwood. The limousines going slowly up the drive glistened in the rain like lumbering black whales. Vapour rose from their radiators into the chill air. The acrid smell of eucalyptus seemed to scent the very atmosphere with bitterness. As we stepped from the car, Hale turned to me. 'I believe I need to stretch my legs before I go inside,' he said.

Someone tried to give him an umbrella, but he refused it. I watched him wander slowly off towards the gardens, knowing he would blame the rain for the wetness on his cheeks. It was the only time I ever saw Hale cry. He wouldn't have liked it if he'd known I had seen through his bluff.

Hale was a pillar of fortitude after that. What self-control he had. How I wish I could have followed his example. I am not a strong woman, I'm afraid, and I wept like Niobe for her children. Poor Hale. I was yet another trial for him to contend with.

'You need a change of scene, Dorcas,' he offered. 'Why not take a trip to New York and do some shopping? See some musicals. *Annie Get Your Gun* is still playing on Broadway. That new show, *Finian's Rainbow*, is a dandy, according to Sam Farkas. Take a friend along with you. I'll get you a suite at the Waldorf and see to the theatre tickets.'

I could not have gone. Sometimes the mere sight of a room full of people enjoying themselves brought tears to my eyes. What was worse, only I knew that it was not sadness that stirred me but fury. I could have dealt with sadness. I had done it before. But the senseless death of my daughter put me in a rage that burns to this day, fiery as a banked bed of coals under a harmless frost of ash. The manner of my daughter's death made her look stupid and foolhardy. I mind that terribly. Dosie was a sensible girl and not given to imprudent behaviour. I will never be satisfied that her death was the result of mere thoughtlessness on her part.

I was quite unprepared for the insurmountable, crushing tyranny of my grief for Dosie. I was completely overpowered and couldn't seem to get a grip on myself. One Sunday afternoon by Ada's tennis court, Hale and I were watching a charity match with a number of other guests when I felt an unpleasant prickling at my cheekbones and discovered that tears were cascading uncontrollably down my face. I touched my highball glass to my cheeks. With luck, people might think I was merely warm and cooling myself with the perspiration from the glass. But I couldn't stop. At last, I excused myself and fled into the house. I found an unoccupied bedroom upstairs and finished my drink, hoping that it would make me doze. Presently, I looked up to see Ada sitting beside me. She took my hand in those long, beautiful hands of hers and told me what had happened when her father died.

'It was very sudden, you see,' she said, 'and a stunning blow to my mother. They were extremely close. I don't believe they were apart for so much as a day in their lives.' She stroked my hand pensively for a moment. 'I've never felt so helpless. Mother was inconsolable. Her sadness was like an impenetrable wall around her.'

'Sometimes I feel like an exile from life. It's all around me, but I can't enter it.'

Ada nodded. 'My mother, too.'

'How long was she like that?'

'Well over a year, and then one morning – it was in April, I remember – she came downstairs wearing a violet dress that had been one of Father's favourites. She wasn't laughing or even smiling, but her face looked serene. I couldn't imagine what had caused the change in her, and I was afraid to inquire. Much later, she told me. "Ada," she said, "your father and I loved each other very much." I was aware of that, I said. "When he died," she went on, "all I could think of was my love for him and how terribly I felt his absence. For the longest time it never occurred to me to consider his love for me. When I did, I realized that while he might be complimented to be so greatly missed, there was nothing he'd like less than to see me suffering. I vowed then and there to respect his memory by putting aside my feelings and doing the best I could, for his sake." Now, Dorcas,' Ada said, 'do you think Dosie would be happy to find you this way?'

I shook my head.

Ada reached for my highball glass and rose from the bed. 'Why don't you take a little nap? I'll tell Hale you're sleeping. We'll wake you for dinner.'

'But I'm not prepared,' I replied drowsily. 'I didn't bring a dinner dress.'

'Hale can run home and pick up some clothes for you. Don't concern yourself, Dorcas. Sleep.'

How typically kind of Ada to have taken me into her confidence like that, in hopes of raising my spirits.

I cannot deny that I resented Andrew and the children for coping with Dosie's absence. I wanted them to find the emptiness in their lives as irreparable and insufferable as I did. I despised the children's laughter. I begrudged them even a moment's comfort in forgetting.

I wanted to keep my daughter's memory alive, and the rest of them wanted to get on with things.

I was alone with my loss. It's true that in time the pain dulled. I became accustomed to my sorrow. But my fury remains undiminished. I have grown quite skilful at concealing it. Only now and then, perhaps if I've unwittingly had a drop too much to drink, does it begin to make me afraid of myself. My anger is an element Hale did not wish to acknowledge. Hale was one of those men who had always to be in control. This was something that raged defiantly beyond the power of either of us to mitigate it. In the end, he thought me merely perverse and contentious. Dosie's death cost me Hale, too, in a way.

Nita Paris

I remember that Drew and I saw each other alone twice more
before that Christmas. I also remember Christmas Eve at Silverwood and how Ada took me aside during cocktails.

'You and I must have a little chat, Nita.' She grasped me by
the elbow. 'Will you all excuse us for a few minutes?'

'Don't be long, Mother,' Drew said. 'Daphne and Dexter have
to be home and asleep before Santa can be about his business.'

'This will only take a few minutes.'

Ada led the way upstairs and held open the door of her
bedroom for me. She closed and locked it, 'Sit down, Nita.'

I sat on the bench in front of her dressing table. Ada remained
standing.

'Do you recall,' she inquired, 'being at the Spinnaker Lodge
lately?'

I could feel a rush of adrenalin. My ears were ringing, as if
someone had hit me with a haymaker. I tried to look composed.
'I've been there many times.'

'You were there this week, I believe.'

'I don't recall.'

'It was the day before yesterday.'

'Oh, that. Of course. I was there to meet a reporter for a
newspaper interview.'

'Really?'

I nodded.

'Nita, I went to the studio yesterday to join Sam for a screening.
I was sitting outside his office, chatting with his secretary, Miss
Kramer, when Tony came in with a script for Sam to read. Miss
Kramer asked him if he was in some way annoyed with her.
Tony looked perplexed and said no, of course not and what made

275

her ask. "But you behaved so oddly last evening. I waved at you across the parking lot at the Spinnaker and you ignored me," she told him. Tony handed her the script and said, "It must have been my brother you saw. I was in a script conference until nearly midnight." Miss Kramer started to add something else, but she just shook her head in confusion. Now, Nita, have you anything to say to that?'

'No. Why?'

'Because after I left, I asked Miss Kramer why she still seemed so puzzled. She was reluctant to say, but it finally came out she had seen Tony and you getting out of your car, walking to a ground floor cabin and going inside. But, of course. . . .' Ada paused. The sound of Christmas music came from downstairs. Dosie was playing 'Silent Night' on the piano and the others were singing. 'Of course,' continued Ada, 'we know it was not Tony, don't we?'

'I needed Drew's advice about something.'

'And what was that?'

'My Christmas gift to Tony.'

'I thought you were giving each other the trip to Sun Valley next week with Drew and Dosie and the Outerbridges.'

'Well, yes, but – '

'Couldn't you have telephoned Drew if you had any questions?'

'There was something else, too. . . .'

She waited.

'Something more personal to do with Tony and me.'

'You still haven't explained why you and Andrew had to meet in a motel room to discuss it.'

'I told you. I was there for an interview. I took a cabin in case I needed to freshen up for photographs.'

'I did a great deal of thinking about this last night and this morning.'

'All for nothing. You shouldn't have been bothered.'

'And then, Nita, I telephoned the Spinnaker and asked if either Anthony or Andrew Prudhomme was registered there. The clerk told me that Mr Anthony Prudhomme had been there the day before and checked out. Explain that. If this was an innocent little encounter, why was Tony's name used?'

'Drew thought it might look – '

'No.'

I glanced up at her. Ada's face was haggard and hard.

'Dosie mentioned that Drew had gone out of town on business that day and stayed late.'

'I can't be responsible for what Drew tells Dosie! Why don't you ask him yourself?'

'I did. He told me the same lie.'

'Then straighten it out with him, why don't you? Why are you putting me through an inquisition?'

'Because I believe you know as well as I do that men are not as strong as women. Both Tony and Drew have a certain hereditary weakness. I'd thought Drew immune to it until you came along. Perhaps if the cause of this – aberration – were to be removed, his family life could go on as before.'

'What about Tony? What about me?'

'Tony would recover. As for you, I'm in a position to give you something Tony says you want badly.'

'And what's that?'

Suddenly Ada's face came alive with triumph. I had grabbed the bait. She'd been right all along and she knew it now. 'You want to get out of your contract with the studio, don't you?'

'You know that's true. I'm not satisfied with the roles I've been getting.'

'If you cooperate with me, I shall make it possible for you to buy your way out of your contract.' She stood there, watching me, gauging my reaction.

I didn't know what to think. What is it about the upper crust that they suppose they can buy off the rest of us? Like Drew paying me off for the abortion with a pair of earrings and a fur coat.

'All you have to do is tell Tony that you realize now your career comes before marriage. You made a mistake. You'll go to Nevada or wherever and obtain a quick divorce. As soon as it's final, the money is yours.'

'What makes you think Drew will go along with your plans?'

'I'll deal with Andrew.'

'How?' I challenged her. 'He's in love with me.'

Ada flinched. 'Do you think for one moment he'd risk my telling Hale Outerbridge and jeopardize his own career and social standing for the likes of *you*?'

'Before you start acting high and mighty, lady, maybe you ought to know that Drew came after *me*, not vice versa. Maybe you also ought to tell Outerbridge that Tony screwed Dorcas. You wouldn't want to leave out anything, would you?'

She went white with anger. 'Have you no principles? Are you so completely amoral that you care nothing for people who can't defend themselves against such outrageous scandal? Listen hard, Nita Paris.' She spoke almost in a whisper. 'I will protect my sons against you. I refuse to let you ride roughshod over their deepest feelings. Moreover, young woman, I will protect my sons against themselves. Before I'd let you destroy Andrew's marriage and drag this family through the mud, I'd see you dead. Believe me, I'll find a way. It's not so difficult, you know.'

The shocking thing of it was, I believed her. Right then, I became absolutely certain that the aristocratic Ada Prudhomme was capable of killing anyone who got in her way.

'My sons are Prudhommes! Do you think I'm going to allow you to bring disgrace to that name? Silverwood and the Prudhommes stand for something fine and noble. You couldn't even begin to understand.'

'Don't try to convince me that you're the high priestess of fair play. It's too late for that.'

She took a deep breath. 'Your opinion of me is irrelevant.'

'I need time to think the whole thing over.'

'You have one week.'

'We'll be in Sun Valley.'

'When you return, then. I'll expect to see you the day after you come back.'

'What do you think your sons would say if they knew you were trying to manipulate their lives?'

She gave me a sleety smile. 'Leave my sons to me.'

I don't know how I made it through dinner. If I'd known then what I know now, I would have laughed in Ada's face and told her to stick it, but as it was, I thought the bitch would stop at nothing to get rid of me. From day one she'd been searching for a reason to force me out of her family and now she'd found it. It hadn't even taken her two months. I glanced across the table at her. Her eyes were bright, and her cheeks were flushed. She looked exhilarated, like she was getting an almost physical gratification out of the contest. I never in my life knew anyone who hated as heartily as Ada Prudhomme. The pleasure she got out of it was the most perverse thing I ever saw. I was convinced that it wasn't Drew's wife and kids she was worried about. Only one thing mattered to Ada and that was the Prudhomme name. It was everything to her, and she'd gone at me like someone fighting for her very life. It occurred to me to wonder if maybe there wasn't something cracked under all that sleek, tight, patrician armour.

It was Tony, not me, who'd wanted to go to Sun Valley. Hale and Dorcas had given Dosie and Drew the trip as a present. Tony liked the idea, and I couldn't come up with any logical argument against it. I had to go along with his plans.

From the start, there were undercurrents. Drew acted preoccupied and restless. Dorcas was uneasy around Tony and me. She had one of those voices that finds fault with everything merely by its tone, and she all but picked me to shreds with extravagant compliments.

After a few drinks, Hale liked to get on his soapbox and lecture. It didn't matter if nobody listened. He'd carry on in that voice of his, rich and potent as his cigar smoke, drumming his fingers on the table for emphasis.

'Now, take your Ralph Gamble, Andrew. The man wears the wrong shoes. Very off-putting. Makes one think twice about investing. One can always spot a gentleman from the shoes. Keep an eye on the shoes, I say.'

'Daddy,' Dosie said, 'Mr Gamble's alligator shoes look very expensive.'

'Exactly. Trying too hard to impress. *En garde*, say I.'

I could tell Drew was bored there. His leg kept him from skiing. Sometimes he went out on the toboggan run, but mostly he read or went early to the bar.

Dosie was in her element at night. Everyone changed for dinner, and that gave her the chance to put on the sable coat

Drew had given her for Christmas. There was Dosie, prancing around in thousands of dollars worth of sable, even though we hardly ever went outside the lodge to eat. The best I could do was last year's lousy fox, the one he'd given me after I had the abortion. I figured she owed me for that sable as much she owed Drew. If it hadn't been for him feeling guilty, he'd never have sprung for it. If it hadn't been for me, she'd probably be thanking her lucky stars for another laundry appliance.

I still had no idea what to do about Ada's ultimatum. I needed to have some time alone with Drew. I had to know how he felt about us and what the hell we were going to do. We couldn't go on like we were. I mean, Tony didn't deserve to wear horns. I felt bad about that, but the thing that drove me nearly crazy was having to watch Dosie get kissy with Drew after she'd put away her usual two sherries every night.

It's an awful thing to admit, but I was glad when Nanny Beale called to say the new baby, Duncan, was sick and Dosie should come home. Not that I wished the poor little kid harm, but I needed to sound out Drew before I could figure out how to handle Ada.

How was anyone to know what would happen? It was one of those situations where you make one little mistake and it gets compounded, like when you drop something and grab for it and break three other things in the process. I never wanted to hurt Dosie. I didn't have any grievance against her. It wasn't her fault we had the same taste in men.

I guess it began with Dosie leaving for Los Angeles. Drew was on edge, not just because of the children being ill but because he and Hale were involved in some big deal. The phone calls and telegrams were beginning to interfere with their holiday. The changeover from wartime to peacetime production was a critical transition for Outerbridge Industries. Hale was tense and talked about cutting the trip short. I was beginning to wonder if I'd ever be able to get a moment alone with Drew.

When Dosie called to say the baby was out of danger and she'd be back as soon as possible, I knew I had to do something soon.

It was Hale who gave me a break. One morning he happened to mention that he'd run into a lobbyist from Washington and they were going to ski the experts' run that afternoon. I told Dorcas that Tony and I would be happy to keep her company. We were all intermediate skiers. Tony was still upstairs, and when he came down to breakfast and discovered what I'd done, he wasn't exactly enthusiastic, but I knew he was too much of a gentleman to bow out of it.

I excused myself from the table and called Drew's room from the lobby.

'I'll be right down. I overslept.'

'That's not why I'm calling. I have to see you. This afternoon.'

'Nita, Hale and I are involved in some important negotiations, and – '

'Hale's going to be on the mountain all afternoon.'

There was a pause. 'What about the others?'

'They're going skiing, too.'

'I'll see if I can spare some time.'

'Goddamn it! You'd better spare me some of your precious bloody time! It may be the last chance you ever get!'

'Cool off, for chrissakes. I'll find a way.'

He came down to breakfast, complaining of a bad back. 'I must have pulled something yesterday when I took that curve wrong on the toboggan run.'

'Get a massage, my boy,' Hale told him. 'Best remedy in the world for a sore back. I'll book it for you.' He rose from the table. 'First thing this afternoon suit you? Meanwhile, you and I have to spend the morning going over some figures. I'm going to check the desk to see if Washington has replied to our wire.'

I walked Tony and Dorcas to the door. 'I think I'd rather skate today,' I said.

Tony looked pained. 'Are you sure? It won't be as much fun without you.'

Dorcas stepped outside. 'It's *cold*,' she accused him.

'Come on, Dorcas.' He threw an arm around her shoulders. 'I guess you're stuck with me.'

I thought the morning would never end. After lunch, I skated for half an hour, just to be seen. Then I went to my room. When the phone finally rang, I jumped like it was an electric shock.

'I got rid of the masseur. Shall I come there?'

281

'No. Tony could always come back. I'd better come to your room instead.'

As I neared his door, a bellhop came towards me from the far end of the hall.

'Mrs Prudhomme?'

'Yes?'

'Telegram for your husband.'

'Thank you. I'll give it to him.' After he went on his way, I glanced at the wire and realized it was for Drew. People were always getting the Prudhomme twins and their wives confused. I folded the wire and put it in my pocket. First things first. I didn't want Drew sidetracked by business complications when I needed his full attention. My whole future depended on the next couple of hours.

I hadn't actually planned to make love with him. What I'd meant to do was sound him out, see if he really cared enough after all these years to cut loose from Ada and the Outerbridges and start over. If not, I wanted out. If I couldn't have Drew, I might as well let Ada pay me off. Tony would be better off without me anyhow.

Right then, though, Drew didn't want to hear anything I had to say. He shut the door and held me against it, pressing close. He was all over me with his hands and mouth. He began to unbutton my sweater. 'Take that damned thing off.'

'Drew –'

'Take it off before I pull it off.'

'We have to talk.'

'Later. It's been hell being near you like this and not being able to put my hands on you.'

'I need to know –'

'Later, I said.' He slipped a hand behind my head and buried his fingers in my hair. He held me tight like that, forcing me down to the bed.

I swear, I forgot about everything except how it felt when we were together. I couldn't help myself. He did that to me.

It wasn't as if we were the only ones capable of making mistakes. Dosie herself did a dumb thing. Why didn't she call from the station or something to let us know she was back? I couldn't believe it. I'd had dreams like that, seeing her face or sometimes Tony's blank with disbelief and then seeing the shock and the pain seize hold. Maybe it was the angle of the light from the hall behind her that made her face look like there were deep cracks in it. She stood there in the open doorway, paralysed, for only a moment. I saw her glance at the number on the door, as if she might have been given the key to Tony's and my room by mistake. Drew turned towards the shaft of light and he made a noise somewhere in the back of his throat like he was going to retch. Dosie never made a sound. She reached for the knob and closed the door quietly, as though she didn't know any way to act except polite.

I turned on the light and looked at the clock beside the bed. God knows, neither of us had realized how long we'd been at it. 'Drew – '

'Jesus Christ Almighty. Nita, didn't you lock the door?'

'Me? Why me? I thought you did. It's your room.'

'I distinctly remember thinking you bolted it.'

'How could I, when – '

'Never mind. Let's get the hell out of here. I've got to find Dosie before the shit hits the fan.'

'Don't look now, but it already has.'

'Shut up and get dressed.'

'Listen, I need to talk to you!'

'Not now. I have to find Dosie before she spills everything.'

'Oh, God.'

'Yes.' He was stuffing his shirt into his trousers. 'Nita, I'm going to tell her we were drunk. It's the only excuse she might go for.' He grabbed his coat. 'Let yourself out and make damned sure nobody sees you.'

I went back to my room, bathed and changed. As I was putting away the clothes I'd worn earlier, there was a knock at the door.

'I can't find her,' Drew said. 'She's nowhere here in the lodge.'

'Drew, you don't suppose she left town altogether, do you?'

'No. There aren't any more trains today. Her luggage is in the room. A bellhop must have put it there.'

'Have you telephoned around?'

283

He nodded. 'I tried every place I could think of. I had her paged.'

'Maybe she didn't feel like answering the page.'

'What's this?' Tony came loping down the hall, his cheeks flushed from the cold. 'Why are you two looking so grim?'

I wasn't sure what to say. I started folding the skirt I had in my hands.

'You haven't seen Dosie, have you, Tony?'

'She's back?'

I felt something in the pocket of my skirt and pulled out the telegram. 'Oh, Drew, I forgot to pass this on. A bellman gave it to me.'

He opened it. When he raised his eyes from the paper, I knew what was in that wire. It wasn't anything to do with Outerbridge Industries at all. Maybe Sigmund Freud would say I'd known all along what was in there, but how could I have? I would have given it to Drew if things hadn't got out of hand. It wasn't as if I had meant to hide it from him.

'How long have you had this?'

I told the truth. 'It arrived about an hour after lunch.'

'It's from Dosie. It says she's arriving this afternoon.'

'Drew, it simply slipped my. . . .'

He gave me a look I can't even describe. He crushed the paper in his hand and dropped it at my feet.

'What's wrong?' Tony wanted to know.

'Dosie seems to have left the hotel, and – '

'Nita,' said Drew. 'I'll handle this.' He turned to his brother. 'Dosie's gone out, and it looks like I'll have to try to track her down.'

'You'd better dress warmly,' Tony told him. 'The weather's getting mean out there.' He gave me a kiss on the forehead. 'How was the skating, honey?'

'Lousy. I made a mistake and took a bad fall.'

Drew turned away and strode off.

He was back in half an hour, and this time Tony went out with him. 'I think they had a tiff,' Tony whispered in my ear as he left. 'We'll find her and be back shortly,' he said.

Christ, but I've never been so low. Drew believed I'd known

what was in the wire and allowed this whole mess to happen. Dosie had obviously run off in hysterics and could blow everything apart with a few well-chosen words. I'd be out in the cold.

Honestly, it never occurred to me that anything awful would happen to Dosie. I thought I was the one it would happen to. I was trying like crazy to keep calm when inside I was afraid my whole world was going to be destroyed. My career, my lover, my marriage were all in Dosie's hands.

You'd think that a few drinks would keep a person warm. I mean, we've all seen those pictures of Saint Bernards carrying brandy through the snow, so it's a natural assumption. How would the average person know that alcohol would make you more susceptible to the cold? Dosie must have put away plenty. She had to have been bombed to go wandering off in a snowstorm in a pair of high-heeled shoes and a new sable coat like she did. That was her second mistake. She never got another chance.

It was no one person's fault really. So what in hell was I supposed to tell Drew after I said how sorry I was? And how come he behaved like I was entirely to blame when he was the one who didn't bolt the door? He laid the whole dreadful thing on me, for pete's sake. And what was I to do? I tried to be understanding. I tried to reason with him. I damn near grovelled before him saying how much I regretted what had happened. And what did he do but look at me like I was something poisonous. Even that, I thought, would pass. I was willing to be patient. What we'd had together, you see, meant something to me. All along, I'd believed it meant something to Drew, too.

It was a while before Ada broached the subject, but I knew it was inevitable.

'Drew and the children are moving to Silverwood,' Ada told me one evening when Tony had insisted we put in an appearance at his mother's. Tony and Sam were in the library, talking business. 'I'll be glad to have them close by,' she said.

'I'm sure you will.'

'He said the other day – I've quite forgotten how it came up – that you get on his nerves.'

'I rarely see him.'

'But you get on his nerves, nonetheless.'

285

'How thoughtful of you to tell me.'

'He can't stand the sight of you.'

'Did he say that?'

'It's easy to see. I don't know what happened,' she said, gazing at me with those ice-blue eyes, 'and even if I did, it couldn't change anything, but I want you to know I hold you responsible. I wish to heaven neither of my sons had ever set eyes on you. You are an insult to everything this family stands for.'

'You're living in a fairy tale, you know that?'

She drew in her breath as sharply as if I'd struck her. For a minute, she seemed to have lost her place in the script. Then, very quietly, she said, 'Young woman, I'm still prepared to keep our bargain, if you'll divorce Tony and leave the Prudhommes alone. Tony's happiness means a great deal to me, if not to you.'

'Don't talk like Tony's suffering. He isn't, you know.'

'I repeat: My offer is still good.'

'I'm staying, like it or not.' I had made up my mind, even before Ada brought it up, that I'd stand pat. Damned if I was going to give Tony up before I knew for certain that it was over between Drew and me. Tony knew a lot of writers and directors, and he could send scripts my way before they were ready for anyone else to see them. Right then, I was reading a script for a picture called *The Trial of Cassie Pilgrim*. The writer thought it was a natural for Anne Baxter, but I knew if my agent could get it to DeWitt Mowbray fast, he could talk the studio brass into buying it and casting me. He did, too. That was the role that got me an Oscar nomination.

After that, I made *Whisper Danger*. It's become a classic suspense movie. I still get a lot of mail every time it plays someplace like the Museum of Modern Art in New York or at one of the film festivals.

I don't know why things unravelled with Tony and me, except that there wasn't much excitement between us. We were both working most of the time on different pictures and by the time we got home we were almost too tired to speak. I never disliked Tony. He really had a nicer disposition than Drew, but the thrill just wasn't there.

It wasn't until Ada died that I found out what a two-bit fraud she really was. Talk about an Academy Award performance! I had to laugh. Tony and Drew didn't think it was so damned funny, though.

It's amazing how, in spite of everything, a person can keep believing in something. Now that Ada was out of the way, I thought if only I could be close to Drew, maybe all the good things we'd once found in each other would be apparent and we might have a chance. I'll admit that's why I talked Tony into moving into Silverwood.

I got along great with the kids. Drew was barely civil to me. Jesus, but that was the last straw. Years later, and he still blamed me for what had happened to Dosie. He treated me like I was Typhoid Mary. Tony and I weren't in the house a month when Drew said he'd bought another place and was moving as soon as the escrow closed. That left Tony stuck with running the estate alone. Drew knew damned well it was too heavy a burden for Tony. It wasn't just the money. Tony didn't want the responsibility of a house that size. He felt Drew was being selfish.

I don't think Drew gave a damn. Nothing seemed to matter to him anymore. He didn't even have much to do with his children. He sent them to good schools and gave them whatever they asked for, but he was like a man tossing juicy bones to a pack of dogs so they wouldn't come any closer.

It was sad, finally. He had become like his mother. He was that cold. When he and Tony decided to sell Silverwood, he didn't even come back for a final look at the place.

PART FIVE

Tony Prudhomme

A few months after Dosie's death, Drew pulled up stakes and moved his entire household to Silverwood. Mother wanted them there, I know. You could see she was suffering agonies for having been the one to suggest that Dosie return to Sun Valley. It was useless to remind her that we all have regrets at a time like that, about things said or left unsaid. I thought she was being unnecessarily hard on herself. Still, she insisted that it fell to her to provide some maternal care for Drew's family now that Dosie was gone. Oddly, she seemed more companionable with her grandchildren than she had ever been with me or Drew. Motherhood, such as it was, came more easily to her at a generation's remove; yet as always she was more at ease with the older children. She showed little interest in the baby, Duncan. Nanny took sole charge of him.

Drew seemed to have surrendered his children entirely to Mother and Nanny. As far as I could see, he'd ceased caring about anything or anyone, including himself. I tried to bring him out of it. So did Nita. We might as well have been talking to a tree. His behaviour went beyond grief. It was as if some process of petrifaction had stolen the life from him, leaving him cool, stony and impenetrable. We were certain, Nita and I, that time would find him his old self. It was a long while before I realized he was never going to change. It dawned on me with some surprise that Dosie's death had permanently altered hs character. I had obviously underestimated my brother's feelings for his wife.

Nita and I were both working most of the time. She made a couple of good pictures, bitching continually that the studio was trying to keep her down when, in fact, they were giving her more than an even chance to overreach her talent. She fancied herself another Katharine Hepburn, though her career was actually a combination of average ability, luck and smart publicity. Needless to say, it would not have occurred to her to think that she had not created the whole thing herself. For a while she simply refused to believe I couldn't somehow lay hands on the cash to buy out her contract. 'Six years,' I told her for what must have been the tenth time. 'That's how long until Drew and I come into our principal inheritance.'

'But we *need* the money *now*.'

'Tell it to the Marines, honey.'

'Maybe you didn't explain it clearly enough to the lawyers. I'm sure you can make them understand, if you'll only try.'

'I've told you before. There's not a damned thing I can do. The trust is unbreakable, every i dotted and t crossed. Don't badger me, Nita. We've covered this ground before.'

'Don't try to dodge the subject. If you loved me – '

'I'd what? Rob a bank? Come up with the loot so you could kiss off the studio and promptly fall flat on your face trying to play Shakespeare?'

'What makes you think I can't play Shakespeare?'

'Oh, for Christ's sake, Nita, this conversation goes around like a broken record.'

'You never said you thought I was a lousy actress. You never hit below the belt before.'

'Limited, not lousy. We all have our limitations.'

'And yours are starting to get on my nerves.'

In time, those arguments constituted the longest conversations we had with each other. I was a slow study, but after being married to Nita for a year and a half, I was beginning to understand that from the outset the only thing we'd had in common was a blind admiration for Nita Paris. At home, we were like a couple of marbles rolling around in a box, colliding occasionally with a short, sharp sound.

I never really got pissed off at Nita until she told me she'd signed to make *Alien Cargo*.

'Shit!' I slammed my hand down on the glass-topped breakfast table. The coffee cups clattered in their saucers.

'It is not!' she retorted. 'It's a brilliant script.'

'You never even discussed the possibility with me.'

'I wasn't aware that you considered yourself my keeper.'

'Were you aware that it's the work of the same redbaiting crew that's been spreading stories about Sam? Writer, producer, director, everyone all the way down the line? They're part of the bunch that's been hotfooting it down to the Biltmore Hotel, carrying tales to J. Parnell Thomas.'

'Who the hell is he?'

'Jesus, woman, don't you know what's going on around here?'

'If it's politics, I'm too busy.'

'So were all those good Germans. J. Parnell Thomas, for your information, is head of the House Un-American Activities Committee. He's come to town to try to dig up dirt on subversives in the movie industry.'

'So what? What's that got to do with me?'

'Can't you see a goddamn thing beyond the end of your own nose? Would it surprise you to learn that you're making a propaganda film for the extreme right?'

'It's a patriotic story, yes. What's wrong with that?'

'I read the script. It's one of those windy melodramas that plays on people's paranoia. If you believed that crap, you'd have kids denouncing their teachers, secretaries informing on their bosses, hairdressers turning in their clients – '

'I heard from a very reliable source that Gene Tierney would have given anything for this role.'

'What do I have to do to get it through your head that you're playing with a crowd that can do a lot of harm? They're saying that Sam Farkas, our friend, is a Communist sympathizer.'

'Is it true?'

'Do *you* think it's true?'

'You work with him. I don't.'

'I certainly never heard Sam spouting the Party line.'

'So what are you worried about? Anyhow, since when has it been illegal for someone to be a member of the Communist Party?'

'It's not illegal. That's why I'm against – '

'The whole business is probably just a lot of publicity.'

'Like hell. People's reputations are on the line. Careers are at stake. Suppose somebody actually has something on Sam? What's he going to do if he can't make a living in the industry?'

'I still don't understand what all this has to do with my making *Alien Cargo*. Why should I turn down the best role I've ever been offered? Aside from your not liking the script – '

'Aside from that, do I care that you're aligning yourself with a smear campaign? Do I care for Sam's feelings? Do I care how Mother will feel? You bet your fucking ass I care!'

'Don't be a fool. It'll all blow over. Nobody's going to give Sam a hard time. His last picture won two Oscars, didn't it?'

After that, I wasn't only concerned for Sam; I was bloody doubtful that anything could rescue my marriage. I was aware of a sense of despondency, steady and dismal as a toothache.

'Pink.' With a turn of his wrist, Sam sent the pastel packet of paper skating across his desk. It landed in my lap.

'What's this?'

'A subpoena. Pink, yet. Nice touch, don't you think?'

'Good Lord, Sam.'

'They served me at breakfast. David couldn't finish his food. He had to excuse himself from the table.'

'Does Mother know?'

'I stopped off on my way to the studio. I didn't want her to hear the news from anyone else.' He rubbed his eyes with his thumb and forefinger. 'She took it pretty hard, Tony. I think it frightens her. We're none of us as young as we used to be.'

'Sam, for God's sweet sake, level with me. Have they really got anything on you?'

'I wouldn't be surprised.'

'Oh, shit. No. Not you.'

'Don't expect me to apologize, my boy. When you're young and idealistic, you're prone to ardent attachments. You become more mature, more informed, wiser – disillusioned even – and you have some regrets. Mind you, I don't regret what I did. I regret that it finally wasn't the best way to solve the world's problems after all. A lot of us had hoped and believed that it was.'

'Do you mean to tell me you were a Party member?'

He inclined his head ever so slightly.

'Oh, fuck.'

'When Stalin signed the nonaggression pact with Hitler, it put things in a new light. A lot of people felt betrayed and disillusioned. The party lost a slew of members. In one fell swoop, the idealists were separated from the cynics.'

I lit a cigarette only, I suppose, to have something to do with my hands. 'Sam, are you saying that what's left is a hard core of cynical subversives?'

'I wouldn't know. It's been eight years.'

'Then that's all you'd have to tell the Committee.'

'Let's not kid ourselves. You think they aren't going to want to know the names of the ones who *didn't* quit the Party?'

'Have you got a good lawyer?'

'The best.' He gave me a wry smile. 'The best who'd touch it, anyway. Tony, forgive me for feeling I have to mention this, but I would prefer this conversation remained confidential.'

The inquiry made front page news daily. Sam and dozens of others from Hollywood had been subpoenaed to appear in Washington.

'It's foolish, isn't it?' Mother said plaintively. We were sitting by the pool at Silverwood after Sunday lunch. 'Why would they include Sam, of all people?'

'Maybe they drew the names out of a hat,' replied Nita.

Mother flicked at the air in front of her face as if she were repulsing a hornet. 'Perhaps reason will prevail, and Sam won't have to appear after all.'

'Mother,' I said, 'don't underestimate the gravity of this investigation.'

'It's nonsense to think someone like Sam could be a menace to the security of the country. It's a shameful waste of the taxpayers' money.'

I watched Sam swimming lengths in the pool, cutting through the placid water with a measured sidestroke. 'People make mistakes, Mother.'

'Then the Committee must be made to see its error.'

Nita got up and dived into the water. Mother rose. 'I believe I shall go lie down.' She waved to Sam.

'For pete's sake, Mother,' said Drew, 'your hands are shaking.'

'Oh nothing, nothing,' she told him, and hurried off, her heels tapping on the flagstone.

Drew looked after her. 'Balls,' he swore quietly. 'Mother *would* have to have picked Sam.'

'She's worried stiff. She refuses to acknowledge the possibility that Sam might be implicated.'

Drew leaned back in his chair and folded his arms behind his head. 'I suppose in time she'd find someone else.'

'Maybe not. You haven't.'

He shot me a look of startled anguish, the kind of look he might have given me if I'd slammed a door on his hand.

'I simply meant to say – '

'Keep off it, Tony.'

I saw Mother once more that week. She was pale and preoccupied and looked, for a woman of her stature, peculiarly fragile. Her eyes were rimmed with red. Her hands flew nervously in the air when she spoke. Her voice was strained. 'A touch of laryngitis,' she told me.

'Mother, even if the worst happens, it's not the end of the world, you know.'

'But it is. You've no idea. It is the end of the world.'

I hadn't an inkling, at the time, of what she meant. Anyway, Mother was inclined to colour things highly. I went back to the studio and knocked on Sam's office door. The tension was beginning to tell heavily on him, too. He looked as if he hadn't had a full night's sleep in a week.

'Sam, have you made up your mind what you're going to do?'

'Yes. Pack.'

'I meant after you arrive in Washington.'

'Strictly between us?'

I nodded.

'The way I see it,' he said, scraping the dottle from his pipe, 'if a fellow quit the Party on account of feeling betrayed and later committed that same offence, he'd become the very thing he abhorred.' He whacked his pipe smartly against the edge of his ashtray and began to refill it.

296

'But testifying before a government committee can't be compared to – '

'It was a sense of principle that attracted me to the cause in the first place. It remains a matter of principle to me still that a man doesn't fink. It was my belief that Stalin compromised himself and a few million other people as well. I'll be goddamned if I will.'

I looked at him across the desk, and he gazed back at me without expression. 'Sam, they'll call it contempt. You'll go to jail.'

'You think I don't know that? Screw them all.' He struck a match. 'In or out of jail, I'm going to have to live with myself.'

'What about David? What about Mother?'

'David understands.'

'And Mother? I saw her today, Sam. You'd think the ground was disintegrating under her feet.'

'Maybe it is, my boy.' He stared absently into the smoke rising from his pipe.

'You're not being fair to her, Sam. She doesn't know you're sticking your head in a noose or why.'

He stood up. 'You're right, of course. I've been putting off telling her the whole story. Tony, you and Drew are going to have to – ' He cut himself short.

'Have to what?'

'We'll cross that bridge when we come to it.'

What he was going to say, of course, was that if he wasn't around, we were going to have to take care of Mother.

I remember the next Sunday very well. It was a hot, dry day with only a feeble wind, the last tired wheeze of Indian summer. A drab, sulphur-coloured haze lay over the city. The air smelled and tasted stale. Nita and I had an argument on the way to Silverwood for lunch. By the time we arrived, we were barely speaking to each other.

'Where's Mother?' I asked Drew.

He tossed aside his newspaper. 'She and Sam are in the library. Have been for over half an hour. David's outside someplace. Dorcas and Hale are in the music room with the kids.'

'And you're sitting here all by yourself?' said Nita. 'For shame. We'll keep you company.'

The door to the library opened. Mother had been crying. Sam looked drawn and pained. For a moment, Mother stood there surveying the drawing room, seemingly unmindful of the three of us, as if she were trying to commit this familiar scene to memory.

She barely spoke during lunch. Occasionally Sam reached across the table to clasp her hand. 'I don't know where to begin,' she said suddenly.

'Beg pardon, Ada?' replied Hale.

'How can I be this enraged without knowing whom I mean to be angry at?'

'I know exactly how you feel,' said Dorcas.

Mother turned to look at her. 'Yes,' she said thoughtfully, 'I expect you do.'

Sam gave her hand a squeeze. 'It's not the first or last time a bunch of people have done the wrong thing for the right reasons.'

Hale snorted. 'That's one of those statements that can be interpreted rather freely.'

'Take it as you please, Hale,' Sam answered him.

Before Hale could reply, Drew changed the subject. 'It feels close in here. Shall we have our coffee on the terrace?'

We straggled outside, Safford following with the coffee tray. David excused himself and went home.

'Come on, Drew,' Nita said. She drained her demitasse cup and set it down. 'Come for a swim. It's too hot to sit here and swelter.'

'You and Tony go ahead. I have to go over some contracts.'

'Ada, you look a bit chalky. Are you all right?' asked Sam.

'My head is throbbing. I feel as though it were about to split open.'

'Here.' Dorcas unclasped her handbag and extracted a small silver pillbox. 'Take these.'

'What are they?' demanded Hale.

'Only aspirin. What on earth did you think they were?'

'Thank you,' Mother said, handing Dorcas back the empty pillbox. She swallowed two tablets and rose from her chair. 'Let

298

me get my dark glasses, Sam, before we go for our walk. The sunlight hurts my eyes.'

'Are you sure you feel up to it?' he asked.

'Why, Sam,' she said, mustering a smile. 'What would Sunday be without our walk?'

After Hale and Dorcas left, Nita and I changed into our bathing suits and went up to the pool. As I lay on my lounging chair, I could see Mother and Sam strolling hand in hand along the shaded path that curved around the contour of the hill above us. Mother's rosy silk dress shimmered in bright relief against the greenery. Sam had removed his jacket and carried it over his arm. Every few yards they would stop to face each other, speak for a while and move on. Once Mother sat down to rest for a moment on one of the stone benches at the top of the steps leading to the tennis court. Sam helped her up. They stood there, clasping each other's hands, looking into each other's faces without a word. Sam reached up and lightly fingered the pearls at my mother's throat, but his eyes never left her face. I don't think they were even aware of their surroundings. For a moment, I envied them. I closed my eyes. I heard Nita dive into the water.

'Ada!'

I sat up. Nita surfaced and swam leisurely towards the shallow end of the pool.

'Ada!' Sam cried again. I had never heard him use that tone of voice to her.

I stood from my chair and shaded my eyes against the yellowing afternoon light. Mother had collapsed. I could see her form lying on the path like a cluster of pink roses fallen to the ground in a heap. The hem of her dress stirred slightly in the breeze. Sam crouched over her, cradling her shoulders in his arms, stroking her cheeks, repeating her name again and again. When I reached them, he looked up at me helplessly.

'The sun,' he began, 'the sun, perhaps, or the heat. . . .'

Nanny Beale

It had been Mrs Prudhomme's custom to have a group for Sunday luncheon. Mr Anthony and Miss Paris would come, often as not the Outerbridges, occasionally Miss Swann and always Mr Farkas and his son, David. The children and I sat with them in the dining room at a smaller table by the window. When luncheon was over, the children would nap and the adults would wander off to amuse themselves quietly until the young ones awoke and stirred them to swimming or a game. After luncheon, Miss Paris and Mr Anthony usually changed into bathing suits and took the sun by the pool. Miss Swann brought out her needlework and moved on to the terrace where the Outerbridges liked to sit. Young David Farkas always brought a book to read while his father and Mrs Prudhomme took their regular Sunday constitutional around the estate.

That particular Sunday was near the end of October, if I recall correctly. I do know that the Outerbridges went home immediately after we left the dining room. It was a very hot day, and Mrs Outerbridge was a trifle under the weather. Mr Outerbridge was acting particularly closemouthed, not nearly his jovial self, even with his grandchildren. I suspect it had to do with Mr Farkas' continued presence in the house because, as he left, Mr Farkas held out his hand to him, and Mr Outerbridge just looked at it and then at Mr Farkas and said, 'I can't, Sam.'

Mrs Prudhomme cried out 'Oh, Hale!' Mr Farkas laid a hand on her arm and gave her a reassuring pat.

We all knew what was afoot, of course. The news was full of it. Mr Farkas and some other of his motion picture cronies had been called to testify before the House Un-American Activities

Committee. It was said that they were subversives, sneaking red propaganda into films.

David Farkas left quickly.

Miss Paris invited Mr Andrew to join her and Mr Anthony at the swimming pool, but he said he had to go over some business papers.

I took Daphne and Dexter by the hands and started upstairs where I could hear Duncan making wakeful sounds.

'Nanny,' Mrs Prudhomme called up to me, 'would you be so kind as to fetch my dark glasses from the little table in the upstairs sitting room? They're in that green needlepoint case that Miss Swann made for me. Sam,' she said to Mr Farkas, 'I've such a frightful headache. I don't know that I can take much exercise today.'

She thanked me for bringing her eyeglasses. I thought her face looked uncommonly strained. I sometimes wonder, usually when I wake up in the night from a dream of Silverwood, if I should have said something, suggested she lie down for a bit, perhaps put a cool compress on her forehead. Who knows but what it might have done some good.

When I saw Mr Anthony come into the house, carrying his dear mother in his arms, my first thought was that she'd been affected by the heat. But no. Something had exploded inside her head. For five days, Mrs Prudhomme lingered in a coma. Mr Anthony and his wife and Mr Andrew kept a vigil for her at the hospital. The end was a blessing, they said. Perhaps it was, for her. For the rest of us, especially the children, it was a great shock.

I was not privy to the provisions of Mrs Prudhomme's will or to what went on between the twins afterward that caused such antagonism. All I knew was that shortly after her death, Mr Anthony and Miss Paris rented out their home and came to live at Silverwood, too. Mr Safford told me the whole thing was Nita Paris' idea, though how he came by that information I don't know.

Within three months, Mr Andrew bought a large stone house on Whittier Drive and moved us out of Silverwood forever. The new place was nice enough, with a pool and some swings and climbing trees, but it was nothing like what the children had enjoyed at their grandmother's. It seemed foolishness to me to give up such a fine establishment, especially since he could share the cost of maintaining it with his brother. Too, I thought it rash of him to uproot the children again so quickly.

What baffled me, however, was that almost at once Mr and Mrs Anthony also quit Silverwood and the premises were put up for sale. I can't imagine what possessed those boys to behave so rashly in regard to something as precious as that grand estate. Perhaps in Mr Anthony's case it had to do with some kind of dispute with his wife. Not long afterward Nita Paris sued him for divorce. She attempted to remain friends with Mr Andrew and the children, but he would have none of it. Blood, I suppose, still ran thicker than water, despite the differences between the twins.

I hear from them on birthdays and at Christmas. Curious, how neither of them has remarried. It's hard to believe that life can skip by so fast, yet it's eleven years since I left Mr Andrew's family. They had no need for a nanny anymore, what with Duncan and Dexter almost eight and twelve at the time and Daphne fourteen. I was with the Buckleys after that and now I'm with the Harrisons. Their children, Martha and Colin, are descended from no less than two American presidents and a gentleman who signed the Declaration of Independence. It's quite something for someone like myself to have been associated for so many years with prominent families like the Prudhommes and the Harrisons. As I made it clear to Daphne in my last letter, I consider myself a fortunate woman. I've been bringing up children for fifty years now, over half of that time with the same family – the Prudhommes. Surely that's why they occupy such a special place in my thoughts. I cared for those people, not only the children but for all the people who were part of the life at Silverwood. I suppose that's the reason I try to keep track of things that passed between them, even though I can't always make sense of what occurred. More happened than I was party to, things I only could guess at. Only the good Lord Himself knows.

Drew Prudhomme

I knew the movie industry was being investigated, of course, and that Sam had been called to testify. I had assumed that Sam, with his Tiffany cufflinks, silk shirts and Scotch tweeds, would serve as a corroborating witness, make little or no impression upon the Committee and toddle off to lunch with some senator. The investigation must have been the furthest thing from my mind that Sunday at Silverwood when I became aware of Mother and Sam arguing in the next room.

'You can't mean it!' she exclaimed.

My first thought was that the sonofabitch was decamping with another woman. I didn't hear his reply. My attention was still half on my newspaper.

'But you must tell them everything!' Mother cried.

Jesus, I thought, he's pulled some sort of financial hanky-panky and she wants him to turn himself in.

The next thing I heard her say was, 'What will happen to us, Sam?'

To us. That meant that whatever mess Sam was in affected Mother. That was when I gave up trying to read the paper and laid it in my lap.

'Sam, what can I do to make you change your mind?'

'Ada,' I heard Sam say, 'what kind of a man do you take me for? I didn't make the decision without a lot of soul-searching, believe me.'

'It means the end of everything I hold dear. Sam, what would I do? And how would David feel? Sam, how would I live without you?'

'You can count on Tony and Drew.'

'I refuse to burden my children.'

303

'They wouldn't see it that way, Ada.'

'Sam, please.' She had tears in her voice. 'You know how much I need you. Reconsider.'

'And spend the rest of my life regretting it and ashamed?'

Mother was sobbing. I was trying to make up my mind whether or not to knock on the door and interrupt them, when Tony and Nita arrived for lunch. Christ, what a grim meal that was. Sam had come clean to Mother and told her her was a goddamned pinko. He'd been a member of some commie conspiracy to put Red propaganda in moving pictures. What's more, he'd decided not to cooperate with the Committee. He was going to play the tough guy, even if it meant being cited for contempt.

To hear Tony tell it, Sam had turned his back on the Party a long time ago. All the more reason to wonder what in hell would make a successful guy like that choose to martyr himself. And where did Sam get off, assuming this self-important pose of bucking the investigation? For what? So he could look down from his high horse on one of the few countries in the world where he could have come clean without fear of being shot? That's what must have really destroyed Mother, that Sam would pull this stiff-necked act of self-sacrifice in spite of what it would exact from her and from David, his own son. If Sam was a traitor, it was to the two of them. None of us realized it at the moment, but Mother had a time bomb ticking away inside her skull, and Sam had just advanced the zero hour. It was an aneurysm that burst and killed her. The doctor wanted to know if she'd been under any undue stress.

How's this for another punch in the gut: When Mother died, she left nothing. Zilch.

On the face of it, it was completely implausible. My first reaction was that she'd given her money to Sam to invest and he'd blown it. Maybe he'd fallen for some stock scam or invested it in a bunch of films that flopped. The lawyers looked at me as if I were a moron. The way they explained things, you'd have thought Tony and I were the last to know. Father had left Mother some stocks, some land, a little money and our home. The crash had taken all but the last. Tony's and my education and upkeep was guaranteed by trust funds. All Mother had to her name was

Silverwood. When Tony told Nita about it, she thought we were trying to put one over on her.

'It's not true.' Nita looked from Tony to me and back.

'Most of the furniture is Sam's,' I informed her. 'All of the good pieces.'

'Jesus! You're kidding! What's going to happen to them now?'

'They were an investment,' Tony told her. 'The way things are going for him, I suppose he'd be glad to sell them to us.'

'What about the house and the grounds?'

'Mortgaged to the sky.'

'Sam was making the payments,' Tony said, 'but he's virtually unemployable now.'

'You're kidding,' she repeated.

He shook his head. 'He was paying for Safford, too. Plus the cook, the gardener and the rest.'

'Christ almighty.' She began to laugh.

'What's so goddamned amusing?' I asked.

'The fact that Sam was keeping her, that's what. All the time she was putting on this queenly act, and we fell for it. What about the emeralds?'

'They weren't in the safety deposit box.'

'Then where are they?'

'They're gone,' I told her. 'She left her jewellery to Daphne, but there were only the pearls to speak of. Who knows? Maybe she hocked them. I'm beginning to wonder if any of us knew what made Mother tick.'

'Tony, maybe Sam knows where they are. What hotel is he staying at in Washington?'

'I'll be damned if I'll call him. He's got enough troubles. At least wait until he comes back.'

'*If* he comes back,' I reminded him.

'When was the last time either of you saw your mother wearing the emeralds?'

'I don't know,' Tony said to me, 'do you?'

'Some occasion or another. I don't recall precisely.'

'In my mind's eyes, I see her with them on, but it's probably the portrait I'm thinking of. I don't think she wore them much after Father died.'

'I intend to locate them,' said Nita.

'Be my guest,' I said, 'but if you do, they're Daphne's.'

'We'll see about that.'

'Lay off it,' Tony told her. 'We have more pressing problems. For openers, what to do about this place.'

Nita had her own ideas about that, too. The first I knew of them was when I arrived home from the office the following Friday and saw the foyer cluttered with valises, hatboxes and wardrobe trunks. I didn't have to ask Safford whose they were.

'Hello, there.' Nita stood on the landing surveying the mess in the hall below her.

'Christ.'

Safford glanced up from the baggage.

'You startled me,' I told her.

'We leased our house day before yesterday. Some Broadway choreographer rented it for six months while he's making a picture.' She gave me that incinerating smile. 'I meant to call and tell you, but I forgot. Moving is such turmoil, isn't it? Anyway, Tony thought you shouldn't have to shoulder this place all by yourself.'

'Don't let me distract you. I'm sure you have plenty to do. Where is Tony?'

'He's working late.'

'I'll have a tray in my room, Safford,' I told him. 'I'm still going through Mother's papers.'

She couldn't have waited, I suppose, until the flowers wilted on Mother's grave, before she made her move to take over as the mistress of Silverwood. I hated that acetylene torch of a smile, cutting slowly through the veneer of civility between us. I hated seeing her use my brother. I hated watching her go through Mother's effects, looking for the emeralds like an animal rooting for grubs. Anyone could see she was out of place at Silverwood. 'Listen,' I told Tony, 'you've got to explain to her that Safford is our butler, not her personal servant. She treats him like a slave, for chrissakes.'

'Where is she?'

'Nanny said she took Daphne someplace. That's another thing. Nanny would rather Nita didn't – '

'Daddy, Daddy! Look at me, Daddy!' Daphne dashed into the room and spun around like a top, her arms flung wide.

'Slow down,' Nita told her from the doorway. 'You're only a blur to him. Give him the full effect.'

'See, Daddy? Don't I look beautiful?'

'For pity's sake, what's been done to you?'

'Auntie Nita took me to the studio. She took me into the makeup department, and a lady there washed and cut my hair and set it, and I sat under a big dryer and looked at magazines, and when it was dry she made me lots of curls.'

'I see. Did Nanny know about this?'

Daphne shook her head. 'It was a surprise. Daddy, don't you like it?'

'I liked you without the ringlets. You were just fine before. I don't like a lot of phony baloney, Daph, you know that. Your mother never even used nail polish. You're pretty enough without a bunch of sausages bouncing around your head. For crying out loud, you look as if you'd finished dead last in a Shirley Temple look-alike contest.'

Daphne started to cry. 'The lady at the studio said I was pretty enough to be in pictures.'

'Have a heart, Drew,' said Nita.

'Run upstairs like a good girl, Daph, and see if Nanny can do something to make you look like yourself again.'

'Drew,' Nita began when she was gone, 'did you have to – '

'I hate to say it,' interrupted Tony, 'but she did look awfully damned cute.'

'She looked like a goddamned celluloid kewpie doll.' I got up and went to pour myself a drink. 'A child Daphne's age shouldn't be concerned with hairdressers. Nita, if you don't mind, please let Nanny see to the children.'

'Spoilsport.' She reached out and put her hand on my rump as I passed her. 'Corduroy. I think it always looks better on *younger* men.'

It was her monkeying with my daughter that first made me think of getting out of there. The problem was, Mother had left her affairs in a mess, and I'd been elected to set them to rights.

Mother's accounts, such as they were, were scattered at random among her personal correspondence. She'd simply dumped the lot into cartons. Her only concession to order had been to label them by year. I was still working my way backward to 1913, the year of her marriage to Father. Before that, she appeared to have kept neither records nor letters. There wasn't so much as a school diploma or a snapshot to indicate she'd even existed before she became a Prudhomme.

'Have you found out what she did with the jewels?' demanded Nita.

I shook my head. 'Beats me. Sam told Tony on the phone that he had no idea where they were. Where is Tony, anyhow?'

'Getting dressed. We're going to a party.'

'I have to talk to him. Safford's given notice. He wants to retire.'

'Who'll run this place?'

'He's shown Mrs Morrill the ropes. She can handle it. Safford deserves to take it easy.'

'Me too. I could use a little recreation. You haven't said anything about my dress.'

'Don't take a deep breath or you'll bust it.'

She came so close I could see down the front of her gown almost to her navel. 'I feel like getting into mischief,' she said with a throaty giggle.

'Here's just the partner for you,' I told her, stepping back as Tony entered the room.

God knows what possessed that crazy broad. Later, when Tony had gone to bed, she came into the kitchen. I was sitting alone at the servants' table, finishing off a piece of pie. I could see Nita was a little tight. She poured herself a glass of milk. 'Helps me sleep,' she said. She came over to me and set the glass on the table. She leaned over me with those big jugs nearly brushing my face.

'I miss my old Drew. Isn't he ever coming back?' Her breath smelled of scotch.

'What do you mean?'

'You know what I mean. You don't look at me anymore like other men do. I haven't changed.'

'Maybe I have. My wife is dead, remember? Do you expect me

to forget how much you wanted her out of the way? If it hadn't been for you, Dosie would still – '

'Don't expect me to swallow that.' She licked the milk from her lips. 'I know better. And don't expect me to belive you've gone celibate, either. You took off the black armband months ago.'

I stood up. 'End of conversation. I'm going upstairs.'

She stepped in front of me and locked her hands behind my neck.

'Back off,' I told her. 'This is dangerous.'

'Am I? Am I dangerous? Are you afraid of me? Are you a scaredy-cat?'

'Goodnight, Nita.'

'Give me a goodnight kiss.'

'I'll rip off your bloody dress. How will you explain that?'

'Kiss me first.' She moved her mouth close to mine. Her pelvis pressed against me. She gave me that flaming smile. Her tongue touched her lips.

I sent her sprawling. 'Slut.'

She looked up from the floor. 'Fuck you, too.'

'Don't ever come near me again.'

She hurled her words at me like sharp stones. 'Drew's a eunuch now! Hear that? He lost it in Sun Valley.'

'Shut your goddamned mouth.'

'You're cauterized,' she said to me. 'You know that? You're cauterized.'

'You're drunk.'

She looked at me in silence for a second, then got up. 'Nevertheless.' She gave me a faint, crooked grin. 'I'm not so drunk I can't see you're cauterized. Poor cauterized bastard,' she said as she left the room.

It was absurd to think we could continue living under the same roof. God knows, the last thing I wanted to do was sell Silverwood, but it seemed worse still to allow Nita to assume our mother's place. I wanted my kids out of there, before she messed with them anymore and while Daphne and Dexter could still remember the way things had been when Mother was the lady of the house. I probably could have swung the place on my own salary until I came into my full share of the trust money, but I didn't feel up to

309

it. I'd had the shit knocked out of me, first when Dosie died and then again with Mother, and I hadn't yet got my stride back.

I knew damned well Tony and Nita couldn't carry Silverwood, so, in a sense, I would force them out by leaving. Hell, maybe that's what I really wanted most. Regardless of what Dorcas thought, I had sufficient respect for my parents and the Prudhomme name not to want Silverwood turned into some kind of three-ring circus with Nita playing ringmaster.

Tony, wouldn't you know, acted as if I'd stabbed him in the back when I said I was moving out.

'For the umpteenth time,' he demanded, '*why*?'

'Too many memories.'

'Bullshit.'

'See here, all three of us work. Who'd look after the place?'

'What about Mrs Morrill?'

'She's a housekeeper, not an estate manager.'

'We could hire someone.'

'Are you telling me you'd pay his salary?'

'When I get another picture, sure.'

'Yeah. Well, I've got three kids to raise. That takes dough.'

'Do they have to go to private schools?'

'Let me get this straight,' I said. 'You want me to economize on my children's education in order to hire some guy to tell us the gazebo needs a new roof and the gardener's taking kickbacks from the seed store. Do I have it right?'

'Aw, Christ. If we could only get our hands on the money Father left us.'

'I wouldn't be in such a hurry, if I were you.'

'Why not?' he asked.

'Nita wants cash to buy her way out of her contract. If you've got lots of the ready, the easiest way for her to lay her hands on it would be to divorce you.'

'That's a hell of a thing to say!'

'You two aren't exactly acting like lovebirds lately.'

'What if I told you I'd give her the money? She wants the two of us to form an independent production company.'

'Or so she says. Don't be a horse's ass.'

'What the fuck has got into you?'

'I get the impression,' I said cautiously, 'that Nita is only looking out for number one. You and I are not as important to her as we might think.'

'You don't know her well enough to come up with an indictment like that.'

'I think I do.'

'I don't give a shit what you think. You sit there like a pompous old fart, looking down on everyone who isn't a Blue Book, white shoe, country club big shot like Hale Hunt Outerbridge – '

'Leave my wife's family out of this.'

'So quit finding fault with *my* wife!'

'I thought,' I said evenly, 'that you wanted to know why I was leaving.'

'What's that got to do with Nita?'

'Not much. Only a little, really.'

'Being coy doesn't become you.'

'Listen, buddy-boy, what do you say we take a swim before dinner?'

'Don't change the subject. First you tell me you're washing your hands of Silverwood, leaving the place for me to run when you know goddamn well I can't afford it. Then, out of the blue, you start making sly digs at Nita, as if she had something to do with it.'

'It wasn't important.'

'*What* wasn't important?'

'It was a lark, buddy-boy. One of those casual things.'

He looked at me as if he wasn't sure of what I was saying, as if he might be waiting for me to tell him I was putting him on.

'That's all it was.'

'When, for Christ's sake? *When?*'

'While you were still at sea. Before you even met her. Listen, it was nothing. It wasn't anything hot and heavy. Nita's not my type, really. She's not the kind of a dame I could take seriously.'

He hauled off and swung at me. He gave me a right to the jaw. I dodged, but the impact still slammed my cheek against my teeth. I tasted blood in my mouth. It took me a second or two to regain my balance. 'Jesus! What was that for? I was trying to break it to you gently.'

311

'What was it for? I'll tell you, *buddy-boy*, it was for having the colossal arrogance to presume that my wife is not good enough to be taken as seriously as Mister Andrew fucking Prudhomme takes his esteemed self.'

'Oh, come off it. You're sore because – '

'You bastard. Why didn't you tell me before?'

'Before what? Before, when you announced you were in love with her? Before, when you'd just eloped with her?'

'Shut up,' he said. 'Listen.'

I could hear the sound of autmobile tyres on the gravel drive outside. It sounded like steam valves blowing.

'It's Nita's car,' Tony said, glancing out the window.

'My mind is made up,' I told him. 'I'm leaving Silverwood.'

He looked at me without expression. After a minute, he said, 'You never cared about anyone or anything except yourself, did you? In your entire life, you never gave so much as a tinker's damn.'

I stood there and took it. It wouldn't have made any difference, by then, to tell him I was doing it for him and for our mother and for my children's mother. Things had somehow gone too far, and we both knew it. There is that one step, never marked by any warning sign at all, past which you plunge and feel yourself falling endlessly, unable to turn back, and the only sound in your ears is the everlasting silence. Not all the king's horses nor all the king's men, as Nanny used to say when we were young, not even they could put my brother and me together again.

Leave it to Nita not to notice anything wrong. 'Look what I found,' she said, tossing her handbag on to the sofa. 'Safford, put it there, please, on the coffee table.'

It was our grandfather's portable writing desk. I remember seeing it as a child in my father's dressing room on top of his bureau and later, after his death, high on a closet shelf. Inlaid in its wood were the initials LGP for Louis Gilbert Prudhomme, my father's father. Its slanted writing surface opened, and inside, where pen and ink and paper belonged, my father had kept his cufflinks, studs, tiepins and loose change. The top, I saw, had been refurbished, the worn, rusty-looking leather inlay replaced with a new one, dark green with a gold-tooled border. Safford set it down and left.

'Where the devil did you come across that?' I asked Nita.

'An antique shop called Wicks and Sharpe. Their claim ticket was in the desk in the library.'

'I thought I was the one who was supposed to be going through Mother's papers.'

'Don't be so damn touchy, Drew,' she replied irritably. 'It was sitting right there, if you'd cared. She'd been using it for a bookmark in the dictionary.'

'It was for Sam,' Tony said. 'She asked me if I thought he'd like it. She had it repaired in order to give it to him for his birthday.'

'Without consulting us? It was our father's, after all.'

'I told you. She asked me.'

'But that's not – '

'Stuff it,' he retorted, and left the room.

Nita looked after him. 'What's eating Tony?'

'Never mind.'

'The claim ticket,' she said. 'I thought it might have something to do with the emeralds. Now I'm beginning to think she must have sold them years ago, before she put the bite on Sam.'

'Why do you seem to be getting such a kick out of this?'

'Because.' She leaned closer and fixed me with that plutonic smile of hers. 'Because, my dear Drew, your mother was a superlative, thoroughgoing, double-dyed fraud. That's what Ada Prudhomme was.'

'Oh, by the way, Tony knows about us.'

The smile disappeared. She stared at me.

'I told him it was nothing significant, only a fling.'

Nita walked over to the sofa, picked up her handbag, took out a cigarette and lit it. She turned to me. For a moment she stood there, shaking her head as if she couldn't quite take it in. At length, she said quietly, 'Does it give you a sense of supremacy, or what, to reduce everyone and everything around you to dust?'

Christ, talk about nerve. If there was ever a case of the pot calling the kettle black, that was a classic. I listened to her footsteps going upstairs and heard the sound of her voice speaking my brother's name. Then their door closed.

I raised the top of Grandfather's writing desk and looked inside. It was empty. It smelled pleasantly of its new leather lining. I went into the library and poured myself a drink. Overhead, I could hear voices raised in argument. Tony and Nita were at it again. Something dropped or was thrown to the floor. A door slammed, and there was silence.

'Mister Andrew.'

I looked up. 'Yes, Safford?'

'I'm afraid I've been somewhat remiss, sir.' He handed me a pair of yellowed envelopes. 'I had these in an inside pocket and quite forgot them until Mrs Anthony brought the writing desk back.'

'What are they?'

'I don't actually know, sir. When Mrs Prudhomme gave me the writing desk to be repaired, I took it to Mr Wicks as she requested. He examined it and found the envelopes wedged behind the interior leather lining. I regret to say they slipped my mind until a few minutes ago. I'd intended to return them to Mrs Prudhomme, but with all that's happened lately. . . .'

'Thank you anyway, Safford. Please, would you take the writing desk up to my room?'

'Certainly, sir.'

I sat down and examined the two envelopes. The first bore a postmark from East something, Illinois. The name of the town was indistinct. I opened it and extracted two sheets of lined paper, the kind that school children use for writing themes. They were covered with bold, upright letters written in ink with a broad nib.

My Dear Mr and Mrs Prudhomme,

Ours is not to know why God in His wisdom sends us such trials as He does. These are matters beyond our comprehension, requiring our firm conviction that somehow divine justice is at work. They are rarely explained in this world.

This makes it all the more difficult for me to account for the behaviour of my late daughter, Roxanne. It weighs heavy on my heart to think that her troubles spilled over into the lives of two innocent people like yourselves, especially as I am aware of how much she enjoyed the months she spent in Mr Prudhomme's employ. I haven't it in me to imagine what possessed her to act as she did. I am ashamed that she should have visited such grief upon you both.

I shall never be able to fully express my gratitude for your efforts to save her from herself. Surely you must know that you were doing God's work and such work is never forgotten in the heavenly annals.

I assure you, I shall always remember you both in my prayers for your Christian kindness in settling her debts and sending her remains home to her family in such handsome style. You are truly good friends in need.

I hope you will find it in your souls to forgive Roxanne.

In fellowship and prayer,

(Rev.) Raymond Pollard

The letter made no sense to me. I didn't know why my father had saved it, if indeed he had. More likely both envelopes had been part of the residue from drawers, files and boxes, carelessly stowed in the writing desk, one step from the trash bin.

The second letter bore a British stamp and a London postmark. The date was indistinct, but inside at the top of the first page was written '25 July.' It was an easy hand to read. The letters were low, precisely formed and slightly slanted to the right. The words were tightly compacted across the page.

Dearest Ada and Victor,

Your letter brought me to tears, as you must have known it would. Though I have not felt up to returning to Langehurst Hall since Poppy's death, the time we spent with you there remains as clear and near to me as if the intervening two years had never come and gone at all. One yearns, at times, for the power to turn back the clock.

I could not have been gifted with a more splendid creature for a wife than my dear Poppy. Memories of her sunny temperament, her charm and her loveliness brighten even these dark days.

I am told by Nessa Cox who was also aboard the *Lusitania* with her that Poppy was in great spirits during the voyage, having had a rattling good time in New York. Nessa remembers seeing Poppy on the dance floor and hearing, as they passed, that she was singing the words to the music in that sweet, clear soprano of hers. The song, she said, was Jerome Kern's 'They Didn't Believe Me.' Poppy was wearing the new green Worth gown she'd bought for the trip and her mother's emerald parure, the same jewels which she insisted that you, dear Ada, wear to sit for your portrait. That painting is now the only memento of. . . .'

I didn't have to read any further. I glanced at the signature, 'Nigel,' and dropped the loose pages on the sofa.

In a sense, by God, Nita had been right in her assessment of Mother, though I loathed admitting it, even to myself. I wondered if I had ever really known my mother. Compared to my father, I thought she'd lacked flair. It amazed me that she'd had the enterprise, not to mention the guts, to piece together such a seamless fabrication. 'The earrings,' I could hear her saying to Dosie, 'can be worn with or without drops, making two pairs instead of one. Victor used to jokingly point out how practical that was.'

And for what? For what, this stubborn lie? To save face, I guess. To convince Safford, the staff, her friends and family that Ada Prudhomme wasn't down yet, that she still had an ace up her sleeve.

'Mister Andrew.' Safford reappeared at my side. 'Will there be anything more before cocktails?'

'Nothing, thank you. Oh, Safford,' I said, as he started to go, 'does the name Roxanne Pollard ring a bell? Or Reverend Pollard?'

'I'm sorry, sir. Neither of them is familiar to me.'

I took the two letters, crumpled them into a ball and tossed it into the fireplace. 'If you'll be good enough to light the fire, Safford, that will be all for now.'

'Certainly, sir.'

I sat there by myself in the library, gazing at the blaze. It pleased me somewhat to think that Nita still belived my mother had owned the jewels. It occurred to me that Mother had manipulated the facts so steadfastly, so often and so skilfully that finally they had conformed to her will. The emeralds had as good as existed. Real or imagined, they had served their purpose. There was no reason, really, why I should be feeling so damned depressed.

I rose and walked into the drawing room. I paused in the doorway, unexpectedly seized by the impression that the room had been tampered with. Something was amiss. I glanced around to be sure. Maybe it was only the mood I was in. I stood there alone in that vast space, taking it in, piece by piece. Nothing in the room was changed. Not a chair nor a lampshade nor so much as an ashtray had been disturbed, yet to me it seemed suddenly a shambles.

Bibi Prudhomme Biddeford

I've no doubt Ada could have remarried if she'd wished. Certainly marriage to Austin Chase, who was still a bachelor, would have solved her financial problems. Austin was extremely fond of her. Then there was Laurence Ward, who was divorced. He squired Ada about for a time. I had to hand it to her for not taking the easy way out of her difficulties. That was how I knew, when Sam Farkas came along, that this was a bona fide love affair. Too, anything less than the genuine item never could have lasted all those years.

When I saw Sam at Ada's funeral, only the sturdy blue serge of his suit appeared to be holding him up. He seemed to have diminished inside it like a nautilus wasting away in its shell.

Maybe if Ada hadn't died just then, if she'd been there waiting for him while he was in prison, his health wouldn't have failed the way it did. After Ada's death, the spirit went out of Sam. 'I was a fool, Bibi,' David said to me not long ago. 'I never understood how much those two meant to each other until I saw what it cost them.'

After Ada's funeral, when we came back to the house, I saw Sam standing alone at the bay window of the drawing room, gazing out over the terraced lawn to the city beyond. In spite of the fact that the room was full of people, he had an air of such isolation that he might have been a man marooned on a reef in a boundless ocean. I went to him and touched him on the shoulder. He started and turned.

'It was you, Sam,' I said, 'wasn't it? You did it all.'

'Did what?'

'This.' I indicated the room. 'You bankrolled Ada. It was you all along. It took me a while but I finally figured you had to be the one who kept this place going.'

He said nothing.

'You see, Sam, I knew what stocks she had. She couldn't fool me like the rest.'

'They don't know yet.'

I glanced across the room at the twins. 'They will soon enough.'

'Let them make of it what they like. I'll be gone by then.'

'But you'll be back.'

'Maybe yes, maybe no.'

He must have seen the expression on my face, because he laid his hand on my arm. 'Never mind, Bibi. I've made my choice. I may be too old to change the world much anymore but I'm damned if I'll let the world change me.'

'You're a stubborn so-and-so, Sam Farkas. I suppose I should be grateful for that, if only on Ada's account.'

'You're probably the only person here who would understand, Bibi, but do you know what I found most affecting about Ada? It was her audacity. It damn near took my breath away. What a poker player she would have made,' he said admiringly. 'I would look at that big, blond Venus of a woman and see someone so fragile and foolhardy that – ' He broke off and stared out the

318

window. 'They're not like her,' he continued after a moment. 'Tony and Drew don't know what it's like to have that fire driving them.'

'Perhaps Duncan will,' I said, looking towards the chair where Daphne sat holding her littlest brother in her lap.

'How's that?'

'A lame joke, Sam. I was thinking of his fiery red hair.'

'Ada couldn't abide it.'

'Do you know why?'

'I do,' he said.

'I wondered if you did.'

Hale chose that moment to present himself and ask for a word alone with Sam. In the nine years since I'd last seen him, Hale had grown heavy and dewlapped. I watched him addressing Sam in a corner, making his case with belligerent thrusts of that fleshy jaw, attempting, I suppose, to talk Sam into cooperating with the Committee. He might as well have been a bull bellowing at the moon for the impassive, distant face Sam turned to him.

Dorcas sat chatting with Andrew's sharpie friend, Ralph Gamble. Her eyes were restless and glittery. Her lipstick had escaped the boundary of her lips, and her mouth looked like a bruised red blossom. She rose and went to greet Elodie Swann. I saw Ralph Gamble reach down and turn over the cushion of the chair where Dorcas had sat. There was a wet stain on the back of her skirt. I wondered if Hale would interpret her incontinence merely as a further example of some fundamental character weakness. The more he could lord his strength over Dorcas, the more satisfied he seemed with his choice of a wife. He was one of those men who had to subjugate others in order to fully enjoy his power.

Nita was talking with Andrew in the doorway to the hall. She reached up and flicked a piece of lint from his shoulder. He recoiled as if she had touched a sensitive area of his skin. Nita looked at him with open annoyance. I had not realized until then that Drew did not get along with his sister-in-law. Nita left him there and joined Tony by the fireplace. She slipped her hand into his and smiled up at him, catching Andrew's eye with an air of having settled the score. Perhaps the rift between the twins had

319

already begun before Ada died. Perhaps even then, like an earthquake fissure, it was blasting upward and outward from the heart of the matter to the surface. It wasn't long afterward, I know, that they ceased to have anything to do with each other.

They were never all that alike, really. It seems to me that Andrew has lived his life like a water strider, moving swiftly and smoothly over its surface, never allowing himself to be fully immersed. He has never quite understood that the only thing more dangerous than taking risks is not taking any risks at all. Tony, on the other hand, plunges headlong into every experience, emerging occasionally dampened but not daunted. Drew has always played the elements of his life against one another, as if investing too much of himself in any one of them might drag him down in a fatal undercurrent. Tony gets in over his head now and then, but he is a strong swimmer. Drew is not. Lately, Daphne tells me, he begins his drinking before noon.

They both look like my brother Victor. Drew has that hard integument of his which was, to my thinking, his least attractive aspect. I suppose Tony's idealism makes him more like his mother.

I did not know her as well as I would have liked to. My part in her life was peripheral. What I did, I did because I was indebted to Victor for his solicitude after Oren died and I was alone, my son away at school.

Ada and Victor had been married for several years by then. Although I had met her briefly at the time of their marriage in 1913 and again a few months later, on their return from their wedding trip to England, we were in no way close as yet. I was surprised when she telephoned me from California.

In those days before dialling and area codes, a transcontinental telephone conversation was a sometime thing, interrupted by static, echoes, earsplitting whines and moments when the line went utterly silent. Consequently, although Ada's call was of the gravest nature, in retrospect it has its comical elements.

'Bibi,' she was shouting into the phone, 'can you hear me at all?'

'Yes!' I cried.

'As I said, it's the girl who works for Victor. You know he

keeps a small office downtown and has a secretary there who. . . .'
Ada's voice faded away.

'Are you still on the line, Ada?'

'. . . and she refused to do anything about her situation. Victor
fired her.'

'And you want me to find her another situation? I don't
understand, Ada.'

'She's in the family way, Bibi.'

So far, the conversation made little sense to me. 'Forgive me,
Ada, but why on earth would you call all the way from California
to tell me about Victor's secretary?'

'Because it's his baby.'

I should have known. 'Oh, Ada, dear, what a hellish – '

'Victor and I have decided to take it.'

'What do you mean?'

'To bring it up. To raise the child as our own. Bibi?' she said.
'Bibi, are you there?'

'Yes.' I was trying to marshal my wits.

'Did you hear what I said?'

'Are you certain this is the right thing to do? What do you
know about this girl?'

'It's what we want to do.'

'What about the girl?'

'At this point, she has nowhere else to turn. She put off doing
anything until it was too late. Now she's almost six months along,
and – '

'Has she no family?'

'Well, yes, Bibi, but her father is an ordained minister, you see,
and she doesn't dare to – '

'Ada, this girl sounds like trouble.'

'She's very scared and not a bad sort, really. Bibi, we need
your help. Victor and I are bringing her east. . . .'

That was when Victor called in the due bills I owed him. He
had been the author of the scenario that Ada related to me long-
distance. Victor had never been one to flout the law, though like
most men of his breed, he had few qualms about circumventing it
when he believed himself justified. In this case, it was more than
a matter of expediency. He wanted a child unaffected by sniggered

rumours and subtle condescension. The baby was to be born at home. My home. His and Ada's names would be on the birth certificate. Ada herself, she told me, would deliver the child.

I was terrified. 'You can't! This is madness. I won't hear of it.'

'Leave it to me, Bibi. Please.'

'Hell's bells, Ada, it wouldn't be safe! What do you know about such things? You've never had a child.'

Victor came on the line. 'Don't ask so damn many questions. I have it all worked out.'

'And the girl will go along with this scheme?'

'For a price. I have a job lined up for her later in Chicago, and I've put some funds in a bank account there in her name.'

'As usual, Victor, you seem to have thought of everything. Still, I can't allow this young woman to give birth under my roof without a midwife or a doctor. It's too dangerous. Ada simply must not attempt this alone.'

'She won't. You'll be there to help her.'

'The devil you say! I refuse to play fast and loose with human life. I won't be a party to this, unless you provide proper care for this girl and child, Victor. Victor?' I waited. 'Victor?' The line was dead.

If it had been up to Victor, he probably would have disowned the bastard and forgotten about the incident. It was Ada who had begged him to take the child. Victor's mistress, for that's what she was, had written in desperation to his wife, spilling the beans. Ada rose to the occasion. She knew all too well that Victor had married to perpetuate the Prudhomme line, and thus far she'd failed to do her part. This entire shabby episode must have seemed a blessing from above, albeit in heavy disguise. In a single stroke, her marriage would be secured, Victor would have his heir and his careless mistress would be out of their lives, unburdened of her mistake. It was, of course, all too good to be true.

Aside from her appearance, the only remarkable thing about Roxanne Pollard was her mediocrity. It was apparent immediately that she was a girl whose startling beauty had always been sufficient to make her exceptional and admired, with the result that the better part of her character remained undeveloped. She had no way of comprehending that her looks, however celebrated, were not enough to bring a worldly man like Victor Prudhomme to his knees. She wasn't a floozy by any means, nor was she sufficiently venal or clever enough to have used the situation to its full potential. When I first met Roxanne, I saw, to my disappointment, only a vacuous girl with snowy skin and sunset hair who seemed bewildered to have found herself over-matched by the company she kept. I confess I had expected more of Victor.

Roxanne looked to Ada with the fawning devotion of a rescued pup, pathetically keen to prove herself worthy of Ada's intervention. Her obsequiousness set my teeth on edge. There was something unwholesome about it, as if it were her way of scourging herself for her indiscretion.

Ada tolerated Roxanne, as she had to, once having set her course. I must say, she showed the girl more compassion than I would have, given the circumstances. I don't know how Ada managed it, coming to grips daily with the increasingly conspicuous proof of Victor's betrayal. I am sure that by that time she had few remaining illusions or dreams about her marriage. Still, I admire the unflinching realism and spectacular spunk that it took to do what she did.

Roxanne, like an Irish setter eager for any small sign from its master, would dog Ada's footsteps, trying to engage her in friendly conversation. Occasionally she begged her, 'Call me Roxy, won't you please?' To her credit, Ada never did. There are limits. I myself would have been inclined to turn on the little wench and order her to make herself scarce.

'Ye gods and little fishes!' I exclaimed to Ada. 'I gasp with relief when that young woman retires to her room. She skulks about as if she'd been whipped.'

'You must admit, she's at somewhat of a disadvantage here. It must be difficult for her, alone with the two of us, wondering what we think of her.'

'I should hope so, but then, I am obviously less brimming with Christian charity than you, my dear.'

'How can I blame her for loving Victor?'

'She might have kept it to herself.'

'Bibi, don't get the mistaken impression that I'm trying to be saintly about this mess.'

'I'm aware that you have your own reasons for what you're doing.'

'And I intend not to have any regrets about it, either. I intend to be able to look back and satisfy myself that I did everything possible to make the situation bearable. I shall be kind to that girl even if every nerve in my body is screaming. Otherwise, whenever I look at our child, I'll be racked with regret. That, you see, is something I cannot afford.'

'All the more reason to call in a doctor when the time comes. It would be much safer.'

'No. The child's secret wouldn't be safe.'

'Who else knows about this?'

'Nobody. Only the four of us. Roxanne used my name when I took her to the doctor in New York on our way here. I said I was her sister.'

'Why couldn't you have carried out that charade to the end?'

'It was too risky. The fewer people involved, the less chance of the cat getting out of the bag. And you never know what a woman will say when she's in labour.'

'But Ada – '

'Bibi, stop worrying. The doctor said her condition is excellent. Besides, I've helped deliver lots of babies.'

'*You?*'

'Certainly.' She caught sight of my expression and went on, 'My parents owned a large ranch at one time, and the ranch hands would fetch my mother when their wives came due. She had a gift for easy deliveries.'

'Great scott, it sounds like life in the primitive wilderness.'

'It was miles to the nearest town. A lot of times my mother called on me to help her.'

'What a shocking experience for a young girl!' (I must confess that, to this day, I continue to find the California penchant for openness unsettling.) 'Regardless, Ada,' I said to her, 'think what might happen if something went awry and you had to accept the blame. Think of the girl. Think of Victor's reaction.'

324

She looked at me without expression. 'He'll leave me anyway, if I don't give him a baby.'

'Are you sure there's no hope for one of your own?'

She nodded. 'The doctors don't know why. It's a lost cause in any case, Bibi. Victor will have nothing to do with me anymore. It's been that way for almost a year. He can hardly bear it when I touch him. I can actually see him steel himself so that he doesn't recoil. Yet anyone else . . . it doesn't seem to matter to Victor who she is, so long as it's not his wife.'

'Some men are like that.'

'And one can't know in advance.'

'Would you ever take a lover?'

Ada looked shocked. 'I don't think I could betray Victor.'

'Not even after this?'

'All I have left is his trust, Bibi.'

It was my impression, from that time on, that my brother didn't deserve a woman like Ada. To people like my cousin Charles and Cornelia who set great store by pedigrees, Ada was an outlander who'd had the good fortune to acquire the noble name of Prudhomme. From my privileged perspective, it seemed to me that the nobility in that marriage was Ada's.

'Are you and Mister Prudhomme close?' Roxanne asked me one day when Ada was out.

'Not very,' I replied, only because I didn't wish to encourage an intimate conversation about my brother. I was somewhat amused that Roxanne persisted in called him Mister Prudhomme, despite the burgeoning evidence of their familiarity.

'He is my dark prince.'

'I should think not,' I quickly retorted. 'You mustn't blow things out of proportion.'

'There's a blackness in him that swallows the light. I'm helpless before it.'

'Applesauce. Don't talk nonsense, Roxanne.'

'He makes me do things. Do you think it's possible to be punished for your sins at the very same time you're committing them?'

'I don't know and I don't wish to continue this discussion.'

'I mean, by being made to do something so degrading that it becomes its own punishment.'

'Stop this nattering at once!' I snapped. To be frank, she was giving me the willies. 'Go to your room, Roxanne. You're supposed to nap in the afternoons.'

She made no further attempts, praises be, to confide in me. She mooned silently about the house, staring out the windows at the falling snow, gazing at the fire in the hearth, occasionally thumbing through a magazine. I had never before met anyone who could be so apparently contented doing absolutely nothing. But then, she was a shallow girl whose only interest, so far as I'd seen, lay in contemplating her own depravity. I refused to believe that my brother had involved her in anything very baroque, but I supposed their doings were nonetheless strong stuff for the conscience of a preacher's daughter.

As the weeks passed, she changed from moonish to morose. Watching her waddle about after that huge belly of hers, I could hardly blame her. Then, out of the blue, she asked Ada, 'What if I love it on sight and can't part with it? My baby, I mean.'

That was the first time I'd heard Roxanne refer to the child as her baby.

'Oh, you'll part with it,' Ada rejoined tartly. 'You'll part with it, or I'll see you both to the door, and then, my girl, you'll be left out in the cold to fend for yourself.'

What Roxanne didn't understand was that she and Ada were in the same boat, albeit at opposite ends. Ada needed that baby easily as much as Roxanne needed someone to adopt it.

'Was I too hard on her?' Ada asked me. 'She mustn't get any ideas about going it alone with an illegitimate child. She hasn't the strength of character.'

'You made your point,' I told her. 'The last thing we need is to have that girl taking matters into her own hands.'

On the last Monday in February, I remember, the weather cleared sufficiently for me to make the trip into Boston to attend to a number of things I'd been putting off. It was getting dark when I returned, perhaps between five and six o'clock, on one of those still, cold evenings when the peal of church bells rebounds from the crystalline amethyst sky and even the bare, grey trees

326

seem to quiver with the sound. I recall rushing towards the house, feeling almost intoxicated with the beauty of that winter twilight and then halting, my breath suspended, when I saw that the place was black, not a light burning downstairs. On the second floor, the lamp in Roxanne's room beamed through a silver in the drawn curtains. I hurriedly let myself in and called out for Ada.

'Up here! Come quickly.'

Roxanne lay on the bed, looking as if she'd been beaten. Her lips were swollen from biting down on them. Her eyes were puffy from crying. Her auburn hair was matted. She was panting like a dying animal. I threw my bundles on a chair and took off my coat. 'Let me wash up. When did it start, Ada?'

'About nine this morning, she thinks. It'll be any time now.'

Roxanne made a high, thin noise like the sound of a wire vibrating in the wind. 'Oh, please,' she whimpered. 'Merciful God, don't punish me any more. I know I deserve to suffer. I know I do, but no more of this, I beg you. I'll do anything, only don't let it hurt me so much.' She broke off and let out a sharp shriek.

'Be quiet,' Ada ordered her. 'Push down the way I told you.'

'Shall I call for the doctor?'

'No, Bibi. It's coming now.'

I went to fill a wash basin with warm water. As I came back into the room, there was Ada, standing by the foot of the bed, holding in one hand, by Its feet, the tiny form of a baby boy glistening and streaked with blood, black hair slicked to its head, its mewling face furrowed and angry-looking. I glanced at her and saw something equally remarkable. Ada's face was glistening like the baby's, shining and blood-streaked. It must only have been perspiration and the high colour in her cheeks. 'There's another,' she gasped. 'Twins!' Her eyes gleamed with triumph. 'I will bring him *two* children!'

Roxanne began to cry softly.

Any tale told often enough tends to pass from fancy through myth to accepted fact. In my mind's eye, I occasionally see Ada heavily pregnant, awaiting the birth of the twins. It's an effort for me to comprehend that it never happened that way. I marvel that Ada pulled it off. For a time, at least, the scheme worked exactly as Victor had intended it should. Roxanne retreated to virginity in Chicago, wearing a handsome outfit Ada had purchased for her and accompanied by a brand-new set of luggage. She didn't seem unhappy to leave. Having seen what a chore it was to deal with two infants, I suspected she thought herself quite fortunate.

We employed a nurse for six weeks. Then Nanny Beale, whom I'd engaged some time before, came to accompany the twins, Ada and Victor back to California.

None of us could have known what Roxanne was going through that caused her to do what she did. As I understood it, she simply swooped down like a Harpy upon Ada and Victor one night almost three years later as they drove into their driveway from a party. She had waited for them there in the shadow of their garage until after midnight. God knows what had coursed through her head, standing alone in the darkness outside the house where her children slept. She wanted some part in the twins' lives, poor girl, to which Victor firmly put his foot down. It was a sorry business. Victor and Ada handled it with great aplomb.

It could be said, I suppose, that Roxanne was as responsible for Silverwood as anyone. She provided Ada with an excuse to move from a house she'd never liked in the first place. Furthermore, it was obvious to me that Silverwood was the prize that Victor awarded Ada for being such a brick. Too, now that he had heirs, the idea of a family seat must have appealed to him. In any case, the creation of the estate provided Ada with a project that absorbed her interest for the next few years, leaving Victor to his own pursuits. He seemed not to care how much she spent, as long as her attentions remained focused on Silverwood. I think that sometimes Ada deliberately went to extremes of extravagance in hope of eliciting a reaction from Victor, in hope that there might be *something* between them, if only a confrontation. But he remained indifferent.

With Roxanne's death, the balance in Ada's and Victor's marriage had shifted. For the first time since their wedding, her own personality began to come forth from the shadow of my brother's like a serene, silver moon emerging from an eclipse.

It was a good thing for Ada that she came into her own during those last few years of Victor's life. No sooner had he died than the market crashed and she lost almost everything. Only someone with inveterate poise could have pulled off such a convincing portrayal of stability when, in fact, the wolf had got past the door and was loose in the halls.

There's no sense in wondering what she would have done if she and Sam hadn't met when they did. At my age, I've learned to accept with equanimity whatever hand fate deals and not to waste time contemplating alternatives. One lacks sufficient energy to tackle the superfluous.

That day at Silverwood, following Ada's burial, was the last time I ever saw Sam. He stayed on until most of the others had left. Elodie Swann departed along with several other old friends of the family. David Farkas left soon afterward. It was late in the afternoon by then. Hale said Dorcas wasn't feeling any too well and they'd better be on their way. Safford began to go through the downstairs rooms, turning on the lights. It was still warm, but the wind had come up, one of those Santa Ana things, and he closed the windows as he went. Nanny took Daphne and the two little boys upstairs to wash up for supper. The minister, Reverend Townsend, was in a corner with Andrew, trying to convince him that a suitable memorial for his mother might be a new wing on the Sunday school. Tony and Nita were in the solarium having a hushed dispute about something. I took it upon myself to walk Sam to the door. In the foyer, his steps slowed, and I saw that he was gazing at Ada's portrait above the stairs. Not wanting to intrude on the moment, I glanced towards the other stairway along the opposite wall where the twins' portrait hung. Two black-haired, dark-eyed, sober-faced boys, immaculately dressed, looked wistfully into the future, towards some time when they would be liberated from starched white sailor suits and the rigours of sitting still to be painted.

'It's not a true likeness, you know.'

I must have given a curious look.

'I believe she was always a country girl at heart.'

'Ada? A country girl?' But then I remembered. 'Oh, yes, she did tell me her parents owned a ranch at one time. I had assumed it was a summer place of sorts.'

'No. It was never like that.' He looked back at her portrait.

'I've always thought it an excellent likeness,' I said.

'She was never as placid as the artist painted her. Not really. Not inside. There was always . . .' he paused and went on, 'this tremendous *energy*.'

'Nobody would have dared call Ada a lazy person.'

'Restless.'

'Perhaps you knew her better than anyone, Sam.'

'She'd have liked to be imperturbable. I think she even wanted to be hard, but it wasn't in her character. She had always to fight her emotions. She was too easily stirred, like a weather vane sent spinning by a breeze.'

I remembered Ada's explosive behaviour on the day of Victor's funeral. 'Generally,' I said to him, 'she hid it very well.'

'She fooled almost everyone. She appeared to be rather Draconian, but the fact is, Ada was never able to let go of things as conveniently as she wished. She accumulated some heavy baggage.'

I waited, not knowing what to say or even what he was getting at.

'What made it particularly difficult was that she was striving, always striving, towards the image of the person she wanted to be.' Instinctively, he reached towards the portrait; then his hand fell to his side. 'If only she had been more forgiving of herself.'

'She could be very forgiving of others,' I reminded him, thinking of Roxanne.

'She allowed for human failings in everyone but herself.'

'That must have been very hard on her at times.'

'At least she didn't have to pretend with me. She understood that we both wanted the same thing.'

'What was that, Sam?'

He turned to me and gave me a look so stark that he might as well have been bare before me. I all but moved a step back.

'I believe,' he said slowly, 'that we both wanted terribly, each in our own way, to be truly good people.'

330

'But you were. You are.'

He might as well not have heard me. 'What is it they say about the road to hell being paved with good intentions?' Wearily, he sat down on the bottom step of the stairs. 'I begin to think there's more than a little truth in that. As for Ada, she couldn't forgive herself for what happened to Dosie.'

'But Sam, that's absurd. Ada had nothing at all to do with her death.'

'She made her go back to Sun Valley. Ada used to say that if only she hadn't meddled, if only Dosie had been allowed to do as she wanted and had stayed in California with her children. . . . Sometimes,' his voice was hoarse, almost a whisper, 'sometimes Ada would wake in the night, crying out Dosie's name. She had nightmares in which she would try to stop her from leaving.'

'She was overreacting, Sam. True, she may have persuaded Dosie to go, but nobody could have foreseen – '

'She didn't persuade her, Bibi. She forced her to go back there.'

'What are you saying?' I sat down beside him on the stairs.

'She told Dosie that Andrew was having an affair, and if she valued her marriage she'd use their holiday together to win him away from the other woman. Dosie didn't want to believe her, but Ada was adamant. She loved that girl and those children. She didn't want to see Drew's family ripped apart.'

'Who was the woman?'

He shook his head. 'I didn't particularly want to know. I have my suspicions, though. Ada was torn up over it. She was afraid it might be a pattern, Drew treating Dosie the same way his father had treated *her*. She was desperate to break the thing up before Drew convinced himself he could get away with infidelity and made a habit of it. Whatever Ada said, it sent Dosie back to Andrew in a hurry and she died the very night she arrived there.'

'From what I hear,' I told him, 'she was intoxicated and probably lost her bearings in the storm.'

'But she normally drank very little. Ada was sure that if she hadn't upset Dosie so – '

'Unfortunately, regrets are a part of growing older. They're as inevitable as grey hairs.'

'Ada had more than her share. That wasn't the worst of them.'

331

He hesitated. 'She also knew, you see, that Victor let Roxanne Pollard die.'

'Sam!'

'I'm sorry, Bibi.'

Despite the late-afternoon heat, I felt suddenly cold. 'God, no.'

'He was capable of that, Ada assured me.'

I nodded, in spite of myself.

'She knew he'd done it to keep the twins or anyone else from ever knowing about Roxanne.'

I took a deep breath. 'Poor Roxanne. If only she'd put the past behind her and been satisfied with the money.'

'Ada never actually disliked her. She never forgot how much she owed Roxanne.'

'But are you sure – '

'Ada knew. It was less than five minutes to the doctor's, yet Victor took almost twenty minutes to get there. He said he'd made a wrong turn and missed the way. Ada was aware that he knew the way very well. He'd driven there before without any difficulty.'

My eyes were smarting. Sam handed me his handkerchief. I wiped them and gave it back. The wind outside had risen. The front door shuddered.

'Ada carried that knowledge with her always. She said the moment Victor drove away, she realized she never should have let him take Roxanne off alone. She blamed herself. Until he returned, she said, she prayed to God that her fears wouldn't come true.'

'Heaven help me, but Victor was capable of anything when it came to his sons. He was mad for those boys. Let me think that's what it was, Sam. Madness.'

He reached over and squeezed my hand. 'Who knows but what seeing things in a better light isn't a kind of forgiveness in itself?' He rose from the stairs, helping me to my feet. 'I'll be going now, Bibi.'

'Oh, Sam. What is there to say? It was clear she loved you so much.'

'Good-bye, Bibi.'

'Thank you, Sam, for all the things you've been to this family.'

I opened the front door. He kissed my cheek briefly, then stepped out into the dusk. The windblown trees made swaying shadows against the stone walls of the house. The moon and stars were visible in the darkening sky. Sam walked slowly down the drive towards home. I watched his form dissolve into the twilight. The hot wind sent the fallen, dry eucalyptus leaves scudding rapidly across the gravel driveway. I remember the sound was exactly like rain.

David Farkas

When I returned by chance to Silverwood that day two years ago, I not only stepped into my past but my future as well.

I'd come back after my long absence to find the place no longer anyone's home and the Prudhommes vanished, or so it seemed, from the premises. I felt as if I had come upon the *Mary Celeste* floating abandoned on the high seas, with no clue as to the fate of its occupants or the reason for the desertion.

After Ada died, my connection with the Prudhomme family was little more than a memory. For one thing, my father's way of dealing with grief was to lock it away in a part of himself so private that I would not have presumed to trespass by mentioning Ada Prudhomme's name or, for that matter, my own mother's. For another, our lives were in a state of upheaval. There were some fast revisions to be made, and we had our hands so full of the present that yesterday might as well have been weeks ago.

The day after Ada's funeral, I drove my father to the station to take the train for Washington, via New York. I remember he kissed both my cheeks, and I, in an uncharacteristic burst of filial emotion, clasped my arms around him and buried my head in my shoulder, catching the familiar blend of his pipe tobacco, cologne and freshly ironed shirt. He extricated himself from my embrace and whispered gruffly, 'Let's chest our cards, Dovid.' He gave me a nod and boarded the train.

My father had been a political liberal, not to say leftist, for most of his life. When we moved to California, his views were well known among his friends and associates, most of whom were at least somewhat sympathetic. I can recall very clearly being with my father one day at the races and running into a well-known Hollywood director who came to sit with us awhile in our box.

'Too bad we haven't seen more of each other lately,' he said. 'It's a far cry from the old days when we got together regularly at the poker game.'

After he left, I asked my father, 'How come you stopped going out to play poker? I remember you went a lot when I was younger.'

'"The poker game" was a euphemism. They were political meetings.'

'What kind?'

'Liberal.'

My father had, in fact, been active in the Party for three years, from 1936 to 1939. I was not surprised when he told me this shortly before he went off to Washington. What surprised me was that, nearly a decade later, anyone would care. Growing up, I was one of those kids who saw virtually every movie that came to the screen. My father used to say I was part moth; I'd watch anything that flickered. From that vantage point, I could recall very little I'd seen that might possibly be interpreted as Red propaganda. The Party, it seemed to me, hadn't exactly flourished in the land of sunshine, swimming pools and celluloid. I'd failed to take into account what Rorschach knew, that people will read into something whatever they please.

'Are you or have you ever been a member of the Communist Party?' my father was asked.

'With all due respect for the government this body represents,' he replied, 'I cannot, in good conscience, answer that question.'

A few days before Thanksgiving, my father was cited for contempt of Congress and sentenced to a year in federal prison.

The following week, the United Nations voted to partition Palestine, clearing the way for the establishment of the state of Israel within a matter of months. At the time, the two events seemed unrelated to me.

At my father's request, I went to the studio to clean out his office. The name on his parking place had been replaced by somebody else's. I parked there anyway. I paused at the guard's booth by the front gate and stuck my head in the door. 'Hi, Matty,' I said. When I was smaller, Matty the guard used to slip me saltwater taffy that his family sent him from Atlantic City. He always had a pocketful of taffy for the kids that came around the studio.

'What are you doing here?'

'I dropped by to pick up my father's things from his office.'

He looked at me coolly. 'He doesn't have an office here anymore.'

'What happened to it?'

He shrugged. 'Maybe they gave it to a loyal American.'

I felt my scalp prickle. 'I came for my father's belongings, Matty, and if I don't go away with them, I swear to you, I'll come back with lawyers and you'll be in a pile of shit.'

He turned his back on me and dialled a number on his telephone. He spoke for a while, then dialled another. He was taking his own sweet time. Finally, he faced me and jerked his thumb in the direction of some dress-extras who were relaxing outside one of the sound stages. 'Behind stage seventeen. In the warehouse next to the prop shop.'

I didn't bother to thank him. The contents of my father's desk, files and bookcases had been haphazardly thrown into a couple of dozen cardboard cartons marked with his name. Two prop men I recognized as having worked for him helped me carry them to my car. Neither seemed to want to discuss what had happened. One of them shook my hand as I was leaving.

That's how my father's career ended. For thirty-five years he had written and produced motion pictures that had made millions of people laugh and care and learn. He had built stars, given some top directors their first big breaks and won enough awards to cover two walls of his study. He'd made a lot of others richer even than himself. In the end, the phone had stopped ringing so abruptly that our housekeeper had thought something was wrong with the line. My father had been cut dead so swiftly that you couldn't even hear the warning whisper of the blade.

He went off to serve his time, leaving me to sell the house and, with the aid of his lawyer, to restructure our finances. He'd made some wise investments, not the least of which was the furniture he'd 'stored' at Silverwood. Tony and Drew each bought a few pieces, but the majority of it was auctioned. Our house brought a fair price, and I saw with relief that we would be able to live modestly without much additional income. The salary of fledgling architects has never been anything to write home about.

It was then I learned that for years my father had paid the taxes, the insurance, the utility bills and the staff's wages at Silverwood. Mrs Prudhomme had had barely enough money to put clothes on her back and food in her larder. My first reaction was that it was a damned shame he'd spent so much of what was now in short supply. Then I began to think about his life with Ada Prudhomme and how she'd made him happy again after that sad time following my mother's death. They'd had a lot of good years together, and if he'd wanted to support her, when he could conceivably have taken up with some gold-digging, free-spending tootsie of a starlet, I had no quarrel with his choice.

A month or so after my father was released from prison he had a severe heart attack. He was never well afterward. We'd rented a small, barn-red clapboard cottage in Santa Monica Canyon, not far from the beach. He would take his typewriter outside, on to the porch, and sit at a card table there, writing. It gave him something to do, but that was about all. Even under a series of assumed names it was impossible for him to sell a script. I know that, at one point, Tony Prudhomme, who'd become an independent producer, optioned a property of my father's, a western called *Slade's Valley*. For whatever reason, Tony never could put a deal together to get the project going and the option lapsed. Every so often, he'd phone my father with some words of encouragement and ask to have scripts sent his way, but nothing ever came of this attempt at collaboration. Our association with the Prudhommes had broken off almost as abruptly as it had started. We didn't move in that crowd anymore.

There was one exception.

The summer my father came home, Aunt Ruth flew out from Long Island. It fell to me to take her to all those places tourists want to see, which was how I happened to run into Ralph Gamble in the Farmers' Market. I was wholly unprepared for the hearty, avuncular enthusiasm of his greeting. To my Aunt Ruth, he said, 'Some kid, isn't he? Used to be a regular stringbean, and look how he's filled out.'

'A *mensh*,' Aunt Ruth agreed.

'Hey! You blushing, David?' He laughed and clapped me on the back. 'Listen,' he said, reaching into his inside jacket pocket, 'here's my card. Give me a call, will you? There's a matter I'd like to discuss with you.'

I called him, if only to be polite.

'How's about lunch, David? Musso and Frank, tomorrow at one?'

We were into dessert before I had any idea why Ralph had asked me there.

'My business is, like they say, booming,' he volunteered. 'Me and my partners have got more work than we can handle. How about yourself?'

'I'm at Hart and Mills, low man on the totem pole, of course, but – '

'You got to be good, if Hart and Mills hired you straight out of college. They're a prestige outfit. How much are they paying you?'

I told him, and he laughed.

'What is it with swells like that, that makes them think you should be grateful for the privilege of working for them? Here.' He cut a piece of his pie and put it on my plate. 'You got to try this. It's a speciality of the house. By the way, David,' he went on, 'how's your father?'

'He doesn't get around too much. He tires easily.'

Ralph looked uncomfortable. 'I wish I could say I had a job for you, but my partner Harry's brother-in-law does all our architectural stuff. You okay, otherwise?'

337

I nodded.

'What I mean, kid, is that I'm pretty solvent these days. Your old man believed in me enough to invest some of his dough once upon a time, when Drew and me were still partners. I'd be glad to return the favour if you, you should excuse the expression, ever run short. No,' he continued, before I could reply, 'no need to discuss it. All you ever have to do is name the figure.'

We were both feeling embarrassed. I told him I appreciated the gesture, but it looked as if my father and I were on solid ground, at least for the foreseeable future.

'You've got my phone number. You can call any time. The offer stands.'

I don't know why Ralph Gamble should have been concerned for my father and me. The reason doesn't matter, I guess. What mattered to me then and still does is that someone we knew so slightly would put himself on the line for us at a time when some of our oldest friends were finding themselves hard put to remember our names.

My father died on New Year's Day, 1950. I pulled up stakes and went to Israel just as if I'd known all along, in the back of my mind, that was where I wanted to live. Maybe, after what had happened to my father, I'd wanted to be someplace where my penchant for idealism didn't seem ironic.

I don't think I realized, until I met my wife, Leah, that Ada Prudhomme had been my first crush. Certainly I never would have dared recognize the fact at the time. At first, I couldn't figure out who it was that Leah reminded me of. When it dawned on me, I laughed aloud. Never mind that Leah was a *sabra*, born in Palestine. She was tall, *zaftig* and fair with the kind of offhand arrogance that's part of the sabra nature. She was a ringer for a young Ada Prudhomme. We were married in '56. Two years later, on her way home from work one Tuesday afternoon, she was killed in a terrorist bombing. One minute she was there, and the next she was not. They weren't even able to identify her remains. I couldn't handle it. Asleep or awake, I was gripped by an overbearing sense of panic. A single idle hour set up a shriek in my head like an icy wind howling through a hollow tree, vibrating against the dead wood, threatening to shake it apart.

338

Leah's father, thinking it would divert my mind, volunteered my services to tour North America raising money for Israel. I accepted, originally without enthusiasm, and found the constant change of scene welcome. I'd made several trips, crisscrossing the continent, making myself useful to my adopted homeland. Now, unexpectedly, I had come full circle back to Silverwood.

I was surprised at how powerfully the memories assailed me of Christmas parties here, complete with dancing, carollers and Jack Horner pies for the youngsters, of Thanksgiving feasts that left me almost immobile and of tranquil summer weekends watching the shadows grow long on the shining surface of the swimming pool.

Now, as I roamed the house again after so many years, I half expected to come upon Safford, white-gloved and correct as always, hurrying along the hallway with a vase of flowers or a bucket of ice. Instead, I met up with my host, Mike Pressman, who glanced quickly at his watch.

'Only fifteen or twenty minutes more,' he said. 'We still have plenty of time to make your plane. Enjoying yourself?'

I nodded.

'There are coffee and doughnuts in the administration office if you'd like a snack. I'll find you, wherever you are, when it's time to leave.'

I bypassed the administration office. There was a crowd around the coffee urn, and I wasn't feeling hungry anyhow. Across the hall was the old billiard room. It was dark and quiet. I stepped inside and waited a minute for my eyes to adjust to the dimness. The billiard table and cue racks were gone, though the large green-shaded overhead lamp remained. I reached for the wall switch and tried it, but no light came on.

'It doesn't work. The janitor's been notified.'

At the far end of the room, a young woman sat at a table in front of the window. The light of the sun, coming through the glass, made it difficult to see more than the silhouette of her face and the stacks of white envelopes before her on the table. Her head was bowed over her work, and her straight black shoulder-length hair had fallen forward from the nape of her neck, making dark crescents around her ears. The sunlight splashed on her hair like quicksilver. After a moment, she spoke again. 'Are you looking for someone? May I help you?'

'No. Thanks all the same. I'm waiting for a friend.'

I saw her glance in my direction. She swivelled her chair to face me. She was wearing a pale gauzy dress. She drew her long legs up and clasped her arms around her knees. Her feet were bare. Her shoes lay under her work table where she had taken them off.

'It's David,' she said, her voice on the verge of incredulous laughter. 'Isn't it?'

'I beg your pardon?'

'It's you!'

I moved towards her across the room, thinking she must be one of the people I had met at the Pressmans' the night before.

She looked up from her chair. 'You don't recognize me.' It didn't seem to bother her.

'I'm sorry.'

'But how could you?' She rose from the chair and took both my hands in hers. Her skin was cool and smooth. As she stepped closer, I caught the unmistakable scent of freesia. 'It's been a very long time,' she said.

She had a high forehead and a light complexion. Her eyes were blue and merry, offset by dark brows and prominent cheekbones. She turned her face up to mine. Her lips were curved in a smile. She shook her head in amazement.

'David,' she repeated.

'Daphne?'

'Of course!'

'Look at you!' I was having trouble catching my breath. 'When I last saw you – '

'You wanted nothing to do with such small fry. I remember it very well. I was crushed.'

'I never expected to find you still here.'

'I'm not "still" here exactly. We moved away a long time ago. I'm a volunteer for ACTS. I'm in charge of sending out the invitations for the annual ACTS benefit.'

'How old are you now?' I held her at arms' length, taking her in.

340

'Twenty-three. That makes you thirty-eight.'

'How did you know?'

'You were always fifteen years older, silly. The last time I saw you, I was ten. It was on the beach at Santa Monica. You were lying on your stomach on a towel, reading a book. I said to a friend of mine. "You see that handsome man there? I know him." She thought I was kidding. I told her I'd prove it, and we came over and said hi. You were polite enough; you asked after my father and brothers, but it was clear you didn't want to be bothered by a pair of little girls like us.'

'Honestly, I don't remember.'

'Why would you? How could you have known that you were my secret heart-throb? For years I collected pictures of Jeff Chandler because I thought you looked like him.'

I was searching for the words to meet her halfway. For some reason, it seemed imperative to make her happy. 'I remember you more clearly than you know,' I said, which was true. 'I used to watch you when you were small and liked to run at a gallop across that wide lawn by the tennis court. You pranced like a frisky colt, arms flung out at your sides, flapping them awkwardly like little wings. You made me think of a young Pegasus.'

'I was one of those lanky, leggy kids who outgrew clothes as fast as they were given to me. At night, when I said my "Now I lay me," I used to pray to be petite. God finally heard me when I was five foot eight.'

'And smashing-looking.'

Her cheeks flushed pink. 'Let's not stand here. There's a sofa behind you.'

She curled into a corner of the sofa and slipped her legs partly underneath her. 'Now,' she said, 'tell me something in between.'

'You knew I'd gone to Israel after my father died.'

She nodded. 'I heard that. But not why.'

'I wanted to cut loose from the past. Things had fallen apart here. I felt at an impasse. I wanted to believe in something, to help build a new country.'

'Are you married? Engaged? Living with someone?'

I shook my head. I hesitated a moment, then told her about Leah. I realized afterward that it was the first time I'd dared to

341

articulate my feelings in the four years that had passed since Leah's death. 'At first, after it happened,' I told her, 'I thought: I can't endure this: I can't carry it. It was like a huge boulder. If I didn't hold it back with all my might, it would roll over me and suffocate me. But finally you find yourself coping with it somehow.'

She reached out and put her smooth hand to my cheek. 'I am so very, very sorry, David.'

'I've been on the move ever since. Selling bonds all over America, raising funds for Israel. I haven't practised much architecture in the past few years.'

'But you can't simply abandon your career. What would your father say? He was so proud of you.'

'Call it a hiatus.'

She looked sad. 'I'm disappointed. I remember the beautiful drawings you used to do when you were studying at SC. All this time, I've imagined you building handsome cities in the Israeli desert.'

'It wasn't anywhere near that glamorous, believe me.'

'Still, even an ostrich has to pull its head out of the sand sometime and look to the future. You seem to have found a handy way of dodging the issue.'

I smiled. 'Are you giving me a pep talk?'

'It does sound like that, doesn't it? Perhaps we should change the subject.'

'Tell me about yourself.'

'I graduated from Wellesley. I wouldn't have gone east to school except that my great-aunt Bibi is in Wellesley. I'm single. A few months ago I broke up with an actor I'd been going with. He went off to New York to do a play. Grandpa Outerbridge died a couple of years back. He left me and my brothers enough money so we don't have to scrounge. I'm a free-lance magazine writer. Grandmother Outerbridge is still living, but I don't see her often. She's. . . .' Daphne paused. 'She's rather difficult.'

'How so?'

'Oh David, you wouldn't recognize her. She refuses to acknowledge that she's an alcoholic. She's become frowsy, and her legs and arms are pitifully thin. The last time I saw her, all I could think of was one of those little bouquets of flowers, a nosegay, that had been dried and crushed between the pages of a book until it was faded and fragile to the point of crumbling. If that weren't enough, after all this time, she still speaks about my mother as if she'd died only recently. It's creepy and upsetting. She's never forgiven Daddy for selling this place. The minute she sees one of us children, she starts denouncing Daddy.'

'It surprised me,' I said, 'that neither your father nor Tony had hung on to Silverwood.'

'There was some sort of *mishegaas* between them, and they both abandoned it like a sinking ship.'

'*Mishegaas*? Where did you pick up a Yiddish expression like that?'

She flashed me a grin. 'Osmosis. You can't grow up in Beverly Hills without absorbing some showbiz slang.'

'What would your Grandmother Outerbridge say to that?'

She gave a little bounce of amusement on the sofa. 'She'd probably think *mishegaas* meant one of the Great Lakes.'

I was studying Daphne's face. 'You belong here,' I said.

'How do you mean that?'

'In a house like this.'

'Am I so old-fashioned?'

'Oh, no,' I corrected her. 'Classic. You've turned into a classic beauty.'

'Now you're embarrassing me, David.'

'It's the truth.'

She looked away. 'Sometimes I wish Silverwood were still ours. I remember how, when we lived here, Grannie would take me for walks around the place, naming all the flowers and trees and shrubs for me. "This is the azalea," she'd explain, "rhododendron over there is its cousin. They originally came from China." The way she spoke of them, I could see them travelling across the ocean, pink blooms floating over the blue water towards Silverwood. She would tell me how the acacia was used by the Egyptians for their pharaohs' coffins and how the eucalyptus can shoot up fifty feet in five years. "You see, Daphne," she'd say, "Silverwood is alive and growing just like you, and you must keep it alive and growing after I'm gone."'

'I doubt I could think of Ada Prudhomme and Silverwood independently of each other.'

'In Grannie's eyes, it stood for something more than privilege. It represented what our family should live up to. Ideas like self-discipline, dignity and philanthropy. Grannie truly believed in those things. I guess she wasn't sure Daddy and Uncle Tony cared about them or about Silverwood as much as she did, so she set to work on me and Dexter. Duncan was too young, and anyhow, she never really took to him, for some reason.'

'It's too bad the place is surrounded by that abominable tract.'

'Silvercrest Estates.' She wrinkled her nose. 'Daddy's pal, Ralph Gamble, is the wizard behind that razzmatazz. The worst part is, all that unrelieved vulgarity has the effect of making dear old Silverwood look pompous and absurd next to it, like Margaret Dumont surrounded by the Marx Brothers.'

'Ralph Gamble once did me a great courtesy. His taste may not be so hot, but I like him all the same.'

'He's a sweet man. He said something to me not long ago that I know was meant to be kind, although I didn't quite understand it. I went to him for some information. We were talking about Silverwood and the family, and he asked me if I ever saw Nita Paris. I said I'd phoned her that very morning but she wasn't home. Then Ralph put his arm around me like a large, tame bear and said in that gruff way of his, "Listen, honey, Nita has a tendency to embroider, if you know what I mean. An overactive imagination, you'd call it. I wouldn't put too much stock in anything she says. You remember that, you hear?" Just then his phones started ringing, and I had to leave, and I never did wring an explanation from him. I was left with the impression he was being gallant in his own funny way.'

Framed by those two crescents of black hair, her face glowed in the shadows like a milk-white moon poised in a dark sky. I found it hard to take my eyes off her and hoped she didn't mind. 'Your father and Tony, how are they?'

'Like oil and water. They don't mix. I see a lot of Uncle Tony, though Daddy doesn't know it. How could I not?' she asked earnestly. 'They're the same flesh and blood. I love them both.'

'Didn't I read someplace that Tony and Nita were divorced?'

'That's ancient history, David. It's been at least twelve years.'

'She was a looker in those days, for sure. Did you ever see her after you phoned her?'

Daphne shook her head. 'Only on TV. She plays on one of the afternoon soap operas.'

'What is that scent?'

A slight frown clouded her face. 'I don't understand.'

'What is that fragrance you're wearing?'

'I'm not wearing any fragrance.'

'Freesia.'

She laughed. 'Honestly, I'm not.'

She had the kind of laugh that would make men search their brains for the wit to amuse her – a clear, sweet, silvery sound like wind chimes.

'David,' she asked, 'will you be staying long in California?'

'I'm leaving today.'

'No. Surely not.'

I nodded. I didn't want to talk about leaving. There were still things I wanted her to tell me. 'The portrait of your grandmother, why was it left here? I'm curious. I always liked it.'

'The truth? If you ask me, Daddy and Uncle Tony didn't want to be reminded that she'd been less than honest with them. She'd made them believe their lives had a firm foundation, and when they learned her affluence had only been a pretence, they reacted like little boys who are angry because their parents allowed them to believe in Santa Claus. Duncan was like that. For a while he didn't even want to speak to Daddy. He was furious about the Easter Bunny, too.'

'Didn't it occur to them that she might have been doing them a favour?'

'Grannie even lied to me,' she said with a smile. 'She told me her emeralds were her Rocks of Gibraltar. Daddy found out they didn't even exist.'

'I'll be damned. They didn't? Did you feel cheated when you found out?'

Daphne tilted her head up defiantly. 'I admired her for pulling it off.' She gave me an apologetic look. 'I wasn't being perverse, really. What I admired was that she'd completely convinced

345

herself and everyone else that the jewels existed, so in effect, they might as well have.'

'Do you live alone?'

'What?' She seemed startled. 'Yes. Why?'

'I wondered, that's all.'

'Seeing you like this makes me sorry we never kept in touch.' She paused and gave me that wonderful laugh. 'Though I can't think why you'd have wanted a teenage pen pal.'

'I doubt your family would have encouraged it.'

'Probably not,' she agreed. 'I sensed from Daddy that he resented the fact that your father was the one who supported this place. He'd like to forget that.'

'That's not entirely incomprehensible.'

'I think it hurt him to learn that Grannie and your father were in cahoots. She levelled with your father and not with her own sons. They felt excluded, that she'd let him in and shut them out.'

I smiled at her. 'How did you get so wise?'

I'd embarrassed her again. She glanced at her hands folded in her lap. 'I love this place,' she said quietly. 'I learned to love it from Grannie. The main reason I do volunteer work for ACTS is that it brings me back to Silverwood. Several months ago, I decided I'd compose a little history of our family and Silverwood.' She stopped and looked up at me. 'Does that sound foolish or self-important?'

I shook my head.

'Our family is scattered now, you see. Uncle Tony and Daddy don't get along. Dexter lives in a commune near Mendocino and raises sheep. Duncan is away at school. It suddenly struck me that everything my grandparents were and did would be forgotten soon. I didn't want that to happen, especially not to Grannie's memory. I want one day to name a daughter Ada and be able to tell her why. Oh dear,' she broke off. 'Am I boring you?'

'Not at all.'

'Well then.' She settled further into the corner of the sofa. 'I did fine on the Prudhomme genealogy, with Aunt Bibi's help, but not on the Willson. I couldn't find any record of Willsons with a daughter named Ada who would have been her age. Agnes, Alice and lots of Annes but not one Ada. It turns out,' she said with obvious delight, 'that Grannie was something of a mystery woman. It's as if she'd sprung like ironclad Athene from Zeus' head. Everyone seems to remember her in different ways and for different reasons. Uncle Tony appears to have developed a sort of grudging admiration for her. When Daddy has a few drinks under his belt, he carries on at length about how Grannie told him the Willsons were an early California family. "Way before the gold rush," she said. Daddy sets great store by breeding. He talks about genes and coming from good stock until you'd think it was Dexter talking about raising sheep.'

I decided I liked the way her lips moved when she spoke.

'After I'd got what I could out of Daddy and Uncle Tony, I telephoned Nita Paris, but when she heard what I wanted, she refused to speak to me. According to Grandma Outerbridge, Nita Paris wasn't fit to kiss Grannie's hem. Maybe that's what Ralph Gamble was implying when I saw him. I wrote to Nanny Beale and she sent me three long letters in reply. Grannie was a great lady, Nanny said. Of everyone, Elodie Swann said the oddest – '

'Miss Swann? She's still alive?'

'Oh yes, but she looked quite frail. Her cheeks were furred and soft, like the pages of a worn book. Her skin was faded and creased and spotted with age. She remembered me immediately, though. She said some queer things. I wasn't sure what to make of them.'

As she spoke, I could hear a piano being played in another room. It was a piece I couldn't identify, a bittersweet melody in a minor key that unexpectedly found me choked with infinite, inexpressible longing of the kind I'd not experienced since I was in my teens.

'Miss Swann said – ' Daphne paused for effect, 'that Grannie was a self-fulfilling prophecy. What do you make of that?' She didn't wait for a reply. 'She looked at me over her tea table, one eyebrow jauntily cocked, and asked if I understood. I didn't. "Have you ever seen a tornado?" she inquired. "It has no substance of its own, really, in spite of the fact that it appears tangible enough. It's merely an illusion caused by the power of the wind to gather up substance. It's dust and debris we see, not

347

the tornado itself. One can't, after all, see the power of the wind except in its effect.'"

'I don't follow you,' I said to Daphne. 'What's that to do with Ada Prudhomme?'

'I'm not altogether sure myself. Miss Swann was quite evasive.'

'What do you think?'

She pursed her lips. 'Having come up against so many dead ends, I wonder if there wasn't some truth to it. When Uncle Tony married Nita Paris and Mummy died and then your father got in trouble, Grannie's hopes and dreams must have taken a battering. Maybe the force that kept her going began to fail her, and that's why she died when she did. Miss Swann was right about one thing: It was Grannie's energy that held our family and Silverwood together.'

'Did you speak to anyone else about her?'

Daphne shook her head. 'As I was leaving, Miss Swann said to me, "Don't go looking, child. You might as well chase the wind." If she knows any more that that, she's not telling.'

'I think Ada Prudhomme and my father cared very much for each other.'

'I should have known that you of all people, David, would understand my feelings for Silverwood. Daddy and Uncle Tony never even speak of it. I guess my brothers think I'm sappy for still caring so much about this place. Anyhow, after I spoke to Miss Swann, I never pursued the project any further. I quite like the notion that there was lots more to Grannie than most people ever knew. I came to the conclusion that the possibility is much more delicious to contemplate than dry facts.' She glanced at me and smiled. 'What are your plans now, David?'

'To go back to Tel Aviv. To take a couple of weeks' vacation.'

'You never considered coming back to the States to practise architecture?'

'I hadn't. By the way, will you give my regards to your father and Tony? How are they, anyway?'

'Uncle Tony hasn't changed much. He never grew up, really. He has lines in his face, but most are the crinkly kind, from laughing.'

'And Drew?'

She hesitated a second or two. 'Daddy's begun to look old. He doesn't stand straight and tall anymore. His posture is stooped, as if he were carrying something terribly heavy. Even his walk has changed. I used to hear his footsteps sounding so brisk and self-assured. Now, when I walk beside him, his pace seems ponderous and slow to me.'

The door to the hall opened, thrusting a wedge of light into the room. Daphne started and blinked.

'There you are!' Mike Pressman exclaimed from the doorway. 'I see you found some company. We should leave to catch your plane in five minutes, if you're ready. What say we meet in the foyer?'

'Right.'

Daphne watched him go. 'I wish you wouldn't.'

'Wouldn't?'

'I wish you'd stay. Even for a little while. It's been so long – '

'Do you mean it?'

She kept her eyes on the door. 'Yes.'

'Look at me.' I touched her chin and turned her to me.

'Yes.'

I remember with utter clarity the extraordinary sense of rapid motion I felt, sitting there. I had, that morning, been pulled into my past with the force of an undertow and now, just as strongly, I felt overturned and drawn swiftly upward, lifted towards the light. I felt myself breaching the present and surging into the future, carried on a wave rushing headlong towards the shore.

She took my hand in both of hers. 'There will be other planes later, won't there?'

I have never asked my wife what was going through her head at that moment, but I knew then, looking into her face so close to mine, that I would not be a passenger on any of them.